A Kiss to Remember

Glynna placed her hands on his shoulders, moved her right leg over the saddle horn, and felt herself being lifted from her mount's back. Then Kane stumbled. Instinctively, her hands moved from his shoulders to clasp the back of his neck, while his arms encircled her waist. They fell to the soft carpet of grass and wildflowers, and tumbled downhill.

When their rolling bodies came to a halt, Glynna was trapped beneath him. He gently placed his hands on either side of her head, his fingers sliding into her hair.

"Are you injured?" he asked huskily.

"It was Jack who broke his crown . . . remember?"

"Jack did not have Jill to cushion his tumble." Kane had eased his weight from her chest, but he made no effort to remove the length of his body from hers.

Their gazes locked, and his mouth lowered ever closer to hers until their breaths mingled. ever so slowly he moved his lips upon hers, seeming to savor their whispery touching.

So this was how it felt to be kissed!

FIERY VIRGINIA JEWEL

ELIZABETH LEIGH

ZEBRA BOOKS
KENSINGTON PUBLISHING CORP.

For my husband,
Michael Thomas Hancock,
whose love, encouragement, and confidence
in my ability have been my mainstay

Special thanks to my dear friends
Caroline Bourne and Lenora Berlin
for their input and support,
and to my three sons—
Michael, Jared, and Whitney—
who try very hard to entertain themselves
"so Mama can write."

ZEBRA BOOKS

are published by

Kensington Publishing Corp.
475 Park Avenue South
New York, NY 10016

First printing: January, 1991

Printed in the United States of America

Prologue

Glasgow, Scotland
March 14, 1753

"I canna understand it, Hugh! Why would anyone want to kill us smugglers? We never harm anyone. Jus' help out, far as I can see. Bring in things people wouldna had any other way. Wiley makes thirteen!" the Scotsman declared, his voice rising in the dimly lit, smoke-filled room.

Jem MacCavendish was well into his cups, but that did not deter him from banging his empty glass upon the stains and nicks of the ancient oak bar and demanding a refill.

The barkeep, who had known MacCavendish for almost a score of years, sighed heavily as he leaned over the counter, his voice low as he gently admonished the man. "I canna, in all good faith, give ye another, ye ol' seadog. Canna ye see ye've had enough?"

Jem's round and weathered face screwed itself into a grimace. "Jus' one more, Hugh. See"—a trembling hand dug into the depths of a worn leather coin-purse, then deposited three pence upon the oaken bar—"I have the coin fer it."

"No need for coin, my good man," a stranger's voice intruded. "Let me pay for this one."

The stranger nodded to the bartender, who reluctantly poured out a draught of Scotch whiskey. Jem had paid little heed to the man; now, however, he turned his attention to the one who sat on his right. Though he searched the limits of his clouded memory, he could not recall ever having seen him before, nor could he remember seeing the man enter the pub. He himself had been there for hours, his intention to drink himself into a stupor. He had just this day received news from Dublin that another of his seagoing comrades had been murdered, running the count to a full baker's dozen. While Jem MacCavendish felt some measure of sadness for the loss of an old friend, his fear for his own hide fueled his desire for strong drink.

The stranger held up his own glass before carelessly tossing upon the wood some coins he had retrieved from a bulging purse. Both his face and his voice exhibited friendliness. "Sorry to hear about your comrade. Murdered, did you say? No one is safe anymore."

Jem warmed to the subject. "Leastaways not from this bastard. I canna understand it," he reiterated.

The stranger tossed down his drink, taking great care not to wince at the bitter brew. He much preferred a smooth brandy, but this was Scotland. Casually he asked, "What makes you think it is just one man and not a group that is after your shipmates?"

Despite the quantity of drink in his belly, the Scot's speech was only slightly slurred. "Oh, 'tis only the one bastard, as I see it. Slices 'em all open, he does, from 'button to button,' they say." As he spoke, he indicated the heinous deed by placing his forefinger on his navel and slowly pulling it upward over his shirt until it had reached his collar. Jem shook his long, untethered hair about his shoulders, then hung his head briefly. His red-streaked, hazel eyes surveyed the path the finger had taken. "What reason could the bastard have? I canna understand."

"Perhaps no reason," the stranger offered. "What sane person understands the workings of a murderer's mind?"

Jem was undaunted. "There be a reason, all right, though which one I know not. But there be a reason. The cap'n, now, he was smart to run off the way he did."

When the Scotsman's gaze once again fixed upon his empty glass, the stranger waved to the bartender to refill it. The brief lull in their conversation allowed him space to survey the occupants of the tavern, none of whom appeared to be paying any attention either to him or MacCavendish.

"Run off, you say? To France, perhaps?"

"Hell, what would he want to do with them Frenchies other than buy their sparkly? Turns a nice profit in London, it does." Jem sipped his scotch, savoring its harshness. "Run all the way to Virginie, he did. Took his wife and family and quite a tidy sum with him, too."

The seaman's words gave the stranger pause. He had not considered this possibility. He had been certain that the smuggler captain was still in hiding on his native Isle of Man, which fell outside the jurisdiction of the British government. Its geographic location, situated as it was between England and Ireland, made it a perfect outpost for smuggling operations. Many Manxmen had amassed small fortunes through this highly profitable endeavor.

"They say the colonies are not so bad. Why do you not go there yourself, if you fear for your life?" the man suggested.

"I'm aimin' to. First ship out of here heading that way. Been tryin' to get me a commission." Jem swished the remainder of his drink around in the glass before swallowing it. Melancholy clung to him. "Never thought I would leave here permanently. Glasgow's always been home."

The tall, well-dressed stranger motioned to Hugh. Laying out a small pile of coins, he requested a bottle of scotch. Jem, who had yet to attain the drunken stupor he so desired, eyed it hungrily.

"My good man," the stranger said, rising from the stool and towering over the smaller Scotsman, "I am in Glasgow on business, which I must attend to come morning. Though my room has only one bed, you are welcome to the floor and as much of my whiskey as you care to drink. I am not without some influence here and will gladly attempt to help you get signed on as soon as my business is concluded."

If Jem MacCavendish had been sober, he might have questioned such kindness from one whom he had so recently met. Instead, he followed the man outside and down the street to a small but clean inn, his bloodshot eyes forever fixed on the bottle of scotch swinging from the larger man's hand.

It was the chambermaid who found him the next morning. Her screams pierced the air, slashing through the gray mist permeating the cobbled streets to reach ears several blocks away.

Jem MacCavendish was alone in the room. He lay on his back upon the bare floor, his legs spraddled wide, his left arm folded upon his bloody chest. The

8

path he had traced the previous evening from his navel to his collarbone lay open. His glazed, bloodshot eyes stared silently in shock and disbelief. His right hand lay upon the varnished boards of the floor, his index finger lifelessly prone and covered with his blood. In the throes of death, the bloody finger had traced a path upon the wood before coming to its final resting place. The double curl it had drawn, now dried to an ugly, rust-colored stain, could have meant any one of several things: a bird in flight, waves upon the sea . . . perhaps even a representation of the letter *W*.

Part One

Deceptions

Chapter One

The soft breath of May meandered down the mountainside, stirring the velvety azure wings of a tiny butterfly to flight. The breeze carried the seemingly weightless creature with it in a gently bounding, rolling motion until the butterfly's vivid blue melded with that of a cowslip growing near the banks of a narrow stream. Silvery shards of light danced fairylike upon the crystal water. From the timberline emerged a graceful doe, her hooves snapping twigs as she made her way to the stream, the noise breaking the mellow silence of the afternoon and causing Glynna O'Rourke to lift her head from the Shakespearean volume resting upon her lap.

Suddenly gaining strength, the breeze changed to a quick gust as it charged up the grassy knoll upon which Glynna perched, scattering a glittering cloud of pollen from the wildflowers growing there and sending a swarm of fat bumblebees off to chase it.

The playful breeze, seeming to laugh softly at the scurrying bees, next plied its mischievousness upon Glynna's dark auburn hair. Her long, tapering fingers smoothed the brittle, windblown pages of her open book, then lifted to tuck wayward wisps behind a dainty earlobe. Her dark lashes half hid her eyes as she read, her features settling into peaceful repose. Then, with a suddenness that startled her, the breeze slapped at the pages of the book again.

With a snap her slender hands closed the heavy volume as her emerald green eyes surveyed the workings of the capricious wind. Just a hint of a smile lifted the slight upward curve of her lips before her brow gathered into a narrow frown.

"My reading is spoiled," she muttered, "and precious little time I have of late to enjoy Master Shakespeare." With a whispery sigh, she tucked the book under one arm and then used her free hand to pull the voluminous skirts of her dress over her knees before pushing herself into a standing position. The brief view of her shapely calves was lost on the wildlife, which, for the most part, ignored the not uncommon sight of Glynna O'Rourke upon the knoll.

'Tis of little consequence, she thought, the frown now easing into her soft features. It is almost time for tea anyway.

Her tiny, slippered feet began to pick a way among the grasses and wildflowers, taking great care not to tread upon the head of even a single blossom.

Though it was only a short distance through the grove of maples to the inn, Glynna chose instead to take the more circuitous route along the banks of the stream. She wished to stretch out the few remaining moments of solitude before she must assist her aunt in the serving of tea. This light meal at the inn was possessed of little of the ceremony which Glynna had learned, through reading and conversation, accompanied its provision in the motherland, yet Aunt Darcie purveyed a delightful and delicious assortment of foods to be taken with her strong brew. To-

14

day the fare included feather-light teacake and Aaron's Bundles—spicy little muffin cakes frosted with maple sugar fudge—two of Glynna's favorites. Despite their lure, she continued her slow, deliberate steps along the rocky path, her eyes searching out the smoother spots while her mind lingered on Rosalind's predicament in the play she had been reading. She still held the volume possessively against her breast, for her uncle's library contained few works of drama and poetry, even fewer of fiction, and these had to be guarded against the ravages of time and the elements.

The works of John Donne, Sir Walter Raleigh, Ben Jonson, and Edmund Spenser were all known to her. She had devoured *Don Quixote, Robinson Crusoe,* and *Moll Flanders,* the only three novels Uncle Galen owned. On occasion, her appetite for literature had even turned to some of the colonial publications her uncle read. These were discussed at length by visitors to the tavern, and there were actually thousands of them in print, ranging from pamphlets to large volumes. Although she had plodded her way through some of the histories written about the various colonies, she'd found much of the writing tiresome. Only that of Benjamin Franklin, especially in the issues of *Poor Richard's Almanac,* appealed to her. It had pleased her to learn that this most versatile and influential man had assumed the office of postmaster general in this year of 1753.

However, it was not his largely philosophical writing or even that of the novelists and dramatists to whom she had been exposed which made her heart sing, but rather the works of the poets. Of these, Robert Herrick and Richard Lovelace remained her favorites. She had read "To the Virgins, to Make Much of Time" often enough to commit it to memory. The poetry of love ran through her veins and fed her heart with romantic notions of chivalrous knights, hulking gray castles, defenseless maidens, and handsome young knights imprisoned without cause and yearning for their own true loves.

When she had first read Herrick's poems written to his mistress Julia, the physical implications had confused her. In the innocence of her youth, she had considered writing about a woman's breasts scathingly indecent. As her own body had blossomed into womanhood, however, she had found herself returning to these poems. While they filled her with an unexplainable warmth, they also left a part of her feeling curiously empty.

To combat these strange feelings, feelings which seemed to lessen the degree of control Glynna wanted to believe she exercised over her emotions, she had turned to Shakespeare. The master playwright's tragedies appealed most to Glynna, especially *Hamlet* and *Romeo and Juliet*. Now Glynna pondered Rosalind's sparkling though tender womanhood in the comedy *As You Like It,* identifying with Shakespeare's heroine in a way she could not quite understand. The girl's femininity seemed to grow more exquisite in the male disguise she had donned in self-defense, so much so that it appeared incongruous to Glynna that the shepherdess Phebe could not see through Ganymede's attire to the softness of Rosalind beneath.

I should not ever be so fooled, Glynna thought as she set her footsteps away from the stream and toward the inn. It would take more than a simple pretense to deceive me! The merry tinkle of her laughter wound its way through forest and underbrush, commingling with a robin's chirping and the coo-cooing of bobwhite quail in peaceful harmony.

"There you are!" called a bright, youthful voice as clumsy feet bounded through the undergrowth, crashing twigs and crunching dry leaves in their wake. Soon the light auburn head of their owner appeared, and the feet skidded to a halt before Glynna, who grasped the boy's hand firmly in her own as they walked.

"You should not be out in the woods alone, Brian," she admonished gently.

"It's all right, Glynna. I heard you laughing, so I knew you were near." His freckled nose wrinkled upward as he slapped an open palm against the leather scabbard which hung from his waistband, then he proclaimed in a haughty voice, "I'm growing up, Glynna."

"Yes, you are. Next month you will celebrate your— How many is it now?" Her dark brows met in a frown over the bridge of her nose as she pretended to calculate the number. "Oh, yes! Six. Next month you will celebrate your *sixth* birthday! Soon you will be off fighting the Indians, and I shall miss you sorely."

If the boy realized the humor with which she spoke, his next words belied that fact. "I shall scalp them all!" he declared, removing his hunting knife from the scabbard and brandishing it before them. Glynna stifled a smile, for the "scalping" weapon had been carved from yellow pine and was no more harmful than Aunt Darcie's broom.

When they reached the steps leading to the ordinary, his wooden knife slicing through the air, Brian scampered off, stabbing imaginary Indians as his war whoops rent the air. Just as Glynna was turning to the door, he whirled around. "Mother wants to see you before tea," he called. "She's in the keeping hall."

As Glynna moved through the ordinary, she was relieved to note that none of their guests were seated at the long tables in the large room, awaiting tea. Seldom did Aunt Darcie summon her, for Glynna was well aware of her responsibilities and prompt in seeing to them. Perhaps an important guest had arrived in her absence and Aunt Darcie wished Glynna to pay special attention to his needs. It might be a British duke or a royal governor—mayhap even a prince from some tiny European kingdom, complete with entourage of aides and servants. Her interest piqued, Glynna joined her mother's sister in the keeping hall.

A small, thin, graying woman whose good nature and robust health had seen her through a multitude of hardships, Darcie Cavanaugh sat, uncharacteristically pensive, her round chin resting on an open palm, her other hand loosely holding a sheaf of papers. Why is it that the past never wants to stay where it belongs? she wondered. Why must it always catch up with you, and then only when you have begun to let down your guard and think you are safe?

Glynna had no idea what had occurred so many years ago. "You should have told her," Darcie fussed aloud, another uncharacteristic aspect of her behavior that afternoon, for, unlike Glynna, Darcie was not given to talking to herself.

This was not an insignificant matter bothering Darcie. How had the baron located them? She and Galen had been so careful in covering their tracks, having severed all communication with anyone in the British Isles shortly before their move to the Virginia frontier. If the baron had found them, then who else might know of their whereabouts? The mere thought

18

sent an involuntary shudder down Darcie's spine.

The soft *whosh* of a door's opening interrupted her disturbing train of thought. With visible effort she cleared her mind of conjecture and brought her attention to the problem at hand. As though coming from afar, her usually mellow voice sounded hollow as she bade Glynna to close the door and sit with her at the oval, hardrock maple table. Soft blue eyes sought the luminous gems in her niece's face as she considered the approach she should take. *Go slowly!* her best judgment dictated.

"You know I have looked upon you as my own daughter, Glynna," she began finally, "and a good and duteous daughter you have been these past fourteen years."

Outwardly, Glynna smiled her appreciation for the kind words. Although her aunt and uncle had always treated her with respect, given her the best education possible, and provided for her every need, kind words and complimentary phrases were not passed out wholesale by the older Cavanaughs. Inwardly, an unaccustomed wariness joined her natural curiosity. Her aunt's words carried the portent of finality in their relationship, a possibility Glynna had never before considered.

Darcie took a deep breath. "As much as I loved my sister and regretted her untimely death, I have never been sorry to have you with us. Now, though"—she sighed, her gaze leaving Glynna to fall upon the papers—"I wish your mother were here to explain all of this."

The near sorrow in her aunt's voice frightened Glynna. Her hopes of entertaining some important personage fled, and she groped for some method of delaying this news. "Can't it wait until after tea?" she offered, wishing that whatever it was could wait forever. A feeling of impending doom began to settle over her.

Misunderstanding the reason for Glynna's discomfiture, Aunt Darcie patted her niece's folded hands. Glynna found herself even more uncomfortable as the recipient of Darcie's patronizing gesture, but she remained respectfully silent, her body tense as she awaited an explanation.

"You shan't miss your cakes, dear. Our guests have been informed that tea will be delayed for the space of half an hour, so that is all the time we have to discuss this" — Darcie paused in her quest for an appropriate adjective, then dismissed the need for one — "matter."

She glanced up as Katie, the Cavanaughs' black cook, lumbered in the back door of the keeping hall, which led, by way of a covered brick walk, to the kitchen. The large woman carried a tea tray, which she set in front of her mistress, a toothy grin splitting her jovial face.

"Them spice cakes turn out jes' right, Miz Dahcie, most 'specially the fudge icin'." She beamed with warranted pride as she set out the tea things, then pursed her ample lips and rolled her round eyes upward as she turned to leave. "I left them two worthless girls tendin' the stew, so's I bes' be gittin' back."

Darcie graciously thanked Katie before she closed the door. "I think we might need this," she said, spooning maple sugar into a filled teacup and taking a sip of the hot liquid before turning her attention once more to the "matter."

"We've discussed at length your mother and father, Glynna, so there's no need to delve into unnecessary detail. You know that your father was Anglo-Irish — "

"Like the writer, Jonathan Swift."

"Yes," Darcie continued. "The Anglo-Irish have been trained generation after generation to serve the Crown, but that is not to say their lives have not greatly touched the Irish people. Your father was a bright lad, but Ireland is a country of limited opportunities. Banking is one of them, and one to which your father was certainly suited. Though not a member of the titled gentry, he was, nonetheless, a gentleman by all rights, an honest, hard-working, brilliant businessman who earned a considerable fortune in his short lifetime. Not trusting anyone he knew in Dublin to handle his business interests properly, he mandated that, upon his death, all of his holdings should be sold and the proceeds put in trust for you."

Darcie paused to take another sip of her tea. "Naturally, he set aside an allowance for your mother, and that, too, went into your trust. In another year, when you have reached your twenty-first birthday, you can take possession of your inheritance, and then you will be a wealthy woman."

A bit of a smile touched Glynna's mouth as she swallowed a bite of teacake, following it with a sip of tea. She knew from the many conversations she'd had with her aunt that the O'Rourkes had been loving parents and fine, stable citizens of Dublin before a disastrous fire had claimed their lives. The couple had been away on holiday, leaving three-year-old Glynna at home in the care of her nanny, when the inn where they were staying had been engulfed in flames. The fire had taken the lives of a score of guests. Shortly after this unfortunate incident Glynna had gone to live with Darcie and Galen.

Glynna pondered her aunt's altered demeanor, still puzzling over the seriousness of the matter at hand. She had grown up in colonial Virginia, following her aunt and uncle's emigration from the Isle of Man shortly after the deaths of her parents. Glynna remembered little of that time in her life. At first they had settled in Williamsburg, where they had lived in a beautifully appointed, three-story townhouse. She had attended a private school for girls, whose purpose was to prepare its students for the life of "polite society." While attending, Glynna had studied mathematics, English literature, the classics, and French. During those early years in the colonies, her uncle had built a tavern on Duke of Gloucester Street, and Aunt Darcie's fine culinary skills coupled with Uncle Galen's warm hospitality and strong business acumen had made the endeavor a major success. Glynna had never understood why her uncle had suddenly sold the tavern and moved his family westward to the frontier. That had been seven years ago.

In many aspects, life on the frontier had not been kind. They were far removed from reliable medical care, and supplies were often slow in arriving, if they came at all. Furthermore, at the brink of the wilderness two of her cousins had lost their lives: Garth had been mauled by a bear when he was but fourteen, and Cullen had fallen victim to a strange fever and had died last winter, at the tender age of twelve. Now Brian remained the Cavanaughs' only natural child, and it was for this reason Glynna, Darcie, and Galen were so protective of him.

As though she knew what thoughts coursed through her niece's mind, the older woman said, "I know, Glynna, that despite the hardships we have suffered here, you have been happy on the frontier. It seems to suit you, to suit the dream world in which you live. Although you have never mentioned it, I would wager that you fully expect a knight in shining armor to come riding through that forest out there one day and take you away."

Glynna's smile over the lip of her teacup acknowledged that the thought had, indeed, crossed her mind.

"By faith," Darcie exclaimed, "that is all you know of courting, love, and marriage; for there are certainly few young swains around here to come wooing . . . but I am straying." She paused momentarily to collect her wits, her eyes raking the contents of the papers before she spoke again. "When you were but a wee babe, your father conducted some business with a lesser baron whose land holdings are in County Galway. The soil there is thin and rocky, and poses a constant struggle for those who wrest a living from it. The baron not only had trouble collecting rents because of this, but his family's fortune had already been diminished by poor investments his father made before the baron inherited the title and the land.

"Though this man was only a lesser baron, he was a baron nevertheless, and this fact impressed your father. If money could have bought him a peerage, Glynndon O'Rourke would have made the investment—and considered it a sound one. At any rate, your father had money, and the baron needed the use of it, that is true. The two men liked each other immensely as well, however, and a close friendship sprang up between them."

Glynna frowned slightly as she daintily touched a linen napkin to her mouth. She asked in confusion, "What are you trying to tell me, Aunt Darcie? What does my inheritance have to do with some lesser baron in Ireland?"

Darcie touched the sheaf of papers again. "It seems that your father died before the debt owed him by the Baron of Ulrich was completely paid. Now the baron and baroness feel that they owe you something. Next year, you will come into your inheritance, and they wish you to spend a year with them in London, where they will provide opportunities for you to meet eligible young men from Britain's elite."

Glynna's brilliant green eyes widened at the thought. Why would this news disturb Aunt Darcie, as it quite obviously had? "Do you mean I am to be treated as a real lady of society? That I will have satin and lace dresses to wear and a maid to do my hair, that I will be able to attend real balls and concerts and go to the theater?"

Darcie poured herself a fresh cup of tea, then gave close scrutiny to her niece, whose tone was filled with anticipation. How could she make Glynna understand the implications? Was it her own possessiveness that made this matter so difficult? She had never allowed herself to entertain the thought of Glynna's being very far away from her, even after marriage. She had grown to love the girl far more than she had thought possible. Now her heart was rending at the prospect of losing her niece, who was more like a daughter. Darcie did not care to admit, either, that she had been overprotective of Glynna. There was much the girl had yet to learn of life, and her aunt had always thought she would be the one to teach her. It appeared now, however, that this duty might well fall to the baroness, a woman Darcie had never met, and one who might not accomplish the task as well as Darcie herself would. With great effort, Darcie forced these thoughts from her mind and attempted a smile.

"I suppose you will have all those things, Glynna. At least that is what I have been able to glean from these papers, which arrived this afternoon by special messenger from Williamsburg."

Darcie Cavanaugh had waged a small battle with herself while she had waited for Glynna earlier. Would telling her niece why they had fled to the colonies serve any real purpose now? Darcie thought not. Such a discussion might become necessary, however, before Glynna left for London. Darcie could feel the tentacles of fate reaching out from across the sea, not quite touching them yet, but too near for her to remain comfortable. Her glance fell to the papers under her hands and a cold chill danced along the length of her spine.

The opaque dreaminess in Glynna's eyes began to dissolve, soon to be replaced by an uncharacteristic coolness as her gaze settled on the papers.

"What else does this missive say, Aunt Darcie?" she asked quietly, her small, lithe frame suddenly overcome with cold dread in the warmth of the May afternoon.

Darcie took a deep breath. She knew Glynna would not take kindly to the baroness's plans. Her niece prided herself on her education, much of it self-taught though well learned. "The Baroness of Ulrich is concerned that your education might be lacking. She is, therefore, sending a tutor to instruct you in the proper decorum for ladies of society, and then to accompany you as your chaperone when you travel to London."

Glynna was aghast. She stood up and began to pace the room, her creamy complexion blotched with ire as she shook her fist at the papers. "I probably know more than most of the fine British ladies my age. In point of fact, I may know more than this tutor! Education lacking? Ha!"

Darcie looked sadly at her niece's set features. "It may be too late, Glynna. This man is now in Williamsburg, arranging suitable conveyance. He should arrive within the week."

"Then he shall just have to return to Ireland, shan't he?" Glynna set her jaw firmly to still the trembling of her lower lip. Her resolve made, she put her anger aside and turned her attention to her duties.

Nimble fingers quickly disciplined the loose tendrils of hair about her forehead, and the smile that touched her lips added bright pinpoints of light to her emerald eyes. "Our guests are thirsty for their tea, Aunt Darcie. I'll have the girls bring in the trays."

Chapter Two

"New to these yere parts, ain't ye?"

The man to whom the remark was addressed sat hunkered in a corner of the forward seat of the bouncing coach, his gray wool tricorn pulled low over his forehead, his eyes shut against both the bright sunlight pouring through the open window and the reversed passage of the Virginia landscape from without. The wheels of the coach seemed to find every rut in the narrow road, some of them so deep as to propel the three passengers completely off the leather seat, threatening to cast them upon the floor or crush their heads against the roof.

Kane Rafferty was growing weary of this journey. Although he was accustomed to travel, never before had he wandered so far. The ocean voyage had proved long and tiresome; its culmination in the charming village of Williamsburg had been a boon, however, to Kane's spirits, for he had found the town both delightfully quaint and wonderfully warm. He had thought, at first, that he might have some problem securing a coach and driver for the lengthy journey to the edge of the frontier, but upon showing the

27

color of his purse, several volunteers had come forward. Not wanting his arrival at the inn to be without preamble, he selected the one with the strongest horse to deliver the letters from his parents, the one with the most commodious coach to deliver his person and his baggage.

The first three and a half days out of Williamsburg had proved uneventful. The road had been wider and smoother at first, as they had followed the James River northward and westward. Gradually, however, the farms had thinned out, and the road had narrowed to a deep-rutted trail, making the journey far less comfortable.

Then, at yesterday noon, Rafferty had hailed the driver to stop as billows of black, roiling smoke filled the coach's interior. Its source, a small farmhouse set back from the road, was engulfed in flames. The quite recent occupants had been rushing wildly about filling buckets from the well and ineffectively tossing water on the fire. Both Kane and the coachman had joined the effort, and though they had worked diligently along with the farmer and his wife, they had not been able to save the small house.

Luckily, the barn had been erected some distance from the dwelling place and had not been affected by the blaze. After all hope for the house had been lost, the four had taken turns dousing their work-weary, grimy bodies in a nearby creek. The couple had managed to save a few of their possessions, including several changes of clothing and some household goods, and these were scattered helter-skelter across the yard. While the woman had prepared an omelet for their supper, the men had set about retrieving what had been saved and stowing these items in the barn. The cow had provided fresh milk to go along with the hens' eggs, and the barn had provided shelter, the four had fallen into the soft hay mows, sleep overtaking them with the swiftness and heaviness of a charging bull.

In the morning, as Kane and the coachman were preparing to leave, the farmer had humbly thanked them for their assistance, and then, to Kane's surprise, had asked if he and his wife might accompany them westward. "Me and the wife've been thinking of moving on Shenando' way. Got relatives 'cross the mountains. They say it's rich, fertile land there in the valley."

His eyes unconsciously straying, Kane glanced at the weathered buckboard by the barn.

"Old Buster never would make it that far if'n he had to pull a loaded wagon," the farmer supplied.

Kane's leaving had, therefore, been delayed a short time while articles were tied into bundles and lashed securely to the roof of the coach. The cow and Old Buster were tied to the back of the vehicle, but the chickens, caged in two wooden crates, rode the interior along with the three passengers. Kane had borne their constant clucking until he'd felt a strong desire to wring their feathered necks.

Yet the farmer's wife had let out a yelp that morning when the coachman had attempted to wrest the crates from her tightly closed fingers. "Them's my babies. They go with me," she had insisted, tears coursing down her cheeks at the thought of losing the noisy birds off the top of the coach. No amount of cajoling or assurance that the crates would be firmly lashed down convinced her otherwise. She now sat next to her husband, cooing to her "babies," her almost nonexistent chin pressed into fat jowls as she patted the crate on her lap. The other one rested upon the floor, providing a footrest for her booted feet. From time to time, she switched the crates, a difficult and noisome task in the crowded confines of the coach's interior. In an attempt to ignore the offending creatures, Kane had tried to sleep, but rest eluded him.

Suddenly pain shot up his left leg as a heavy boot made contact with his shin. Lazily he opened one eye, setting its steel gray gleam upon the offending boot, the toe of which was bare of the fresh red mud caking its sole. His gaze traveled slowly to the white stocking on his left leg. A large dollop of gooey clay clung tenuously at the point of contact, its weight demanding release as the silk quickly absorbed its sticky moisture.

As Kane reached for his own handkerchief, the farmer pulled a plainly hemmed square of coarse brown homespun from his waistcoat pocket and handed it over sheepishly. "Sorry. I didn't mean . . ."

Kane's lean fingers applied the nut brown square to the lump of mud, catching it in the middle of the handkerchief, then twisting the coarse fabric around it. He used the corner of the piece of cloth to rub roughly at the spreading stain before returning the messy bundle to the farmer.

"Just trying to be friendly. Couldn't seem to git your attention no other way. Sorry we weren't introduced last evening. Cyrus McGinty's the name." The farmer stuck out a gnarled brown hand, which Kane took, a hint of a smile lifting the corners of his wide mouth. Although almost twenty-four hours had passed since he had stopped to aid the farmer, the two had, indeed, been too preoccupied with survival to spend much time conversing. Among the lack of amenities had been proper introductions.

"You are new to these yere parts, ain't ye, mister?" Cyrus McGinty reiterated. A brief nod served as the farmer's answer. McGinty was undaunted. "Got business up the road?" A nod again. "Got a name?" Now here was a question that required a verbal response from the reticent stranger!

Kane pushed his gray tricorn back and sat up straighter, his smile growing wider and lighting his gray eyes. The farmer certainly had perseverance, an admirable quality in his estimation. "Rafferty," he said, his voice deep and well modulated. "Kane Rafferty."

McGinty grinned. "Well, now, how do you do, Mr. Rafferty? And what brings you to these parts, besides rescuing two crotchety, backwoods people?"

"A girl's education, or rather, her lack of one." Kane Rafferty did not mean to be rude; he simply could think of little he wished to discuss at the moment, having allowed himself to become absorbed in his own annoying thoughts. He was outdone with his mother. It was strictly on her behalf that he had agreed to this venture, and he could think of a number of other available options he would rather have pursued, not one of which would have placed him in a bouncing coach in the wilderness with a talkative farmer and a dozen clucking chickens for company.

McGinty shifted uncomfortably, then turned his gaze to the open window. "Beautiful horse country here. Folks've been raising Thoroughbreds around here for more'n a score o' years now."

"Is that so?" Rafferty asked absently, his attention now diverted to the view from the window. He had paid little heed to the countryside since leaving Williamsburg five days ago, having quickly become bored with the never-ending ripple of tobacco rows, their green shoots just inches high. At some point, though—the tutor wasn't sure just where—the plantations had given way to gently rolling hills, the occasional mansions to houses with dormers and tall

31

chimneys, patches of corn and small plots of tobacco nestled nearby. A thick carpet of verdant green covered the landscape, its brilliance darkened in dappled patches where stately oaks spread thickly leaved arms wide or a popcorn cloud obscured the sun's rays. For a brief moment, his heart constricted before he cast aside the ridiculous notion that had caught him unawares. Nowhere on earth could the green match that of his beloved Ireland.

From the crest of a hill the proud head of a chestnut stallion appeared, his long, lean forelegs sending tufts of earth and grass flying. For a moment the horse paused, turning his head back to look down the hidden side of the hill, his sleek body a tense silhouette posed against the blue breast of the sky. Rafferty found himself touched, quite involuntarily, by the pastoral beauty of the scene.

"In a couple hours we'll be there."

Kane had become lost in reverie again. "And where is that?" he questioned.

Cyrus McGinty pursed his leathery lips as he considered the well-dressed and obviously well-educated man in front of him. Didn't he know where he was headed? "Cavanaugh's Tavern, o' course. Ain't that where ye're goin'?"

Suppressing the enthusiasm of his natural curiosity, Kane asked flatly, "Have you been there?"

"Naw. Just heared about it. Me and the wife'll be spendin' some time there until we can git word to our folks in the valley to come and fetch us."

The farmer's correct assumption as to their destination gave Kane pause. "How did you know where I was going?"

" 'Cause Cavanaugh's place is the end of the road. Ain't much else 'tween here and there, 'ceptin' a few farms. It just seemed the likely place."

My God! Did all the people in rural Virginia have such poor grammar and atrocious diction? Were there no schoolmasters to teach the king's English? Would his pupil speak so? If she did, he certainly had his work cut out for him.

Kane Rafferty, eldest son of the Baron of Ulrich, had been so absorbed in his own private irritations that he had given little thought to the young woman he would attempt to teach. Now, though, he paused to consider this task his mother had set for him. What kind of tutor would he be? His own school masters had been hard and brittle, demanding much of their pupils and tolerating no laziness. He could not quite see himself in this role, yet a part of him yearned to discover how well he could teach.

Would his pupil be amenable to his instruction? What would she be like? Tall and gangly? Short and fat? Totally undisciplined? Loud and boisterous? Or shy and reserved? He found his imagination running from one end of the spectrum to the other.

There was also the matter of the jewel-encrusted tiara—the real matter that had spawned his journey. What would his mother say if he failed to locate it? Indeed, what would his father do should he ever have to be told that it had been lost in the first place? The tiara had traditionally been worn by the brides of Ulrich, a tradition that had spanned almost four centuries. To even consider that this priceless headpiece might be lost forever bordered on treason.

Perhaps conversation with McGinty would ease his irritated spirit. The man certainly seemed inclined to talk. "Tell me about Virginia," Kane requested, settling himself back into his corner as the farmer accepted the challenge.

* * *

Although the day had begun like any other, with the family and slaves arising before dawn to begin the daily regimen of chores, an air of expectancy pervaded the crisp, bright morning. Four days had passed since the messenger had arrived. Today—Friday—was the earliest, by Glynna's and Darcie's calculations, the tutor could make it that far in a coach. Would he arrive?

Darcie and Glynna had both avoided discussing the distinct possibility of his arrival on Friday. As the week progressed, Glynna's resolve to send the man packing had strengthened. The more she had thought about it, the more outraged she had become. How dare the baroness think of her as illiterate and uncivilized!

Dusting the gentlemen's parlor was one of Glynna's Friday chores. Just thinking about the highly probable imminent arrival of the tutor had her dander up, and she attacked the room with a vengeance. Within minutes she had knocked over the inkwell on the desk, the dark liquid puddling on the thick coating of beeswax. Although she managed to clean it up before it damaged the furniture, the task left purplish-black stains on her hands and nails. A short time later she dropped the pipe rack, breaking half a dozen of its clay pipes. As she knelt on the floor, surveying the damage, Aunt Darcie walked in. The look she gave Glynna was neither one of condemnation nor of sympathy but rather one of calm acceptance.

"Perhaps we had better swap jobs this morning, Glynna," she suggested. "You go finish weeding my tomatoes, and I'll clean up this mess."

Glynna nodded, standing up and brushing absently at her apron. As she moved silently through the doorway, her aunt called good-naturedly, "Be sure to pull the *weeds*—not my tomato plants!"

The slaves were responsible for taking care of all the crops, both in the fields and in the gardens, except the tomatoes. These they refused to tend, claiming that the tomato was the poisonous fruit of the devil. Accepting their superstitions, Aunt Darcie planted her tomatoes in a separate plot just off the walkway connecting the kitchen to the keeping hall, where she could tend them personally. Glynna knelt carefully among the tender, young plants, and found that jerking weeds from the moist earth suited her black mood well.

Just short of an hour before noon, Kane Rafferty noted a distinct difference in the terrain. The gentle ascents had given rise to much sharper inclines, and plateaus had replaced the mildly sloping descents. He found the wild, untamed beauty of the land both exhilarating and frightening. Thickly leaved evergreens dotted the slopes, their dark green needles glistening in the bright sunlight, their solidity obscuring much of the view, which was broken only by an occasional outcropping of rock. At one such break in the trees, Rafferty caught a breathtaking glimpse of the valley below, a glimpse that filled him with so much amazement and wonder that he almost called out to the driver to stop the coach. The stark beauty of Virginia had surprised him—nay, shocked him. He had not expected such loveliness from this wild land.

It occurred to him that he had yet to see a native, one of those savage Indian beasts who, according to the rumors touted about Great Britain and the Continent, roamed the land, torturing and killing unwary white settlers. These savages painted their faces

35

and chests and wore only loincloths to hide their nakedness . . . or so he had been told. Their bronze skins glistened with bear grease and their dark eyes stared wildly from deep sockets. Were it not for fear of losing his scalp, Rafferty thought he might like to encounter one of them.

His musings came to an abrupt halt as the coach itself halted. So . . . At last they had arrived at Cavanaugh's. Rafferty stifled the desire to crane his neck in an attempt to secure a look at the place, which was visible only from the opposite window of the coach, and sat calmly until the coachman opened the door and beckoned the passengers to disembark.

Kane Rafferty stood aside, his view of the tavern still obstructed by the coach. The McGintys descended, Cyrus assisting his wife with the chicken crates. Watching the man's heartfelt solicitousness convinced Kane that the presence of the noisy, smelly creatures had not been so offensive after all.

The coachman handed him his valise, a large, handsome black leather bag which boasted a brass lock and plate bearing his engraved initials, and the tutor followed the McGintys around the back of the coach to the brick walk which led to the inn's ordinary. The sight of the tavern took Kane Rafferty completely by surprise. Its size far surpassed that of any other at which the coach had stopped along its journey, but it was the stateliness of the inn which really stunned him.

The gleaming white structure sat atop a slight rise, spreading its wings outward to embrace the landscape. The stepped walk curved in a gentle S as it wound its way around two tall sycamores to reach the columned porch at the center of the inn. This must have been the original building, he surmised, his approving gaze surveying its two galleried stories, on either side of which rose tall brick chimneys. The wings sported dormers whose windows, like those of the lower floor, were gracefully draped with simple, white, tie-back curtains. Black shutters defined the windows that broke the expanse of the ground floor of the building, while a myriad of tiny, multicolored flowers filled windowboxes on the wings. The inn bore an air of understated elegance.

A petite, gray-haired woman with a warm smile and sparkling white apron greeted the passengers as they passed through the doorway and into the front hall. The tutor, entering last, had made his way more slowly, in large part due to his absorption with the large, elegant inn. The woman spoke to the McGintys, her voice so low he could not hear her words, though he could see her pleasant smile and the warmth of understanding in her soft blue eyes. Without argument, the farmer's wife allowed the servant to take the crates from her and deposit them out of the way on the porch. Once the couple was inside, the tiny woman motioned to a young, red-haired boy playing on the front lawn. The lad obediently picked up the two crates of clucking hens and headed around the sprawling building with them.

"You have my deepest gratitude, my lady," Rafferty said softly, his free hand waving her inside ahead of him. A knowing smile touched her eyes, crinkling their corners and lighting their blue depths as the sun's rays give light to the delicate hue of a Scottish bluebell. He could not help thinking what a lovely woman she was, how beautiful she must have been when her youth had blossomed into womanhood. Such a shame that she had been indentured, forced into a life of servitude while her dazzling youth slipped away from her. He pondered the nature of her crime and the length of her contract.

Despite his attempt to hide it, Rafferty knew his surprise showed clearly on his face when she introduced herself.

"Welcome to our corner of the world," she said, her voice soft and fluid. Her intonation carried a pleasing drawl similar to that he had heard on occasion in Williamsburg. "I am your hostess, Darcie Cavanaugh."

The tutor quickly recovered his poise. "Ah, then it is your niece I am to educate. I am Kane Rafferty." Her delicate eyebrows rose slightly as her mouth formed an O, a hint of mischief joining the smile in her eyes. Misunderstanding her expression, he added, "You did receive the baron's correspondence?"

"Oh, yes," she hastened to acknowledge, her eyebrows resettling themselves but the mischief still in her eyes. "Yes, indeed!"

Searching for some explanation of her attitude, Kane suggested, "But you were expecting someone . . . older?"

Blithely she ignored his question. "We are so pleased to have you stay with us, Mr. Rafferty. A private room has been prepared for you, and I will have someone take your valise there now and unpack it for you. You must be tired from your journey, and hungry for a good meal, I would think." A small, expressive hand gestured to the open doorway of the ordinary where two neatly dressed, gingham-aproned black girls were putting onto several tables platters and bowls laden with an assortment of foods, the odors given off blending in a mouth-watering fragrance Rafferty could not ignore. "The gentlemen's parlor is through that doorway," she added, indicating a room on the opposite side of the front hall, "should you care to wash up before dinner."

Kane found her reference to the noonday meal as dinner rather than luncheon strange, as he had many other aspects of language he had heard since arriving in Virginia. "Thank you. I would," he said, "but I would also like to meet my charge as soon as possible. Where might I find her?"

The mischief, full-blown now, fairly danced in Darcie's eyes as she pointed toward the back wall of the ordinary. "Go through that door, across the keeping hall, and out the back entrance onto a covered brick walk. I believe you will find my niece quite alone in the garden. Please pardon my sending you by yourself, but I must supervise the serving."

"I shall be able to manage, I think," he said, turning first to the gentlemen's parlor as she had suggested.

Darcie stood in the hall for another minute, staring at the parlor door and considering the gentleman who had finally arrived. Since receiving the baron's correspondence earlier in the week, Darcie had thought of little else but her niece's future. This man was now part of that future, for the time being at least. What will Glynna think of such a handsome young man? she wondered, certain that her niece would be as surprised as she had been at both his youth and his good looks. The man had been correct in assuming her expectance of an older man . . . a much older man, in fact, and not one named Rafferty. Darcie smiled. And Glynna was prepared to send him packing.

There was a new bounce to Darcie's step, and the tune of an Irish ditty was upon her lips as she moved into the ordinary to see to the needs of her guests.

Glynna raked the back of a dirty hand across her

damp forehead as she sat back on her haunches to survey her handiwork. The day had grown warm, its heat intensified by the vigor with which she had attacked the bothersome weeds. Her stomach grumbled noisily, reminding her it was time to eat. Knowing Katie, she was certain that efficient woman already had the big wooden washtub in the kitchen filled with steaming water for a bath. It was also highly probable that the much-loved slave had prepared a plate of food for Glynna and was keeping it warm on the kitchen hearth. As soon as Glynna plucked the yellowed leaves from the lower stalks of the tomato plants, she would head for the kitchen. Perhaps she could cajole Katie into singing to her in her pleasant contralto voice. Glynna loved its soft cadence and delighted in the poignant eeriness of the minor keys of Katie's favorite songs.

With the grace of a cat, Glynna stretched her aching arms, pulling hard on her shoulder muscles in an effort to relieve their distress before turning her attention to the delicate plants once more. She neither saw nor heard anyone approach, so the rather soft "Excuse me" startled her almost as much as a thunderclap might have. Her hand involuntarily jerked up the plant she held, and she found herself looking at a gossamer cluster of tiny roots.

"Oh!" she gasped, distress scrunching her delicate features into a tortured mask. Quickly, she dug her fingers into the soft black earth until she had made a hole large enough to accommodate the root ball. Gently, she tamped the soil around its stalk, and when she saw that the plant would stand up straight, she breathed an audible sigh of relief.

The stranger, who had paid little heed either to her or to her deed, was looking around the garden for that one he sought. His eyes lit on several wooden benches along the narrow walkways branching into the gardens, and he noted that an assortment of shrubs, roses, and perennials were planted here, many of which had already begun to bloom. It was a pretty, peaceful place, seemingly laid out with carefree abandon. Closer scrutiny, however, indicated it to be masterfully planned in order to blend the stateliness of the inn with the wildness of its surroundings.

Seeing no one else around, Kane turned his attention once more to the girl who was working with the tomato plants. Lord, she was a mess! Her long, unruly locks cascaded down her back, their weight caught up in a kerchief which covered the top of her head and whose ends were tied underneath the mass at the nape of her neck. The kerchief, once white, bore a myriad of dirty handprints as did the apron which covered a nondescript calico dress. The girl's face, arms, and hands also were darkened by soil. Curly tendrils of auburn hair had escaped the confines of the kerchief to cluster about her grimy face. She resembled the street urchins he had seen the one time he had gone slumming in London.

Glynna, having finished the replanting, glanced up to see a white stockinged leg planted on the walk in front of her. This was the intruder who had startled her into pulling up one of Aunt Darcie's treasured tomatoes. The stocking bore an ugly red mud stain which appeared quite incongruous on this otherwise immaculate person.

"Pardon me," he said, at last capturing her attention, "but would you know where I might find a Miss Glynna O'Rourke?"

The young woman revealed wide, brilliant green eyes. He had thought her to be prepubescent; he now placed her age at about ten and six.

"Yes, I might know where she is." Glynna had no desire in her present state to acknowledge her identity. "Whom may I say is asking to see her?"

Kane Rafferty's eyes narrowed in angry irritation. In his father's home, servants were not allowed to speak so impudently. "Tell her I am the tutor the baroness has sent to see to her education. I shall want to see her as soon as I have eaten and seen my room. Her aunt will know where to find me." *Damn!* Why was he explaining himself to a servant?

The words were clipped, almost angrily spoken, most definitely carrying a certain haughtiness and arrogance which Glynna found delightful. It would not be difficult at all to bid this insolent man good day.

Yet, as he turned on his heel to walk away, she could not help noticing the rippling of muscles down his long, lean thighs or the width of the shoulders beneath his frock coat. His hair, black as a raven's wing and caught into a queue, glistened in its unpowdered beauty. Though his gray eyes had snapped authoritatively from their hard depths, Glynna had thought of the soft gray feathers of a dove as she had looked into them. And then there was the stain on the white silk of his stocking, totally inconsistent with the stark immaculateness of his attire, yet it indicated a certain human vulnerability.

Glynna smiled behind her grimy hand as she walked toward the kitchen and her much-desired bath.

Chapter Three

He really is an insufferable lout.

But you have to admit he's the most handsome man you've ever seen.

Recently, maybe. But there has to be more to a person than good looks to make him attractive.

Sure. There's cow dung on a man's boots, or the rancid odor of unwashed flesh and the gleam of yellowed, rotting teeth, or a year's growth of scraggly beard to catch a girl's eye and warm her heart.

He thinks I'm ignorant and uncultured.

And you had no preconceived notions concerning him before he came? Why don't you give him a chance?

Glynna studied the bare toes of her dainty foot which was propped on the edge of the oversized wooden tub in which she sat. The warm water, having soothed her aching muscles and cleansed her dirty body, had now grown tepid, a condition which she had only recently begun to note. The dark mass of her damp, freshly washed hair hung over the side of the tub, its unruliness yet untamed by a comb, its curling ends lying on the white linen towel Katie had laid out on the clean-swept bricks of the kitchen floor. Glynna watched lazily as the quickly disappearing bubbles, their faint English lavender fragrance wafting up to tease her senses, swirled around the soft mounds of her breasts, the pink crests standing erect. A cooling breeze sailed through the open door, sending a tingle down her spine and ironically warming her deep within. The new sensation startled Glynna and caused her to turn her attention to the one other occupant of the kitchen.

"Hrrumph," Katie bellowed, settling her bulk upon wide knees beside the tub as she took up comb and hair and began untangling the mess. Her body blocked both the breeze and the sunlight from the open door, a mixed blessing for Glynna, who had been enjoying the touch of the sun's rays upon her bare limbs. The breeze, however, had proved to be the harbinger of those new sensations she had neither expected nor prepared for. A part of her felt no remorse for its abrupt disappearance.

Katie pursed thick lips, her quick, bright eyes assessing her young mistress. Glynna had learned at an early age that there was little, if anything, which could begotten past the Cavanaugh's robust cook. Katie's body might not possess much agility, but her mind certainly did. Glynna had the distinct feeling that Katie had heard every one of her thoughts as she had argued with herself over what to think of the tall, dark stranger who had sought her out in the garden.

"You feels bettah now, Miss Glynna?" Katie's soft, mellow voice crooned. "I best git this hair dressed an' git you outta that cole water 'fore you catches your death." Her large hands put the comb aside and reached for a brush, her meaty arms pulling its bristles through the thick mass with surprising gentle-

44

ness. Glynna relished the unwarranted attention, for she was accustomed to performing such chores herself. Her eyelids drooped lazily, their thick fringes fanning skin pink from recent scrubbing. A long sigh of self-gratification escaped her as she lifted her neck from the edge of the tub to allow Katie's brush to complete its ministrations.

"Pardon me."

The deep male voice rudely intruded on the soft quiet of the early afternoon. Quickly, Glynna slipped deeper into the tub, her hand groping for the large linen towel Katie had hung on a rack close by. Although Katie's bulk sat between her and the unwelcome visitor, Glynna had no intention of allowing him to see even a bare toe. How dare he stand there in the open doorway when he could plainly see she was indisposed? And *he* intended to teach *her* manners and courtesy?

The man stood stock-still, his patience tried as he waited for the towel to be draped across the open expanse of the wooden tub. From all appearances—he could see only the tumble of auburn tresses in the dim interior of the kitchen—the tub's occupant was the girl he had seen weeding in the garden earlier, the one who was supposed to have informed Miss Glynna O'Rourke of his arrival. Why, she was no more than a chit, too young and certainly too common to be overly concerned with modesty.

Katie's large head twisted around on the folds of her ample neck, her dark eyes narrowing as she surveyed this impertinent man. "You must be lost, suh," she said, her voice quietly respectful, belying the indignation sparking in her bright eyes. "This here be the kitchen, where we's *cook* the food, not serve it." She paused, allowing time for the man to acknowledge her observation of his misdirection. When the

45

intruder neither said anything nor removed himself from the doorway, she continued, "An' where we doan 'spect no outsiders to come call in' when we's usin' it for a bathin' house."

Despite the chilling effects of the cool water and the breeze which was becoming stronger by the minute, Glynna felt a warm flush spread over her, beginning at her neck and traveling swiftly through her trunk and limbs all the way to her bare toes, which were now covered by the towel. She squeezed her eyelids tightly shut, thinking, quite foolishly she later realized, that if she couldn't see him, then he couldn't see her either.

"I was told I could find Miss Glynna O'Rourke here."

A sharp intake of breath from the vicinity of the tub momentarily drew Katie's attention. A quick glance from the cook in her direction assured Glynna of Katie's discretion.

"You go on back up to the house," Katie ordered, her words drawing a tiny smile from Glynna's coldly set lips. "I'll find her and send her on up there directly."

"You do that," the man said, turning on his heel, then calling over his shoulder as he walked back down the covered path, "and you tell her my patience is growing thin."

Katie chuckled at his retreating back, bracing her hands on the edge of the tub and pushing herself up. As she turned to close the door against further intrusion, she laughingly said, "You can come on out now, Miss Glynna. He be gone, but you done made that man real mad."

"I don't care!" Glynna declared petulantly, her arms crossing behind her neck to lift her hair as she stood up in the tub. Katie held the towel, which she had managed to retrieve before Glynna's sudden movements doused it in the water. When the young woman stood, dripping and shivering, Katie used its length to dry her creamy skin.

"Lord High and Mighty's not nearly so smart as he thinks he is." Glynna laughed despite her anger. "Why, that's twice now he has found me, and he still doesn't know it! I wonder who he thinks I am anyway."

Stepping from the tub, she lifted her arms over her head to receive the clean chemise Katie pulled down over her bosom. To herself, she mumbled, "I wonder who *he* is."

Katie frowned slightly, puzzled. "He's that teacher, ob cose, sent by that lawd or whateber he be." Although Glynna was aware of no direct conversation with the cook concerning the tutor's imminent arrival, she remained unsurprised by Katie's knowledge. Katie knew everything that was going on at Cavanaugh's Tavern, and usually she seemed to know what everyone was thinking, which would have unsettled Glynna had she not become accustomed to it over the years. She had, in fact, learned to appreciate Katie's gift, for it removed the necessity for explanation much of the time and allowed for an easy camaraderie between them.

"I know that," she minced, pirouetting so Katie could lace up the back of her fresh day gown. "What I don't know is his *name,* and he knows mine, which puts me at a disadvantage, and you know I don't like to be at a disadvantage." She reached for the hairbrush, grasping its handle so tightly that her knuckles turned white, and began to pull it through her tresses once more. "I had better not take the time to braid my hair and pin it up," she said as much to herself as to Katie. "Lord High and Mighty awaits."

Turning toward the cook, she asked, "You don't know what his name is, do you, Katie?"

When the black woman shook her head, Glynna persisted, not quite convinced her friend had not heard his name somewhere. "Think, Katie. Are you sure you don't know?"

Katie gave her a toothy grin. "I reckon you'll find out soon enough, Miss Glynna." She shooed Glynna toward the open doorway. "You best run along now and be properly innerduced to the fine gempmum from 'cross de sea. He done come a long way to see you." When Glynna hesitated, Katie gently ordered, "Run on. I gots my work to do an' you in the way."

Glynna took a deep breath and ran her open palms down the bodice of her dress, smoothing its wrinkles. The deed brought her attention to the ink splotches staining her hands. She eyed them critically, chagrined that the scrubbing had failed to erase them, although their dark starkness had been diminished. "I wish . . ." she began, letting her voice trail off.

Katie turned from the chopping block where she had begun to peel potatoes in preparation for supper. "You still here? I thought I tole you—"

"I'm going," Glynna countered, her voice sharper than she had intended it to be. Softer, not quite so sure of herself, she repeated, "I'm going."

She took a few tentative steps toward the door, then turned and almost ran over to Katie, her slender arms reaching out to encircle the larger woman's almost nonexistent waistline. "I love you, Katie. Thanks for the bath and dinner and . . . well, thanks for understanding." Her small frame shuddered slightly against Katie's bulk. "Wish me luck?"

Katie's meaty hand, wiped clean on a towel, patted the top of Glynna's head. "Jes' be yo'sef, chile," she whispered. "Jes' be yo'sef."

Resolutely, Glynna pulled away from the black woman's bulk and walked slowly through the doorway and down the covered path to the inn. She straightened her back and wiped all traces of trepidation from her face. In her mind, she rehearsed again the lines she had so carefully planned. She supposed she would have to put up with the man for a few days. He would want to rest some before beginning his journey back to Williamsburg. So, what were a few days? She could bear anything—even *him!*—for that long.

Absorbed in her reverie, Glynna had not noticed the darkening sky. A sudden, rather loud clap of thunder ended her measured steps and sent her scurrying for the door to the keeping hall, though she chided herself for such skittishness. Whatever had happened to her today? Everything seemed to startle her. She was not some mouse to be devoured alive by his lord and highness. She stopped before the door, her hand upon its knob, her head held high once more. *He doesn't scare me. Nothing does. I will politely dismiss him and he will return to Ireland next week.*

Despite her bravado, Glynna found herself immensely relieved when she opened the door to a room empty of occupants. Her quick perusal of both the ordinary and the gentlemen's parlor failed to produce the tutor. Where had he gone? She stood in the front hall, her brow gathered in thought, when Aunt Darcie came through the door carrying chair cushions she had retrieved from the porch.

"Glynna!" Darcie exclaimed, shoving the cushions into her niece's arms. "Where have you been? Oh, never mind. Put these up while I get the rest of them. It's going to storm."

Glynna could not help smiling at her aunt's short sentences punctuated by quick movements. She was neatly stacking the plump cushions in the cabinet under the stairs when Darcie called to her from the porch, "And then go meet Mr. Rafferty. He's waiting for you in the ballroom."

Rafferty. So that was his name.

"The ballroom? Why there?"

"I thought it best. No interruptions. Now hurry!"

First Katie and now Aunt Darcie! Why were they so eager for her to meet this man? Sedately, and decidedly unhurried, Glynna mounted the stairs, her slippered feet padding softly on the thick carpet of each tread as she ascended to the second floor of the tavern. Outside, thunder rolled as the first fierce slashes of rain pelted against the window glass. Glynna watched them splatter against the panes of the landing window, her heart leaping into her throat when a jagged streak of lightning tore across the pewter sky, its flash momentarily blinding. She wanted with all her heart to run to her room and fall upon the counterpane, burying her head underneath her pillow while the storm spent its wrath. But the ballroom door beckoned.

Kane Rafferty had pulled a wing-backed chair from its usual corner out onto the bare, highly polished oak floor and turned it to face one of the large, western-faced, front windows. The oversized room, almost barren of furniture, lay shrouded in shadows. No lamps had been lit against the near darkness brought on prematurely by the fast-approaching storm. Only flashes of lightning, which were coming with increasing frequency now, heavy rolls of thunder presaging their occurrence, served to light the room. Their brilliance limned the planes of his face, the firm lines of his jaw, and fired silver

50

streaks into the gleaming blackness of his hair. The high back of the chair coupled with the lack of sufficient light successfully cloaked both his posture and his demeanor, but Glynna felt distinctly that this man was totally relaxed—and quite unaware of her entrance.

Without taking her eyes off him, she reached behind herself to close the door. Its metallic click brought his back up ramrod straight.

Amused, she watched him rise stiffly and turn toward her, his brow gathering into a frown as he peered into the grayness darkening the entrance. Self-consciously, she tucked her ink-stained hands into the folds of her skirts, which she lifted slightly as she dipped her lithe frame in a most becoming and respectful curtsy.

"You wished to see me, Mr. Rafferty?" she asked, molding her voice into the most dulcet of tones as a few steps took her closer to him. A flash of lightning illuminated her face then, drawing an almost inaudible gasp from the stranger.

"You? But you're—"

"Miss Glynna O'Rourke." She forced her mouth not to twitch, but merriment at his discomfiture sparkled in her green eyes.

Still, he seemed unconvinced. He stood chiding himself. He should have known. Her aunt had told him plainly that he would find her quite alone in the garden. But no. It just couldn't be.

"But you're the girl from the garden, and the one in the—" He caught himself then, not wishing to embarrass either of them further. Yesterday, he'd had no great desire to spend a year in this godforsaken country and attempt to teach a bumpkin how to be a great lady. Now he was intrigued by the prospect.

My God! Just look at her! She's neither chit nor

51

common. There's a regal aura about her—and there's passion in those eyes.

His right arm crossed his midsection and he afforded her a cursory bow, which she theorized was in deference to her act of courtesy.

"And I am Kane Rafferty, sent by the Baron and Baroness of Ulrich to prepare you for London society."

Did she detect a slight hesitation in his introduction of himself, or was it just the acceleration of her pulse, making her ears pound, that made her think so? Glynna could not be certain. What she did know was that her alter ego had been right: he was the most devastatingly handsome man she had ever seen, recently or otherwise. The planes of his face appeared sculpted, so perfectly artistic were their proportions. His nose, which would have seemed overly large on a face more finely boned, bridged the broad, unlined expanse of his forehead, and his decidedly wide mouth was defined by lips neither too thick nor too thin. His clear gray eyes had darkened, whether with emotion or the lack of light in the room Glynna could not be certain, to a color akin to that of the storm clouds gathering outside. His skin was lightly tanned, marred by neither an underlying ruddiness nor sallowness. Despite her earlier resolve, Glynna found herself quite taken aback; she tried to force a haughtiness she did not feel.

"And what if I do not wish to become a member of that group?" she asked more demurely than she had intended.

A smile graced his lips, placing a dimple in his left cheek. "I believe," he said levelly, "that it would be to your distinct advantage to allow me to stay."

An affectation of haughtiness was no longer required. "My advantage!" she railed, making a sharp quarter-turn to her left, away from him, and striding several paces into the room. Her hands left her skirts to fly ceilingward, her fingers splayed in anger. "Are you suggesting"—she whirled around, facing him again and dropping her arms as she noticed his gaze fall upon her ink-stained palms—"that I am ignorant and uncultured?"

The dimple deepened. "Isn't that what *you* think?"

Glynna fought for composure. "I really don't think that's your concern, *Mr.* Rafferty!"

"Ah, but that is where you are wrong, *Miss* O'Rourke, for what you are inside—how you feel about yourself—is as important as how you look, and is often the deciding factor in how you act. My purpose here is to shape you into the lady which you are to become, and it is with your soul that we must begin." He regarded her with amusement, an attitude Glynna found uncomfortably condescending. She regarded him with fierce animosity, an attitude which Rafferty found decidedly attractive. "I think I might enjoy my task after all," he admitted, surprising himself while reminding Glynna of her prepared speech.

" 'Tis a task which will never be undertaken, sir," she said flatly, without emotion, "for I have no desire to have you—or anyone else—tutor me."

Some of the amusement left his face. It was one thing to voluntarily return to the baron's estate in County Gal way and inform his parents that Miss O'Rourke was uneducable, and quite another to be forced into returning and imparting the information that his services had been declined. The latter would make him appear incompetent, possibly even undesirable, and would be certain to incite the baron's wrath. *That* he could stand, for he was no stranger to the baron's barbs. But her rejection of him stung

53

his pride. He must do something to convince this girl—dare he think of her as a young woman?—to allow him to stay, at least until he had discovered her potential, or lack of it. And, more importantly, until he had discovered whether or not his mother's tiara had come to Virginia with Miss O'Rourke.

He would try a different tactic. Perhaps all was not lost—yet. "And what do you suggest I do with myself for the next few days, for I am far too weary to return to Williamsburg just yet."

Feeling triumphant, Glynna moved toward the door, turning to bestow a winsome smile upon him as she reached it. Somehow, she could not imagine his ever being bored, his ever lacking a way to keep himself entertained. "We have stables here where you will find several fine Thoroughbreds from which you may select a mount, should you wish to ride. And my uncle's library boasts many fine volumes, both of British and American extraction, from which you may select reading material. If conversation is more to your liking, you will find the ordinary often packed with our guests and neighbors, some of whom are quite knowledgeable and given to debate." She paused, waving a graceful arm toward the harp, cello, and harpsichord which occupied a corner of the ballroom. "And, as you can see, there are instruments you may play should you possess the talent and be so inclined. We are not without some culture here, although our entertainment is primarily of our own making. I think you will survive, perhaps as much as a week."

"What?" he asked aghast, attempting humor. "No theater? No opera? No ballet?" The total incongruity of his questions was softened by an upraised brow and the return of the dimple to his cheek, causing Glynna to smile again despite herself. His next words denied her recent thoughts. "I am quite unaccustomed to creating entertainment and diversion for myself and shall require some tutoring in that regard." He moved closer to her then, and she saw that his eyes were again the clear gray they had been earlier in the garden, except this time they were not hard and brittle but the soft gray of a dove's wing as she had imagined they could be. Her pulse quickened as he gazed deeply into her eyes, his silently pleading for understanding and cooperation.

Then he took her hands in his — her hands that were lightly calloused and splotched with ink — and she thought, I can't send him away, but if I don't, my cause is lost.

Her fingertips tingled where they rested in his palms, and then the tingle traveled up her arms, turning her elbows to jelly in its journey to her heart. She knew she should take her hands away. She could. He did not hold them tightly. Yet, she could not. For the moment, her hands were as surely imprisoned within his as if he had tied them to him. She opened her mouth to speak, which words she did not know. Since none came, it did not matter.

"Will you help me fill this time, then, Miss O'Rourke?" His voice sounded hoarse, almost, Glynna thought, as a lover's might. "Will you teach the teacher?"

And she knew that she would not be able to refuse him this one simple request. After all, it was only for a week.

Chapter Four

Reverend Mitchell's colorless, totally unanimated voice droned on incessantly as he elaborated on the obscure text he'd chosen from one of the minor prophets in the Old Testament. Glynna couldn't remember from which book he had read, nor did she honestly care. Her attention, since the onset of the service, had been diverted by the man who sat beside her.

She had tried to concentrate, even more so than usual, for the fat reverend's sermons seldom failed to bore her to distraction. That was the one thing on which she could rely as she sat primly on a backless bench on Sundays. Still, Sundays held a certain attraction, for services were held at the inn — in the ballroom, which was transformed by the addition of the benches. The small community had not yet the wherewithal or the need to build a meeting house, so everyone from miles around came on Sundays, bringing with them baskets laden with a delicious assortment of foods. These were spread out on tables in the interim between services. A time of fellowship and socialization followed, a time to catch up on all the local happenings and goings-on. Glynna enjoyed those parts of Sundays even if she couldn't work up much excitement over the sermons.

On this particular Sunday she sat sandwiched between Brian and Rafferty, whose broad shoulders seemed to occupy more space than the short bench allowed. Usually the end of the bench was hers entirely. At one minute she found herself irritated by the intrusion on her space; the next she welcomed their guest's presence — the warmth of his long thigh so close to her own; the soft rustle of his silk frock-coat as he wriggled uncomfortably from time to time; the faint, manly fragrance he exuded, a combination of soap, tobacco, and leather, which wafted close to tease her senses.

No matter how hard she tried, Glynna could not seem to shift her thoughts from his closeness to a subject more benign. Everything around her reminded her of him, of the almost forty-eight hours he had now been at the tavern. When she focused her attention upon the windows, she did not see the brilliant yellow shafts of sunlight pouring through their many panes but rather the dark gray of storm clouds and of eyes that matched their mystery. As the hymns were played on the harpsichord, she did not hear their pious refrains but rather the melodious strains of the concerto Kane Rafferty had played for her the previous afternoon.

Indeed, it was a pious refrain from the harpsichord which finally served to recapture her attention. Mechanically, she stood with the other members of the congregation, only to consider once again her new tutor as her clear soprano blended harmoniously with his rich baritone. Was there no end to his talents? Or his boldness? Now that they were standing, there was no real need for his shoulder to be pressed so firmly against her own. Again she felt that inner conflict, the intellectual part of her wanting to shove him toward the aisle while her heart demanded that she lean even closer to him.

Glynna heard her voice falter before her mind assimilated the fact that the hymn was finished but she had kept on singing. Her cheeks tingled hotly from embarrassment as she forced her eyes to remain trained forward. When she heard the minister call upon Deacon McLaird to pronounce the closing prayer, she found herself fervently asking God to fill the verbose man's mouth with even more words than usual to allow her time to recuperate from her discomfiture. Her prayer was answered.

When the deacon's loud "Amen" ended his lengthy oral dissertation, everyone filed out reverently. The hushed silence ended at the foot of the stairs, however. Free at long last, the children scampered outdoors, but their play would be hampered by the fact that it was Sunday. Dressed in their best and admonished by their mothers to stay clean, they limited their activities accordingly. The women moved into the ordinary, chattering brightly as they began to unpack the baskets and arrange the food, while the menfolk assembled across the hall in the gentlemen's parlor. Although Glynna often wondered what transpired behind that closed door, on this day she was thankful for the temporary separation of the sexes. It gave her a bit more time away from Kane Rafferty. She had felt his eyes on her back as they had descended the stairs and knew, without actually seeing it, that his mouth had twitched in amusement at her blunder.

Someone else was obviously amused. Glynna whirled in irritation as an unbridled giggle erupted behind her. Hepzibeth Jenkins, who detested her name and insisted on being called "Beth," quickly clamped a hand over her mirthful grin as she followed Glynna into the keeping hall.

"I'm sorry. I couldn't help it," Beth managed between giggles when the door had closed behind them. "You made it all so obvious! Does this mean I get Edwin all to myself now?"

The mention of Edwin's name dissolved Glynna's anger. Edwin McLaird, youngest son of the long-winded deacon, had, by age seventeen, reached the ungainly height of six feet eight inches. For the past six years, everyone in the community had waited for him to fill out. If anything, though, the man seemed to have grown leaner—and clumsier.

"Dear old Winnie," Glynna almost choked on her own laughter. "He's always been yours, Beth."

"Don't let him catch you calling him 'Winnie'! You know how he hates that childish endearment. Were you a man, he'd probably strike you for it."

"I wonder how he manages at home. Aunt Darcie says his mother still calls him that." Glynna piled freshly ironed table linen onto Beth's outstretched arms.

Beth grunted. "You know Mother McLaird could get away with mayhem. She rules the roost. No wonder Deacon speaks so long at Sunday meeting! He is probably never allowed to utter a word at home."

Glynna stopped piling linen momentarily, the focus of her attention not on the McLairds but on her friend Beth. Two years Glynna's junior, Beth Jenkins had the look Glynna so wished had been given her. The younger woman's hair, caught in the cascade of ringlets which fell from her crown, gleamed golden blond even in the meager light of the keeping hall. Her flawless complexion appeared almost translucent in its whiteness, combining with the stark paleness of her blue eyes to create a vision of helpless femininity. And she stood a full head taller than the diminutive Glynna, her body willowy and graceful. She and Edwin were destined to have tall children, were they indeed to become man and wife.

"Whatever did you mean by 'You made it all so obvious'?" Glynna queried, suddenly remembering her friend's giggling outburst. "I made *what* so obvious?" A part of her immediately set up a defense.

Beth's wide smile beamed conspiratorially from her lovely face. "Why, your interest in *him* of course—and don't pretend you don't know who I'm talking about. He's absolutely the dreamiest thing I ever saw! Girl, do I envy you! But you needn't worry," Beth hastily added. "I'm not interested in your tutor. I'm just thankful you're now out of the running for Edwin's attentions."

"And you will never know how much I wish I were in your place, Beth." Glynna wanted to confide completely in her friend, but duty beckoned. "We'll talk later," she promised, "but if we don't get these linens out there soon, Aunt Darcie will come looking for us."

The aromas of fried chicken and potato salad commingled with that of freshly baked bread and apple pie to tempt the appetite. Glynna, as usual, was ravenously hungry, and Beth again elapsed into giggles as she watched her friend pile her plate with food. "I don't know how you manage to eat so much and stay so tiny!" she observed without malice, her own plate sparsely filled. "Why, if I ate like that—"

"You'd look like Mother McLaird?" Glynna finished for her.

"Sh-h-h! Someone will hear you!"

Ignoring the stares their mirth provoked from some of the women, the two young conspirators moved onto the front porch in an effort to gain a small degree of privacy, leaving the adults and smaller children in the comfort of the ordinary. On pleasant Sundays, such as this one, the older children took their plates onto the lawn—as far away as they could safely get from their parents.

Glynna and Beth settled themselves comfortably into the two white, slat-backed straight chairs, which they had turned to face each other; a small wooden table had been set between them to hold their tall glasses of milk. Beth sat stiffly for a moment, absently spearing green peas with her fork, her brow slightly puckered. "What's wrong with Winnie?" she asked in an unusually quiet voice.

Glynna smiled as best she could, her mouth being full of succulent chicken, and was grateful for the moments it took her to finish chewing and swallowing. "Nothing is wrong with dear old Winnie," she proclaimed, hoping her voice would remain steady despite the subject.

"Then why don't you want him?"

"Because you do."

Beth was unconvinced. "You think he's too gangly. You needn't deny it. I've heard you say so myself. And you think he's just a country boy. A clumsy, uneducated country boy. You needn't be so high and mighty, Miss Glynna O'Rourke!" Her voice gained in both pitch and volume as she delivered her speech, causing the children on the lawn to raise their heads and gaze at the two young women on the porch.

Glynna feigned hurt. "Hepzibeth! You wound me! I've oft heard *you* make those very same observations." She bit into a soft roll, studying her friend's pale features as she chewed. "You love old Winnie, don't you?"

61

"It's that obvious?"

Glynna nodded.

"I only wish he were in love with me." Beth set her plate, the food barely touched, on the table and sighed wearily. "Maybe with you out of the way, he'll finally see me."

"Of course he will," Glynna reassured her, realizing that while her words seemed to agree with Beth's viewpoint, an argument would serve no purpose. She could not recall Edwin ever having courted her, even remotely. Nor could she say that he had ever bestowed any special attention upon Beth. He was just dear old Winnie, forever the courteous gentleman, though a bumbling one. That he would make Beth a good husband Glynna was certain, so long as they were not required to live under the same roof as the elder McLairds.

Beth visually relaxed, a slow smile curving her perfectly formed lips. Glynna smiled in return, happy to see her friend's frown dissipate. In short order, however, Glynna's own brow creased in vexation.

"Tell me about your new beau. Where is he from? How old is he? How long will he be here? Aren't you thrilled to your toes?" The questions gushed from Beth's mouth, allowing Glynna no quarter.

I will not be defensive! Glynna promised herself, taking a deep breath and letting it out slowly before speaking. "Hepzibeth Jenkins, he is my *tutor,* and he is here quite without my invitation. I have no need of his services, but I seem to be stuck with him for the time being. His personal history is of no interest to me, and as to the duration of his visit, I sincerely hope it will end soon."

Despite being called by her full name, Beth was undaunted. "What does Aunt Darcie think of him?" she asked, her pale eyes wistful.

The question conjured up a vision of the sparkling mischief in Aunt Darcie's blue eyes as she had rushed Glynna upstairs to the ballroom on Friday. "I-I'm not sure," Glynna stammered. "We haven't discussed it."

"And Katie? What has she said?" Beth knew that Glynna valued Katie's opinion above all others—and that the black woman never hesitated to offer her viewpoint, especially where Glynna's welfare was concerned.

"Nothing," Glynna answered honestly, for she and Katie had yet to discuss Kane Rafferty, "except to call him 'that fine gempmum from 'cross the sea.'" *And I suppose he is that,* Glynna reluctantly admitted to herself. "But I don't want to talk about Mr. Rafferty anymore. If I have my way, he'll be gone soon." She ignored Beth's disbelieving glare. "Let's talk about the dance instead. What are you wearing?"

Her question produced the desired effect, for Beth's face became animated as she described the ice blue silk dress she was making for the event, which was to be held the following Saturday evening at the inn. They had sorted out their gowns and accessories and digressed to how Beth might achieve Edwin's undivided attention when Aunt Darcie interrupted to remind them it was time to help clean up the ordinary.

The afternoon service was no easier to bear than the morning one had been. Glynna gave up trying to pay attention to the sermon and allowed her mind to wander where it would. She tried to imagine Beth and Edwin married, and saw in her mind's eye the lovely bride Beth would make. She envisioned her friend swathed in ice blue silk, the very same gown Beth was making now, and her mind's eye traversed the length of the dress, seeing the creamy lace ruffles cascading from Beth's elbows and adorning the skirt in an inverted V all the way to the hemline. As her eyes traveled back to Beth's glowing face, it was not that palest of complexions and eyes she saw, however, but rather the peachy tone of her own skin and the brilliant green of her own eyes. She darted a look at the groom and almost gasped aloud when he was not dear old Winnie but Kane Rafferty.

That self-same man stirred at her side, causing her to think that perhaps she had actually gasped aloud. A surreptitious glance squelched her fear, for she saw his attention sharply focused on Reverend Mitchell, his features almost rapt as he listened intently to the sermon. How could he be so engrossed? Glynna wondered, looking at the minister and seeing only his sweating face, hearing only the ever-increasing volume of his gritty voice. She tried to concentrate on the words . . . "why you have not gone to hell, since you have sat here in His divine worship, provoking His pure eyes by your sinful, wicked manner. Yea, there is no other reason why you do not at this moment drop into hell . . ."

Glynna shivered involuntarily. Had she provoked His pure eyes? Was she destined for hell? She did not believe she was either sinful or wicked, although she was quite certain the egotistical Reverend Mitchell thought so. She had gleaned enough from his sermons to know that he thought he was saved but everyone else was lost. Glynna refused to allow the somberness and fiery intensity of his words to ruin a perfectly beautiful day.

At long last the sermon ended. Reverend Mitchell wiped his damp brow with the handkerchief that had started out pristine white but was now pale gray and soaked with his sweat. Everyone rose and filed forward to receive the sacrament.

Those families who lived closest remained for tea, but most of them, including the Jenkinses, climbed into their buckboards immediately afterward. Glynna stood on the front porch and waved goodbye to Beth until the Jenkinses' wagon bounced over a hill and out of sight. When they returned the following Saturday, they would stay at the tavern through Sunday services. Glynna looked forward to such weekends, for Beth always slept in her room. The two had been known to talk until the wee hours of the morning, stifling their giggles lest Aunt Darcie hear. Neither wished to run the risk of ending the privilege of sharing Glynna's room on such occasions.

As Glynna turned to reenter the tavern, she found her way obstructed by a man's lean chest. Only one man could be that tall. Dear old Winnie. She tilted her head back to gaze into his smiling face. So . . . He *was* interested in Beth after all. "You have a horse," she declared. "You don't have to wait a whole week to see her again, Edwin. Why don't you ride over one evening and sit with her?"

Edwin's thickly lashed brown eyes blinked down at her. "Ride over and see who?" he asked, his angular face a study in confusion.

"Whom," Glynna automatically responded, then realized this was Winnie, not Brian. The bewilderment remained. "Beth, of course. You should ride over and see Beth."

The brown eyes blinked again. "Why would I want to do that?"

Glynna felt like stamping her foot in frustration with the overgrown lout, but he was standing so close to her she might stomp him instead of the planks. If he hadn't come out to see Beth once more, then why was he here? She asked him as much.

65

He shook his head, obviously an effort to clear the cobwebs, for his eyelids ceased their infernal blinking and he smiled sweetly at her. "Your aunt sent me. Tea is being served." He opened the door and held it for her, then followed her like a little lost puppy into the ordinary, stumbling over his own feet and almost falling as he crossed the threshold. Kane Rafferty was nowhere in sight. Glynna's eyes searched the limits of the large room for him while her intellect berated them for doing so. When she would have sat with Brian, Uncle Galen, and Aunt Darcie, Edwin gently guided her to a separate table in a dark corner. Glynna was taken aback. Perhaps Beth had been correct in her assumptions about dear old Winnie's romantic interest.

They drank their tea and ate their cakes in silence, for which Glynna was grateful. She sat with her back to the wall, able to view the entire roomful of guests, and engaged in one of her favorite pastimes: studying people. The most interesting by far were the middle-aged couple who had arrived with Kane Rafferty. They enjoyed their refreshment with obvious relish, their mutual girths suggesting that this was generally the case. Aunt Darcie had told Glynna about the fire's destroying the McGinty farm and she had mentioned Kane's generous assistance in providing for the couple's immediate welfare, even to the point of sending his coachman on horseback across the mountains to the Shenandoah valley in search of the McGintys' relatives. The pair would remain the Cavanaughs' guests for at least another fortnight, or until such time as someone came for them.

Uncle Galen had offered the use of a buckboard to transport the McGintys and their few possessions, since the fine carriage the tutor had hired was not suitable for travel through the Blue Ridge Mountains, but the McGintys had declined. Their family would come eventually, they knew, and they had not the wherewithal to pay for a lost or damaged vehicle should misfortune overtake them. In fact, they were so distressed over their lack of funds that Cyrus McGinty had insisted on helping out in the barn and stables while his wife had volunteered to assist Katie in the kitchen. The black woman's ready acceptance of assistance had surprised Glynna, who had thought no one outside of Katie's two daughters would ever be allowed in that domain.

As Glynna further scanned the group, she realized that Reverend Mitchell was also missing. Never before had she known the man to forgo an opportunity to eat. Since his farm lay only a few miles to the southeast of Cavanaugh's Tavern, he always remained on Sunday through teatime, and then took with him a large bundle of food for his supper, there being neither missus nor servant to cook for him. Glynna could not help but wonder, though rather absently, what had become of the minister.

The afternoon grew late. Long shadows had begun to creep eastward, their fringes dappling the dormered roof of the tavern as the last guests rode away. Darcie found Glynna perched on one of the front porch chairs, her green eyes staring wistfully at the pink streaks in the western sky, her face in complete repose. The older woman sat down beside her niece and allowed her own mind and body to rest, allowed the beauty of the early evening to cleanse her soul as only nature's wonders can. There was an unspoken camaraderie, a gentle understanding between the two, that speech could never replace.

It was speech which broke their silence, however, when Brian came bounding around the house leading Reverend Mitchell's gelding. "Gabe's all ready for you, sir," he called loudly, his freckled face alight with pleasure at being asked to accomplish this task.

"Just hold him for a minute, Brian," Darcie said, half rising from her chair. "I need to get the reverend's food. He's coming."

"No, Aunt Darcie," Glynna insisted. "You stay here and rest. I'll get it." Remembering the minister's absence from tea, she turned as she reached the front door. "Where *is* Reverend Mitchell?"

"You should find him in the gentlemen's parlor," Darcie smugly replied, settling herself once more into her chair.

The parlor door stood ajar; the harsh grittiness of the minister's voice ground its way into the front hall, his argumentative language clearly audible as Glynna crossed the wooden floor. "I must dispute that viewpoint, sir. I find this 'age of light' to be contrary to the teachings of the Divine Word—and to logic and experience as well. The deists are concerned only with attacking and downgrading conventional Christianity!"

In sharp contrast, the voice that answered was firm and well modulated. "I hold no argument with your philosophy, Reverend, only with your ability to think for yourself."

The two men were hidden from view by the partially open door, but Glynna now knew where Kane Rafferty and Reverend Mitchell had closeted themselves during tea. Aunt Darcie had always insisted on good manners, and Glynna was aware that she should not eavesdrop, but the temptation to hear these two debate was too great for her to make her presence known. She had never before heard anyone argue with Reverend Mitchell, and her tutor seemed to be confidently holding his own. Besides, she wanted to know what he had meant by the minister's not being able to think for himself.

A harsh intake of breath immediately followed. "Whatever do you mean?" Mitchell sounded as if he spat out the retort. "Of course, I do my own thinking!"

"I beg to disagree. I, too, am familiar with the works of Jonathan Edwards, sir. Your sermon this afternoon came almost directly from his most famous speech. Did you honestly think no one would recognize it?"

That explained her tutor's rapt attention. *Bravo, Mr. Rafferty!* Glynna waited patiently for the older man's response. When none came, she decided, much to her displeasure, it was time to rescue him. She knocked lightly on the portal before pushing it wide. Two plates covered with crumbs and two teacups rested upon a small table, attesting to the physical gratification of the men within. From the pleased look on Kane's face, he must have enjoyed the repartee, but Reverend Mitchell stood stiffly, his heavy jowls beet red, his bulbous eyes narrowed in anger. Glynna had difficulty maintaining a serious mien as she informed him that his horse sat ready, and, that done, she immediately darted off to the keeping hall to collect his bundle of food.

She remained in the front hall as he took his hasty departure, then finally allowed herself to burst into laughter when he had safely, though somewhat awkwardly, mounted his horse.

"Laughter becomes you, Miss O'Rourke. You should indulge in it more often." Rafferty had not moved from his chair by the hearth. Someone had laid a neat pile of firewood against the encroaching coolness of the early May evening, and Glynna felt rather than saw his eyes follow her as she crossed the room and set about lighting the wood.

"Why did you not summon a servant?" he asked, his voice lacking the irritation Glynna felt and did not try to hide when she answered him.

"Why should I?"

"Because great ladies do not light fires. That is why one employs servants—or, in the case of your aunt and uncle, why one purchases slaves." His tone clearly indicated his intolerance of the latter institution.

Glynna ignored him, refusing to snatch at the bait as the poor Reverend Mitchell must have done. When she had piled sufficient kindling on the ready wood and seen it ablaze, she straightened her back and settled herself comfortably on the hearth rug.

Kane Rafferty regarded her in some amusement. "Great ladies do not sit on the floor, either."

"I like sitting on the floor."

"You must learn that not all things will be to your liking." The corners of his mouth quirked upward. "Now come," he coaxed, "take the reverend's chair so that I may study your posture."

Reluctantly, Glynna arose from her place by the fire and moved as gracefully as she consciously could to the chair, sitting on its edge so stiffly and primly she felt as though she might break. Indeed, this man made her feel like a crystal vase as he held his hands under his chin, fingers splayed and touching each other, his cold gray eyes scrutinizing her, seeing through her.

"Sit back," he ordered. "You look as if you were poised for flight."

Glynna performed as instructed, wriggling her buttocks backward until her spine touched the back of the chair.

It was Kane's turn to burst into laughter. "You poor child!" He nodded toward her feet, which hung

70

limply from her ankles, their slippered soles several inches off the floor. "I had no idea you were so short."

How dare he ridicule her and call her a child! Glynna fought the suffusion that threatened to flood her cheeks. "Perhaps you have a solution, sir. Can your superior knowledge make me taller? Or perhaps you brought with you a torture rack which you can employ to stretch my height?"

The total ridiculousness of her suggestions caused him further amusement, but this time, humored by her wit, she laughed with him.

"There is a solution, albeit one which has no bearing on the application of my knowledge or of a rack." Her brows lifted in question. "That chair was constructed for a man," he explained. "European salons are furnished with smaller chairs for ladies. Perhaps your own ladies' parlor is thusly equipped."

"My legs are still too short," she admitted. "That's why I sit on the floor."

" 'Tis a habit, then, that you must break. We shall work on it—tomorrow." He continued to smile at her, a smile so disarming it caused her to drop her gaze to her lap. The sun had almost set, and no candles had been lit against its absence, the only light in the room coming from the fireplace. Fearful that he might take further offense, Glynna hesitated to correct the problem. If she had had any notion what a fetching picture she made with the golden firelight dancing on her face and cavorting among her ringlets, turning her hair to molten copper, she would have chanced his ire. Instead, she waited patiently for his dismissal.

It was Aunt Darcie who rescued her. "Goodness me," she declared in her no-nonsense way, showing no surprise at finding the two of them in the gentlemen's parlor. "Light some lamps, Glynna. It's dark in here. Katie is laying out a cold supper, which will be served within the hour. Perhaps Mr. Rafferty would like to hear you read in the interim." She bustled out of the room as efficiently as she had entered it.

When Glynna had finished lighting the lamps, she retrieved the Bible that lay on the mantel. Yes, she would read to him—something which would show him she had her own ammunition should she ever manage to hold a debate with the egotistical Reverend Mitchell. Her fingers quickly located the Book of Psalms, from which she read the sixth. " 'O Lord, rebuke me not in thine anger, neither chasten me in thy hot displeasure. . . .' "

She lifted her eyes to his, saw his pleasure in her clear voice as she read the words with feeling. He would see that she did not need his tutoring, and then he would return to his homeland, allowing her to return to sitting on the floor.

Chapter Five

Kane Rafferty was not, by nature, an early riser. On Monday morning, however, he greeted first light with more vigor than he'd ever thought he could muster at such an hour. Indeed, he had rested extremely well since his arrival at the tavern three days ago. The fresh air combined with the quietness of the countryside worked on him like a drug. He knew, without having to be told, that everyone in the household arose quite early, and his internal clock was beginning to adjust to country timekeeping.

He found his hostess in the ordinary, clearing away crumbs from two of the tables and extinguishing lamps as the meager rays of early morning slanted through the windows. "You'll find corn muffins and jam on the sideboard and tea on the settle," Darcie said, raking the last of the crumbs into her apron pocket. "I'll bring fresh milk from the springhouse and tell Katie to start your omelet—unless, of course, you would rather have something else this morning."

"Katie's omelets are quite delectable. That will be fine." Darcie was on her way through the door to the keeping hall when he added, "But I will be happy to wait for the others, Mistress Cavanaugh."

He was so proud of himself, Darcie hated to tell him. "They've already broken their fast, Mr. Rafferty. Even the McGintys. Do, please, make yourself at home. Things are so hectic around here at this time of day, we expect our guests to act like family."

Kane found clean cups, sugar, and cream for his tea on the sideboard. Embers glowed in the fireplace but a slight chill pervaded the room, not so much from its lack of heat as from its lack of occupants. He watched the steam rise from his delicate porcelain teacup as he settled himself at the table on which Darcie had left a lamp burning. The hot tea warmed him, as did his consideration of the utter simplicity of this room and the cordial charm of its owners. Virginia had proved to be more of a jolt to both his senses and his intellect than he could ever have imagined. For the first time in his life, he was discovering how most of the world lived. He found it not nearly as abominable as he had once thought he would.

His pupil, too, had not met his expectations, but failed to in a most delightful way. He had offended her last evening when he'd called her a child. Dammit, he was trying very hard to think of her that way. He needed to think of her as such, lest he fall prey to her charms and forget his mission. She was so tiny—no, petite—so childlike—no, fresh and naive. So different from Valerie.

Tall, willowy Valerie. It was the first time he had thought of her in days. She had wept when he'd told her he was leaving Ireland for a year, clung to him and begged him not to go, extracted his promise to write—and not to forget her. "How could I?" he had assured her, kissing her temple even as his hands roamed where they would down the length of her torso. That she would always please him, both as lover and wife, he had no doubt, but she lacked Glynna's spunk. No fire lit Valerie's cold blue eyes; there was no warmth in her laughter. He was betrothed to her, however, and must find the tiara for her to wear on their wedding day.

Where might it be, if indeed his mother was correct in her assumption that it was among Glynndon O'Rourke's personal possessions? There was no excess baggage at the inn, only the bare minimum of necessities. Should Glynna have received her father's things, where might they be stored? The Cavanaughs appeared to be upright, law-abiding citizens. Perhaps he should just tell them about the tiara and be done with it. His mother had thought there might be some problem with Galen's past, though. He would wait . . . and watch and listen.

Katie appeared with his omelet, her smile broad as she laid the warm plate in front of him and set about retrieving muffins, butter, and jam from the sideboard. "Miz Dahcie say to tell you if'n you want to ride, one of the stableboys'll saddle you a hoss. Jes' doan ride too far till you learn the lay of the land." She refreshed his tea, then pursed her ample lips and surveyed his place setting, assuring herself that he had everything he needed. "Us wouldn't want you to come to no harm, Massah Kane."

She was the only one in the household who used his given name, though she always prefaced it with "Massah." Kane surmised that she considered "Rafferty" too much of a mouthful and found himself pleased rather than offended. He wondered what Katie would think if she knew his title would one day be "Baron of Ulrich" and how she might pronounce it.

His deception, though slight, nettled his sense of honor. Thinking he would find the Cavanaughs backward peasants and discover the whereabouts of the tiara in short order, he had not argued with his mother's reasoning. Now, however, he thought they had both made a grave error in judgment. If Glynna did accompany him on his return to Ireland, the Cavanaughs were certain to discover his true identity. What a tangled web his mother had woven. He was beginning to wish he had never agreed to be a part of her scheme.

At his parents' estate in Ireland, he would never have stooped to ask a servant to dine with him. He had not planned to breakfast alone this morning, however, and he approached the possibility with little relish. Were he to explore his feelings fully, he would have to admit that it was Glynna's company he desired. "Have you had breakfast, Katie?" he asked.

"Yassuh, I have."

"Would you have a cup of tea with me, then, while I eat?" The baroness would faint if she knew.

"Thankee, Massah Kane, but I doan have much time. That kitchen full of dirty dishes, and lunch ain' gonna cook itself." Katie rolled her dark eyes at him, amazed that he would suggest such a thing.

"You'll just have to come back for my plate, Katie," he reasoned. "You might as well pour yourself some tea and sit down while I finish this omelet."

The black woman reluctantly agreed with his logic, but she refused to sit down, pouring her tea and standing close to the fireplace as she sipped it.

"Why did Mistress Cavanaugh suggest I ride this morning?" Kane asked, eager to begin his tutoring. "It was my understanding that all of Miss O'Rourke's duties were to be suspended while I am here."

"Her chores, yassuh. They be taken care of."

76

"Then where might I find my charge?"

Katie grinned, exposing the wide gap between her front teeth. "In the garden, Massah Kane." She took up his plate, silver, and linen, along with their empty cups, tilting her head toward the back of the inn. "Jes' follow me."

Despite Katie's assurances of suspended chores, Kane half expected to find Glynna on her knees weeding tomato plants again. He could see her dirt-smeared face as the emerald brilliance of her eyes seared him, hear her say, "You don't have to remind me — great ladies don't pull their own weeds." Instead, it was the brilliance of the sun-kissed dew he saw and the sweet melody of birdsong he heard as he followed Katie down the brick walk. The tomato patch was devoid of a weed-puller. Glynna was nowhere in sight, and Katie had disappeared into the kitchen.

Kane stood still, absorbing the wonder of the crisp morning, luxuriating in its freshness. A pair of squirrels scampered across the brick path, their furry tails erect as they played their game of chase. His gray eyes followed their course until he spied a dainty slippered foot swinging to and fro from behind a rhododendron. "No, Brian, not that way!" Glynna's lilting voice gently chided. "Let me show you."

The two sat comfortably upon one of the benches, Glynna with her right leg folded and tucked under her left knee, her left leg swinging, Brian with both feet flat on the bench, his knees pointed skyward. Upon his thighs the boy held a slate on which he had written chalk letters, including the one in question, which Kane supposed was a *G*.

Brian saw him first. "Hullo, Mr. Rafferty. You're up early! Glynna is teaching me my letters."

"So I see." Kane smiled broadly at the enthusiastic five-year-old. "I thought *I* was the teacher."

"Oh, you're Glynna's teacher and she's mine. Maybe one day I will have someone to teach."

Glynna straightened her legs, smoothed her apron over her full skirt, and sat up primly. "We hadn't expected you to be up so early. Brian and I will be another hour at his lessons," she explained, her tone apologetic. "Everyone else is busy with chores, but you have the house and stables at your disposal. Shall I meet you in the ballroom later?"

Although she did not realize it, she was offering him his first opportunity to snoop. He hastened to consent and then made his departure. The tavern was quiet and apparently empty of additional occupants. Just to be certain, Kane leisurely walked through the first-floor rooms before ascending the stairs. The guest rooms were located either in ground-floor wings or on the third floor. Upstairs, the ladies' parlor lay opposite the ballroom. Kane walked through the ballroom to a door in the opposite wall, which he had learned led to the family quarters. Beside it, he paused, listening intently but hearing no sound. Stealthily—he felt like a thief—he opened the door and entered a hallway.

Golden shafts of sunlight flooded through the windows on the right. On the left, two doors stood open; the third door, at the end of the hall, was closed. He knew where he wanted to start looking, and a quick glance into the two rooms on his left convinced him neither was Glynna's. His heart sinking, he decided to try the closed door anyway. The knob turned smoothly in his palm. It wasn't locked.

Although as tastefully yet simply decorated as the other bedchambers, this one so closely reflected Glynna's personality that it took him completely by

78

surprise. The furnishings were diminutive, almost child-size but full-blown in style, from the cherry fourposter to the crewel rug on the floor.

And that rug dominated the room, lending it its color scheme—peach, blue-green, and cream. Kane could not resist bending to touch the cavorting Jacobean flowers expertly embroidered with fine wool threads on its light background. It was truly a work of art, one of the most beautiful rugs he had ever seen. He turned up a corner, looking for the maker's signature, and gasped when he saw it: "Made by my own hand and completed this 3rd day of January in the year of our Lord 1751. Glynna F. O'Rourke." The words had been backstitched on a square of linen which had been carefully stitched to the wrong side of the rug.

He dropped the corner and let his heart examine her room. His mind had absorbed the teal-colored damask draperies and bedhangings, the peach walls, the graceful curvings of the Chippendale-style cherry furniture. Now he noted the basket of dried flowers on the candle stand, arranged, he was sure, by her hand. He saw her name embroidered once again, this time on a cross-stitched sampler hung over the fireplace. One corner of the room boasted a miniature cottage, complete with thatched roof and hand-carved door; another held a blue damask-covered settee with gently scrolled arms and arched back. A tea table in front of the settee held a miniature porcelain tea service. The room was further adorned with two small theorem paintings, a handsome hand-decorated firescreen, a large bisque doll whose jewel-encrusted, emerald green gown seemed oddly out of place, crewel-embroidered pillows, and a stack of painted boxes. It was to the latter that he turned his attention.

The boxes were round, their colors various shades of peach and blue-green. Kane reached to remove the smallest one, which was on top, and cursed under his breath even as his reluctant hands touched its sides. He couldn't do this. Just standing in this room made him feel that he was invading her privacy. There must be a better way to discover whether or not Glynna actually had the tiara in her possession! His mother, to whom he felt a great loyalty, would be expecting a letter from him, though. If he just looked in this one box, then he could honestly tell her that he had begun his search. A lie to his mother would set with him no better than his invasion of Glynna's personal possessions.

He removed the lid. A tiny pair of embroidery scissors and crewel needles of varying sizes nestled amid skein upon skein of fine woolen threads. Its contents weren't so private after all. With far less trepidation, he moved the box to the top of a chest and opened the next one. There were six boxes in all. Each contained items used in fine handwork. Kane carefully restacked the boxes, stood back to survey the small tower, and, finally convinced that he had left no evidence of his intrusion, retraced his steps to the ballroom to await his charge.

The lesson with Brian had gone well, Glynna thought as she stepped into the kitchen for a sip of water before going upstairs. She had been working with him every weekday morning now for several weeks, and found him an attentive and enthusiastic student, a joy to teach. Like most children his age, especially boys, he had a minor problem with manual dexterity, but Glynna knew that his skills would improve with time. No one had thought to tell Kane

Rafferty about Brian's lessons; of course, they had all expected him to continue his habit of staying abed late.

Katie said as much as she dumped yellow cornmeal into a large earthenware bowl. "That Massah Kane, he ast me to sit with him this morning," she continued, shaking her head in wonderment. "He sho'ly is a nice man, Miss Glynna. You best hurry up 'fore you vex him."

That Kane Rafferty knew how to charm women Glynna now had no doubt. Katie was not easily influenced. Yet, he did not seem so closely bent on charming Glynna. The memory of his calling her a child still rankled, but it also explained his attitude toward her. As long as he considered her immature, her cause was lost. Why did people think your size affected your mental or physical capabilities? She remembered how proudly Aunt Darcie had shown Mother McLaird Glynna's crewel rug when it was finished. The tall, raw-boned, overweight woman had looked down her nose at Glynna and said, "How could anyone that small make something so beautiful?" Other memories of similar incidents rushed around in her head as she climbed the stairs. She would show Mr. Rafferty! And anyone else, too! With that resolve, she strolled into the ballroom, head held high, her green eyes flashing defiance.

He paced the length of the polished floor, his gaze directed toward his feet, his hands clasped at the small of his back. When Glynna cleared her throat, he whirled around, his countenance troubled. She stretched her neck, stiffened her back. She could do battle as well as he. She would not let him disarm her.

Even when the frown disappeared and he smiled warmly at her, she held fast to her resolve. His smile

81

widened, dimpling his left cheek, but there was something almost secretive behind the pleasantness, almost as though he knew what she looked like in her shift. The very thought sent tiny prickles down Glynna's spine.

"The weather is too nice for self-imprisonment," he said, the clear gray of his eyes assessing her apparel. "Do you ride?" At her nod, he added, "Then, why don't we both change into suitable attire. I'll meet you at the stables."

The morning retained its original crispness. Glynna had gambled that it would when she'd chosen her bottle green velvet habit over the black bombazine. The garment was constructed with a tight-fitting, high-necked jacket ending in a point over her flat stomach, full sleeves, and an even fuller skirt made to accommodate a lady's saddle. Contrary to fashion, it was barren of adornment, a deliberate calculation on Glynna's part when she had made it. On her bosom she wore a large pearl and amethyst brooch, which had been her mother's. A small-scaled but rakish hat completed the outfit, its plumes reiterating the lavender and cream colors of the brooch. The riding habit made her look every bit the woman she was—and Glynna knew it.

Kane knew it, too. He finally gave up trying to keep his eyes off her narrow waist, straight back, and saucy hat, and began to enjoy the sight. She sat a horse well, handling her mount, a prissy mare named Sheena, skillfully. There would be no need for lessons in equestrianism.

Glynna had set for them a northwestward route, taking them deeper into the foothills. Wildflowers bloomed in profusion as did a multitude of wild fruit trees and shrubs. Kane became the pupil as Glynna pointed out the many varieties, most of which were foreign to him. The Blue Ridge Mountains rose in majestic splendor, their peaks hidden among wispy clouds, but Glynna seemed to accept the wild, unadulterated beauty of the land with a nonchalance bred, Kane supposed, from having grown up here.

Reining in her mare in a grove of mountain laurel, Glynna suggested they dismount and give the horses a rest. Accustomed to riding alone, she had stopped near a small tree, planning to use one of its low-hanging branches as an aid in removing herself from Sheena. Before she could accomplish this task, Kane appeared at her side, his arms held in readiness to accept her small frame. "I can manage quite well," she insisted, removing her kid gloves.

His cheek dimpled again as his gray eyes, now bright with merriment, measured the distance between her saddle and the sloping ground. "But why should you, when you have me willing to lend my assistance?"

Since she could find no ready retort, Glynna placed her hands on his shoulders in resignation. The act sent delicious tingles up her arms, reminding her of the one other time they had voluntarily touched each other—the afternoon of his arrival. When he placed his capable hands on each side of her midriff, however, she felt her skin burn beneath his palms. Just yesterday Edwin had touched her, but her body had not responded. Why was it so different with this man?

Glynna had little time to ponder the question. As she moved her right leg over the saddle's horn, her body was lifted upward. His holding her felt so right! The realization sent a jolt through the length

83

of her. She wondered later if she had actually jerked and caused her tutor to lose his footing or if something else had been the cause. Whatever the reason, Kane stumbled. Instinctively, her hands moved from his shoulders to clasp the back of his neck, while his arms encircled her waist. They fell to the soft carpet of grass and wildflowers, Kane's back absorbing their weight, and tumbled downhill, their arms clutching each other more, perhaps, than was absolutely necessary.

When their rolling bodies finally came to a halt, Glynna's length was trapped beneath his. Concern filled his countenance as he gently removed his hands from around her waist and placed them on either side of her head, his fingers sliding into her hair. The saucy bonnet lay uphill, as did most of the pins which had held her locks secure.

"Are you injured?" he asked huskily.

"It was Jack who broke his crown, remember?"

"Jack did not have Jill to cushion his tumble." Although Kane had removed his weight from her chest, propping himself on his lower arms, he made no effort to remove the length of his body from hers. His fingers moved gingerly upon her scalp. "No bumps here," he said, his head lowering as though he wished to examine her more closely.

Their gazes locked, his concern dissipating as his eyes clouded. Glynna's own eyes searched his face, seeing there a look different from any she had ever before observed, on his face or any other. His mouth lowered ever closer to hers, until their breaths mingled and her lips tingled in delightful anticipation. His hands tightened their hold on either side of her head, gently lifting it, bringing her mouth ever closer to his. When his lips brushed hers, Glynna thought she would scream in blissful agony, yet she held her mouth firmly closed, waiting to see how far his kiss would progress.

Ever so slowly, he moved his lips upon hers, seeming to savor their whispery touching. Her scalp tingled beneath his fingers; a shiver of delight coursed the length of her spine. She continued to wait, knowing instinctively there was more to lovemaking than this, until she lost patience with the waiting. With conscious direction, her lips pressed harder against his, then moved of their own accord upon the sweet softness of his mouth. He answered their pressure by turning his head, slanting his lips across hers and holding her more tightly. Glynna, lost in sensation, was disappointed when he released her mouth for a hair's-breadth until she felt the tip of his tongue traverse the width of her lips. In surprise, she parted her lips as she felt the sensual response of her body beneath his. His tongue touched her teeth, gently raked her gums, and then thrust into the recess of her mouth when she gave it access. Her fingers sought his head, their tips luxuriating in the crispness of his hair as her palms held his head closely against her own. So this was how it felt to be kissed!

With a sudden savageness, catching Glynna completely off-guard, Kane pushed her head back to the fragrant grasses and rolled away from her. For a moment she lay panting, feeling disoriented . . . and, somehow, empty. Unbidden, a tear trickled out of her left eye, leaving a hot, moist trail before puddling in her ear. Angrily, she wiped at it, but not quickly enough.

"Please accept my apologies, Miss O'Rourke," he almost hissed. "I don't know what came over me. It won't happen again."

But I want it to! her mind screamed at him. Had it

been so awful for him, then? Her arms ached for him. Her scalp still tingled where he had held it. Her lips felt swollen and bruised, but pleasingly so. With all her heart, she wanted him to hold her again, to kiss her again. All the while her heart ached, her eyes watched with detachment as he stood up and brushed himself off, brushing her off as well.

Fighting the tears which threatened to spill onto her flushed cheeks, Glynna sat up and ran her fingers through the tangled mass of her hair. She would not allow herself to look again at Kane Rafferty, although she heard him moving around on the hill. Moments later, her hat fell upon her lap, its crown holding her hairpins. With jerky motions, she twisted her heavy locks into a coil and pinned the mass securely to the back of her head, then turned the bonnet over in her lap, her hands smoothing its slightly crushed felt before they placed it upon her head. When she would have pushed herself to her feet, he grasped her upper arms and pulled her up with a roughness that belied his former tenderness and erased her desire for closeness.

The ease between them was gone, shattered by his reaction to their embrace. Suddenly she shivered in the growing warmth of mid-morning. And she knew that, next week when he was gone and for a long time thereafter, she would remember his hands entwined in her hair, the weight of his body bearing down on hers, the softness of his lips upon her own, the response of her body to his touch. Then, and only then, she would let loose the tears she now held at bay.

Ignoring his halfhearted offer of assistance, Glynna remounted Sheena and pushed the mare into a fast gallop toward the inn.

* * *

Darcie and Katie were busily pulling tender heads of cabbage from the black earth of the garden when Glynna came riding hard into the stableyard.

"Now what you s'pose she in such a hurry for?" Katie asked, not really expecting an answer.

Darcie answered with her own question. "Didn't she go riding with Mr. Rafferty?"

Katie shook her large head in exasperation. "I *tole* her to be nice to that young man."

"Don't push her, Katie. You know how independent Glynna can be." A secretive smile lifted the corners of Darcie's mouth. "Mark my words, everything will turn out right for Glynna. I just know it will."

"I hope you right, Miz Dahcie. I sho' hope you right."

Chapter Six

"Take care of Sheena!" Glynna snapped at an openmouthed stableboy who could not recall her ever being anything other than polite. "And make sure she gets a good rubdown," she called over her shoulder, stalking from the stable and almost running headlong into Kane Rafferty, who had dismounted and was leading his stallion through the doorway.

He let go of his mount's reins and grasped her upper arms. She winced, not so much from pain as from his touch. "I told you I was sorry," he said, his usually mellow voice reverberating harshly in the large, open space.

"Take your hands off me," she hissed.

"We have to talk."

"That is where you are wrong, Mr. Rafferty. We have nothing to discuss." She wriggled from his hold and continued stalking across the stableyard.

Kane handed off his horse, hastily expressed his gratitude, and followed her. "No, Miss O'Rourke, you are wrong. We have much to discuss. If I am to work with you for the better portion of a year—"

Glynna abruptly stopped stalking and whirled around. "Not a year, but a matter of days, Mr. Rafferty." Her green eyes shot sparks at him. "If you will recall, I never agreed to being tutored, by you or anyone else. My only agreement was to accommodate your inability to entertain yourself for this week. When your coachman returns from the valley, you will return to Williamsburg, and from there go wherever you wish. As for your entertainment . . . after this morning . . . well, I don't honestly care how bored you become!" With another whirl of her full skirts, she continued on her way toward the inn, leaving, for the second time in minutes, someone else openmouthed.

Why did I kiss the chit? She's acting like no one ever did before. He remembered the way her slight frame had trembled at his touch, her hesitation in kissing him back, the single tear she had so quickly wiped away, her jerking movements as she repinned her hair. *No one ever has!* The realization startled him, for he was quite certain his wandering thoughts had stumbled upon the truth. His gaze followed her path even as his feet began to trace her steps. Had he glanced toward the garden, the grinning faces of Darcie and Katie might have undone his determination.

Kane caught up with Glynna in the front hall. Her fingers fiercely plucked at the ends of her kid riding gloves while her chest heaved from exertion mixed with anger. His own ire had mounted with every uphill step he had taken in pursuit of her stiff-backed figure, yet he now found himself wanting to take her in his arms to plant his mouth firmly upon hers. The urge was so great, he almost gave in to it. Instead, he consciously softened his voice and afforded careful consideration to his words before he spoke.

"Glynna, please, can't we be friends? I'm a stranger in a strange land, and I need your friendship."

"I do not recall granting you permission to address me by my Christian name." The retort came out not nearly so sharply as she had intended. She worked at pulling off the close-fitting gloves, the pounding of her heart beginning to recede as her anger and fatigue ebbed. Having, from her point of view, summarily dismissed him, she began her ascent of the stairs.

She underestimated Kane Rafferty. He continued to dog her steps. "What did you expect, *Miss O'Rourke?* I'm only human. Any red-blooded man would have done what I did."

Glynna knew she had set out that morning to prove her womanhood to this man—and prove it she had! It was not the kiss that had upset her, rather his rejection of her afterward. She also knew she was not about to reveal this to him. At the landing, she removed her plumed hat and placed her gloves in its crown. "I would not expect such behavior from a *gentleman,* Mr. Rafferty." She shoved the hat under her left armpit, caring not that she crushed it further, and began to undo the frogs which held her jacket closed as she started up the next flight of stairs.

"Why are you making so much of one kiss?"

She answered him with a baleful glare tossed over her shoulder, her fingers completing their task. The jacket now gaped open, revealing a cream-colored silk bodice beneath. Her bosom had begun to heave again. Kane had some difficulty in keeping his eyes from its up-and-down motions when she turned around at the head of the staircase. Glynna placed the hat on a small table, shrugged out of the velvet jacket, laid it across her left arm, and retrieved the hat and gloves.

He followed her into the ballroom. "You can't deny that you enjoyed it."

"And you can't expect me to dignify that remark." Her demeanor as haughty as she could make it, she crossed the wide space and opened the door leading into the family quarters.

Kane was becoming quite exasperated with her. "Let's put this morning behind us and start over. Just tell me what you want to learn, and that's where we'll begin."

Without realizing it, he had followed Glynna down the full length of the hallway. Even when she opened her bedchamber door and entered her room, he dogged her. "A *lady* would know how to employ some diplomacy."

Glynna deposited her jacket and hat on the bed. "I suppose now you will attempt to convince me that you had my education at heart, that the whole incident was just an experiment to see how I would react. Such convoluted logic does not impress me, sir." She moved her hands to the back of her skirt and began to work at unfastening the hooks. "Unless you want to prove your baseness by watching me disrobe, I suggest you take yourself elsewhere."

Much as he'd have liked to stay, the chit did have a point. Kane gave her a cursory bow—and left.

By the time Glynna had changed her clothing and refreshed herself—she wanted a bath, but knew there wasn't time—dinner was being served. She stood for a moment in the doorway of the ordinary in utter confusion, for the McGintys sat with the three Cava-naughs and no place had been set for her. Katie's two daughters moved about the room, placing steaming plates of food and glasses of milk in front of the diners. When they had completed their tasks and, trays aloft, exited through the keeping hall, Glynna's roving gaze settled momentarily on her aunt. Darcie smiled and inclined her head toward the corner table where Glynna had shared tea with Edwin the previous afternoon.

There Kane sat, looking for all the world as though nothing untoward had transpired between them that morning. Although he was by himself, an extra plate had been set upon his table. Glynna fought the urge to stamp her foot and leave the room, knowing such a display of temper would weaken her stance. With as much dignity as she could muster, she walked sedately to Kane's table and did not argue when he moved to seat her.

"How dare you!" she hissed so only Kane could hear her, her back now to her aunt.

His eyes widened at her attack. "Not I."

"What a good actor you are. Perhaps you missed your calling."

"How would you know? You have yet to allow any lessons."

Glynna would not allow a change of subject, either. "If not you, then . . . No. Aunt Darcie would never—"

"But she did. She doesn't know about our, shall we say, disagreement."

"No, I don't suppose she does."

"She is eager for us to begin."

Glynna ignored the remark. Apart from Kane's occasional questions about the food, much of which

92

was new to him, and Glynna's unadorned answers, the meal passed without further conversation. She passed the time pondering her predicament, testing one plan and then another in her mind as she became more determined than ever to avoid Kane Rafferty. He passed the time reliving the morning, running every word, every movement, every feeling through his head, refusing to allow guilt passage into his thoughts.

Chair legs scraping against the bare wood floor signaled the end of the noon repast. Glynna glanced at her half-full plate in surprise, not realizing until now that she had eaten little. "Excuse me, Mr. Rafferty," she said politely, though without sweetness. "I am not feeling well. Perhaps an afternoon spent resting will settle the ache in my head."

And with that declaration, she mounted the stairs to her room.

There could be no mention of the tiara, for the baron was certain to read any correspondence from Kane. He reread the letter he had just penned, double-checking it to be certain the code his mother had set for him had been followed.

    Cavanaugh's Tavern
    Colony of Virginia
    May 14, 1753

Dear Father and Mother,
    You will be pleased to know that I have arrived safely and in good health. This land is almost the jewel Ireland is — quite green and fertile. My arrival was met with so much

warmth and kindness, I was stunned. This inn
is rather a far distance from the coast. . . .

The remainder of the missive detailed his journey
and highlighted the few newsworthy events since his
arrival. He did not consider this morning's events
newsworthy. But it was not the rest of the letter
which concerned him, rather those first few sentences. They sounded stilted to him, yet they carried the
required message to his mother: "No jewel so far."
The code she had contrived was simple—the sixth
word of each sentence until the message was complete. He realized he had used "know" for "no," but
his mother would understand.

Satisfied, he folded the letter, sealed it with wax,
then placed it in a drawer. When the coachman returned from the valley, he would give it to him to
post in Williamsburg. Kane made a mental note to
ask his host how often they were able to post letters,
knowing it might be weeks before he could send another to his parents.

Then he settled himself into a comfortable wing
chair beside a window and picked up a book he had
borrowed from Galen's library, but he found himself
unable to concentrate on the historian's words. It
was his mother's story which commanded his
thoughts.

In the spring of 1736, just months before
Glynndon O'Rourke and his wife, Brenna, had died,
a rash of jewel thefts had occurred on Irish estates.
Almost seventeen at the time, Kane was away at
school; his father, a member of Parliament, had

been called to London. When word reached Lady Catherine Rafferty, Baroness of Ulrich, that the thieves had struck an estate in a neighboring county, she knew that she must take defensive action, so she carefully sewed necklaces, bracelets, earrings, brooches, and rings into the hems and linings of her clothing, but she could find nowhere safe to hide the jewel-encrusted tiara. She moved it from place to place, never satisfied that the thieves would not find it should they enter her domain.

For several days she fretted over the tiara, not sleeping well and becoming increasingly jittery. Its preservation was more important than that of all the other jewels, not only because of its value, which was great, but due to its historical significance and its place in family tradition.

Sigmund, a former Baron of Ulrich, had fought beside the Black Prince at the Battle of Poitiers, France, in 1356 during the Hundred Years' War. It was a great victory for the English, and Sigmund had distinguished himself in battle. He'd then returned to his estate with the spoils of war, including the tiara which had been confiscated from a French château. Still a young man, the baron had not yet taken a wife. When he did, he insisted she wear the tiara atop her wedding veil. Since then, the headpiece had been reserved for weddings, and all the brides of Ulrich had worn it.

That virtually everyone knew of its existence, there was no doubt. Catherine feared the thieves would ransack her home, looking for it. Therefore, it must be removed from County Galway. But where would she take it? And whom could she trust with its safekeeping?

Glynndon O'Rourke was more than a family acquaintance. He was a close and trusted friend. Risking being robbed by highwaymen, Catherine ordered a coach, packed a bag, and traveled to Dublin. She arrived without mishap. Glynndon assured her the tiara would be kept securely until the threat of thievery was past. She assumed, much to her later regret, that Glynndon had put the tiara in his bank vault.

It was not until midsummer that the clever thieves were finally caught. By that time, Glynndon and Brenna were away on their holiday. Having endured a lengthy Parliamentary session, the baron had just returned to Ireland when news of his friend's death arrived. Wary, though not unduly concerned about the safety of the tiara, and respectful of his grief, Catherine did not tell her husband what she had done. Glynndon had given her a receipt, and this she presented to his solicitor, one David Garvin, a few weeks later when other business took the Raffertys to Dublin. The man had not seen the tiara; he offered to ask the bank's officers if they had any knowledge of its disposal, assuring Catherine he would be discreet. Unfortunately, no one at the bank had ever seen it.

This knowledge led Catherine to believe Glynndon must have taken the tiara to his home. Since Garvin was handling the sale of the house along with its furnishings, he made a careful search for the tiara. It was not there, either.

Brenna's sister and only close relative, Darcie Carmichael, had already collected Glynna and her possessions by this time. David Garvin had but little knowledge of the aunt, and this he passed on to Catherine: the Carmichaels lived on the Isle of Man; Darcie's husband, Galen, owned and operated a fishing boat; the aunt, a petite woman who strongly favored her sister, seemed uninterested in Glynndon's fortune.

Catherine retained David Garvin to continue making discreet inquiries and to learn what he could of the Carmichaels. When she saw him again a few months later, he regretfully informed her that Galen Carmichael had met with some misfortune and left the Isle of Man. His informants had not been able to learn much from the closemouthed Manx, but it looked as though the Carmichaels had fled the country.

Everyone knew that many a Manx family had accumulated fortunes smuggling contraband to the British mainland. French brandies and champagnes, Jamaican rum, and Oriental silks all made their way to the independent island strategically located in the Irish Sea between England and Ireland, and not subject to English duty. Under the cover of the mist which often cloaked the isle, the Manx sailors ran goods across the water at quite a lucrative profit.

Carmichael owned a fishing boat. His wife was not interested in money. Perhaps he did more than fish with his boat. Perhaps this "side business" had produced more trouble than Galen Carmichael wanted to face.

Catherine agreed that David Garvin's conclusion had merit. It brought her no closer, however, to locating the tiara. Feeling no guilt in the matter, for she had done no more than she thought necessary under the circumstances, Catherine considered telling the baron. But her husband had suffered an inordinate amount of stress for the past several years, as he'd attempted to recoup the family fortune his own father had gambled away. This, coupled with his Parliamentary duties, was almost more than he could handle. And now he grieved over the loss of his dear friend, Glynndon O'Rourke, who had personally loaned Thomas Rafferty a rather large sum of money and then included a clause in his will absolving the baron from further debt. Catherine could not bring herself to increase her husband's burdens.

The longer she kept this knowledge from him, the harder it became to broach the subject. The baron never mentioned the tiara, never asked to see it. Kane reached his majority, but he seemed in no hurry to marry, which would require her to produce the missing headpiece. When her husband began to talk of finding Glynna, feeling he owed something to the child, Catherine fueled his desire to do so. Intuitively, she knew the tiara must be with Glynna.

They had traced the Carmichaels to Williamsburg. That had been seven years ago. Then the family had disappeared again, but the Raffertys had learned that the family name had been changed to Cavanaugh, both facts serving to confirm David Garvin's assumption that Galen was running from something. Ill health befell the baron for a while; this had been followed by several years of good fortune, a favorable turn of fate but one which required much of Thomas Rafferty's time. When events finally reached a plateau, the baron resumed his search for Glynna.

"What will you do for her, should you find her?" Catherine had asked her husband. "She is almost old enough now to claim her trust, so she has little need of your money." Thomas agreed, adding that if Glynna were at all like her father, she would want to abide by Glynndon's wish that the debt be erased.

"She's been in the colonies now for seventeen years. In all probability, her education has suffered," Catherine suggested. "Nor would she have much opportunity to marry well in that heathen land. Perhaps we could send a tutor, then give her a season in London."

Her suggestion, the result of careful thought and planning, fell on willing ears. When the baron received word from his colonial contacts that the Cavanaughs owned and operated a tavern on the Virginia frontier, Catherine easily convinced her husband that their eldest son, Kane, should be sent.

For almost a decade there had been strife between the two Rafferty men. Once Kane had completed both the university and the Grand Tour, Thomas had thought his eldest should marry and start a family. His spell of ill health reminded him of the uncertainties of life. He wanted a grandson—an heir—before he died. But Kane refused to cooperate.

Until now. At thirty-four, Kane had finally decided upon a mate—Valerie Sherman. Thomas was far from thrilled. In his estimation, the twenty-two-year-old daughter of his friend, Squire Leland Sherman, left much to be desired. Granted, she was a beauty, but she was also haughty, self-centered, and aggressive. Kane deserved better. Perhaps, if his son spent some time away from his betrothed, he would realize her shortcomings. He might even fall in love with Glynna O'Rourke. Thomas Rafferty could think of no match more appropriate.

A totally different reason prompted Catherine's eagerness to send Kane to the colonies. She could not trust a stranger to return with the valuable tiara, should it be found. Kane would understand the need for discretion—and it would be in his best interest to locate the tiara as well. Presented with the facts—Catherine purposely omitted the reason his father wanted him to go—Kane reluctantly agreed to his mother's plan.

Glynna awoke from her nap, a smile upon her face. She stretched upon the counterpane, wriggling her bare toes as she held her body taut, luxuriating in the mellowness that suffused her being. She had never intended to go to sleep, but sleep she had—a deep, restful sleep through which a delightful dream had flitted. She relaxed her limbs, folding her knees and drawing them up into her stomach as she rolled onto her left side. Her eyelids closed. She willed the dream to return, wanting to see it from a conscious state.

Bits and pieces of the dream's fluff crossed the horizon of her inner eye; her knight, replete in shining armor, riding like the wind upon a white stallion; storm clouds gathering in a pewter sky; ancient gray stones mortised into the walls of a hulking castle. There was no color, only black and white and shades of gray. A haunting melody, plucked upon the strings of a harp, accompanied the flying hooves of the stallion and the congregation of dark clouds approaching the castle.

Abruptly, the images disappeared, leaving only the music to attest to their existence. Glynna let the music wash over her, through her . . . lulling her, filling her with a peace unlike any she had ever known. The knight of her dream returned, the eye of her mind moving ever closer to him until the helmet that covered his head filled the frame. A visor covered his face, a mail collar his neck. Gauntleted hands reached upward and removed the shiny metal helmet, its crest of feathers blowing gently in the wind. Her gaze followed the path of the helmet as it was held first in silhouette against the darker gray of sky and then held almost as a shield in front of the knight's face. Slowly the helmet was lowered, exposing first a shock of raven black hair, then a wide expanse of forehead, and finally a pair of dove gray eyes.

Glynna gasped, her thoughts in disarray, the dream shattered. No! Kane Rafferty is not my knight! she railed silently. Without her usual economy of movement, she donned her clothes, pulling on her gown before her petticoats, her shoes before her stockings. When she was finally dressed, she jerked open her bedroom door. The harp's music drifted down the hallway, beckoning to her, soothing her frayed nerves. She followed it as docilely as sheep followed Pan's pipe.

Kane sat at the harp, his head bowed as his long fingers plucked the vibrant strings. The notes resounded in the stillness of the ballroom, then wafted softer . . . slower . . . as the piece wound to a close. As fluidly as his fingers had moved upon the strings, his capable hands removed the weight of the harp from his right shoulder and set it solidly upon the floor.

"That was beautiful," Glynna whispered, her eyes misty.

"This is a beautiful instrument, almost as lovely as the one in my mother's music room." Kane did not move away from the harp but waved an arm toward a nearby chair, inviting her to sit with him. "Do you ever play it?" he asked softly when she was seated.

She shook her head in negation. "Will you teach me?" The question stunned her, for it was uttered without conscious thought, but she didn't take it back.

"My pleasure." Kane smiled broadly, exposing his

dimpled cheek. "Do you know the harp is the oldest of stringed musical instruments? The Bible says it was invented by Jubal."

"And it was the instrument David played," Glynna supplied.

"In fact, a double harp like this one is sometimes called David's harp."

"I have never heard it played so well," she admitted, surprising herself again. Where was her anger, her rebellion?

"Everyone in my family plays the harp—everyone except my father, that is. You should hear my mother play it."

"Did she teach you?"

Kane grinned impishly. "Yes, but not willingly."

"Didn't she want you to learn how to play it?"

"She *demanded* we all learn. My mother is of Irish ancestry and our home is there. The harp is an emblem of Ireland and was the favorite instrument of the old Irish poets. Mother said if we became proficient at no other instrument, we would be at the harp. She hired one teacher after another, but none pleased her, so she finally gave up and taught us herself."

"Do you have many brothers and sisters, Mr. Rafferty?"

"One of each—both younger."

Glynna sighed. "I wish I did. Oh, I know I have Brian, and he's like a brother to me," she added quickly, "but it's not the same." She had never told anyone this, not even Katie or Beth.

"Do you miss your parents, Glynna?" He watched her expression closely, seeing there no visible sign indicating her further objection to his use of her Christian name. Instead, she dropped her eyes to her lap and sighed.

"Not in the way you might think. You see, I never really knew them. I was so young when they died." She poured out the story, telling it to Kane exactly as Darcie had told it to her over and over again. It was not a happy tale, but it was a part of her heritage, and as such she had requested its repetition until she had committed it to memory. When she had finished, Kane leaned forward and, with the balls of his thumbs, gently wiped away the tears that had spilled onto her cheeks. He wished he could as easily wipe away her grief.

"Come, little one," he said, so tenderly Glynna was touched rather than offended by the reference to her size. "Let me show you how one supports this heavy instrument." He laughed. "I was not quite your size when Mother began my lessons!"

Chapter Seven

The ballroom was ablaze with candlelight, but the blaze emanating from the emerald gems set in Glynna's face was powered by its own source of energy. Kane's hand held hers with a gentle firmness as he guided her through the steps of the minuet. She moved gracefully through the complicated pattern of steps, rises, dips, and curtsies as the slowly played, three-quarter-time music flowed through her. She knew that all eyes were trained upon her and Kane as they demonstrated the dance, and yet she felt almost a spectator, as though she, too, watched from the periphery.

At some point in the past week she had stopped resisting Kane's tutoring. She had thought herself so knowledgeable — and, indeed, she was — that she had not realized the extent of her ignorance. Had Kane approached their sessions with arrogance, as she had fully expected him to do, Glynna would have continued to rebel. Instead, he had worked his way into her life with a patience and singleness of purpose which had melted away her icy resistance. Not once had his attitude been patronizing. He recognized her intelligence, using her current knowledge as a foundation on which to build. And she was discovering there was much he could teach her.

He had not touched her again, either. Not as a man touches a woman. When he had taught her the minuet, he had maintained an impersonal aloofness as he had guided her through the steps. Glynna refused to analyze her feelings about this new attitude. It was the easy route to take. Perhaps he would behave himself, after all.

She had not, however, decided that he could stay for the proposed year. The coachman had not yet returned from the valley, thus postponing the need for a final decision. A part of Glynna hoped such a need would not arise for a few more days. She had begun to enjoy Kane's company.

As a final bow and curtsy completed the dance, the ballroom exploded in applause. Reluctantly, Glynna became Edwin's partner as Beth became Kane's. This arrangement had been worked out in advance of the demonstration to make teaching the minuet to the others easier. This dance, so popular in the ballrooms of France, had yet to become widely known in the colonies. In contrast to the bouncing country dances to which Glynna was accustomed, the graceful minuet was a delightful change. Kane had promised to teach her the gavotte and the allemande as well, but for the moment she must contend with Winnie's bumbling steps.

Out of the corner of her eye she watched Beth and Kane. They seemed to be managing much better than she and Edwin were. A tiny stab of jealousy pierced her heart; this she blamed on her sudden lack of grace. She had not minded being under scrutiny as long as she had Kane to guide her steps. She had already begun to think of Kane as being exclusively her own, but she had yet to fully acknowledge that fact.

A few more duos joined them. Glynna smiled when

she noticed Darcie and Galen move onto the dance floor. Her uncle towered over his wife, yet they moved with a fluidity that belied their differences in height. Was this how she and Kane looked when they danced together? she wondered, hoping it was so.

She hadn't considered the absurdity of her dancing with Edwin, who stood more than half a head taller than Kane, until she looked up into his beaming face, the corners of his dark eyes crinkling as his mouth widened. Didn't he realize how ill matched they were? Just to look into his eyes, she had to bend her neck so far back it hurt. Were the musicians never going to end the piece? Her turn with Kane seemed to have passed swiftly in comparison.

At long last the dance ended. Before dear old Winnie, who forever seemed to be at a loss for words, could invite her to share a cup of punch with him, Kane appeared at Glynna's elbow. She silently breathed a sigh of relief, not so much, she told herself, because she would rather have Kane's company as because she knew Beth wanted Edwin's. The musicians had ceased playing to take a short respite, and a crowd congregated around the refreshment table. Others moved into the hall, ostensibly to take momentary advantage of the comfortable chairs in either the ladies' or gentlemen's parlors although many intended to seek out the appropriate water closet. Kane led her to the hall, but when they reached it he ushered her out the open door and onto the upstairs gallery.

Glynna shivered in the cool night air, upon which a multitude of floral fragrances wafted, yet she reveled in its freshness. Although the windows on both sides of the ballroom stood open to the evening breezes, she had grown warm within its confines.

"Are you cold? Would you rather go back inside?"

Kane's voice was low and mellow and solicitous.

"No," she answered quickly. "It is refreshing out here." Besides, she silently added, I'm out of Edwin's sight now. She could not understand his sudden interest in her.

"Shall I get your shawl? Or, perhaps, a cup of punch?"

Glynna leaned her bare forearms on the railing and inhaled deeply of the crisp air. "Thank you, but no on both counts, Mr. Rafferty. Perhaps later on the punch."

Kane, too, leaned on the railing; the silk fabric of his sleeve lightly caressing her naked arm and sending a delightful shiver down her spine. She fought to control it. For a few moments they stood thus, each absorbing the nearness of the other in the guise of absorbing the fragrant air.

"When are you going to start calling me 'Kane'?"

His question caught her off-guard. "It hardly seems appropriate for a pupil to call her teacher by his first name." As soon as the words were out of her mouth she realized what she had said, but it was too late to call them back.

"So. You have decided to allow me to be your tutor." He sounded pleased.

"No . . ." She floundered. "I misspoke."

"Then you have no reason not to call me 'Kane,' " he said so matter-of-factly she could not be certain how he felt now.

She turned her head slightly, bringing his profile into her field of vision. The moonlight played upon the planes of his face, softening its angles. His gaze seemed fixed upon some far-distant star; his mouth he held in a firm line. Realizing she had dug herself in rather deeply, Glynna sought a response. She returned her gaze to the night sky, for she found that when she looked at Kane she could not think clearly. It did not seem to matter, however. The man's presence filled her heart, obliterating logical thought. The knight of her dream, that self-same man as the groom in her daydream, returned to haunt her.

Where reason failed, fate intervened.

"Here you are!" Beth's bright voice came from the open doorway. "Edwin and I have been looking everywhere for the two of you." She joined Glynna at the railing. "By faith, it's chilly out here!" she declared, hugging herself.

Glynna laughed softly.

"You gloat in my discomfort?" Beth sounded offended.

"Not at all, my dear. You just reminded me of an ongoing misunderstanding with Brian." Glynna's eyes sparkled, their corners crinkling in merriment. "Several years ago, when he was about three, I suppose, I was tucking him in one wintry night and I said, 'Bundle up, Brian. It's chilly outside.' In his child's mind, he conjured up a vicious monster named Chilly, of whom he has been terrified ever since!" Glynna sobered then. "I shouldn't laugh about it. For Brian, the fear is quite real."

"It's amazing, don't you think?" Kane said. "The way people misunderstand situations, I mean, and then create for themselves a fear that has no foundation. Children are not the only guilty parties."

That there was double meaning in his words Glynna had no doubt. The confusion lay in knowing exactly what he'd intended.

"For my part, I'm not so sure Brian isn't right," Edwin said. "The cold can turn into a vicious monster, one a man had better respect if he doesn't want to freeze to death."

The three at the railing turned their attention to

him, though he stood behind them. Glynna's and Beth's expressions registered surprise at his being argumentative, which was certainly out of character for him. Kane viewed him with a new respect.

Music flowed through the doorway, signaling that dancing had resumed.

Edwin grasped Beth's elbow beneath the cascade of ecru lace. "You are chilled," he observed. "You have goosebumps, Beth. Let's go back inside."

Kane shrugged, then waved an arm at the couple's backs. "Shall we?" he asked without enthusiasm.

Glynna misinterpreted his lack of eagerness. "I thought you liked to dance."

"I do."

You just do not wish to dance with me.

Neither moved. Both watched Beth and Edwin disappear into the hallway. Glynna's eyes misted as she considered Kane's ready admission. She willed the tears away and took a deep breath to soothe the hurt. "You will find many assenting partners. You needn't concern yourself with my disposition." She took one step toward the doorway before Kane moved quickly in front of her, his hands reaching out to grasp her upper arms in a firm hold.

"Glynna O'Rourke, you suffer from a lack of understanding as great as Brian's." His words were spoken through clenched teeth. Roughly, he pulled her into the shadows.

Green eyes flashed sparks. "You bask in demonstrating your superior strength, Kane Rafferty!" Glynna's chest began to heave due to her anger. "Unhand me, or I'll—I'll scream!"

"No, you won't, you little she-devil!"

She struggled against his hold, but her efforts served only to increase his purpose. "I will," she threatened again, jerking her head back to look up at

109

him. Shadows swathed his countenance, allowing her no indication of his intentions. She opened her mouth to make good her threat, but to her dismay, it was a moan she emitted, not a scream.

Kane's mouth descended quickly upon hers, his lips and tongue staking a claim as his hands moved to her back, pulling her closer. Glynna placed her palms on the hardness of his chest and pushed against him, but he ignored her struggles. His assault eased into a caress as his hands roamed the length of her back, and his lips softened their hold on hers. Unwillingly, Glynna felt the anger depart from her stiff limbs, to be replaced by a sudden weakness over which she exercised no control. Without her willing it, her hands traveled upward to rest momentarily on his shoulders before continuing their journey to the back of his neck. Her fingers invaded the hair at his nape as the heels of her hands molded themselves to the contours behind his ears. She offered no protest when the tip of his tongue flickered over hers before raking the roof of her mouth. Her own tongue reached upward to touch his. Kane's lips became firm against her own once more as their tongues danced to the music coming from the ballroom.

Except for a brotherly peck on the cheek, no one had ever kissed Glynna before Kane had on Monday. Do all men kiss this way? she wondered. His mouth tasted good . . . fresh and clean. She breathed deeply of his essence, luxuriated in its starkly masculine crispness.

She sighed when his tongue retreated, his lips leaving hers to journey across her cheek and then downward to her throat. His hands moved, too, pausing briefly under her arms before their palms covered her breasts. Her heart pounded against the gentle squeezing, her nipples answering his caresses by growing hard beneath her thin chemise. She felt incredibly strong and deliciously weak at the same time. The pressure of her palms against his head brought his mouth back to hers while his hands resumed their fondling journey to travel down her sides and cup her buttocks, pulling her completely against him. Glynna reveled in the mixture of her softness against his hardness until she felt the evidence of his manhood pressing against her stomach.

Horrified, she pushed at him, wrenching her mouth from his and almost falling when he released his hold of her. "How dare you!" she hissed, her fingers pulling at her bodice and then smoothing her skirts. Her breath was coming in short pants and she refused to look at him. His chuckle fueled her ire.

"What a delightful little tease you are, Miss O'Rourke. Just how many hearts have you broken? It must be many, indeed, for you are certainly well schooled in the art of lovemaking."

A resounding slap echoed in the stillness of the evening air. Glynna hoped his cheek stung with the same intensity as her palm. She then allowed herself that act of immaturity she had repressed since his arrival: she stamped the sole of her right foot hard against the planks of the gallery. After doing so, she gathered her dignity about her and, fighting the urge to run, turned on her heel and sedately walked away.

Glynna fought the demon that seemed bent on keeping her awake. Somehow she had made it through the remainder of the evening with her dignity intact, but only, she was certain, because she had managed to avoid Kane completely. What would she do tomorrow, and the next day and the next . . . until the scoundrel finally left the tavern? Glynna had never been a very good actress. Her emotions and feelings showed through, despite her best efforts to contain them. Aunt Darcie—and the ever-perceptive Katie—would know something was wrong. Whatever would she tell them?

Her thrashing about and heavy sighs elicited a giggle from Beth. "Whatever did he do to you, Glynna, to upset you so?"

The answer came swiftly. "I don't want to talk about it."

Beth was unperturbed. "It might help." When Glynna failed to respond, Beth got out of bed and lit a candle. Instead of climbing back under the covers, she sat cross-legged on the counterpane, drawing her bare feet under her thighs and pulling her long nightdress over her legs. She propped her elbows on her knees and rested her chin on her open palms. "I'm your friend—your confidante. Remember?"

Glynna could not help smiling when she rolled over on her back and spied Beth's pose. She piled two pillows against the headboard and leaned comfortably against them. "It might help," she agreed, albeit reluctantly.

For several moments they sat thus, Beth waiting patiently for Glynna to continue, Glynna trying to decide how to broach the subject without embarrassing herself. In the interim, Glynna plucked nervously at the bedcoverings. Finally, she took a deep breath and asked quietly, "Has Edwin ever kissed you?"

Beth grinned mischievously. "Do you mean kissed, or"—she opened her eyes wide and dragged out the word—"*kissed?*"

Glynna could not avoid smiling herself, much more at ease with the subject now. "*Kissed.*" She mocked Beth's pronunciation.

"Edwin has not so much as kissed me on the

cheek," her friend admitted.

Glynna pulled one of the pillows from behind her back and threw it playfully at her friend. "Then why didn't you say so in the first place?"

Beth giggled. "It was more fun leading you on." She settled her pale features into a more sober expression then. "Is that what he did? Kane Rafferty, I mean. Did he kiss you?"

Glynna nodded.

"Whew! For a second there, I thought you meant Edwin had committed the deed. What a relief!"

"For you, maybe."

"Didn't you like it?"

"I . . . I'm not sure. It scared me." Glynna started plucking the counterpane again.

"It might scare me, too — to be *kissed*. But I think I might like it! Tell me, how did it feel?"

"I can't really describe it. You'll find out when it happens to you. It may be different for you."

Beth considered this for a moment before replying, "I can't fathom why it should be any different for me."

"Because" — Glynna floundered — "because I'm not sure all men kiss like Kane does." She felt the redness staining her cheeks in embarrassment at this admission, and she dropped her gaze once more to the bed-coverings.

Her friend stifled the urge to laugh. How could any girl reach the age of a score of years and be so ignorant about something so basic? she wondered. Especially one as attractive as Glynna O'Rourke! Beth had thought Glynna to be far more experienced than she, but Glynna's discomfiture belied that conclusion. Beth's voice was soft and understanding when she said, "I think all men kiss the same way when they are in love. And I think all women feel the same way

113

when they are kissed by someone they love."

It took a minute for Glynna to comprehend fully the meaning of Beth's speech. When she did, her eyes flew open and she gasped. "You think Kane and I are—are in love?" she asked incredulously.

Beth shrugged. "That's the way it appears to me."

Her tone was so matter-of-fact Glynna was further taken aback. "That's just not possible."

"I don't know why not."

"But . . . I haven't known him long enough."

"Oh, yes you have. Glynna O'Rourke, can't you see that Kane Rafferty is that knight in shining armor you've been looking for so long?"

"No!" Glynna fervently declared. "He can't be!" She searched her friend's face in the dim candlelight and saw in it the firm conviction Beth's words had carried. Glynna could see no point in further argument. The hour was late and dawn would come far too soon. "Blow out the candle, Beth," she said gently. "Let's go to sleep."

Beth's conviction haunted Glynna through the next day and the next. Her usual robust appetite waned, and so rare was this occurrence both Darcie and Katie noticed it. Darcie feared some malady might be afflicting her niece and fussed over her as a mother hen fusses over her chicks. Katie harbored no such fear. She knew from whence the pale cheeks and distaste for food derived. Glynna intercepted Katie's knowing looks more than once and counted herself grateful for the black woman's silence on the matter.

Glynna accepted Darcie's clucking as though she, too, thought she might be ill, besides which a firm denial would only bring questions she was not yet ready to answer. If her aunt had other ideas, she cloaked them completely. Darcie had asked Glynna in a most delicate way if her physical problem stemmed from some feminine ills, providing an easy excuse for her niece and erasing any question of contagion.

Too late, Glynna realized that this reason would not excuse her from further contact with Kane Rafferty. Getting through Sunday was not too difficult, since she had Beth's company. Nonetheless, she breathed a sigh of relief when Kane chose to sit next to Galen during church services. But the time came when the Jenkinses must leave, as Glynna had known it would. This Sunday, she gratefully accepted Edwin's exclusive attentions at tea, especially since Reverend Mitchell and Kane took theirs in the ordinary with everyone else.

She spent the remainder of the afternoon and evening in her room, her hands busy with needlework. Her mind, on the other hand, seemed bent on dwelling on the events of the previous evening and on Beth's startling revelation. Glynna refused to believe Beth was right. It's just not possible! she repeatedly assured herself, but as the days wore on, her conviction lessened.

If Kane noticed anything different about Glynna, he made no comment. The supposed malady gave her reason to take her meals and tea in her room, thus avoiding his presence in the ordinary. Try as she might, though, she could not avoid him altogether. He insisted on lessons anyway, although he tailored them to fit Darcie's requirements, those being shortened sessions which involved no physical activity. And that meant no dancing, for which Glynna was thankful. She did not think she could bear his touch again. If she never learned the gavotte and the allemande, then so be it.

Kane thought otherwise. "Dancing often and danc-

115

ing well improves much," he told her. "Good posture and graceful movement are obvious by-products of the art, but dancing affects far more than that. A person who is at ease on the ballroom floor will find himself—or herself," he hastily added, "at ease in almost any situation. There exists a grace of the mind, of the soul, as well as that of the body. If you will recall our initial conversation, you will remember that it is your soul with which I am most concerned. When you are feeling better"—Glynna could not help noting the amused glint which suddenly appeared in his gray eyes at this point—"we will resume our dancing lessons. Until then, we will practice the art of conversation."

"I know how to talk, thank you!" Glynna quipped.

"Just as you know how to sit, I suppose." A twitching at the corners of his mouth joined the amusement which remained in his silvery gaze. "A proper lady *never* crosses her legs, except perhaps at the ankle. Nor does she, as I have already pointed out, ever sit on the floor."

"And when did you see me with my legs crossed?" she demanded.

"In the garden. When you were giving Brian his lesson."

"But I would never sit like that with an audience!" she insisted.

"Habits, easily formed though they may be, are quite difficult to break. You must never sit that way at all, whether alone or otherwise." For a moment he continued to regard her with amusement before the business at hand claimed his attention. "Now, what shall we discuss? Politics? Science? Philosophy?" Her delicate features registered her surprise at his suggestions. "In the salons of France, all are socially accepted topics of conversation."

Glynna's French teacher in Williamsburg had spent some time in France and had incorporated a knowledge of the French people into her lessons. Glynna had, therefore, some understanding of French culture and knew that aristocratic French women were not only allowed but actually encouraged to exhibit their intellects. She also knew that this was not true in England, and that was her supposed destination, not France. English women were schooled in the feminine arts: needlework, painting, literature, music, and French. For an English woman to be brazen enough to discuss politics, science, or philosophy was unheard of!

Yet she did not want to start an argument with Kane. Besides, this was untraveled territory for her and the journey might prove interesting. She supposed her future husband could be disposed to indulge in private intelligent conversation with his wife. She considered his proposed topics and made her selection.

"Philosophy it shall be, then," Kane agreed. "What do you know of Voltaire, Rousseau, or Montesquieu?"

"Nothing of the latter two," she reluctantly admitted after a careful searching of her brain for some remembrance of their names.

"No, I don't suppose you would, since they have only recently begun to publish their ideas. And quite revolutionary they are, too. I shall have to enlighten you."

Later that evening as Glynna, closeted in her room, faced a supper tray piled higher than usual, she found her thoughts returning without her bidding to the afternoon she had spent in Kane's company. His lack of arrogance in his role as tutor continued to amaze her. He had answered her questions with an innate in-

117

telligence unmarred by presumptuousness. Why must he approach their personal relationship so differently? she pondered. Although a niggling voice prompted the thought, Glynna refused to question the fact that a personal relationship with Kane Rafferty was totally inappropriate.

She was amazed at herself, too—at her ability to forget her anger with Kane when the two of them assumed the roles of teacher and pupil. Despite her resolves, Kane's charm coupled with his natural talent as an educator obliterated her resistance.

Still, the man was certainly not worth losing her good health over, she suddenly decided, attacking the food with more relish than she had been able to muster since the ball.

The coachman had been gone now for almost two weeks. Would he ever return from the valley? Perhaps Mr. Wilson had been waylaid by Indians, attacked by a mountain lion, or lay stricken with some dread disease. Glynna berated herself for even thinking such unkind thoughts, yet she reluctantly acknowledged her unwillingness to send Kane Rafferty away.

She was sopping up the last bit of gravy with her second slice of bread when Katie arrived to collect the tray. The cook's unexpected frown upon seeing the clean plate gave Glynna cause for further reflection. Her sated appetite won the battle with her overactive mind, however, and she soon dropped off into a deep and pleasant sleep.

Chapter Eight

Glynna O'Rourke was not one given to complaint. Darcie had often marveled over her niece's quiet acceptance of the basic isolation of Cavanaugh's Tavern. Granted, there were the weekly church services and occasional social gatherings which brought their scattered neighbors to the inn. Visitors came and went, also, but few of these were from the aristocratic elite. Most were surveyors, trappers, or pioneers en route to points westward. Although her niece seemed blithely unaware of any need for more social interaction, Darcie knew such a need existed.

It was for this reason, if no other, that she was privately thrilled by both Kane Rafferty's presence and the baron's plans for Glynna. She could not have planned better herself. This way, Glynna would be afforded the opportunities Darcie wished her to have, and without threat of exposure to Galen and herself. The placid, rather uneventful life which she and her husband had chosen out of necessity, but to which they had now become accustomed, could continue.

Or so Darcie thought.

The upheaval which both adult Cavanaughs had

feared would someday disrupt their lives had already begun to approach, and it was only a matter of time before their peaceful existence would be menaced.

Jarvis Whitfield was a man accustomed to getting what he wanted. There was a presence about him, an aura which lured and charmed the weak-minded into his various webs of deception. He felt no compunction when the silky strands he had spun entrapped a victim, even when the entrapment meant death. In his estimation, that left one less fool to populate the planet. The more he considered this premise, the prouder he became of each dastardly deed, for eliminating one fool surely resulted in eliminating several. Did not fools beget fools? he reasoned, then answered, as surely as intelligence begets intelligence.

If Whitfield had ever begot anyone, he owned to no knowledge of it. The possibility certainly existed, for he was a man accustomed to getting what he wanted. He wanted women, among other things, and he had them often. He took a woman with so much skill that seldom was he asked to pay for the privilege. The few who had dared request coin from him did not live to spend it. Whores he grouped with fools, and he cared not if his seed had ever been planted in one. In recent months, however, he had begun to think that perhaps he should seek intelligent female company from whom he might select a worthy mother for his son. He was, after all, the last of his lineage. He owed his father an heir.

If Jarvis Whitfield were capable of loving anyone, including himself, the one person upon whom that gentle emotion would have been bestowed was his father. What Whitfield felt for his progenitor clothed itself in a complexity of loyalty, admiration, and gratitude, as love itself often does. But what Whitfield felt was not love. Gentleness, tenderness, compassion were unknown to this man. For him, the truth lay not in beauty or kindness but rather in compensation and retribution.

Seeking the truth had proved to be an expensive endeavor, but Jarvis Whitfield had borne the expense without regret. He had spent every brass farthing he could beg, borrow, or steal—or even, at times, earn. He was so adept at the former options he could choose when to exercise the latter, and this method of obtaining money he reserved for those times when it suited his purpose.

This was such a time.

Jarvis Whitfield was convinced the man he sought, the one who had been responsible for his father's death, was in the colonies. What better way to travel there than with someone who would pay his fare? The fact that the arrangements he had made provided him with necessary cover sweetened the pot.

He had joined a theatrical troupe in London, having easily, with a superb audition, convinced its manager of his professional acting ability. In truth, Whitfield had acted professionally for most of his adult life, though never before with a troupe. He was a master of disguises, a virtuoso at whatever role he chose to play. His role, for the moment, was that of an actor playing Shylock in Shakespeare's *The Merchant of Venice,* the play with which the touring company would open when they arrived in Williamsburg.

Although Whitfield was pleased with his present coup, he nonetheless chafed at the delay in departure. During the daytime, the members of the company were engaged in painting sets, making costumes, and rehearsing their parts in preparation for the move to Virginia. Four nights a week, the troupe performed at a London playhouse, honing their skills while maintaining a living wage. They were a congenial, spirited lot who took Whitfield under their wing, teasing him about how well he played the evil Shylock. If they had had any inkling of how close their compatriot came to possessing the same personality as the character he was playing, their teasing would promptly have ceased, and Whitfield would have found himself without the cover he so desperately needed.

But Jarvis Whitfield was smarter than that. Like a chameleon, he altered his persona to fit the occasion. The members of the theatrical company warmed to his own jesting and posturing. Entertainment was their profession and provided their livelihood, but they grew tired of always being the entertainers. He understood this about them and gave tit for tat. He worked — nay, slaved — right along with them, and they mistook his enthusiasm for professional pride, just as he had intended they should.

The harder Whitfield worked, the closer they came to departure. That time could not come soon enough for him.

A fortnight had passed since Kane Rafferty had arrived at Cavanaugh's Tavern, and he still had no clue as to the whereabouts of the tiara. Glynna's supposed illness had confined her to her bedchamber for most of the previous week, thus precluding its accessibility to him. The few hours each day when her room was vacant, she was with him. Kane had not discounted the possibility of the tiara's being hidden elsewhere in the inn, but he could not believe he would find it in any of the public rooms, and those were the only ones available to him at present.

He had spent much time in Galen's library, ostensibly seeking reading material when actually searching diligently for his family's jewel among the books and bric-a-brac. His search won him nothing, as he had expected, for Galen offered the use of his library too freely. Kane was convinced, as he had been since his arrival, that if the tiara were, indeed, hidden somewhere at the tavern, it was either in one of the family bedchambers or the attic. Thus far, the mere existence of attic storage space was an assumption on his part, since the majority if not all of the upper floor was occupied by guest rooms.

His immediate problem lay not in discovering whether such storage space existed, but rather in convincing Miss O'Rourke to allow him to remain at the inn as her tutor. The coachman he had hired in Williamsburg was due to return from the valley any day now, but Kane had decided that he would remain at Cavanaugh's, regardless of his pupil's whims. As a paying guest, he could stay as long as he desired, and the chit could like it or not. He had his father's wishes to consider, however, and the baron wanted his friend's daughter to receive a suitable education before her season in London. Should she refuse Kane's tutoring, the baron would send another to take his place, and then the tiara might never be located.

Why he found her so desirable he could not understand. He would just have to keep his hands off her. This would be easier to accomplish were she repulsed by his advances, for he was certain that the evidence of his arousal had only frightened her. He could not forget how she had molded her softness against his length, how her hands had moved upward from his chest to his shoulders and had pulled him closer. Her lips had tasted ever so sweet; her skin had felt incredibly silky beneath his palms. And every time he looked at her, he wanted to take her in his arms again.

Am I using her as a substitute for Valerie? he wondered. *Or is there more to this than I want to admit?*

Glynna sat primly on the edge of a mauve velvet-covered wing chair, her small slippered feet planted firmly on the polished wood of the ballroom floor, her hands demurely folded in her aproned lap. *Let him demean my posture this day! Or my countenance!*

Although she wore her usual weekday attire—gingham day gown, sparkling white bibbed apron, black leather slippers, and diminutive white lace cap—Glynna had taken especial care with her toilet this morning. Her burnished locks she had pulled up, securing the heavy mass at her crown and then freeing a few thick tendrils to fall in loose ringlets down the back of her head. To the back of her lace cap she had added a tiny nosegay of violets fashioned with loops of narrow white ribbon, leaving the ends of the ribbon long to mingle with her ringlets. The cap tilted saucily upward, covering the knot she had made from the length of her tresses.

Today Kane could not accuse her of looking like a serving wench. Proper ladies, perhaps, did not wear plain gingham gowns or protect them with aprons, but this was the Colony of Virginia and the frontier of that, no less—not some fancy parlor in London. Had he not also plainly stated that one recognized a lady by her demeanor not her dress? A hint of a smile lifted the corners of Glynna's mouth, setting a tiny dimple in one cheek, as she contemplated his surprise upon seeing her.

But when he entered the ballroom minutes later, he scarcely glanced her way, turning his attention instead to a book he opened and placed upon his lap after seating himself in a chair which faced hers.

The smile congealed on her lips while tears of anger and frustration glazed her eyes. The man was insufferable! Glynna had lived with predictable behavior all her life and was, therefore, accustomed to gauging reactions, but she never knew what Kane Rafferty was going to say or do. One day he plied his suitor's charms, the next he maintained an aura of unquestionable authority when he assumed the role of tutor. But always he was a man, Glynna reminded herself, and whether or not he gave any indication, he saw her as a woman. *So look at me! Show me you approve of what you see!*

His gaze remained on the open book.

" 'I have attended the opera in England and in Italy,' " he read, " 'and saw the same pieces with the same performers; and yet the same music produces very different effects on the two nations: one is so cold, so phlegmatic, the other so lively, excited, that it is almost incredible.' " He paused, waiting for her reaction.

I can be just as unpredictable as you, she thought, realizing as she listened to his mellow voice that, whether he approached her as a lover or a teacher, she consistently fell prey to his charms.

The silence between them continued. Glynna had opened a window on the east side of the ballroom when she had entered earlier, and now the sounds of birds chirping and squirrels chattering drifted up to them. Katie's pleasant alto joined nature's chorus as the black woman lifted her voice in song. Glynna breathed deeply, filling her lungs with the fresh morning air, and said quietly, almost to herself, "It's going to rain."

She could not have secured Kane's absolute attention more easily had she thrown a screaming fit.

"How do you know?" he asked incredulously. "And what does that have to do with Montesquieu?"

She chose to answer his questions in the order in which he had posed them. "I can smell it, as can anyone who is attuned to nature's signs. As to what the weather has to do with Montesquieu, I have no idea, since I know nothing of this man."

His gray eyes left the printing on the page then and began a slow perusal of her, starting at her feet and traveling upward to the checkered green of her skirt, moving onward to the clasped hands in her lap, and pausing when they rested on the tight bodice of her gown. His inspection traversed the length of her bare neck, caressed the peachy glow of her cheeks, then finally halted when it reached the lace cap perched upon her head.

"Whatever have you done with your hair? Stand up and turn around. I want to see it better."

Glynna didn't move. She didn't like his tone, which sounded almost disapproving. Neither did she appreciate being commanded to do his bidding. "You haven't told me about Monsieur Montesquieu. Wasn't he one of those revolutionary French thinkers you mentioned a few days ago?"

His gaze left her cap. Gray eyes locked with green, but neither pair gave the other quarter. Glynna wished she could see beyond the mist which cloaked his visage, for she was certain that Kane Rafferty was hiding something. Just where that certainty came from she did not know, but suddenly it was there, lodged in her heart. She knew it just as she knew it would rain. She had told Kane she was attuned to nature. Was she also becoming attuned to him?

Kane saw the subtle change from defiance to distrust in her eyes. Whatever could have caused it? he wondered and found the thought disconcerting. It was he who finally broke the transfixion when he dropped his gaze once more to the book upon his lap. "Montesquieu argues"—he cleared his throat—"that governments are shaped by their physical environments. In his estimation, climates profoundly influence behavior. He uses the differences in the opera as an example. 'England's wet and windy weather encourages suicide,' Montesquieu continues, 'while the Mediterranean sun leads men to love sensuality for its own sake.' "

Glynna emitted a small gasp. No one had ever used the word "sensuality" in her presence before.

Kane ignored her temporary lack of composure, his cheeks dimpling as he grinned up at her. "Well, well, my dear Miss O'Rourke. It appears the rain you predicted and this Frenchman's philosophy are related. Did you, perchance, sneak into my room and borrow this volume?"

Her cheeks flamed crimson with immediate ire. "How dare you suggest such a thing!" she seethed, standing abruptly and whirling away from him in her anger. Inwardly, she fought for control, trying to still her short panting breaths and the quick beating of her heart. The chuckle that erupted behind her served only to augment her fury.

"At last," he gloated, "you exhibit your coiffure."

Although she desperately wanted to confront him, she dared not, for she could not seem to stop the heaving of her bosom. It was better that he view the stiffness of her back, even if that meant a closer scrutiny of her modestly adorned ringlets. The fact that she had arranged them so carefully for his benefit did not enter her head.

There followed an abrupt silence in which neither of them moved. Glynna thought she heard the soft *swoosh* of the book's closing behind her, but she could not be sure. Moments passed. A cooling breeze sailed through the open window, and she shivered in its aftermath. Her anger had eased in the interim, but it did not disappear entirely. The threat of tears clung to her eyes, and she squeezed them shut in an effort to contain the moisture. Her hands remained closed in tight fists against the front of her apron. She wanted to escape to the refuge of her room, but in her profound annoyance with Kane she had turned toward the upper hall. To flee downstairs presented the possibility of having Katie's quick eyes assess her discomfiture, and to turn around most assuredly meant having to face Kane. Momentarily she would have her face in order, she reasoned, and then she would seek her asylum.

When Kane's hands touched her shoulders, her whole body jerked in startlement. She could feel the warmth of his fingers beneath the thin fabric of her gown, could feel the length of his digits as they gently massaged her tense muscles, could feel his thumbs inexorably drawing circles at the base of her neck. She was aware that her eyelids relaxed, but they remained closed, though now from the sensations his fingers were causing rather than from frustration. Her fingers loosened their grip on her palms, and she felt the sting of the deep impressions her nails had dug in them. Gradually, as his ministrations continued, her stiff muscles relaxed as well, and when he gently turned her around, she did not protest.

Still she did not open her eyes. A part of her persisted in fighting the languidness that seemed bent on consuming her limbs, but the battle was ill fated and she knew it. When Kane planted a forefinger under her chin and a thumb in the indentation under her lip and tilted her face upward, she did not — could not — protest. His lips brushed hers ever so lightly, then

128

moved to a corner of her mouth and plucked delicately at its sweetness. She felt as though a butterfly had landed there, fluttering its fragile wings against the sensitive skin as it sought the nectar of her mouth. She swallowed hard to prevent a moan from escaping the confines of her throat.

His hands left her shoulders and slid down her arms without exerting any more than the slightest pressure against the fabric of her sleeves. He circled her wrists with thumb and middle finger, and she forced her curved fingers to retighten into fists. Her efforts were short-lived. Kane's thumbs left her wrists and coaxed loose her hold; then he used the balls of his thumbs to caress the tender skin along her lifelines. She felt her fingers splay and then close over his thumbs as a shiver trickled down the length of her spine. His hands moved from her wrists to cover the backs of her hands while his lips still danced their fluttering waltz upon her mouth.

One of them moaned. Perhaps they both did. Neither knew, nor honestly cared.

Defeated, Glynna moved her lips against his, savoring his taste and texture. She breathed deeply of his essence, languished in unbridled desire when he pulled her hands to his shoulders; and she wantonly pressed her soft breasts against his hard chest. Kane cupped her cheeks with his open palms, his thumbs now planted at the corners of her mouth as the tip of his tongue teased the seam of her lips until they willingly parted. Her own tongue invited the heat and moisture of his.

For a space, time—and reason—were suspended, yielding to the needs and desires of the flesh. The room grew dark with the approach of the storm, but nature's impending assault offered no match for that which raged between Glynna and Kane. She relished the movement of his hands as they forged a warm trail from her cheeks down the sides of her neck and then slid down her shoulders and slipped beneath her raised arms to continue their journey to her waist. When the heels of his hands grazed her breasts, she felt their peaks harden. Moisture clung to her brow, her upper lip, and trickled into the crevice between the soft mounds of her flesh. Deep within her, an ache like none she had ever felt before was growing, Kane's kisses and the press of his length against hers fanning its flames until she thought she would faint from the heat.

What it would take to cure this ache Glynna did not know. Kane had taken her beyond rational thought. She did know that her body yearned for surcease and that she was willing to grant it. The low moan of the wind and the ever-darkening interior of the great ballroom intensified their feeling of aloneness, not only in the tavern but in the whole world as well.

Glynna felt her knees buckle beneath her at the same moment a knock sounded at the door. With a swift, fluid movement, Kane's right arm slid behind her knees and he effortlessly lifted her into his arms while his lips reluctantly removed themselves from hers. Her eyelids flew open and she found herself trying to read the expression in his heavy-lidded gray eyes, but she saw there only a hue as leaden as the storm clouds from without. As the sharp rap of knuckles upon the portal sounded once more, she considered the import and began to struggle against his hold of her.

"Sh-h-h, little one," he whispered, then called out, "Come quickly! The child has fainted!" Immediately she understood his ploy and went limp in his arms, closing her eyes and attempting to breathe shallowly, which was an extreme effort.

"Your arms!" he hissed, turning his back to the door, which flew open to admit Darcie Cavanaugh. Glynna hoped her aunt had not witnessed the movement of her hands as they released their hold on Kane's neck and slipped down his chest. For greater effect, she allowed her left arm to hang loosely at her side. Stifling the giggle which threatened to make a liar out of her tutor, she wondered how she could possibly think the situation comical.

Darcie's voice was hushed, concerned. "What happened?"

Kane had begun walking toward the door which led to the family quarters; Glynna could hear her aunt scurrying to open it for him.

"We were dancing. I suppose she became overwarm."

This time there was a tinge of anger in Darcie's tone. "But I gave instructions —"

"She insisted she was better. I had promised to teach her the allemande and she was eager to learn it. Apparently the exercise coupled with the heat and humidity were too much for her."

A second door opened and then Glynna felt her body being lowered to the bed. With gentle motions Kane laid her on the counterpane and eased his arms from beneath her slight form. She wanted to open her eyes, but dared not. She could hear the splashing as water was poured from the ewer into the wash bowl. Soon, her bed creaked as Darcie sat on its edge. The cool, damp cloth her aunt applied to Glynna's face felt wonderful against her clammy skin. She supposed now was the time to regain consciousness, and she cautiously fluttered her eyelids before opening them completely.

Darcie's clear blue eyes met Glynna's shadowed gaze. "How are you feeling, my dear?" Darcie crooned, her fingers tenderly pushing back damp tendrils of Glynna's hair. "You gave me quite a scare."

"I feel . . . sleepy." She had not thought of it, but she was, indeed, feeling a bit tired. The ache, the yearning that had sent her senses reeling just moments before had vanished, leaving in its wake an emptiness, a lack of fulfillment. And she was chilled. She wished Darcie and Kane would leave her alone so she could strip down to her chemise and wriggle under the covers.

"And sleep you shall." Darcie patted Glynna's shoulder affectionately. "There will be no more lessons today, Mr. Rafferty." These last words were spoken sharply and carried a tone of reprimand.

Glynna could not see Kane, but she surmised he stood near the open doorway when she heard him reply, "As you wish."

"I'm going down to the kitchen to make you a cup of herb tea, Glynna. It will help you rest." Darcie rose from the bed and returned the cloth to the bowl. "You, sir," she instructed Kane, "will stand here by the door until I return. Call out if she faints again."

With her usual briskness, Darcie left the room. Kane watched her until she had crossed the ballroom and then he took her place at Glynna's side. Glynna opened her mouth to protest, but he quickly covered it with his hand.

"What an accomplished little actress you are!" he teased. "She thinks you really did swoon." He removed his hand from her mouth, and she gasped when he bent to remove the slippers from her feet. Kane was taking liberties she knew she should not allow.

In spite of this knowledge, she smiled at him. " 'Twas your lie saved us." Glynna's smile dissolved as she considered the reason for their subterfuge.

"Kane," she said a bit timorously, her glittering emerald eyes transfixed on his face, "what is happening between us?"

It was a question she would not have asked before this morning, but she was now convinced that Kane thought of her as no mere dalliance. There was too much tenderness in his touch, too much passion in his kisses. It might not be love, but it was something special, and Glynna wanted Kane to tell her that. She wanted to hear it with all her heart.

Chapter Nine

When he didn't answer her immediately, she watched him closely, saw the shield of his defenses move into place, masking his recent lightheartedness. His gray eyes were no longer warm, but neither were they cold. They clouded and became a dull pewter color that lacked emotion. His expression lacked emotion as well, and though his eyes looked into hers, Glynna wasn't at all certain he actually saw her.

She waited, holding her breath, suddenly wishing she had not posed the question. After what seemed an eternity to her but was actually only a matter of seconds, joviality returned to his face, the twin dimples which gouged his cheeks giving him a boyish look. It was not a look that pleased her, despite its pleasantness. She wanted him to look at her again the way he had the day he'd first kissed her.

"Are you not going to chide me for calling you a child again?" he asked.

I can play your game, she thought, simultaneously disappointed and relieved. "It was your line," she calmly replied.

Kane's brow beetled in his confusion. "My line?"

"In the drama we were acting out for Aunt Darcie's benefit."

"Oh . . . of course." His response lacked conviction.

"If you are attempting to ignite my wrath—"

His wide smile appeared again and he hastily raised his right hand. "Heaven forbid!" A glint of humor took possession of his gray eyes, lending him a devilish guise.

Glynna laughed, both at his expression and at the memory of their playacting. "Whatever made you say I'd fainted? I've never fainted in my life!"

Kane shrugged his broad shoulders. "It was just the first thing I thought of to explain our . . . um . . . embrace." His eyes opened wide then, the evidence of his good humor full-blown in their sparkling gray depths. "You didn't want me to tell your aunt the truth, did you?"

She sobered at his question. "The truth is usually best. I have never held much fondness for subterfuge." Glynna paused, considering their situation and the unanswered question she had asked of him just moments before. Perhaps if she expressed herself with less bluntness, she would get her answer. "However, I'm not at all certain I know what the truth actually is—the real truth, I mean."

She waited for his response, her eyes never leaving his face. He continued to regard her with some amusement, though not as much as before. His dark eyebrows arched quizzically, and she thought, He knows what I mean. Still, he did not reply.

"The deeper truth," she supplied, but he refused to accept the bait.

As she had watched the play of emotions on his visage, she realized that she knew very little of this

135

man. If something special *was* happening between them, she should know more about him. Besides, it was quite obvious he did not intend to be candid with her. Her insistence on the truth only caused tension between them.

"Have you prior experience—professional, I mean—in drama?" she asked teasingly in an attempt to rekindle their bantering while she gained some knowledge of Kane Rafferty's background.

"Merely as a member of the audience, my dear."

"And you have attended the theater many times?"

"Inquisitive all of a sudden, aren't you?" Though the indulgence never left his face, he reached out and stroked her cheek affectionately. "Yes. Many times."

The warmth from his hand felt good on her cool cheek. He was actually answering her questions, which was more than she had expected. There were so many she wanted to ask! Ofttimes she had wondered how much the baron was paying him, and what he would do with his life when his time in Virginia was over. It would be indelicate to ask the former, so she settled for: "Will you be a tutor all your life?"

This question obviously took him unawares, for the smattering of remaining humor abruptly left his eyes and his lips tightened in a firm line. Kane wanted to answer all of her questions truthfully, if he answered at all, but the truth might lead to further questions he did not want to answer. He considered his words carefully before he said, "No, not all my life. I have done many things, and there are many more vistas I want to explore before I die. But for now, being a tutor suits me fine."

He hadn't said "being *your* tutor." Glynna refused to allow the slight to penetrate. Despite this resolve, her good humor was dented, for when she honestly considered his answers to her questions, she had to admit he had given her very little concrete information. She was framing another question in her mind when a booming noise emanating from the center of the tavern caught her attention. It sounded like Katie lumbering up the stairs.

Kane heard it too, and he quickly removed himself from her bed and took up his post by the door. In moments Katie entered the room, bearing the cup of herb tea. She bestowed upon Kane a withering look, cursorily dismissed him, then clucked over Glynna, who had difficulty maintaining a pained expression.

"Miz Dahcie, she be mighty worrit 'bout you, Miss Glynna. You ain' never been sick, not really sick. You ain' never passed out before." Katie stood by the bed, her hands moving restlessly as she talked, her quick black eyes darting about the room. Glynna sipped her tea, trying to recall ever having seen Katie *un*busy before. The woman was a veritable mountain of nervous energy, and she fretted now as she impatiently waited for Glynna to consume the contents of the cup.

"You come on now, Miss Glynna, and drink up so's I can hep you outta those clothes and git you in the bed. Hit's so dark outside maybe you can git some sleep. I'm gonna make you some beef stew. You ain' been eatin' right here lately. That's part of what ails you. You gots to git yourself well so's Miz Dahcie won't worry 'bout you no more. That poor woman's got enough to worry her."

Glynna handed Katie the empty teacup, a slow smile spreading across her face. "But you're not worried about me, are you, Katie?"

"Hrrumph," Katie groaned, her fingers now happily occupied with unfastening Glynna's gown. "I 'spec I know what your real problem be, but doan you concern yourself. I won't be telling Miz Dahcie . . . long as you doan go faintin' agin. You done sceered her right good, and there ain' no call for it."

Glynna was grateful her back was turned toward Katie. Just having to listen to her friend rebuke her was bad enough. She didn't want to watch her do it.

She had known deep down that Katie must be aware that she was lovesick. Yes, that's what it was, too. Lovesick. She didn't like the way the word echoed through her brain. Lovesick. It sounded like something ailing a cow. Or an adolescent. Disgust distorted her delicate features.

Glynna stepped out of her dress, climbed back onto the bed and slid beneath the covers, lying on her side and keeping her back to Katie. She mumbled her thanks to the black woman and listened intently until Katie's rumbling steps died away.

Contrary to her usual reaction to it, the distant rumble of thunder soothed her. A gentle rain splashed softly against the window panes and plopped upon the brick walks below. Glynna sighed contentedly, pulling her knees up into her chest.

Lovesick!

Maybe the word didn't sound so disgusting after all.

It rained all that day and the next. At Darcie's insistence, Glynna remained in her room, and her frustration grew with every plopping raindrop. She tried alternately to read and embroider but achieved little success at either. Although Glynna's eyes moved over the pages of the books Darcie brought up from Galen's library, the words remained, dully, on the pages, refusing to come to life as they usually did for her. As for her efforts with the needle, she spent the second day of her imposed isolation picking out the wayward stitches she had put in on the first day.

Glynna knew it would be unseemly for Kane to enter her bedroom, yet she longed for his companionship. Without her bidding it, her mind conjured his image and the sound of his mellow voice. And her inner voice asked her repeatedly, Do you honestly want him to leave? In return, she argued that while he remained, she was lost. His touch robbed her of will. His countenance destroyed her own identity. His words, though often couched in teasing, eradicated her wit. When she was with him, she was different, and she was having great difficulty getting to know or like the person she became at those times. Still, her inner voice taunted her with its incessant question, while her ears remained finely attuned to the noises from without, forever listening intently for the sound of gravel crunching beneath the hooves of the coachman's horse.

Her body betrayed her as well. Each time she lay upon her soft mattress, a yearning deep within her belly begged for surcease. Her legs balked at the confines of her room when she was up and about, and to her chagrin she would suddenly realize that her feet had ceased their pacing and begun to move rhythmically to music only they could hear. Her whole being seemed bent on treason.

The various roots and stems of her frustrations gradually blossomed into anger's full bouquet so that by the end of the second day Glynna was in a rage. This is all his fault! she silently proclaimed. If he had never touched me . . . if he had never kissed me . . . if he had never told Aunt Darcie I had fainted . . . if he had never come here in the first place! If! If! If!

But he was here, and she knew she could not force him to leave. The darkness of her anger matched that of the landscape, depriving her of her appetite, although Katie had thoughtfully prepared Glynna's favorite foods for supper. She forced down the meal, knowing that a half-empty tray might well extend the length of her restriction. Anger of this depth and dimension was a stranger to her, and her instincts rebelled against its intrusion.

By the time Katie arrived to collect the tray, Glynna had decided what she must do to clear her mind of the littered petals of her wrath. She gave no notice to the black woman's arched brows as Katie surveyed both the clean plate and the triumphant look on Glynna's face. The moment Katie ambled away, shaking her head as she closed the bedchamber door, Glynna assembled her writing materials and set about closing another door—a door without substance, and yet one more formidable than the heavy oak portal which marked the entrance to her uncle's tavern.

A harsh haze greeted Glynna's serene gaze the following morning. She stretched luxuriantly, enjoying the contrast of tensing and then relaxing muscles and the subsequent effect that had on her well-being. For the first time in more nights than she could readily count, she had slept peacefully. She threw back the light cover, noting its almost undisturbed state, and rose to open a window. The air was not as fresh as she had hoped it would be, for it bore a sweltering humidity. Small lakes pocked the lawn, their surfaces obscured by the thickness of rising vapor.

In amusement, Glynna watched a lone hen waddle across the muddy barnyard, its feet sinking deeply into the mire with each step. A severe shaking of each foot as it was pulled from the muck punctuated the hen's progress, an action which set its feathered tail atremble. The hen squawked its irritation until it finally gained the refuge of the henhouse.

That's what I've been doing, Glynna thought. Trying to walk in quicksand.

But that was all over now.

The warm bath Katie's daughters brought further soothed Glynna's nerves, and the time she spent in the cooling water strengthened her resolve to face each day with equanimity. There would be no more vacillations of spirit for there would be no more private contact with Mr. Kane Rafferty. His days as her tutor were over. Her letter to the Baron of Ulrich had accomplished that fact.

She had reread her missive that very morning while awaiting her bath. As she had intended, its tone was warm yet forthright, appreciative of his concerns yet firm in her refusal of his gift. She expressed her desire to visit him and the baroness, should she ever return to her parents' homeland, but she assured him such a journey would occur in her own time and be one of her own choosing. She had avoided bitterness when she'd mentioned Kane's tutoring, insisting instead that she felt no need for it as she felt no desire to leave Virginia permanently. She was a woman of the frontier, she explained, and should she choose to marry, her husband would have to share her love for this wild land.

Her message was simple and direct: *I am who I*

am, and the choices that are made concerning my life will be made by me and me alone. Strictly to herself she acknowledged that she had once and for all put the fanciful and totally unrealistic dream of her knight in shining armor behind her. She had been thinking and behaving juvenilely, but that was all over. If Kane Rafferty's brief visit had accomplished nothing else, it had, at least, helped her grow up.

Although she was eager to end her imprisonment and quit her room, she took the time to mop her floor after the tub bearing her bathwater had been removed, and then she decided to strip the damp, stale linen from her bed and replace it with fresh. Her aunt and uncle might own slaves, but their duties did not extend to the care of the family's private quarters. Glynna usually cleaned her bedchamber on Saturdays, and though today was only Thursday, she felt the need to rid the room of its mustiness. Her revitalized spirit sought physical activity, and she attacked the chamber with a vengeance.

Midmorning arrived before she completed her task. The heat had ebbed somewhat as the intense humidity had dissipated. The little lakes on the lawn lay placid in weak sunlight, their glistening surfaces now mirroring puffy clouds and patches of the robin's-egg blue of the spring sky. The fresh breath of an occasional breeze wafted through the open windows, lending its multifloral fragrance as it chased away the dampness.

As Glynna worked, she mentally fashioned her speeches to Aunt Darcie and Kane. She would take the same approach with them she had with the baron: simple, firm, and direct. There would be no brooking her judgment on this matter. There would be no more shilly-shally wishy-washiness.

142

Near noontide, she practically skipped downstairs, energized by the lightness of her mood and the erratic pulsing of her blood. Swinging the bundle she had made of her sheets, she pursed her lips in a carefree whistle. Darcie should he alone in the ordinary, setting the tables for dinner. She would talk to her first.

Glynna's merry mood quickly dissolved when she bounded into the common room and came face-to-face not with her aunt but with the mud-spattered coachman.

"Oh!" she gasped softly. "You have returned." It was not a very polite greeting, and the words rang flatly in the large room. Glynna blushed in her embarrassment and hastily attempted to redeem herself. "We were beginning to harbor some concern for your health and safety." She peered around the large fellow but did not spy her aunt or anyone else in the ordinary. "You must be hungry and tired and wanting a bath. You may wash up in the gentlemen's parlor while I see about having a room prepared for you and getting you some dinner." Despite her endeavor to make him feel at ease, he shuffled his feet and his mouth twitched nervously. Whatever was the man's name? Glynna searched her memory but could not recall it.

"Thank you anyway, but Mistress Cavanaugh is already seeing to those things for me. I'm . . . I'm waiting for your uncle." His callused workman's hands twisted his hat over his round stomach, and his small, pale eyes darted about.

Whatever is the man so nervous about? Glynna wondered absently, then mentally shrugged it off and excused herself—politely, she hoped. She crossed the ordinary with her soiled linen still in tow. On her way

143

to the laundry house she encountered Darcie returning from the kitchen.

Her aunt seemed distracted and showed no signs of relief at seeing Glynna's healthy glow and spritely step. "Glynna, I need your help," Darcie blurted out, her manner almost as nervous as that of the coachman. "The girls are too busy with the final preparations for dinner to see to Mr. Wilson's room." Yes, Glynna remembered, that was his name! "I'm putting him in room twelve. Please check to see that all is in order there and get one of the stableboys to take the tub up. The girls are heating the water now."

Before Glynna could say anything — and there were questions she wanted to ask — Darcie scurried by her and into the keeping hall. Katie would know what was going on, but there was no time now to talk to her if Glynna were to comply with Darcie's requests. She deposited her bundle in the laundry house, secured the services of the stableboy, and hurried upstairs to room twelve. By the time her tasks were completed, Katie's daughters were serving dinner. Her gaze wandered over the ordinary and noted that Wilson, the coachman, had disappeared and Galen Cavanaugh was nowhere in sight.

Whatever is going on? Glynna wondered, feeling the tension and knowing the coachman was now delivering his bad tidings to her uncle, wherever the two men were. Darcie was absent also, and Brian sat alone at the family table. As Glynna moved to join him, she caught a glimpse of Kane seated in a front corner, but she ignored him.

Brian seemed to sense things were awry, for he had subdued his normal exuberance. She sat down and began to sort through the possibilities. Perhaps the McGintys' valley relatives were in trouble, or had moved or even died. If such were the case, the couple had yet to be informed, for the two conversed amiably as they satisfied healthy appetites. Perhaps some harm had befallen the horse Galen had lent Mr. Wilson, but surely such a small matter would not warrant so much anxiety. There must be trouble in the Shenandoah Valley.

A shiver of dread sluiced its way through her. She knew from the many conversations she had overheard between fur traders and her uncle that the farms in the valley were too widespread for disease to be a problem. Storms and fires, though immediately life-threatening, spent themselves eventually. No, the news Wilson brought carried a portent far worse. That left only one possibility: Indian trouble.

But the Iroquois had been friendly for years! The English-speaking fur traders who visited the tavern on their journeys back and forth between the eastern seaboard and the deep woods of the Northwest spoke highly of the Iroquois, who as middlemen secured furs from more remote tribes. She did recall, however, their complaints about the French fur traders, who bypassed the Iroquois and dealt directly with the Algonquins, the traditional foes of the Iroquois. The footloose and fearless French fur trappers and traders penetrated deep into the interior, made friends with the Indians, lived among them, and took squaws for wives.

She wished she had paid closer attention to the conversations of the traders. What specifically had they complained about? She could not remember.

Glynna sighed in relief when Darcie took her place across the table. "Aunt Darcie," she whispered, "please tell me what has happened."

The older woman shook her head then stole a

glance at the McGintys. "Later," she mouthed.

They ate their meal in strained silence. Glynna looked up once and saw Kane's attention directed at her. He was obviously puzzled. *He feels it, too. And no wonder! You could cut the air in here with a butter knife.* The McGintys seemed ensnared in their own particular brand of euphoria. Perhaps that was best for now.

When she had eaten her fill, Glynna pushed back her chair and half rose to leave before Darcie's hissed "Wait" stopped her. Momentarily Katie arrived and collected Brian, whose protests were immediately hushed by the beloved cook. "You doan have no bizness in here now, Massah Brian. You come with me." It was just as Glynna had thought: Katie *knew.* Katie always knew!

The door to the gentlemen's parlor opened then; Galen and Mr. Wilson traversed the hall with heavy feet and stopped just inside the ordinary. Their faces were grim. A stunned silence followed their entry. Glynna could feel a pulse pounding fiercely in her throat, and her stomach knotted in apprehension.

"Mr. Wilson has brought distressing news from the valley," Galen began, his sharp gaze slowly sweeping the occupants of the room and finally settling on the McGintys. "Although this news most directly affects your decision to move there, I fear we shall all feel its repercussions." He paused briefly, his brow puckering in consternation. "The French have laid claim to the Ohio Valley and have begun to build a chain of fortifications along the river to make good their claim."

Small wonder Uncle Galen is upset, Glynna thought, for her uncle was a member of the Ohio Company, a group of Virginia land speculators who

146

looked to the country across the mountains as a profitable field for their operations. There had always been border disputes within the American wilderness, but the most serious of them concerned the ownership of the Ohio Valley. The French wanted to control this direct route between Canada and Louisiana, which were both their possessions. Surely the British government would rise to the defense of its territorial rights. Understanding of the far-reaching aspects of the French encroachment then began to dawn; her uncle's next words confirmed her worst fears.

"As if that were not enough," he continued, "the ill-begotten French have also incited the Algonquins against the Iroquois, a task none too difficult,'tis true, yet one coldly calculated, I am afraid. War is imminent."

Chapter Ten

It was a cool and dismal morning in early June when the sloop named *Charming Bess* sailed with the tide, but the penetrating mist failed to dampen the spirits of the fifteen members of the Prescott theatrical troupe who were aboard. Although the tide carried them swiftly away from their native England, the prospect of challenge in the New World buoyed their already adventuresome spirits. Theatergoing in London was a common enough pastime for its residents, and even superb stage performances were often taken for granted. Colonists, on the other hand, had little opportunity to attend a play. William Prescott's spirited band of players planned to charm the colonists with their performances.

One of the members in particular breathed easier when the mouth of the Thames lay in the wake of the *Charming Bess*. By now, someone had surely discovered the slashed body he had left behind. Whitfield's usual late-night forays among London's dockside pubs had finally won him the prize he sought. As he had entered the Cock and Crow, a group of drunken colonial sailors were boasting loudly of smuggling

West Indian sugar, rum, and molasses into the colonies, a defiance of Parliament's twenty-year-old Molasses Act which put a high duty on foreign sugar taken to Great Britain's possessions in the New World.

"That's nothing!" challenged a British seaman, also in a euphoric state. With much gesturing and swearing of oaths, the tar related tales from his own smuggling days, "long since behind me now, though I would not mind returnin' to 'em," he averred, the loud cackle of his laughter reverberating in the smoke-filled confines of the common room. "Cap'n Carmichael, now, he knew how to slip right past the king's warships. Dead 'o night it always were, and us burnin' no lamp to guide our way. The cap'n, he swore to kill any one o' us ever dare light a pipe, though I don't reckon as how anyone could see such a tiny spark through the thick cover of Manannan's Mantle."

The colonial sailors, unfamiliar with the mist which often cloaks the Isle of Man in the Irish Sea, requested an explanation and then snickered derisively when one was given.

" 'Tis true Manannan Mac Lir be the lord of the sea and a sorcerer to boot," the limey declared, raising his raspy voice to be heard over the laughter. The practical, common-sense colonials shrugged away the tales, returning to their ale and ignoring the British seaman's sputtering — and thus paving the way for Jarvis Whitfield to comfort the object of their derision. This self-same object had easily succumbed to Whitfield's charm, and just as easily had lost his life as a result.

Jarvis Whitfield possessed no knowledge of the total number of men who had worked for Galen Carmichael at one time or another, but he did know they now numbered fifteen fewer. It was not the crew members who really interested him anyway. Captain Carmichael was the one he wanted to bring to justice—to his own form of justice, that is. That Carmichael was adept at slipping by the British naval authorities Whitfield had no doubt. Had the man not slipped through his fingers more than once?

But not this time. If his seventeen-year-long search for Carmichael had taught Whitfield nothing else, it had taught him patience. He had learned that all he had to do was frequent public rooms and listen; eventually someone would talk. The fewer questions he asked, the less attention he brought to himself. This time, no one would be the wiser. No one would warn Carmichael of his imminent danger.

The mist gathered in minute droplets on Whitfield's dark, uncovered head, and the folds of his black cape billowed out around him like bat wings as he stood at the rail of the *Charming Bess*. His senses, always finely tuned, had some moments before noted the quiet, tentative approach of Violet, a young and buxom member of the troupe. At ease now with the sureness of his purpose, he turned to her, his outstretched arm offering her comfort. She settled against him and sighed as he wrapped his cloak around her. Whitfield allowed himself to feel her softness, to smell her sweetness, and when she rubbed her breasts against his enfolding arm, the two turned in mutual longing and made their way with some haste to his private cabin.

Wilson, the coachman, was gone. And he traveled to Williamsburg alone.

Glynna stood on the upstairs gallery and watched the ironbound wheels of his coach churn mud as the sun rose in magenta splendor behind her. Within a week Governor Dinwiddie would know about the trouble in the western territories. Such knowledge did not preclude the imminent arrival of His Majesty's troops, however. Galen had supposed—and Kane supported his theory—the governor would appeal to the king for guidance before any action would be taken.

Galen had assured his family that he needed no outside advice concerning what actions he should take, however. He had spent many a day in the past seven years driving a rig to the closest mill to sell his grain and buy flour. As he aged, he tired of these necessary trips. For some time now, he had talked of building his own mill, which would not only benefit himself but all the other local farmers as well. Now that war with the French appeared certain, travel would become unsafe if not seriously dangerous. He had sent an order with Wilson for the large iron gears he would need. By the time they arrived, he planned to have the basic structure already built on the nearby creek.

Darcie and Galen had also talked of converting one of the downstairs rooms into a general store. Convenience for themselves and their neighbors as well as additional revenue had been their only reasons until now, and they had never made the effort. The threat of war necessitated action, however, so Wilson was also carrying a large order for food staples, dress goods, shoes and boots, kitchen utensils and dishes, nails, medicines, gunpowder, wagon wheels, tools, and other supplies to be sold in the general store.

The room Darcie planned to use for the store was a small one at the far end of the house. It had an outside door and had been serving for some years as a lumber room. She had commandeered Glynna, Kane, and Brian to go there with her that Thursday afternoon, following Galen's announcement and subsequent decisions, to help her to begin clearing it out.

"What a mess!" she had apologized with a laugh. "I've put anything and everything that I didn't know what else to do with in here, and I've been doing that for years." She had stood with hands on hips surveying the none too neat stacks of wooden crates, broken furniture, and discarded personal items, all of which were covered in a thick layer of dust. The spiders had done their work here, as had larger, more destructive varmints, for the musty odor of dust and disuse combined with the acrid smell of ammonia, and there were trails of tiny black droppings everywhere.

"This will not be an easy task — nor a clean one." Darcie had turned her attention to Kane, her merry blue eyes quickly assessing the fine cut and fabric of his breeches and waistcoat. "Perhaps, Mr. Rafferty, you had better change into something less . . . fragile."

He had winced inwardly at the prospect of their chore as well as at her choice of adjectives. Never in his life had he, the son of a baron, performed physical labor. But he had not come to Virginia as the son of a baron, he reminded himself, this line of thought also reminding him of his purpose in being at the tavern. Until this moment, he had not been aware of the use of this room. If neither Glynna nor her aunt and uncle were aware of the existence of the tiara, then that jewel might very well be hidden somewhere among this rubbish. A slow smile had spread across his face as he had considered that possibility.

"I have no workman's clothing with me," he had said, Darcie and Glynna mistaking his smile for one of humorous chagrin. "If I ruin these garments, then so be it. I have others."

Darcie's mouth had formed an O and her eyes had opened wide at the very idea. "This will take more than one afternoon, I'm afraid. How many suits are you willing to destroy?" Before he could answer, she had quickly supplied an alternative. "Brian, fetch your father's blacksmithing apron for Mr. Rafferty. And you, sir, remove your waistcoat and roll up the sleeves of your shirt. I will not be responsible for the ruin of such fine garments." Her bright eyes had then inspected his person from silk cravat to the sparkling buckled shoes. "Tonight I shall look through my husband's old clothes. You are of approximately the same height as he, and his girth has not always been so wide. Perhaps I can find something for you to wear tomorrow."

Glynna had never heard her aunt utter one critical word about Galen Cavanaugh, and she had known this admission was probably as close to criticism as she ever would hear. No one could call Galen fat, but his thickly muscled torso had become somewhat flaccid with the combination of age and a diminishing of heavy chores as he had purchased more slaves over the years. Galen now supervised the labor both in the fields and in the stables and barns. He had also found a willing and capable smithing apprentice among his slaves, and that man had gradually taken over all the work at the forge.

Darcie had then turned her attention to her niece. Since Wilson had arrived with his distressing news that morning, she had been so busy she had not given any thought to Glynna's illness. She now noted the healthy glow on Glynna's cheeks and the sparkle in her green eyes, but she worried that her niece had not regained sufficient strength to accomplish work such as this room obviously demanded.

"And you, miss"—Darcie's voice was as gentle as always, but it carried a firmness that brooked no argument—"will tell me *immediately* if you feel the least bit weak." She had upturned an empty crate, erased most of the dust from it with one of the cleaning rags she had brought with her, and instructed Glynna to sit upon it. "Your task will be to sort through the contents of these crates as we bring them to you. Under no circumstances are you to lift anything that weighs more than a stone, or back you go to your room."

The four of them had worked diligently all that afternoon and the following day. Darcie had organized the room's contents into three categories: personal family items with sentimental value that needed to be stored elsewhere, practical items that could easily be repaired (most of these she sent to the slave quarters for dispersal), and pure rubbish that should have been burned years ago and most assuredly would be burned now.

Brian and two black boys about his age had carried the lighter items and dragged the heavier ones outside, dumping them into the appropriate piles on the flagstoned walkway. Kane had provided the muscle within the room, lifting and moving packed crates and pieces of furniture as Darcie had directed him.

Though she would never tell her aunt, Glynna had thought her task to be the most tedious and tiresome of all. The backs of her thighs still burned where the edge of the crate upon which she had sat that first afternoon had cut into them. Someone—and she felt certain it had been Kane—had thoughtfully brought her a chair from the ordinary yesterday morning, placing it in the storeroom before she'd arrived. There was an ache between her shoulder blades that a good night's rest had not removed, and the muscles in her upper arms were sore. Even her hands hurt.

Glynna now used those aching hands to pull her wrapper more closely about her as she watched Wilson's coach disappear behind a hill. The meager warmth of the rising sun could not reach her here on the western balcony, but it was not against the morning's chill that she sought warmth. Wilson carried not only her uncle's lists. He carried her letter to the Baron of Ulrich as well.

She had yet to gain either the courage or the opportunity to talk to Darcie or Kane about her letter. Everyone assumed Kane would remain at the tavern as her tutor, and no one had thought to ask for her opinion. There existed a general distraction from common, everyday events. Although she understood the urgency of their situation, she could not bring herself to believe they would be in any real danger here. Miles and miles of thick woods — even a whole mountain range — separated them from the Ohio Valley. Surely whatever trouble might be occurring there would not move this far eastward.

Darcie had kept her so very busy that Glynna had had no time to think about whether or not she really wanted to send Kane away. It had become obvious within a short time on Thursday afternoon that he was unaccustomed to labor, yet he'd worked hard and without complaint. Sweat had poured from his wide brow, mingling with the dust and cobwebs clinging there to mottle his skin with ugly brown patches. The fine linen of his shirt would never be white again, and Glynna had wished as she had stolen glances at him that her aunt would allow him to remove the stained garment completely. Of course, Kane had not embarrassed his hostess by asking her if he could.

Glynna could not help wondering what he looked like beneath his clothing, and she blushed deeply for even thinking such a thing. He had removed the silk cravat and opened his shirt at the throat, exposing a patch of crisply curling black hair. Glynna was accustomed to seeing as much of her uncle, for Galen never wore a cravat except on Sundays, but seeing a bit of

Kane's chest had sent delightful tingles all the way to her toes.

As Kane had worked, he had earned her grudging respect. Now that she honestly thought about it, she had considered him to be a bit dandified, for in her limited realm of experience real men worked with their bodies as well as their minds. The past day and a half had shown her a different Kane.

She turned from the balcony and walked back to her room, her heart now filled with an ache as big as that in her shoulders. She felt like a traitor, not only to Kane but to the baron and her father as well. They had been dear friends, the baron and her father. That letter could very well hurt the baron's feelings. After all, the man was only doing what he thought her father would have done for her had he lived. Now she wondered how gentle her words had actually been. Would they sound selfish when he read them? Would he think her ungrateful and inconsiderate?

If she dressed hurriedly, she might be able to overcome the coach and retrieve that letter from Wilson. She drew her nightdress over her head and flung it upon the unmade bed. There would be time to put it away and straighten the covers later. Now she must hurry! Hurry! Hurry! Or Wilson would gain too much distance for even her spirited mare to surmount.

Kane tied the length of rope Brian had supplied around his waistline, cinching Galen's old breeches tightly. He grinned as he considered how he must look in the rough workman's clothes that were a mite too big for him. If he were home, he could steal a glance in his cheval mirror, but the only one at the tavern stood in the ladies' parlor and he didn't want Glynna to catch him looking. He did not stop to wonder why he cared what she thought. Since she had fainted in his arms—whether she had actually swooned or not did not matter; he knew she would have in a few more minutes anyway—he had begun to realize how important she was to him.

He had also begun to hope that she shared this intense but delightful feeling. Perhaps it was true. She had not insisted he return to Williamsburg with Wilson as she had so often promised she would do. In fact, she had not mentioned his leaving at all this week. When she had come downstairs to dinner on Thursday, she had looked vibrant and healthy—and happy. There had been a peaceful look on her countenance that Wilson's news had not marred even a whit. Perhaps, at last, she had come to terms with their relationship.

When she had asked him what was happening between them, he had wanted to answer her, but he did not honestly know how. None of his previous emotional experiences had prepared him for this. This was not only different . . . it was special. It went far beyond what he felt for Valerie, which he recognized now as a warm fondness, and that mostly for her body. He had thought intelligent conversation could only be enjoyed in the company of men, that wives were not meant to be companions. Glynna had proved him wrong on those accounts as well as a number of others.

Satisfied that he would not suffer embarrassment by having his breeches fall down, he stooped over the pier glass, which was hung too low to accommodate his height, and combed his sleek black hair, then tied its length with a plain dark ribbon. His brow puckered as he thought about the contents of the lumber room, most of them now cleared out and stacked in the yard. The tiara had not been found, although a crate of small items which had belonged to the O'Rourkes had been discovered among the rubbish. Glynna had given its contents a hasty look before sending the whole box to her room to be sorted through at her leisure. He had wanted to beg her to go through it then and there, but such a plea could only serve to arouse suspicion.

Kane could not believe that the Cavanaughs were purposely hiding the tiara. He had been at the tavern long enough now to know they were good, decent, honest people. He wished he could just come right out and ask them about it, but to do so would expose his real identity and lead to further questions that would compromise his present position.

If his mother had been honest with his father, none of this subterfuge would have been necessary. He was sorely tempted to write a letter plainly asking her to tell both her husband and the Cavanaughs about the tiara. And to hell with her blasted code! He knew the baron would be furious at first, but he would eventually capitulate. He always did.

The Cavanaughs—and Glynna—were another matter entirely. How could he ignore his growing feelings for Glynna? But how could he tell her he was in love with her, for love was surely what he felt, without telling her who he really was? That he was not a tutor by trade but the highly educated eldest son of a baron and therefore in line to inherit the title and all it entailed? Would she even agree to marry him if that meant leaving her beloved Virginia?

What if she found the tiara when she examined the contents of the crate in her room? He imagined the scenario: Glynna squealing in delight, bolting to wherever her aunt was at the time, the two of them exclaiming over the magnificence of the piece and then wondering how it had come into Glynndon O'Rourke's possession. Yes! That's what they would do, and then they would write to Glynndon's solicitor in Dublin and ask if he had any knowledge of it. He, in turn, would contact the baroness, and all would be well.

All except the part which required him to tell Glynna why he had been sent instead of a real tutor.

His thoughts had come full circle and he still had concocted no workable plan.

Perhaps fate would intervene in his behalf and solve his problems without damaging his relationship with Glynna. Kane didn't relish leaving his future in fate's fickle hands, but for the moment he would have to.

Breakfast and the lumber room awaited.

The stableboy rubbed his heavy-lidded eyes and yawned sleepily as he removed Sheena's bridle from the tack room and handed it to Glynna. Massah Galen had told him he could go back to bed after he had assisted in the harnessing of the coach horses, and he had done just that, drifting off almost immediately into dreamland. Miss Glynna never rode before breakfast, but he dared not question the square set of her shoulders and the determination in her clear green eyes. If he had been more alert, he might have questioned her haste.

As soon as she had checked the security of the girth straps in the cinch rings, Glynna mounted Sheena and pushed her into a canter. The mare's hooves sent clumps of mud flying across the stableyard as Glynna guided her horse toward the coach road.

"Hurry! Hurry!" she urged Sheena in a whispery voice. The full face of the sun now sat in crimson glory upon the horizon; she rushed toward it, oblivious of the biting wind upon her cheeks and the blur of familiar landscape speeding by. Swiftly, Glynna calculated the passage of time between Wilson's departure and her own and determined it to be no more than twenty minutes. If he were moving at half Sheena's pace, another twenty minutes would pass before she could possibly catch up with him. Allowing time for Sheena to rest, Glynna belatedly realized she would be gone almost an hour. She should have told someone — even the sleepy stableboy — where she was going.

Thank goodness Aunt Darcie was not a panicky person! Given the circumstances, Darcie would most likely think Glynna was still asleep. Should she discover her missing, the stable would be the first place she would check. And when Glynna returned home, she would say she had taken an invigorating ride and was now ready to return to work in the lumber room. Right after breakfast. Lord, but she was hungry!

Silently she protested the brilliance of the sunlight in her eyes, the twisting of the road as it wound around the hills. She could not change the position of the sun nor her eastward destination, but she could shorten the distance she must travel by cutting across the lower hills. After all, she was not driving a rig!

Glynna gave Sheena her head as she turned her off the road and upward over the gentle slope of a rocky hill. The sure-footed mare mounted the somewhat slippery slope with ease, sailed down the other side and back onto the road, which they followed until it appeared to bend around another hill. Again, Glynna took the hill. This one was a bit steeper and dotted with scrub pines and cedars. Glynna leaned low in the saddle, her eyes watching the ground closely for the tangle of a blackberry vine or the presence of a rabbit hole.

When she looked up she saw, to her surprise, not the road at the base of the hill but a narrow grassy space and another hill ahead. Where had the coach road gone? she wondered absently, certain that if she continued to travel eastward she would find it again.

Sheena leaped from the bottom of the hill into the thick, bright green meadow grasses. Almost immediately, Glynna realized her mistake in leaving the road. The two days of steady rain had created a marshy bog in this low-lying area which remained shaded by the twin hills for most of the day. The mare's vault from the road into the grass abruptly jarred Glynna as one of Sheena's hind feet landed in the mire and sank up to the fetlock.

In reaction, Sheena brought both of her forefeet down hard in an attempt to maintain her balance, not allowing Glynna enough time to recuperate from the initial jolt. She had already lost her seat before Sheena's remaining hind foot struck the soft earth, and this final jounce sent Glynna flying, her arms treading air and her heart leaping into her throat.

Instinctively, she had stiffened her muscles as her body left the sidesaddle and hurtled in an arc over the left side of Sheena's head. She hit the bristly marsh grasses with a resounding *thump,* her left side receiving the brunt of the fall.

A black void engulfed her.

Chapter Eleven

Over a hearty breakfast, Darcie and Kane discussed their plans for the day.

"I think Glynna and I can complete the sorting this morning," Darcie said, "while you and Brian work at eliminating those piles! One never knows when it will rain this time of year, besides which, tomorrow is Sunday and I wouldn't want our neighbors to see that mess."

Kane completed his final ablutions with his napkin and laid the linen square beside his plate. "We might as well get started then," he offered as evenly as his weary body would allow. "Where are Miss O'Rourke and Brian?"

"Still abed. I'm afraid Glynna has overdone it these past two days, and Brian is not accustomed to such labor. If we are tired, just imagine how those two must feel! But I'm certain they will both be up and about soon," she quickly added, "and they will know where to find us."

Glynna fought the reeling vortex that threatened to

pull her back into its seductive chimera where pain did not exist. With sheer force of will, she compelled her eyelids to open, feeling that should she allow the blackness to envelop her again, she might never regain consciousness. Even so insignificant an action increased her pain. Her small frame had received a tremendous jolt, and now every part of her rebelled at even the tiniest movement.

Myriad tiny flecks of gold danced before her eyes, their harsh glint brutally searing. Steeling herself against the pain, she blinked several times, trying to clear her vision, then resignedly closed her lids again to ease the intense burning. The glittering flecks diminished in number but refused to disappear completely.

After a while, the spinning in her head and the ringing in her ears began to subside, leaving a dull ache behind her eyes. Gradually, awareness of specific physical agonies penetrated her jaded state. Sharp splinters of pain pierced her left wrist, her throat and lungs felt scorched, and a deep throbbing pulsated in her left thigh. The anguish that afflicted her heart momentarily obscured all other pain, however, when Glynna opened her eyes, her vision blissfully clear now, and saw that Sheena, frightened and devoid of rider, had bolted.

As her mind assimilated her predicament, her other senses began to awaken. She choked on the fetid stenches of stagnant water, stale mud, and bitter marsh grasses. A thick, black, malodorous slime clung to her left cheek and oozed into her ear, and the sharp, irritating tattoo of a woodpecker grated on her taut nerves.

Home! she wailed inwardly. How will I ever get home?

163

Glynna used her right arm as a brace to push herself up out of the muddy grasses, bending her right knee and pulling it toward her chest as her torso left the ground. The effort was a supreme one which left her panting, the quick breaths burning her sore lungs. She hung her head over her right shoulder and winced at the quivering muscle spasms racking those parts of her which supported her weight. For several minutes she remained thus, her back arched, long tendrils of hair trailing in the bog, until her breathing evened and the spasms ebbed.

What she wouldn't give for a stump or a bush or a fence post—anything stationary she could use to pull herself up. But she had landed squarely in the middle of the marshy area. There was nothing here but sharp grasses covering several inches of thick mud. And even if she managed to stand on her own, she wasn't sure her weakened and aching legs could get her through the soggy muck.

She straightened her right arm, tested the strength in that wrist and elbow and found it adequate. Slowly, painstakingly, she crawled back to the westward hill from whence she had come, using her right arm and leg in alternate push-and-pull motions until she had gained firm ground.

For a long moment Glynna lay upon it, considering her best course while waiting for some semblance of strength to return to her trembling limbs. She rubbed her cheek against the soft hillside grass, transferring some of the mud to its green blades before she turned her head to the left, her eyes searching the landscape for the road. It was not in sight. She looked upward then at the scrub pines dotting the hill. Were it not for them, she might not be in this predicament, but she saw them now as a means of salvation.

Grasping their small trunks, she hobbled from one to another, dragging her injured left leg as she zigzagged up the hill. When she reached its summit, she fell to her knees and wished she could allow herself the inward cleansing of a good cry. But her lungs were weak enough already. She could pray, though, and this she did fervently.

Now was as good a time as any, she supposed, to examine her injuries. She started with her left wrist and sighed in relief when she found no broken bone, adding a quiet "Thank you, Lord" to her prayer. The throb in her left thigh had spread so that now that whole side ached intensely. She rolled onto her right buttock, pulled the heavy skirt of her riding habit up to her hipline, and gasped at seeing the large area of discoloration on her thigh. Pressing tentative fingers against the bruise, Glynna winced at the pain her action caused. In even this she rejoiced, though, for a mere bruise would not stop her from getting home, even if she had to hobble the entire way.

How far had she come? she wondered. And how long had she been gone? When Sheena appeared at the stable riderless, someone would come for her. Surely someone would come.

Glynna's pulse pounded in her ears as her eyes found the winding muddy ribbon of the coach road below her. From her heightened viewpoint, she could now see how it wound in a wide *C* instead of in the double curve she had expected. If she had just stayed on the road, she would surely have caught up with the coach by now.

The coach! In her physical misery she had forgotten why she was out riding so early. Now the intention of her ride came back to her, causing her additional heartache. Without Sheena, Glynna could not possibly retrieve the letter. She reluctantly admitted that, even had Sheena not run off, her own physical condition would have necessitated going straight home. She would write another letter to the baron, a letter of apology and retraction. And, uncertain as mail service was between the continents, he might never receive the letter Wilson now carried, or it might arrive with the second one.

But she couldn't write another letter until she got home. How was she ever going to get there?

Glynna pulled herself up, her gaze ricocheting around the immediate territory in a vain search for Sheena. She took a deep breath, placed her fore and middle fingers in her mouth, and whistled shrilly for the horse. With bated breath, she looked westward, watching and waiting for the mare to appear. Sheena did not.

Refusing to give in to utter despair, Glynna began her descent, continuing to use the scrub pines for support. Although going down strained her muscles less, she had to exercise caution to avoid slipping and falling. She examined the ground closely as she carefully made her way down, hoping to spy a fallen limb she could use as a crutch, but the small scrub pines did not provide one.

At long last she reached the road. The heavy wheels of Wilson's coach had cut deep ruts into its soft surface, turning the mud outward into lumpy, grotesquely shaped lips. Glynna tried to avoid these as she stepped into the firmer center but her left boot raked across the pair, digging a shallow rut in a diagonal slash.

As Glynna limped toward home, she realized that more than her game leg impeded her progress. Fully exposed to the sun now, the mud had begun to dry in

166

large, light gray patches on her black bombazine habit, its weight combining with the water her full, already heavy skirts and petticoats had absorbed and increasing her discomfort. The damp hems kept sticking to her muddy boots, threatening to trip her, and most of her hair had come loose from its hastily fashioned knot, the recalcitrant strands' damp, muddy ends flopping in her eyes. Without thinking, Glynna repeatedly pushed them back with her right hand, wiping more mud, from her glove, into her darkly stained and badly tangled auburn locks. The streaks of mud on her left cheek were drawing her skin tighter and tighter as they dried.

Oh, what she wouldn't give right now for a horse and a bath!

"It was a fool's errand," she muttered. "And I am a fool several times over. A fool for writing that letter! A fool for sending it with Wilson! A fool for thinking I could overcome him! A fool for resisting the love of the only man I've ever known who could excite me in so many ways!"

A solitary tear trickled out of her left eye, its moisture diluting the drying mud as it coursed slowly down her cheek, leaving a somewhat wavy trail from her eye to her jaw. She fought back the tears that threatened to follow, knowing she was on the verge of a deluge.

I will get home, even if I have to limp every step of the way, she promised herself. I couldn't be more than two or three miles from there.

The ache in her thigh continued to worsen with every step she took. Without a crutch, she was forced to put some weight on her left foot, and each tread sent shards of pain from her knee to her hip. I won't ever make it home if I don't stop thinking about the pain. I'll think about something else. I'll think about Kane.

But his name rhymed with "pain," and she could not seem to keep from linking the two of them together in her mind. She tried singing, but the tune which came to her lips was one of Katie's soulful ballads. It wrenched at her heart and made her throat burn. She finally settled for mentally reciting poetry, inserting her own brief petitions to God in odd places where they seemed to fit. At any other time, the utter insanity of this combination would have seemed completely absurd to her.

" 'That is my home of love; if I have not ranged, Like him that travels, I return again' "—*Lord, please let me return again*—" 'Each step trod out a lover's thought and the ambitious hopes he brought, Chained to her brave feet with such arts' "—*Release these chains on my feet, Lord!*—" 'I follow, lo, the footing still of my lovely cruel, Proud of herself that she is beauty's jewel. And fast away she flieth' "—*Oh, for a horse, Lord, to fly away on! Please, send me a horse.*

So engrossed was she in the snatches of verse that came to her mind and the accompanying prayers she sent heavenward that she did not at first hear the horse's whinny behind her. Even when the soft neighing and tinkly jangle of harness penetrated her thoughts, she assigned them to her imagination. It was the sound of a familiar voice calling "Whoa!" that finally claimed her attention.

Unmindful of her bedraggled state, she turned eager eyes eastward and smiled broadly, pleased for the first time ever to see the fat paunch and smug face of Reverend Mitchell. The golden orb of the sun, its glistening fingers radiating in a glowing halo behind him, had never shone so brightly.

The yellow flames leaped skyward, their efforts at standing straight thwarted by an occasional gust of wind. Brian giggled gleefully as he tossed fuel upon the fiery furnace. Never before had he been allowed this close to a bonfire, and although the heavy black smoke tossed by the wind stung his eyes and the flames' heat burned his cheeks, he took no notice.

"Stand back, Brian," Kane directed, "while I stir this fire." Kane had become concerned about Glynna and wished he could check on her, but he could not leave the blaze. Galen had taken every able-bodied man except Kane with him to the woods, where they were felling timber for the mill, so there was no one to relieve him. Perhaps, he told himself, he worried for nothing. Surely Darcie would see about her. Maybe she had come downstairs already and was even now at work with her aunt in the lumber room. Still, he wished he were not stuck here behind the tobacco barn with no clear view of the house.

Sheena's snorts awakened Josh, the stableboy. He found the mare standing in front of her stall shaking her head and pawing nervously at the straw-covered floor. Miss Glynna must have been in some awful hurry to leave Sheena in the stable like this and not even remove her bridle. The young miss had probably called to him and he hadn't heard her. Josh worked quickly at removing the tack and putting it away. If all went well, he would finish currying Sheena and have her safely in her stall before anyone would be the wiser.

Josh liked his job in the stable. He'd certainly rather be here than in the tobacco fields, but if he weren't more careful, that's exactly where Massah Galen would put him.

"Massah done complain oncet 'bout my laz'ness. Lawd, keep everyone away jes' a little bit longer," he muttered.

Darcie sighed wearily. Midmorning had yet to arrive and already her shoulders and back ached. I'm getting too old for this, she thought, realizing that the energetic company of the younger trio had lent her a vitality she could not now muster alone. Brushing the dust from her apron and opening still another crate, she fought the urge to awaken her niece. The stack had diminished considerably, so that now there were only half a dozen crates left. If Glynna had not appeared by the time she had opened and sorted through those remaining, she decided, she would go upstairs and check on her.

Glynna lay in the back of the buckboard, her eyes closed against the brilliant sunlight, and listened to the rhythmic *swoosh, slush, swoosh, slush* noises the softened earth made as it alternately sucked at and then released the wooden wagon wheels. She thought she had never heard so comforting a sound.

Reverend Mitchell would not have been her choice of a rescuer, but who was she to question Divine Providence? The good Lord had answered her prayer, and in a matter of minutes she would be home . . . home, where it was safe and secure . . . home, where she could have a bath and then crawl into the sweet comfort of her own bed. . . .

Consoled with thoughts of home and lulled by the warmth of the sun and the jangle of harness, she laid her left arm over her eyes and allowed herself that special peace of darkness she had earlier denied herself.

The bonfire roared and crackled as it made short work of reducing the pile of rubbish to ashes. Kane wiped his damp forehead on the coarse fabric of Galen's shirtsleeve and watched in relief as the flames consumed the remaining few items. He was glad he had started this task early, for the sun's heat had increased. Now, if he could just convince Brian to back away from the fire and into the shade of the tobacco barn . . .

"Mr. Rafferty! Kane!" The gasping voice came from directly behind him, and he turned to see a distraught Darcie Cavanaugh, the color drained from her face and her breath coming in short pants.

Concerned that she might collapse, he grasped her upper arms in a firm but gentle hold. "What's wrong?"

"It's . . . Glynna," she gasped. "She's gone . . . I can't find her."

"Gone? What do you mean?" There was a sharp edge to his voice. "Gone where?"

"I don't know!" Darcie's blue eyes glistened with unshed tears and one of her hands worried the other.

"But how do you know she's gone? Did she leave a note?"

Darcie shook her head. "No, but Sheena—" Her voice broke then, and tears spilled from her lower lids.

Kane increased the pressure of his hold on her

171

arms. He could not believe Darcie Cavanaugh would panic over nothing, but he could not help her until she told him what she knew. "What about Sheena? Where is the mare?" he asked quietly, refusing to allow his ever-growing panic to overtake him. One of them had to remain calm.

"She's—she's in the stable."

Kane sighed in relief. "Then Miss O'Rourke must be nearby. Perhaps she is taking a walk, or in the kitchen with Katie."

"No . . . you don't understand." Darcie gulped air. "Her bed is unmade, and her black riding habit is the only missing garment. And I've looked everywhere! No one has seen her this morning except Josh, the stableboy. He said she rode out early—right after Mr. Wilson left—and he didn't see her when she came back."

"Then he can't be certain she did come back." Even through the fabric of her sleeves Kane felt the goose-bumps erupt on Darcie's flesh.

"Something terrible has happened to her! I just know it has!" Darcie wailed.

A terrified scream pierced the crackling air, and they whirled in unison toward the fire. Brian was running away, toward the fields, his little-boy voice bellowing in pain.

There was a hole the size of a small watermelon in the back of his shirt, a hole that grew larger with every breath as the licking yellow flames which had created it spread outward and upward in an all-consuming fury.

Glynna came fully alert with a start.

She still lay in the back of the buckboard, but the

gentle swaying and bouncing motions had ceased. A starkly blue sky greeted her as she rolled onto her back and removed the shading arm, and she breathed a silent prayer of thanksgiving.

She was *home!*

The deep throbbing in her thigh reminded her of the morning's events, but one of Aunt Darcie's poultices would ease that pain. She wondered where everyone might be and sat up in bewilderment. Her pale brow furrowed in deep consternation as she surveyed her surroundings.

Why had Reverend Mitchell brought her here? His farm was no closer to the spot where he had found her than was the tavern.

He had parked the buckboard in front of the barn, and Glynna could hear him muttering to his draft horse from within. She thought she heard the expression "hoity-toity" and something about comeuppance, but she could make no sense of it. Nor could she make sense out of what he was doing. Not wanting to believe that he had actually unharnessed the horse, she turned around to see for herself.

The singletree lay upon the ground, a stark testimony of the deed.

Glynna almost called out to her savior before her intuition stopped her. This was not right. Reverend Mitchell had said he would take her home. Allowing him the benefit of the doubt, Glynna reasoned that perhaps something had gone awry with either horse or wagon. She thought to extricate herself quietly from the latter so that she might investigate, but as she slid her buttocks across the planks of its bed, a sharp splinter pierced her already tender skin and, involuntarily, she shrieked in pain.

Reverend Mitchell appeared immediately, his fea-

173

tures a study in concern. "Let me help you out," he offered, extending his meaty arms toward Glynna.

She accepted his assistance with some trepidation, not entirely convinced, despite his courteous manner, that all was as it should be. "Why did you not take me home?" she asked when her feet were planted firmly on the ground and she could see nothing broken on the wagon.

His answer caused her hackles to rise.

"You *are* home."

Darcie screamed. And screamed and screamed.

Later, when Kane had time to think about it, her screaming jolted him. According to his estimation of her character, he would have expected her to remain completely calm in the face of an immediate, tangible crisis. Kane might have understood her reaction better if he had known she had already lost two sons. Memories of their deaths, coupled with Glynna's disappearance, were more than Darcie could bear.

But Kane's primary concern was not for Darcie's hysteria. He called to Brian, instructing him to stop while he himself ran after the boy, his long fingers fretting with the knotted ties of Galen's leather smithing apron as he ran. For a moment, time stood still for Kane, whose whole being totally absorbed the vocalized pain of both mother and child. Despite Kane's directive, Brian did not stop running.

And Darcie did not stop screaming.

Kane, with his long legs, reached Brian in a matter of seconds. He hurled the apron upon the child's back, wrapped its ample width around Brian's small body and swooped the boy up into his arms, his mind now blocking out both Brian's whimpers and Darcie's screams.

Frightened, uncertain of what to do next, Kane never stopped running. The tobacco barn stood close to the stock barn, and when Kane spied the trough, he knew what to do. With utmost care, he lowered Brian into the cool water. Tears washed his own cheeks as the water washed over the boy's burns and he watched Brian's pain-distorted, deathly white features visibly relax. A sheen of clammy dampness clung to Brian's freckled face. The little boy seemed unnaturally calm.

Tenderly, Kane opened the leather apron and laid its ends over the sides of the trough. His fingers worked loose the fastenings on the front of Brian's shirt, but he realized how much easier it would be to remove the garment if he had a knife. At any other time, he would have had a virtual army of slaves at his command, but now a deathly stillness hung over the farm. Even Darcie's screaming had ceased.

Then, as if he had willed their appearance, Josh, Darcie, and Katie all came running. Now quiet and much calmer, Darcie seemed to have gained some measure of control over her rampant emotions. Josh stood with mouth agape. But Katie, her astute mind quickly assessing the situation, took command with her usual brisk efficiency.

"You, boy, go fetch Massah Kane a knife—and doan run with it. You li'ble to hurt yo'sef. An' you, Miz Dahcie, go tear up a clean sheet and turn back Massah Brian's bed. Massah Kane, when you git that shirt off'n that boy, bring him up to his room. I gots to git some hog fat for them burns and then I'll meet you there."

The three left the barnyard as quickly as they had arrived, each scurrying to accomplish the task set for them. Brian turned pleading, frightened eyes to Kane.

175

Not wanting to draw Brian's attention to his own emotional anguish, Kane would not allow himself the comfort of wiping away the tears that clung to his cheeks. Instead, he forced the semblance of a reassuring smile to his chiseled lips and tried to answer Brian's silent questions. "No, Brian, I don't think you're going to die. But I do think you will be quite miserable for a while. We're going to make you as comfortable as we possibly can, and you will have to do exactly as you're told."

Josh came back with a large, wooden-handled utility knife. Kane would have preferred a smaller one, but this one would have to suffice. He worked the long blade under one sleeve and pulled its edge against the fabric, rending it easily. Kane continued to ply the sharp blade until he could lift the shredded pieces of the shirt away from Brian's torso. The boy lay perfectly still, his clear blue eyes mirroring his trust.

"Can you turn onto your side?" Kane asked softly. When the child's face failed to register any understanding, Kane gently moved him onto his left side.

Kane stifled a gasp when the tight, shiny red flesh on Brian's back was exposed. Charred pieces of fabric clung to the crimson skin and patches of blackened flesh mottled the affected area. He scooped up water in his folded hands and splashed it gently onto the boy's back in an attempt to clean away the scraps of burned fabric. When the burned flesh was relatively clear of foreign matter, Kane, careful not to touch Brian's back, lifted the boy from the trough.

When Brian had been safely deposited upon his own bed, with his mother and Katie in attendance, Kane motioned to Darcie to follow him into the hallway.

"I'm going to look for Glynna now," he told her. "Can you give me any clue as to where I might start?"

Darcie shook her head in despair. "Ask that fool boy Josh. Maybe he watched her leave." Tears glistened in Darcie's blue eyes as they searched Kane's face. "I am so very ashamed of my earlier behavior, Mr. Rafferty. I owe you much more than mere words of gratitude. Brian could have died had you not acted so quickly. Now I may owe you for my niece's life as well."

As Kane turned to leave, Darcie hurried after him. "And, Mr. Rafferty, I have one more favor to ask of you. Please send Josh to the woods to fetch Galen. I'm certain that after he talks to Brian, he will join you in your search."

"Don't worry, Mistress Cavanaugh," Kane said with more confidence than he actually felt, "we'll find Glynna. She was probably just thrown and is even now walking home."

Part Two

Discoveries

Chapter Twelve

Glynna fought the bile rising in her throat. Reverend Mitchell's root cellar smelled of mold and mildew and other noxious odors she had no wont to define, but it was not the stench of the cellar which nauseated her, rather stark memories of her treatment at the hands of her vile captor. No bonds kept her from roaming the narrow confines of the dark space today, and though she needed exercise, the twittering of tiny creatures combined with the lack of sufficient light kept her from wandering too far. Her previous incarceration in this ebony prison had taught her not to fear the minuscule residents of this dank room; she simply had no desire to tread upon one of them or to destroy one of their nests with a wayward step.

Her leg had yet to convalesce fully from her accident, but it was somewhat stronger—no thanks to Reverend Mitchell! At least she could move around today without intense pain. She tried to ignore the dull ache in her thigh, tried to repress the horror of the past twenty-four hours, tried to concentrate on an escape plan, for it was clear to her now that she would have to accomplish such a feat on her own. And escape she must.

Her fingers plucked nervously at the overlarge, gaudily trimmed red gown Mitchell had provided that morning. The dress was inches too long, requiring Glynna to hold up its skimpy skirt as she paced, lest she step upon its hem and trip or, worse, tear the garment. Its cheap fabric smelled of dry rot, and Glynna had no clue as to whether her jailor possessed another.

An entire day and then some had passed since she had so foolishly ridden out after Wilson. Mitchell — Glynna refused to think of him in terms of the clergy anymore — was now gone to the tavern to conduct the weekly church services. A wry smile wreathed her swollen face for a moment as she considered the hypocritical prayers he would lift heavenward in her behalf this day. God knew what despicable deeds his supposed servant had committed, but Darcie and Galen were, quite obviously, not privy to such information.

In spite of her own concern for her immediate safety, Glynna could not help worrying about the travails her aunt and uncle must be going through. That they had diligently searched for her she had no doubt. She realized now that they would never suspect their friend and neighbor of abducting her — and worse! The men who had visited Mitchell's farm yesterday were, more than likely, only seeking information. Glynna had been allowed more time than she would have chosen to consider alternatives, and it was her conclusion that Darcie and Galen and everyone else she loved probably thought some trapper or other itinerant had taken her. Until they had exhausted all other possibilities, they would probably cling to the hope that someone kind had taken her to his home and was even now nursing her back to health.

Unbidden, the stark memory of yesterday blossomed in full kaleidoscopic color in the darkness before her. Expecting someone to follow the wagon tracks to his farm, Mitchell had wasted no time in trussing Glynna up like a harvest festival turkey and leaving her tied to a supporting pole in the root cellar. Her efforts at fighting him had only caused her additional pain.

An indeterminable time later, she had heard the pounding approach of horses' hooves followed by male voices raised in question. Mitchell and the men had remained outside while they talked, their voices muffled by the thickness of the farmhouse walls and the double floor above her head. Although she had kicked out at a stack of crates, hoping to make enough noise for the men to hear and realize something was wrong, her legs were not long enough to reach them. Mitchell had tied a scarf over her mouth to prevent her from issuing a cry for help.

Until she had heard their departure, Glynna had thought the men who were looking for her would surely search Mitchell's house and find her. After all, she had left her footprints in the soft middle ground of the road. The only other tracks along that section were those of the coach and of Mitchell's buckboard, and since her prints pointed westward, surely her deliverers would realize what had happened to her.

She had conjured up an image of the coach road then, and had seen several sets of hoof prints among all the other tracks. Those hoof prints would make it almost impossible to determine how and by whom she had been rescued — or abducted!

For the first time since Mitchell had said, with such finality, "You *are* home," Glynna had allowed the hot tears she had been holding back to flow forth. But when she had choked and gagged on her emotion, she had staunchly forced herself to stop crying. Her cheeks and eyes had burned with moisture she could not wipe away, for her wrists were bound behind her back. She had dried them as best she could by lifting her shoulders and inclining her head, and had worried that Mitchell would see that she had been sobbing.

She had refused to let him think he had bested her, though at that point, she had had no earthly idea why he had abducted her. Even now she had her doubts as to his real purpose.

It had been almost dark when he had finally raised the hatch in the kitchen floor and descended the ladder. She had winced inwardly at the sight of the long-bladed knife he had wielded, and had wondered—even after he had used it to slice through the ropes which held her—if he did not intend to plunge it into her heart. Instead, he had beckoned to her to climb the ladder behind him.

As much as Glynna had wanted to comply immediately, she could not. Blood had rushed painfully to her hands and feet once the bonds were cut, her back and limbs were stiff, and her thigh throbbed where she had fallen on it. She pushed back the hot threat of tears as she forced her bent knees to straighten, but when she tried to stand up, her knees buckled under her. She had then turned pleading eyes to her captor; it had been a vain effort. Mitchell continued to stand at the foot of the ladder, his right foot perched on its lowest rail, a sneer twisting his too-thin lips. With a lazy shrug of his broad shoulders, he taunted her. "You can spend the night here if you so desire, my fine lady slave." This was the first indication he had given of his purpose in abducting her. "Or you can pick yourself up and get upstairs. I'll not be carrying you."

Emerald sparks had flashed from Glynna's red-rimmed, swollen eyes. Who was he to think he could treat her or any other human being this way! she had silently protested. Physically exhausted, emotionally drained, she had seriously considered remaining where she was, but without either lamp or candle, or—her body reminded her—food or water or chamber pot, none of which he had provided, any other alternative had seemed better.

Now confined to the root cellar once again, Glynna was not so certain she had made the right decision the previous evening. The resident mice and spiders made no demands of her and kept a respectful distance. The darkness, which lightened slightly once she became accustomed to its embrace, she accepted as a friend. The dank mustiness of the cellar she just accepted. Neither the creatures nor the darkness nor the close atmosphere were dangerous. She now knew that Reverend Mitchell was.

Employing sheer willpower the previous evening, Glynna had forced her aching muscles to yield to her demands. The ladder was steep, the rungs placed too far apart for easy maneuvering, but she had climbed it, wondering with each painful step upward what treatment she would encounter at the hands of her abductor. At that point, she had thought nothing could be worse than banishment to the dark, smelly root cellar.

She had been wrong.

* * *

Kane Rafferty's icy gray gaze studied the set mask of Reverend Mitchell's florid features. There was something different about the preacher today, something indefinably different, some subtle alteration of his mien, his posture, his speech. Although Kane had never liked the man, his opinion had been based solely on the minister's pseudo intellectualism. Now, however, Kane added distrust to the short list. If a man could not be truthful about what he knew and didn't know, if he pretended others' thoughts and words were his own, could he be counted faithful in other realms?

Kane didn't think so. Yet his own dishonesty nagged at his conscience. He knew himself to be an honorable man, but he had placed himself in a dishonorable position, one from which he feared it might prove difficult to extricate himself.

Kane put his private concerns aside. Now that he thought of it, now that he had rested his mind and body from the rigors of the previous few days and the horrors of the last one in particular, Kane was not at all certain that Reverend Mitchell had been truthful yesterday afternoon when he had denied seeing Glynna on the coach road.

Galen had caught up with Kane near the bend where Glynna had fallen from Sheena. Kane had already found the evidence of her accident and subsequent return to the coach road: the disturbance in the bog where she had fallen, the broken scrub-pine limbs scattered over the hill, the diagonal slash her boot had made in the mounded earth paralleling the ruts in the road, the impression of her boot prints which indicated she was dragging her left leg, and, finally, the total disappearance of those prints. He and Galen had followed the road westward, toward the inn, until a set of wagon tracks had left the

186

road heading south. At that point, Galen had breathed an audible sigh of relief. "This trail leads to the preacher's place," he had explained to Kane, "and the tracks are fresh. Maybe Samuel knows what happened to Glynna."

If Samuel Mitchell did know anything about Glynna's whereabouts, he hadn't told Galen and Kane. They had found him lazily reclined in a straight chair on his front porch, an open Bible upon his lap, a large, ugly cur at his feet. Despite his pose, he had greeted them with alacrity, as though he had been expecting them. When Kane had mentioned this to Galen later, the older man had reasoned that the preacher seldom had guests at his place and would probably have greeted with the same enthusiasm anyone who came to visit him. Kane did not think so. There was too much enmity between them for Mitchell ever to respond enthusiastically to a visit from Kane. And he did not believe Galen's presence would appreciably alter the minister's attitude.

Staring Kane in the face as well was the fact that Mitchell had not invited his visitors indoors. Granted, the weather was pleasant and Galen had wasted no time in revealing their purpose; yet propriety demanded the offer of refreshment. The minister had too quickly assured them of his ignorance on the matter, had too quickly hastened them on their way, without even offering a dipper of water from his well.

Galen and Kane had spent the remainder of the day looking for Glynna—to no avail. She had simply disappeared without a trace.

As Kane listened to the prayers being offered in Brian's and Glynna's behalfs, he toyed with a plan. Mitchell was certain to remain at the tavern for the balance of the day. If I pretend illness, he thought, I can ride over to his farm now, while everyone is further occupied, and look for Glynna.

He mentally calculated the amount of time such an action would require and decided his plan had merit. He harbored no compunction about getting caught, so long as no one followed him immediately. He had to have time to search Mitchell's house and the outbuildings before anyone else showed up. If he were discovered too soon, Mitchell could have him arrested for trespassing, and then who would find Glynna? Kane knew that he would never convince Darcie and Galen—or anyone else, for that matter—of any wrongdoing on the reverend's part. Not unless he caught the man red-handed. Kane shuddered inwardly when he thought of what this supposed man of the cloth might do to Glynna.

If Kane had had any knowledge of what Mitchell had already done to her, he would probably have killed the man right then and there, in front of God and everyone else, the consequences be damned.

"Come on, if you're comin'," Mitchell had called down to her the evening before, his voice and manner brusque. "I don't have all night to wait for you.

He had stood to the side of the hatchway, holding the planked cover at an angle while Glynna had manipulated the final two rungs. When the upper half of her body had cleared the opening, Glynna had fallen upon the bare kitchen floor, her chest heaving from the exertion of the climb.

"Move your feet, girlie, 'less you want me to close the hatch on them," Mitchell barked.

The moment her feet were clear, she heard the

heavy trapdoor fall back into place. She remained on the floor, hunched on her knees, while she attempted to catch her breath.

"I'll be wantin' me some supper directly. You'll find meal in the larder and there's fresh greens in that pan over there." He waved his stubby arm toward the dry sink. "Course you'll have to start the fire, but I brought in plenty of wood. When I come back from feeding the stock, I'll bring some milk from the springhouse." He walked toward the back door as he delivered the final instructions, and when he opened it, Glynna heard a low, fierce growl.

Fearfully, she glanced upward to see a large mongrel crouched in the doorway, his one yellow eye gleaming savagely at her, his pointed teeth clenched and bared. The other eye was missing, its socket grotesquely gaping. The dog's hunched form filled the lower half of the opening, the long hairs of its heavy gray coat standing out in silhouette against the pale sky of early evening. Large patches of its fur were missing, as were two toes on one of its front paws. A long, bloody welt, obviously fresh, ran from the corner of its empty eye socket to the back of its neck.

"And don't get any ideas about running away, unless you want some ugly scars to carry with you the rest of your life." Mitchell's meaty hand caressed the dog's head, the feral gleam in his eyes matching that in the mongrel's. "Lucifer here is well trained. You wouldn't get past the barnyard." Then, in a voice filled with compassion, he spoke to Lucifer. "What happened, boy? You get in a fight with a coon? Bet you whipped that rascal! Come along, and I'll rub some salve on that cut."

Though Glynna had prepared the meal as best

189

she could, for she knew little about cooking, Mitchell complained loudly about the greens being gritty and not seasoned well; the cornpone, he said, was hard and tasteless. Glynna had no firsthand knowledge of the food since she had been relegated to a chair in the farthest corner from the fireplace and given a glass of milk for supper.

"Why are you doing this?" she queried as he ate, her voice soft but firm.

Instead of responding verbally, he glared at her as though she were some totally insignificant being not worthy of an answer.

"You will not get away with it," she prodded.

He shrugged his massive shoulders lazily. It was a gesture he employed often and one that was beginning to irritate her.

"If you want a slave, why don't you purchase one? Or perhaps an indentured servant would suit your financial status better. Either way, you would be operating within the realm of the law and would receive much better service than I am trained to give. Allow me to return home and I will say nothing about this."

At last he responded, but not as she had expected him to. "Who said I wanted a slave?"

"You did."

His bushy, graying eyebrows rose in protest. For someone who enjoyed filling up endless hours on Sunday with his own speech, this man was being uncharacteristically taciturn. Or perhaps, she thought, this is the real Reverend Mitchell.

"Earlier you referred to me as 'your fine lady slave.' "

"And so you are, for the time being."

That was all he would say. When she had delved further, he had cut her speech short, his beetled brow and pursed lips indicating supreme irritation with her questions.

Later, after she had scoured the dishes and mopped the kitchen floor, both tasks accomplished under Mitchell's ever-watchful and critical eye, he insisted that she retire to the parlor with him and read to him from the Bible. He chose the sixth chapter of Ephesians, catching Glynna unawares until she reached the fifth verse.

" 'Servants, be obedient to them that are your masters according to the flesh,' " she read, struggling to keep her voice steady, " 'with fear and trembling, in singleness of your heart, as unto Christ.' "

With all her heart, she wanted to pitch the volume at him, hurling forth at the same time the accusations she dared not voice. But Glynna knew that she must keep still, at least until such time as her body had healed. Thus far, Mitchell had not struck her, but that he was capable of inflicting physical punishment she had no doubt. Nor did she want him to bind her again. Her wrists and ankles burned from the ropes' chafing, which had been augmented by her feeble struggles to free herself. Perhaps, she decided, if she played the part of submissive servant, as the verse suggested, he would slacken his hold of her and she would find a way to escape.

Mitchell's farmhouse was small. In comparison to the tavern, it was tiny. Built in accordance with typical double cabin structures of the time, the downstairs consisted of two rooms: a parlor on one side and a hall on the other with a double fireplace serving both rooms. The hall functioned as both kitchen and dining room. The second story contained two bedchambers. Glynna assumed she would be occupying the one opposite Mitchell's.

Again, he proved her incorrect.

When he had tired of listening to her read, Mitchell had accompanied her to the necessary, an act which increased her discomfort more than it relieved it. Knowing he was standing just outside the flimsy portal, listening to her perform her ablutions, was unnerving. When they returned to the house, he retrieved a blanket from a chest in the parlor and tossed it at her. "The floor is good enough for the likes of you," he said, returning to the back door and whistling for Lucifer. The dog limped in, favoring his injured paw. "Watch," Mitchell commanded. Lucifer lay down in the doorway, resting his broad chin on outstretched paws.

A shiver ran the length of Glynna's spine as she realized the full impact of this deed. Treating her with complete disdain was not enough for this felon; he must force her to sleep with his mangy dog as well!

Glynna had had enough. Her stomach growled from lack of food—the one glass of milk he had allowed her, plus a few sips of water were all she had consumed this day. Her body ached from her injuries and the subsequent bonds and gag he had employed. Her skin, hair, and clothing retained the mud they had collected that morning. And, when she yearned for rest, he expected her to sleep on a bare, hard floor in the same room with that stinking mongrel dog!

She forgot her resolve to keep still. With more energy and greater strength than she had thought she could muster, she flew at him, her long nails curved like talons, her eyes burning bright with ire. A long, low growl, as ferocious as that Lucifer had released earlier, issued from her throat, and it was a similar growl which stopped her. The dog stood

MORE PASSION AND ADVENTURE AWAIT... YOUR TRIP TO A BIG ADVENTUROUS WORLD BEGINS WHEN YOU ACCEPT YOUR FIRST 4 NOVELS ABSOLUTELY *FREE*
(AN $18.00 VALUE)

Accept your Free gift and start to experience more of the passion and adventure you like in a historical romance novel. Each Zebra novel is filled with proud men, spirited women and tempestuous love that you'll remember long after you turn the last page.

Zebra Historical Romances are the finest novels of their kind. They are written by authors who really know how to weave tales of romance and adventure in the historical settings you love. You'll feel like you've actually gone back in time with the thrilling stories that each Zebra novel offers.

GET YOUR FREE GIFT WITH THE START OF YOUR HOME SUBSCRIPTION

Our readers tell us that these books sell out very fast in book stores and often they miss the newest titles. So Zebra has made arrangements for you to receive the four newest novels published each month.

You'll be guaranteed that you'll never miss a title, and home delivery is so convenient. And to show you just how easy it is to get Zebra Historical Romances, we'll send you your first 4 books absolutely FREE! Our gift to you just for trying our home subscription service.

BIG SAVINGS AND FREE HOME DELIVERY

Each month, you'll receive the four newest titles as soon as they are published. You'll probably receive them even before the bookstores do. What's more, you may preview these exciting novels free for 10 days. If you like them as much as we think you will, just pay the low preferred subscriber's price of just $3.75 each. *You'll save $3.00 each month off the publisher's price.* AND, your savings are even greater because there are never any shipping, handling or other hidden charges—FREE Home Delivery. Of course you can return any shipment within 10 days for full credit, no questions asked. There is no minimum number of books you must buy.

4 FREE BOOKS

TO GET YOUR 4 FREE BOOKS WORTH $18.00 — MAIL IN THE FREE BOOK CERTIFICATE T O D A Y

Fill in the Free Book Certificate below, and we'll send your FREE BOOKS to you as soon as we receive it.

If the certificate is missing below, write to: Zebra Home Subscription Service, Inc., P.O. Box 5214, 120 Brighton Road, Clifton, New Jersey 07015-5214.

FREE BOOK CERTIFICATE

4 FREE BOOKS

ZEBRA HOME SUBSCRIPTION SERVICE, INC.

YES! Please start my subscription to Zebra Historical Romances and send me my first 4 books absolutely FREE. I understand that each month I may preview four new Zebra Historical Romances free for 10 days. If I'm not satisfied with them, I may return the four books within 10 days and owe nothing. Otherwise, I will pay the low preferred subscriber's price of just $3.75 each; a total of $15.00, *a savings off the publisher's price of $3.00*. I may return any shipment and I may cancel this subscription at any time. There is no obligation to buy any shipment and there are no shipping, handling or other hidden charges. Regardless of what I decide, the four free books are mine to keep.

NAME

ADDRESS _____ APT _____

CITY _____ STATE ____ ZIP ____

( )
TELEPHONE _____

SIGNATURE _____
(if under 18, parent or guardian must sign)

Terms, offer and prices subject to change without notice. Subscription subject to acceptance by Zebra Books. Zebra Books reserves the right to reject any order or cancel any subscription. 019102

GET
FOUR
FREE
BOOKS

(AN $18.00 VALUE)

ZEBRA HOME SUBSCRIPTION
SERVICE, INC.
P.O. Box 5214
120 BRIGHTON ROAD
CLIFTON, NEW JERSEY 07015-5214

AFFIX
STAMP
HERE

poised, ready to attack upon command from his master.

That self-same man roared in derision, his paunch shaking in jelly-like fashion as his cold, hard eyes bored into her. "I always thought you had more spirit than you have shown me this day," he said, "and I shall enjoy breaking that spirit." His frosty gaze then traveled the length of her small frame, causing Glynna to tremble as his eyes raked her. She had never before noted how very evil his countenance could appear, for he had been careful to maintain a blandness of both voice and face while he'd occupied the pulpit. She and Kane were not the only people, Glynna realized, who were capable of playacting.

"You are too dirty to sleep in my house, even on the floor," Mitchell observed, his voice riddled with scorn. Without further explanation, he beckoned her to the kitchen and instructed her to heat water.

He's going to allow me a bath! she thought, stoking up the fire and hanging the kettle on the hook with a measure of genuine enthusiasm. A good deal of her anger dissipated as he dragged in a large, wooden tub from the back porch before returning outdoors to draw more water from the well. While he was gone, she let down her hair, running her fingers through it in an attempt to dislodge some of the tangles. When the tub had been filled, Mitchell produced clean towels and a large bar of sweetly scented soap. Perhaps she should have rebelled earlier, she reflected.

Glynna stood by the steaming tub, waiting with forced patience for him to retire to his chamber; instead, he pulled a chair away from the table and set it in the middle of the room, straddling it backwards and resting his double chin on its top rung.

In his right hand he held a flask from which he sucked occasionally.

"I'm waiting," he said, his voice deceptively soft.

"No-o-o!" she wailed, her anger full-blown again, pearly tears of frustration gathering in her eyes. So this was to be her punishment for lashing out at him!

The characteristic lazy shrug touched his shoulders then. "Lucifer!" he called, his cold stare never leaving her anger-ridden countenance. Despite the injured paw, the mongrel appeared almost immediately, teeth bared and black nose quivering. "I grow tired of this delay. If you value your precious hide, you will remove those filthy garments and get into that tub."

Glynna had never felt so degraded, so very humiliated, so vulnerable. Until that moment, she had not known what it meant to hate someone, but she was quickly discovering that capability in herself. As she removed her boots, she stole a glance at the mongrel, saw him crouched, his single yellow eye watching her, his pointed ears listening for the command to attack, his pink- and gray-splotched tongue lolling out of his mouth and dripping saliva on the floor. Turning her back to Mitchell, she removed her black bombazine habit, letting it puddle on the floor at her bare feet. Before her captor could protest, she stepped into the tub still wearing her chemise.

With an angry roar he was on his feet, filling his large palm with the loose skein of her hair, closing his hand around the thick strands like a vise. He jerked her hair hard, pulling her head backward so that she was painfully forced to look up at him. "You *will* obey me in all things," he ground out, his face so close to hers she could smell the stench of

194

his breath. He let go of her hair then, with the same sudden savageness with which he had grabbed it, and just as savagely, snatched her clothing from the floor and hurled it into the fire.

Her vision bleary, she watched in horror as the flames swiftly consumed her garments. He won't defeat me. I won't let him defeat me, she promised herself over and over, taking up the bar of soap and lathering it between her soft palms. Attempting to forget that he sat behind her, his cold wolf's eyes watching her every movement, she scrubbed her face and arms and feet until her skin turned pink. She washed her hair, too, thankful, despite herself, finally to be rid of the dried mud.

Still, she found little joy in this bath. The memory of another bath taken weeks ago—the bath she had enjoyed the day Kane Rafferty had arrived at the tavern—assailed her. Her anger at Kane's intrusion in the kitchen that afternoon seemed mild in comparison to that which she now felt. She realized then how very naive she had been, how very sheltered and protected her life had been.

Mitchell had not moved. His breathing had become increasingly labored as she had bathed, and while a part of Glynna's mind wondered what further degradation of spirit he had planned for her, another part of her—a stronger part—refused to contemplate those possibilities.

The sheer fabric of her wet chemise had molded itself against her skin, leaving no portion of her anatomy in question. She would not stand up without at least asking Mitchell to allow her some privacy, but he laughed at the suggestion.

"No, missy. I want to see you. *All* of you. *Now!*"

In the close darkness of the root cellar, with no one to see her but the mice, Glynna blushed furiously at the memory of the previous evening. The animal—Glynna searched her mind for some more appropriately condescending name for him, but could come up with nothing else—had ripped the wet, soapy chemise from her frame, then had run his beefy palms over the length of her torso, cupping her bare breasts and drooling at the sight of her pink nipples. She shuddered to think what he might have done next—had she not retched sour milk all over him.

He had slapped her soundly, a blow that had sent her head reeling. But Glynna hadn't minded. For the time being she was safe from his lecherous advances.

She had been forced to sleep naked, the rough woolen blanket prickling her skin. Lucifer had slept in the doorway, and each time she had repositioned herself in an attempt to gain some comfort, he had raised his head and growled low. When at long last dawn had arrived, Mitchell had roused her with a rough shake and gifted her with the red gown. He had allowed her to eat a few crusts of bread while he'd consumed a huge breakfast, and then he had locked her in the root cellar.

As soon as she had heard him ride away in the morning, Glynna had climbed the ladder and pushed with all her might against the trapdoor, but it would not budge. Mitchell must have set something heavy on top of it. Even if she did get out, she realized, that damnable mongrel, Lucifer, would tear her to pieces.

Why, oh why didn't someone come?

Where are you, Kane? her heart cried, while her soul willed him to hear her anguish.

The object of her heart's plea paced the length of his room nervously as he awaited Galen's summons. He alternately clenched his hands into tight fists and then released his fingers, splaying them wide.

If that bastard is holding her captive, I will strangle him! I swear I will. Or anyone else who harms her.

Kane's plan had been foiled. Immediately following the prayer session that morning, Galen had asked Mitchell to suspend services for the day so that the men could search for Glynna. The minister had agreed, albeit reluctantly, knowing that any protest from him would raise suspicion. He had not been completely able, however, to mask his frustration.

At long last, the noise from the ordinary, where the womenfolk were preparing packets of food, abated, and Kane listened closely for the sounds of footsteps mounting the stairs to his room. Momentarily, a knock resounded in the stillness, and he opened his door to find Galen standing in the hallway.

"We're ready to leave now," Galen informed him.

Kane hesitated as he quickly assessed the situation. Perhaps he had been wrong to think the minister was holding Glynna, and yet doubts continued to assail him.

"Are all the men going?" he asked, his interest centered on only one of them.

"Of course," Galen answered. "We're a small but closely knit community. You'll find we band together in a crisis."

Kane realized how callous it would seem if he did not join in the search, though he wanted to strike out on his own. Perhaps their combined efforts would lead them to Mitchell's place. If not, surely

197

he could find a way to break away and go by himself. Mitchell could not be in two places at the same time.

He asked for a few minutes in which to change into his riding clothes, and then he, too, was ready to go.

"I almost forgot," Galen added. "Brian wants to see you before we leave."

Chapter Thirteen

"I'm sorry, Mr. Rafferty."

Kane gazed down at Brian with sympathetic gray eyes. The boy was lying on his stomach, his face turned toward Kane, his back swathed in loose strips of white linen through which yellow splotches of lard had oozed. The rosy bloom of youth was absent from Brian's face and his blue eyes were listless. "I'm the one who should be apologizing, Brian, for not watching you closer than I did."

"But you told me not to get too near the fire. You told me how dangerous fire is. I'm sorry I didn't listen to you."

"Does it hurt much?" Kane knew it hurt him to ask.

"In some places. Katie said it burned so deep that it burned away the hurt." Brian's sandy-red eyebrows met in a frown for a moment. "I'm not sure I understand what she meant, Mr. Rafferty."

Kane sat down in the chair that had been pulled alongside Brian's bed, took the boy's closest hand, and began rubbing the back of it gently. "Can you feel that, Brian?" The boy nodded. "You were created to feel things when you touch them or when they touch you," he explained. "Sometimes the touching feels good, and sometimes it feels bad. Touch is one of your five senses, like hearing and seeing. If you had seriously injured one of your eyes, you might not be able to see out of it. That's what Katie meant. The burn hurt your back so severely in some places that you can't feel it. Where you can feel the pain is where the fire didn't burn as deeply. Do you understand it now?"

A slight smile touched Brian's lips. "You explain things real good, Mr. Rafferty."

"Well." Kane immediately wished he hadn't automatically corrected Brian, for the boy's cherubic features screwed into a grimace. But when he spoke again, Kane realized that he probably hadn't even heard the correction.

"Where is Glynna? She hasn't been to see me at all." A crystalline tear rolled out of Brian's left eye and down his cheek.

Kane regarded him with bemusement. Hadn't the Cavanaughs told their son about his cousin's disappearance? Or was this another subject Brian had difficulty comprehending? "Didn't anyone tell you she had an accident when she was riding Sheena?" Kane hedged.

Brian nodded again. "But that stubborn mare has thrown her before. Glynna's never hurt. Not really. I want to see Glynna!" He began to cry in earnest, and Kane breathed easier when Darcie entered her son's room.

I want to see her, too. Kane's heart pounded as he walked swiftly toward the stairs, descended them quickly, then jogged down the hill to the stable. *And when I do see her, I know exactly what I'm going to say to her.*

As luck would have it, Kane was assigned to the same group as Mitchell, along with Edwin and his father. At the deacon's insistence, they had ridden north, toward the McLaird farm, for the older man wished to change mounts. Edwin had ridden his own gelding to the tavern that morning, but his father had driven the wagon bearing Mother McLaird and their younger children. Deacon McLaird seldom sat a horse anymore, and then only a particularly sedate mare he had had in his stable for a number of years. He refused to ride long or far without being mounted on Blossom.

There had been another reason this foursome had taken the northern stretches as their territory for the search. Deacon McLaird and Reverend Mitchell would, of necessity, have to return home by dark, for the livestock on their farms required their attention. Kane and Edwin, on the other hand, suffered from no such restrictions. They would continue to look for Glynna, and they might be gone for days. A stop at the McLaird farm would give Edwin the opportunity to change clothes and outfit a pack-horse for their journey. Other small groups of men would perform similar extended searches in other areas.

Kane had attempted reassignment to the group heading south, but Edwin had fervently insisted they travel together, making Kane feel like an insensitive lout for suggesting otherwise. Perhaps he was wrong about the minister. Everyone else thought Glynna had been taken by Indians, or perhaps by a French trapper traveling eastward from the Ohio Valley to Williamsburg. These were possibilities that could not be ignored. If such were the case, the more the men dallied, the farther Glynna moved away from them, and—Kane shuddered when he considered it—the closer she came to vile treatment, if such had not already been her fate.

The encompassing darkness of the root cellar allowed Glynna no knowledge of the passage of time. The minutes dragged by, taking with them her jumbled thoughts while increasing her intense displeasure. After a while, cold, hard reason settled in, and Glynna began to formulate an escape plan.

In her mind she ticked of the three necessary elements of this plan as she paced: disable Mitchell, disable Lucifer, ride Gabriel back to the tavern. The immense complexities of accomplishing the first two points were staggering, for Glynna could not imagine disabling both Mitchell and Lucifer at the same time, and if she did not, the one fully functioning was likely to incapacitate her. If she were to conquer these two adversaries, they must first be separated.

She conjured up first one situation and then another, mentally visualizing each, realistically assessing its possibilities, then discarding those factors which were not feasible while cataloging those which were. Glynna had no desire to kill either of her foes, but she would if it came to that.

She considered which weapons she had at her disposal and how she might employ each one. Mitchell did not allow her the use of a knife unless he was present; she found a blade the least favorable of her few alternatives anyway. He did own a blunderbuss, but this she had totally discounted since she had no firsthand knowledge of its use. However, there were many heavy objects at her disposal with which she could stun one or both of her jailors were she swift enough in the wielding. If she were just allowed to go outdoors, she thought, she could get her hands on any number of plants whose leaves, berries, or flowers could be distilled to make a mildly poisonous brew.

As she weighed the various merits of each available weapon, it was to the last option she kept returning. Purple foxglove, rhododendron, larkspur, mountain laurel, mistletoe, oleander, and wild mushrooms all grew near the farmhouse—and all had poisonous parts. She must devise a way to secure one or more of them!

When the swift, hard pummeling of a horse's hooves sounded over her head, Glynna's pulse skipped a beat. Hope swelled within her breast as she listened closely, her heart waiting expectantly for either Kane's or Galen's voice to call her name. She opened her mouth to sing out, but reason closed it before any sound was uttered. If the horse was Gabriel, then its rider was Mitchell, and she dared not push her luck too far.

Darcie planted the gentlest of kisses upon her small son's pale cheek, then leaned back in the chair and studied his face, which was in repose.

The evidence of tears was strongly etched upon his features. His eyelids were red and puffy, his forehead puckered. She had not wanted to tell him about Glynna—not yet. Surely one of the groups of men out searching would find her this afternoon and that part of the nightmare would be over. But Brian sensed something was wrong. Nay, she corrected herself, he *knew* something was wrong. Nothing short of her absence would have kept Glynna from his bedside, and Darcie's assurances that she would come had lost credibility with him.

It had been a long afternoon. Brian's dressings had required changing, a long and arduous process but a necessary one, for infection must be prevented at all costs. Katie had concocted a batch of oak-bark tea, and this she and Darcie had applied to Brian's back after the old dressings had been carefully removed. His reddened skin was now horribly splotched with large blisters, and the tea helped to loosen the dead skin as it cleansed the burned area.

Daily debridement for the removal of dead or contaminated skin was also necessary. Brian had remained calm throughout the ministrations, although Darcie noticed that he occasionally tightened his mouth or squeezed shut his eyes when those ministrations became painful for him. When the debridement had been completed, lard had again been applied to his back, and clean, thick dressings had been gently wrapped around his torso once more.

While he was sitting up, Darcie spoonfed him a cup each of beef broth and herbal tea, for an intake of liquids was vitally important to his recovery. He had tried to sip from the cup himself, but the use of his arms involved the use of the muscles across his back, and the effort had caused him intense pain.

Darcie sighed wearily as she watched the only son left to her sleep. With Brian not yet out of danger and Glynna heaven only knew where, she closed her eyes and submitted yet another silent plea for the safety and well-being of both.

The June sun hung low in the western sky, its fiery tentacles brushing the sparse gathering of clouds just above the mountaintops, painting the cottony puffs in delicate shades of apricot and mauve. The ridges stood in slate blue relief against the pastel palette, its gently sloping sides swathed in dark forest green, its base shadowed in deep gray. Clusters of rhododendron dominated the foreground, the pink and red of their blossoms glistening where the pale yellow light touched them, eclipsing into dusky hues where the absence of light extinguished the vibrancy of their colors.

It was a scene begging for a rendering on canvas, one in which the artistic side of Kane Rafferty would have gloated under other circumstances. However, its pastoral beauty was now lost on both men who hurriedly established camp.

The sweet scents of wildflowers clung fragrantly to the heavy warm air; the songs of a multitude of birds blended harmoniously with the crisp chirp-chirping of insects and the throaty croaking of tree frogs as afternoon slipped into evening.

Kane smelled nothing more than his own sweat, heard nothing more than the erratic beating of his heart, as he gathered wood for a fire and filled a large goatskin flask with water from a clear mountain stream. Edwin removed an oilcloth-wrapped package of food from the packhorse along with two blankets and the makings for tea. The two men worked in silence, each occupied with his own conjectures and misgivings.

They had chosen for their campsite a semiflat, grassy spot protected by an outcropping of rock. When their tasks were complete, they sat cross-legged, facing each other from opposite sides of the small fire, their hands holding tin cups of hot tea.

Their lack of success in finding Glynna bore heavily upon them. The four had searched vainly for most of the day before Deacon and Mitchell had taken their departure, yet they had found no tracks other than those of wild animals, no clothing fragments, no limbs broken off bushes — no indication that the person or persons who had taken Glynna had traveled north.

Kane had suggested that he and Edwin return with the two older men, but his proposal had met with opposition, especially from Reverend Mitchell.

"Let the others do their jobs. You do yours," the minister had admonished. "We will stay with the original plan."

Before the men had split up at the tavern, it had been decided that each group would thoroughly comb the area assigned to it. If, after two or three days, Glynna had not been found or if substantial evidence of where she might be had not been discovered, the extended search groups were to return to Cavanaugh's. Should they find her, they would naturally return immediately.

Kane's thoughts kept backtracking to Mitchell, however. The man was hiding something. Kane knew it with his mind and with his heart.

Edwin broke the tense silence born of their individual fears for Glynna's safety. "No one disappears into thin air."

Kane slowly nodded his agreement. "And there were no signs of a struggle." He sipped the steaming brew. "You've known Glynna longer than I have. No matter how badly she was hurting, don't you think she would have offered some resistance or found some way to leave a clue if she had been taken against her will?"

Edwin smiled over the rim of his cup. "She is most definitely a woman of spirit, especially when she's riled." His smile melted into a slight frown.

"But we can't ignore all the possibilities, Kane, and there are so many of them. Someone on a fast horse could have just scooped her up as he rode past. Then she might have been bound or tied to a horse, leaving her unable even to break a twig. Someone may have found her already—or she could be miles away by now." Edwin's face and voice became grim. "And we have to realize we may never find her."

"But we can be reasonably certain a human being is responsible for whatever happened to her, can't we? An animal would have left tracks in that soft earth." An animal would have left more than tracks, Kane knew, but he refused to give voice to the remainder of his thoughts.

"Yes. Someone took her. The questions now are who and where and why."

Kane studied the raw-boned face of his companion as they both finished their tea. He saw strength and intelligence there, and warmth and good humor. He saw a man who was willingly giving his time and energy to search for someone he cared about. Edwin might ridicule Kane's notions, but it only made sense to try his theory out on him.

"I think I know who and where. Thinking about the 'why' scares the hell out of me," Kane said quietly.

Edwin's eyebrows rose, registering his surprise at Kane's words. He had unfolded the food packet and taken a baked chicken leg out of it, and now he held the piece in midair, his appetite forgotten.

"Hear me out," Kane requested, waiting for Edwin's slow nod before continuing. "I've been thinking about nothing else all day and have become convinced that I am correct." He reached for the teapot and refilled his tin cup, that action reminding Edwin of the drumstick he held. Edwin put it back in the packet, giving Kane his undivided attention.

Beginning with finding Glynna's tracks on the coach road, Kane told him everything he knew, and then he elaborated on his theory. Edwin listened carefully, nodding his agreement from time to time, his eyes occasionally opening wide, for he found Kane's ideas shocking, yet he could find no ready argument. When Kane had finished, the two sat quietly for a space, the soft whispering of the night wind through the treetops the only sound in their reflective silence.

"If you're right—and God help her if you are!— then we're out chasing rabbits when we should be fox hunting." Edwin chewed his lower lip. "And I think I can supply the reason."

The harsh scraping of wood against wood convinced Glynna that it was Mitchell who had ridden up. Anyone looking for her would have called her name or at the very least spent some time searching through the outbuildings and the interior of the farmhouse before checking the root cellar. During the several minutes that had passed since she had heard the horse's approach, Glynna had hoped that a rescuer had arrived. Although sounds came to her dimly, she could hear outside movement. The interim had been silent. Glynna supposed Mitchell had spent those minutes unsaddling and currying Gabriel.

While her immediate hopes were dashed, she refused to relinquish hope altogether. Somehow, some way, someone would find her . . . or she would find some means of escape.

The trapdoor creaked open, and a shaft of light illuminated the stairway. "Get on up here, missy," Mitchell called down to her. "It's getting late and I missed tea at the tavern, thanks to you." He cackled in unmitigated glee. "They've got the entire male population of this area out looking for you. Think the Injuns took you!" His mirth turned to scorn as he watched her negotiate the steep ladder. "As worthless as you are, I don't know why anyone cares what happens to you. You surely aren't worth stirring up a hornet's nest over."

Glynna blinked involuntarily as she cleared the opening, the dying sun's feeble rays dancing upon eyes long since grown accustomed to darkness. Her tone matched his scornful one when she spoke. "You honestly believe you'll get away with this, don't you? How long do you think you can keep me here before someone figures out where I am?"

"For someone with your education, you are incredibly dense-witted," he said as he lowered the hatch and replaced the rag rug he used to keep it covered. Glynna's gaze traveled from the rug's faded colors to the large oaken tub, still full of water, which sat beside it. Small wonder she had not been able to budge the hatch cover! "In this community, my reputation is above reproach. Who would ever think me guilty?"

Kane Rafferty would.

Glynna quickly lowered her head, hoping as she brushed the dust and cobwebs from her red skirt that Mitchell had not seen that sure knowledge in her eyes. Yes, Kane would think this man guilty. Kane knew this man to be a fraud. Everyone else might think their minister a man of integrity, but Kane knew better.

Then why, her heart cried, does he not come?

209

The evening passed much the same as had the previous one, with a few notable exceptions. Glynna was beginning to feel faint from lack of food, but she resisted begging for sustenance. She would be of little use to her captor if he continued to starve her, and Mitchell knew that as well as she. This evening he allowed her a full meal, although he limited her portions. Glynna could not help agreeing that her culinary skills were sadly lacking, but she did not voice this opinion.

How she longed for Katie's cooking! For the privilege of sitting at a table, surrounded by those she loved, instead of having to balance her plate on her lap as she ate in her corner, listening to Mitchell's noisy chewing and incessant complaining about the fare.

Nor did he require her to bathe again, thus sparing her additional humiliation. Instead, he used his tongue to ridicule her and her aunt and uncle while she cleaned up the kitchen. She made as much noise as she could safely get away with in an effort to drown him out. Again, he walked her to the necessary; again, he had her read to him, this time from the works of Jonathan Edwards; again, he brought Lucifer inside and made her sleep on the bare parlor floor with the beast guarding her.

At least he had allowed her to retain the ill-fitting garment, she thought later as she sought some comfort in the prickly blanket. Had it only been a matter of weeks since she had fancied herself in a similar situation? Where had the guileless maiden locked in a stone tower fled? Where was the romance in this adventure? Her fairy tale had come to life, and the malevolence of the flesh and blood antagonist far surpassed her previous notions about villainous antiheroes.

Where was her knight in shining armor?

It was time for him to rescue the damsel in distress.

The night, mountain air had grown cold and the earth beneath him seemed bent on preventing rest. Never before, in all of his thirty-four years, had Kane Rafferty, future Baron of Ulrich, slept on the ground. Never before had he tried to sleep fully clothed, either. Following Edwin's lead, Kane had removed nothing more than his boots. He lay wrapped in his blanket, his head resting on his saddle, listening to Edwin's soft snuffling snores, wondering how his friend could sleep in spite of the damp chill and pebbly ground.

Yes, he realized with a start, Edwin is my friend. How his life had changed these past few weeks! When he thought of his British friends, he now remembered their stiffness, their eccentricities, their arrogance, their snobbery. Why had he not seen them before in this light? he questioned, and acknowledged with chagrin that he had been equally as stiff, as eccentric, as arrogant, as snobbish as they. His sojourn in this new world had changed all that. Would he ever be able to return to his old way of life now? he wondered.

Not without Glynna.

Kane could not imagine spending the remainder of his life without her. These past two days had been hell. In retrospect, the previous three weeks had been heaven. Wherever he went, whatever he did with his life, Kane wanted Glynna with him. She filled the emptiness in him in a way no other woman — not even Valerie — had been able to do.

Was this what his father had been trying to tell

him about marriage? "A wife should be more than a lover," Thomas Rafferty had said, "more than a mother to your children, more than a hostess to your friends. A wife should be your best friend, your confidante, your companion. Do not confuse lust with love."

Kane had privately scoffed at his father's advice. Who wanted to marry for friendship? He wanted a warm, willing, attractive bedmate first. Now he realized he could find a lover anywhere, but never would he find another woman like Glynna—a woman who could fulfill every wifely role, a woman he could respect.

That she could completely satisfy his lust, as well, he had no doubt. He felt his body grow warm with the memory of her caresses. He felt her soft palms on his neck, her pliable lips upon his mouth, the willing press of her small frame against the hardness of his larger one. He felt his own body respond to the dream maiden he held close to his heart, felt the staff of his manhood rise in wanton need of her.

Dammit, he wanted to be the one to take her maidenhead! Not some French trapper or renegade Indian or—he shuddered—that fat, pompous Reverend Mitchell! For once, neither selfishness nor jealousy played a part in his feelings for a woman. Glynna deserved to be wooed, to be treated gently, to be loved by the man who possessed her. And he was that man.

If he had believed he could find his way in the dark, he would have saddled his horse and traveled south right then. He had tried to convince Edwin to leave immediately after the younger man had told his gruesome tale, but Edwin had warned of the dangers of night travel: predatory creatures, snakes, and rabbit holes. If Edwin's story was factual, Mitchell posed no threat to Glynna's virginity.

Still, Kane wanted with all his heart to find her, to hold her close, to tell her how very much he loved her. Every passing minute fanned brighter the flames of his anger and frustration. When he found her, he vowed, he would never allow her to be separated from him again.

He did not question her willingness to comply.

Chapter Fourteen

"Are you absolutely certain you want to do this?" Edwin fastened the cinch straps on his gelding, tested their security, and waited for an answer from Kane.

The reply was another question. "What other choices do we have?"

Edwin mounted his horse, then held the reins loosely as he turned to Kane. "Keep looking around here, I suppose. But you're right. No one's been up here recently except the two of us."

"Chasing rabbits," Kane hastily added, his tone one of irritation and impatience—and neither with Edwin. The younger man had been much more receptive to Kane's theories than he had expected him to be. But the night had been a long one, and Kane's body felt stiff and sore and his head ached miserably.

"Let's go find that fox."

"It's Monday, and I don't have to do my own washing."

Samuel Mitchell leaned back in the straight chair and rubbed his palms over his protruding stomach. "Your cooking's improving, girlie. Think I might just keep you 'round for a while. I kinda like having someone to do the cooking and cleaning."

Glynna didn't hear the last sentence. Her mind zeroed in on the keeping around part. What else had he planned to do with her? She asked him as much, trying not to cringe when he used a fingernail to pick a piece of gristly ham out of his teeth.

" 'Tain't none of your business." He glowered at her. "And don't you go gittin' any foolish ideas about ruining the food on purpose. I've got ways of making you behave, and you ain't even gotten a good taste of 'em yet."

The man projected a more fraudulent guise than Glynna had thought. This morning he had dropped all pretense, his truer self evident in both his speech and his manners.

"When you get finished with them dishes," he continued, "you can take the dirty laundry down to the crick and wash it. Lucifer and I'll go with you, and he'll stay so you don't run away." He laughed then, a deep, throaty guffaw that chilled the blood. "I've got it all in a nice bundle for you, 'long with the soap."

Without being aware of it, Mitchell was giving her the opportunity to collect pieces of poisonous plants, and Glynna planned to take full advantage of it. She hurriedly scoured the final dirty item in the kitchen, a heavy iron skillet, all the while considering ways to conceal the plants until she was ready to use them.

Her heart sang with the joy of freedom as she hefted the heavy bundle of soiled linen and cloth-

215

ing over her shoulder and started toward the creek. If Mitchell had not walked with her, or the bundle been so heavy, she would have skipped, so light-hearted was her mood.

The morning sun bathed the green hills with its soft golden light and lent its precious-metal glimmer to the fringes of a few small cotton puff clouds. Wildflowers bent their heads in deference to a wayward breeze, then lifted them upward to offer their sweet nectar to the horde of insects flitting among them. What a pretty bouquet I could make, Glynna thought, then realized she had inadvertently stumbled upon the solution to her earlier dilemma.

Nothing was going to spoil this mood—not her stiff, aching muscles or her unstockinged feet, which were quickly sprouting blisters; not even Lucifer, who tagged along at her heels or Mitchell with his asp's tongue. She would not succumb to despair; she would triumph over it.

They walked almost a quarter of a mile before they came to the creek. The stream gurgled noisily, its crystal clear water flowing swiftly over stones eroded to a glassy smoothness through the years by the constantly moving liquid. This was the same creek that flowed down from the mountains near the tavern. Were it not for Lucifer, Glynna could follow it upstream for some three miles and be home. The going would be slow along the rocky bank, the journey tiresome to her bruised limbs, but she would gladly have attempted it. Even without Lucifer to stop her, though, she would not be able to make much headway before Mitchell discovered she was gone. And with the advantage of horseflesh, he would catch up with her long before she reached safety.

She quailed when she recalled his recent threat: "I've got ways of making you behave . . ." Glynna didn't think she wanted to learn firsthand what those ways were. Her right cheek still stung from the blow he had administered two nights before, and her tender skin had swollen to an ugly purple. No, she would bide her time. When she did make good her escape, neither Mitchell nor Lucifer would be able to stop her. She would see to that.

When Mitchell had left her alone with his ugly, mangy cur, Glynna removed her boots, then tied a linen towel, which she had taken from the bundle, around her waistline. She reached between her legs to pull the back of the red skirt up; this she tucked into the strip of linen at her middle, leaving her bare feet and calves exposed.

While washing clothes was a task she had never before been given, she had watched Katie's daughters perform this chore. Mimicking their activity, she waded a few steps into the creek, took a piece from the open bundle on the bank, and wet it in the stream. Using the bar of lye soap Mitchell had given her, she rubbed the cake on the fabric and used the smooth stones as a scrub board.

The warmth of the sun's shimmering rays eased the soreness of her muscles and filled her heart with renewed hope. Without conscious direction, her thoughts turned to the discussion she and Kane had had about French philosophers. Which one had written about climate affecting mood? Montesquieu. Yes, she decided, that's who it is. And how correct he had been! She had every right, every reason to feel downhearted and depressed, yet her spirits soared in the bright sunlight.

A portion of that buoyancy was due to the fine weather, she knew; her partial freedom—freedom from the dark root cellar, freedom from the ever-watchful eye of Samuel Mitchell—accounted for another portion. But it was her dauntless love for Kane, a deep, abiding love she had only recently begun to acknowledge, which was most responsible for the rise in her spirits.

The water splashed coolly around her ankles and soothed her blistered feet as she worked slowly but diligently. Knowing Mitchell might appear at any time to check on her, she dared not dawdle, yet she could not help wanting to take as much time with this chore as was prudent.

When she had finished washing the garments and spreading them to dry on low bushes near the stream, Glynna picked up her boots and started back down the trail toward the farmhouse. She had momentarily forgotten about Lucifer. The mongrel emitted a low though quite ferocious growl as he pounced on her, his weight easily throwing her to the ground. Glynna's heart lodged in her throat as she fell, a voice within her screaming, He's going to kill me! Dear, blessed Lord, he's going to kill me! Did her throat give voice to her panic? She was so frightened she wasn't sure whether it had or not.

She lay still, her pulse thumping loudly in her ears, her lungs gasping for breath, her body tense as she waited for the dog's teeth to sink into the soft flesh at her nape. She had felt Lucifer's claws dig into her shoulders and the backs of her thighs as he'd leapt forward. For a long moment, she continued to lie prostrate on the dry, grassy spot in the sun where she had landed, not comprehending that the danger had passed.

Timorously, she lifted her head. There, stretched out in front of her on the warm earth, lay Lucifer, his tongue lolling, his one yellow eye upon her. She could smell his dog's stench, which fused rankly with her own stench of fear. The combination was nauseating, and she turned her face away from him and snuggled into the grasses, using her arm for a pillow. She would have to wait for Mitchell now, and she was afraid to move again.

Her tired body yearned for rest. The ground was much softer than Mitchell's parlor floor, the sun is a more desirable blanket than the prickly woolen one. In time, her breathing evened and she fell into a deep, restful sleep.

The journey to Mitchell's farm took longer than Kane had anticipated. Not wanting to meet anyone else, thereby exposing themselves to unwanted opposition, Edwin and Kane had carefully skirted the farms between their campsite and Mitchell's place. It was midmorning when they finally arrived at their destination, and with each passing minute, the tension between the two had grown.

Edwin and Kane had had difficulty coming to an agreement concerning how they would handle Reverend Mitchell. Edwin did not believe he could confront this venerated member of the community with an accusation of felony, even if Kane actually voiced it, were Edwin present, he would be guilty of the deed by association. Although he categorically agreed with Kane's theory, Edwin's ingrained respect for members of the clergy warred with the supposition of guilt. He had his own reputation in this community to consider, he reminded Kane. If they were wrong, Edwin would bring shame upon himself and his family.

Kane harbored no such compunctions, yet he respected Edwin's ethical obligations. Neither liked the idea of subterfuge, but that seemed the only viable alternative.

They had basically followed the creek downstream, giving it a wide berth at the spot Galen had selected for his mill. They stopped to rest the horses less than a half mile from Mitchell's farm and spent those few minutes solidifying their plan.

Edwin rode in alone. Kane tethered his horse in a copse within sight of the farm and waited in under the cover of the trees, watching.

Mitchell opened the front door of his farmhouse and walked out onto the porch as Edwin reined in. His ruddy features registered a look of surprise when he saw who his visitor was. "Praise be to God!" he exclaimed. "Someone found Miss O'Rourke! Is she all right?"

Bastard! Kane thought as he watched Edwin shake his head in negation.

"No, Reverend. No one has found her yet — at least, not that I know about."

Mitchell's wide brow furrowed deeply. "Then why are you here? You and Mr. Rafferty are supposed to be out searching for her."

"Whoever took her didn't go north. We came back this morning."

The minister shuffled his feet nervously. "Look here, young man. If you've come to fetch me for another search party, well, I can't go with you today. There's work to be done on this farm and no one else to do it but me."

"No, sir, that's not why I'm here." Edwin took a deep breath, for what he was about to say could shape the remainder of his life. "This business with Glynna got me to thinking. What if it had been Hepzibeth instead?"

Mitchell shrugged broadly. "What if it had been?"

"I think I would be going crazy with worry by now. I—I love Hepzibeth Jenkins. I want to make her my wife."

The minister chuckled. "You're asking the wrong man, Edwin. I'm not her father."

"But you will perform the ceremony?"

"Certainly. Who else would you get? You didn't need to ride all the way over here to ask me that! You'll need a fortnight to publish the banns. What date did the two of you have in mind?"

"We haven't exactly discussed it. I was hoping you and I could talk about it first—you know, about marriage. There are some theological questions I want to ask. Could we go inside and sit down?"

Mitchell turned and opened the door. "For a spell, I suppose. I do have work to do."

Kane had begun to skirt the property as soon as Edwin stepped onto the porch. Before he left the shelter of the trees, he double-checked to make sure they were both inside. Mitchell's farm was small; there were only four outbuildings: a barn, a smokehouse, a necessary, and a springhouse. Kane started with the smokehouse, which sat in closest proximity to his hiding place. Edwin had thought this the most likely of the four to be employed as a "jail," since it would not be in use this time of year.

The interior was dark and redolent of hickory

smoke, but it did not yield his prize. Quickly, Kane left the smokehouse and ran to the springhouse, which had been built over a sluice. From there he headed for the necessary, and finally made his way to the barn. He had been ever watchful of the house as he'd moved from one building to another, but Edwin and Mitchell remained closeted there.

The barn was not overly large, and there were few places Mitchell could have hidden Glynna. Kane looked in the tack room, checked the corn crib, and climbed the ladder to the loft. He poked the length of his arm into stacks of hay and combed the lower floor in search of a trapdoor. Edwin had assured him of the existence of a root cellar—every farm in the area had one—but he hadn't known how Mitchell's was accessed. Kane could tell him it was not from the barn.

There was virtually nowhere else to look. Kane had felt certain that if he didn't find Glynna, he would at least uncover some shred of evidence indicating Mitchell had brought her here, but there had been nothing. Not one single solitary thing.

His spirits sagging, Kane slipped out the back of the barn and into the copse to wait for Edwin. He entertained little hope now that Glynna was somewhere inside the farmhouse. Mitchell would not have allowed Edwin inside if she were.

Kane scratched his head in utter frustration. Where could she be?

A sharp pain in her rib cage awakened Glynna. She opened eyelids puffy with sleep to view booted feet, then allowed her blurry vision to travel upward until it took in the broadly smiling face of

Samuel Mitchell.

"They came looking for you, girlie!" he boasted, his paunch shaking with laughter. "And you weren't there!"

With a trembling hand, she brushed the hair off her forehead, mentally brushing the cobwebs of sleep away. Who had come looking for her? she wondered as she sat up, the impact of Mitchell's revelation piercing her soul with daggers of despair.

His next words answered her unspoken question—or had she whispered it?—and thrust the knife points deeper. "That so-called tutor of yours and the McLaird boy came snooping around. Edwin concocted some fool excuse about wanting to marry the Jenkins girl to divert my attention while Rafferty searched the outbuildings. If you ever see that uppity Englishman again, you can tell him he ain't very good at sleuthing. But, of course, you won't ever see him again. It don't matter none, anyways. They won't come looking for you here anymore."

Glynna squeezed back the rush of hot tears that threatened to flood her eyes. With irritable, jerking motions she pulled the dry garments off the bushes and slung them across her left arm. The day had lost its brilliance, the air had lost its freshness, and she had lost her hope. She didn't see the band of pewter clouds scurrying across the gray-blue sky or feel the weight of the damp, humid air as Mitchell hurried her back down the path. They were crossing the yard before Glynna remembered the wildflowers she had planned to gather.

A loud crash won her attention, and she slowly lifted her gaze from the wagging tail of Lucifer upward to the heavens. A bold streak of lightning rent the gray sky asunder, its jagged path forking downward and seeming to touch the distant hills as it plunged to earth. Just a few weeks before, such a sight would have left her quivering, but now it had lost its power to disconcert. It was the evil in mankind she now feared, and not nature's wrath. Upon reflection, it seemed incongruous to her that she had ever trembled at the mere sound of thunder.

An index finger prodded her forward, its nubby end pushing into her spine. "Get a move on, girlie. It's started to rain."

And, indeed, it had. Big drops stung her cheeks and arms as the clouds hurled them earthward. Glynna had not noticed.

From the long windows in the ballroom Kane watched the leaden sky unleash its fury. He had just come from Brian's room. The boy certainly had gumption. Today was Brian's birthday. His sixth. A child should be able to celebrate such a momentous occasion with unreserved joy. Kane thought life terribly unfair to have inflicted on the lad a double cause for concern right now.

Glynna's disappearance weighed more heavily on the boy's mind than did his own physical incapacity. Kane had so wanted to bring her home to assuage his own worry as well as that of the Cavanaughs. If he ever found her, he silently vowed, he would never let her go. Every minute he spent away from her now, every heart-crushing minute brought him closer to the realization that she was more important to him than his beloved Ireland, than his future title and position as Baron of Ulrich, than the jeweled tiara his mother had sent him to find, than anything else he had ever dreamed of having or being. Though he knew it not, he was on a collision course with that realization, time and circumstances hurtling him toward it.

As he watched the rain, he thought of Ireland, where downpours occurred with such regularity the isle was commonly and quite vulgarly referred to as the Urinal of the Planets. His purely English forebears had not loved this land as did his father, who had passed that love to his eldest child. How fortunate it had been, Kane thought wryly, that one of his ancestors had found favor with the king centuries before and had thus been doubly gifted, with an estate in County Galway and the title of baron.

The Irish people as a whole looked upon their English landlords with unmitigated disdain. In a calculated effort to erase that contempt, Kane's father had committed the unpardonable: he had married an Irish girl. Then he had set about further dispelling the inherited ill will between himself and his tenants by treating them justly, demanding no more of them than they were able to give. Not once had Kane ever heard his father make light of the Irish or make them the brunt of ethnic jokes, as did so many Englishmen. Kane blushed in shame at the memory of doing just that as a young man at Cambridge when, in self-defense, he had learned to refer to potatoes as "Irish apricots" and a false witness as "Irish evidence."

Virginia, wild though it was, reminded him a great deal of Ireland. He could come to love this land almost as much, perhaps, as he loved the emerald expanses of his homeland.

But only with Glynna at his side.

Without her, he might as well go home, marry Valerie, and accept the feudal title and estate that were his inheritance.

Kane chafed at the day's turn of events. The rain seemed a fitting end to the disappointment of not finding Glynna at Mitchell's farm. He had been so certain! Everything pointed to the contemptible man. The story Edwin had told him over the campfire had sealed that certainty, and Kane shivered involuntarily as he recalled the details of the narrative. But Edwin had seen nothing inside Mitchell's house to lead him to believe Glynna was there or ever had been.

Somewhere, someone had a clue. Surely someone had seen her. If this were Dublin or London, Kane would hire men to find her. He would post a reward for her safe return, advertise her disappearance in the newspapers. *Do* something! Here there was so much wide, open space, there were so few people on so much land; and Kane was a virtual stranger in Virginia and considered a foreigner to boot.

He walked without knowing he did, his feet moving of their own accord, taking him from one side of the room to the other as he paced. The booming thunder rattled the glass in the paned windows and the rain pelted against the roof in a steady staccato, but he did not hear the effects of the storm. He forced aside the torrent of emotion that insisted on clouding his thinking, refusing to allow his abhorrence of the obese minister to color his reason further, and settled his mind on the alternatives Edwin had offered.

If Glynna had been taken by Indians, she would

most likely never be found.

If she had been taken by a French trapper, or some other unsavory character heading east, they were almost to the coast by now.

Kane ignored the former, concentrating instead on the latter assumption. Williamsburg lay to the east. The colonial capital of Virginia was Williamsburg. Governor Dinwiddie lived in Williamsburg. There was a garrison of the king's soldiers at Williamsburg. A newspaper was published there.

If he had no other choice, he would go by himself, but he knew he would rather travel with Edwin. When it stopped raining, he would ride over to the McLaird place and ask him to go along. They would leave on the morrow. Or he would. If he rode hard, without the encumbrance of a coach, he could be there in three days. One way or another, he was going to Williamsburg. And he was going on the morrow.

Unconsciously, Glynna had built an invisible wall around herself. It was an act of desperation, of self-preservation, an act over which she exercised neither knowledge nor control. The wall shut out all feeling, all emotion, and thus all the pain. She moved through her assigned tasks as one moving through a dreamworld, utilizing innate intelligence to make up for lack of skill and experience as she accomplished each chore, her mind focused on a tandem beam: survival and escape.

Vaguely aware of her surroundings, she nonetheless noted that Mitchell was sitting at the rough-hewn table in the hall, his Bible open before him, a lamp set close by to illuminate the printing in the grayness of the room. She also noted the perspiration that sprouted with maddening regularity upon her brow as she set the irons to heat on the hearth and then used them to press the garments and linens she had washed that morning. And she noted the orange flames dancing in the fireplace, the pot of rabbit stew hanging over the fire, the tender soreness of her muscles as she tended to each.

The dim gloominess waxed into utter darkness as she worked, and the storm waned as the ebony canopy of night encompassed the farmhouse. Rain fell in soft patters upon the roof; its diminished cadence might have been soothing to Glynna given other circumstances, and had the mental fortification she had created allowed her inner sensation.

She ate without tasting, moved without conscious direction, and slept without dreaming.

Chapter Fifteen

Duke of Gloucester Street, the mile-long, ninety-nine-foot wide, foot-deep main thoroughfare of Williamsburg, gaped before the pair of dust-laden, hungry, and weary travelers. "You ought to be here in the spring or autumn," Edwin told Kane, "during the Public Times when the General Assembly and the General Court meet. This place is so crowded then even the halls and stairwells of the taverns are utilized for sleeping."

But it was summer, and the sleepy town yawned in the hot stillness of midafternoon. Only a few of its tenants stirred about. Kane spied one weeding his garden, another carrying to the cobbler a shoe that obviously needed mending. He recalled how much busier this very street had been just a month before, how difficult it had been for him to secure private sleeping accommodations and then a coach and driver to take him to the edge of the wilderness. *Just a month ago!* It seemed like a lifetime, as though he had not started to live until he'd met Glynna. And, he realized with a shock, he would not live again until he found her. Until that time, his life could have no meaning, could be nothing more than a mere existence.

"The barber, the stable, the tavern, or the government offices." Edwin called them off. "Where do you want to stop first?"

Kane groaned in indecision, one hand reaching upward to trace the dark, bristly line of three-day stubble on his jaw. "If you think our mounts and stomachs can wait, the barber. I don't want to see anyone without first having a bath and a shave."

His companion nodded his agreement, then pointed across the street to a standing pole with two red balls on it, above which hung a shingle, inert in the windless air, proclaiming the establishment to be that of "Barber and Peruke Maker."

"There's a barber's sign. May the water be hot and plentiful, and the razor well honed!"

An hour later, clean and freshly shaved, Edwin and Kane sat in an anteroom of the governor's office, a small outbuilding in front of the Governor's Palace, waiting to see a Lieutenant Reed. The interval was of short duration.

A young man lean as a leather strap motioned them into a small cubicle off the anteroom and with typical military brusqueness inquired as to their business. The two minced no words, being as eager as the lieutenant to conclude the matter and be on their way. Reed offered to circulate a description of Glynna among the soldiers along with the particulars concerning her disappearance, but he offered little hope that she would be easily located. He agreed with Kane, however, that an advertisement in the *Virginia Gazette* could not hurt their cause and an award would sweeten the pot. He also graciously agreed to serve as liaison between Kane and any civilian who came forward with information.

The building housing the printing office, post office, and bindery was on Duke of Gloucester Street just a block west of Henry Wetherburn's Tavern, where they planned to stay. The steamy heat of early summer followed them into the small clapboard-sided building.

When they asked to see the printer, they were both taken aback to hear the diminutive, blond-haired young woman who had greeted them declare, "Then 'tis I you want to see. I'm Samarra Seldon, but you may call me 'Sam.' How may I help you?" Her round, cheerful face smiled sweetly up at them, her dark brown eyes crinkling merrily at the corners. She watched their bemused gazes travel over her ink-splotched apron and then return to her beaming countenance. "Always takes newcomers by surprise. Whatever your printing needs may be, I can accommodate you."

Samarra had grown accustomed to openmouthed stares over the six years she had been plying her trade in Williamsburg. Ladies, she knew, were not supposed to work as tradesmen. It was considered quite unseemly. Nor were they supposed to be addressed by their Christian names by people they barely knew. She had learned, however, that men — and the vast majority of her customers were of the masculine gender — were more comfortable dealing with a woman who put simpering courtesy aside and talked to them in the straightforward, business-like manner a man would use.

It was Kane who found his voice first. He gently nudged his openmouthed companion as he introduced Edwin and himself. Then he removed a sheaf of papers from the leather packet he had brought with him and began to itemize his requirements. The packet contained a charcoal sketch of

231

Glynna, and when Edwin saw it, his mouth dropped open again.

"I had no idea Glynna had sat for an artist," Edwin exclaimed.

"She didn't — at least, not for this sketch," Kane replied.

Edwin's brow furrowed in his confusion. "But how . . . when . . . who?"

"From my own hand, my own memory. The night before we left the Cavanaughs'." He returned his attention to Samarra Seldon. "Can you make an engraving from this sketch? It is a reasonable likeness—"

"An *exact* likeness," Edwin corrected, his words drawing a wry smile from Kane's lips.

"Of course," Samarra said. "How soon do you need it?"

"The sooner the better." Kane briefly explained the urgency of the situation. He ordered two hundred flyers advertising Glynna's likeness and the reward he was offering for information leading to her safe return. Some of these would be mailed to newspapers and government offices in other colonial cities, the remainder posted around Williamsburg.

Samarra studied the charcoal sketch and was amazed at the deftness with which this devastatingly handsome man had drawn the young woman. That there was more than talent involved she had no doubt. Love had guided the piece of charcoal, adding a depth of character and personality generally missing from works of art accomplished without the benefit of a model. She raised her gaze to his and witnessed that love shining in the softness of his dove gray eyes. Would there ever be someone special for her? she wondered, knowing he would have to be special to accept her vocation without reservation.

"It's almost time to close up shop today," she said, as much to herself as to the two men. "Tomorrow is Friday. If I work straight through, I can have them ready by Monday noon. You're fortunate this is not the busy season." And that I have succumbed to your charm, she silently added, for it was unusual for Samarra Seldon to submit herself to such pressure.

Lieutenant Reed had told them that the *Virginia Gazette* was published every Wednesday, so there was no need to rush to the newspaper office. If Samarra could have the engraving finished by Monday, Glynna's sketch could be included in the newspaper advertisement. Kane and Edwin decided to postpone their visit to the *Gazette* until the morrow, for their hunger had not abated.

A half-hour later, over tea at Christiana Campbell's Tavern, they discussed their disposition over the next three days while they awaited the printing of the advertisements. "How do the men here occupy their leisure?" Kane asked as he cut into a succulent cherry tart.

"Cards, cockfights, and horse racing."

"Sounds like fun."

"If one has the coin to enjoy such sport."

Kane hefted a heavy purse from his waistcoat pocket, and holding it between thumb and forefinger, jingled it in front of Edwin's long nose. "I have the money. Can you get us into a card game tonight?"

A wide grin split Edwin's face, exposing strong teeth tinted pink from the thick cherry filling. "I believe I can."

* * *

233

A week had passed since Glynna's accident; five days had passed since Edwin had visited Mitchell while Kane searched the outbuildings for her. No one had set foot on Mitchell's property since then. Glynna's injuries from the accident seemed minor now. Her left wrist was still sore, but the large bruise on her thigh had almost completely healed. The additional injuries she had received at the hands of the self-righteous reverend obliterated those resulting from the accident.

Glynna had continued to cook and clean by day, and now she submitted herself to the minister's groping hands by night.

When Mitchell had told her three nights ago that she would be allowed to sleep upstairs, she had thought he meant the guest bedchamber. Thinking only of the comfort of a mattress, she had climbed the stairs without trepidation. Though she was to be allowed the luxury of a bed, it was not to be the one in the guest chamber.

When he had pulled her roughly into his room, his meaty fist squeezing her lower arm so tightly it left a bruise, the wall she had built around herself came tumbling down. She kicked and screamed and clawed at him, all to no avail. He laughed at her feeble efforts. But when she called him a whore's son—one of the few vulgar expressions in her vocabulary, he hit her. The blow came swiftly from his open left hand, the pads of his knuckles striking her right cheekbone with so much force she thought he had broken it. One of his fingers caught her in the eye, and instead of bringing his hand away from her stinging cheek, he closed it tightly around the hair above her right ear, pulling so hard on her tresses that Glynna cried out for mercy.

"I'll give you mercy, you devilish wench, I wish I could give you the kind of mercy you deserve for flaunting your wares before a righteous man's face and then resisting when he wants to sample them."

His left hand unrelentingly held her hair, while his right grasped the scooped, bulging neckline of the red dress and pulled downward, ripping the bodice all the way to the waistline. Since he had ruined her chemise that first evening and had not supplied her with another, she wore nothing underneath the overly large garment. Glynna's hands flew to the gaping fabric, but when she would have used them to hold the pieces together, Mitchell grabbed her wrists, cuffing them in his large right hand while his left tugged harder on her hair.

She cried in earnest then, her tears soothing the swelling of her right eye but her sobs making her heaving chest burn. Mitchell's gaze locked onto the undulating flesh, and for a long moment he held her in his painful grip, salivating, his Adam's apple bobbing. Then, with a sudden fierceness, he released his hold and pushed her upon the counterpane.

When he stalked violently to a highboy, Glynna rolled from the mattress, intending to bolt downstairs. Lucifer's menacing growl halted her at the doorway. The mongrel sat upon his haunches, guarding the opening, his single yellow eye glazed, the loose flesh of his chops trembling above bared, fanglike teeth. She felt Mitchell's hands upon her arms, jerking them backwards. The wooden planks of the floor vibrated beneath her bare feet as he sank to his knees behind her. The softness of silk grazed her lower arms, then tightened around her wrists as he wound a stocking around them and

235

then tied it securely.

He whirled her around by her shoulders, sank his hands into the waistline of the ruined dress, and yanked at the time-weakened fabric, separating the skirt as he had the bodice, opening the dress the rest of the way down the front. Glynna shivered, terrified, as she watched his wolf's eyes rake her exposed flesh.

What was he going to do to her? She shuddered to think what he had meant when he'd said he wished he could give her what she deserved.

He dragged her back to the bed, threw back the covers, and hurled her onto the tick. With eager fingers he tugged the shredded edges of red fabric over her shoulders. His thick, red tongue licked his lips as he raped her with his eyes. Glynna closed her own eyes tightly, wishing he would extinguish the candle he had left burning on the small table by the bed, trying without success to regurgitate her supper. She writhed inwardly in total agony at this ultimate humiliation, willing the dark curtain that shut out pain to fall.

He began to touch her then, his too-soft palms cupping a breast, squeezing a buttock, rubbing her stomach. Tears flowed unheeded from her eyes, which she continued to keep closed in an effort to blot out some of the degradation.

At long last, he stopped, blew out the candle, turned his back to her and promptly went to sleep, his body still fully clothed, his boots upon his feet.

Each night since he had repeated the roving quest of her quivering flesh, never further violating her, always binding her wrists with one of his stockings and threatening to beat her should she show anger toward him again. Yet, he goaded her, almost begging for a display of spirit, as though he

236

wanted to strike her again but could not bring himself to do so without cause.

"Your little cousin's bad hurt," he had told her, sniggering. "That tutor of yours let him get burned. Real intelligent man, that Kane Rafferty is."

She didn't believe him.

"You better enjoy the easy life while you can, missy," he had taunted at another time. "Gonna trade you when the trappers come through. You ought to bring a passel o' money, purty as you are. Can't sell you, though, as damaged goods. Aw, them little bruises'll heal 'fore you get to Williamsburg. It's the permanent kind of damage I'm talking about, so you don't have nothing to worry about on that score."

She had known all along he had something else in mind for her. If he did mean to trade her, how much time remained? Probably not much. If she was going to escape, it would have to be soon.

She now allowed him to remove her gown—a salmon-colored one gaudily adorned with cheap, scratchy lace and as large as the red one had been. He had produced this one the morning after the red dress had been ruined, and Glynna was beginning to wonder how many such gowns he had and where he kept them. Whose had they been? Glynna could not recall ever hearing that the minister had once been married. Regardless of how he had obtained the dresses, there could not be an endless supply, and she had no desire to go naked.

Her right cheek was swollen, the skin tinged a dark bluish purple. Her scalp was extremely tender above her right ear, and her right eye was bloodshot where Mitchell had stuck his finger in it. Her wrists were ringed with red welts from the bonds

Mitchell regularly superimposed on them. She had applied vinegar to the bruises, a remedy Katie had taught her. It eased the pain and swelling some, but every time she touched the tender skin she remembered—graphically—how it had become bruised and sore.

The wall would not rebuild itself. The inner pain and humiliation had returned, and although Glynna had learned to exercise some control over her emotions, she could not shut out the ill feelings. A deep, abiding hatred began to take root in her—a hatred that knew no bounds.

Kane marveled over the bulletins Samarra had printed for him. The engraving she had made was an exact replica of his sketch, the lettering precise and clear, the arrangement pleasing. She helped him prepare the ones that were to be mailed—she was also the postmistress—and thanked him sweetly for his patronage when he paid her.

"You are an unusual woman," Kane complimented her, "and a very talented one. You will never know how much I appreciate the expediency and accuracy you applied to this job."

"I just hope these advertisements help you find your young lady," she replied. "This Glynna O'Rourke must be very special to you, Mr. Rafferty."

"She is."

"I wish you good luck—and will you let me know how this all turns out?"

"Of course. And should you hear or see anything that might help me, I'm staying just down the street at Henry Wetherburn's."

Kane and Edwin had yet to uncover a shred of

evidence that indicated Glynna might now be or might recently have been in Williamsburg. They had spent the past three days circulating among the taverns, boardinghouses, and shops in this colonial capital, listening and asking questions to no avail. They had visited doctors, apothecaries, and parsons; blacksmiths, tinsmiths, and gunsmiths; bakers, storekeepers, and cabinet makers. They had ridden east to Yorktown, boarded every ship in port, and had learned from the portmaster that no ships had sailed that week. They had played cards and attended cockfights and horse races, always listening to the talk around them and making appropriate inquiries. While Kane's purse bulged with the money they had won, that was all they had to show for their time.

Kane met Edwin for lunch at Wetherburn's, gave him a handful of the flyers, and the two went their separate ways.

Their first task Friday morning had been to visit the offices of the *Virginia Gazette,* where they had made arrangements to purchase advertising space in the next edition. Now Kane made his way there again, taking with him the copper printer's-plate engraving Samarra had made. Edwin was waiting at the newly opened coach office, for a coach was due to depart for Yorktown in the early afternoon. He would post some of the flyers at the depot and send more on to the constable at Yorktown. There was an outside chance that whoever had taken Glynna would use the public coach for transportation to the port at Yorktown, which was on the York River. Investigating this possibility was worth the short delay.

Kane rode next to the governor's office, where he left more of the flyers. He readily accepted Lieutenant Reed's offer to have some of the redcoats under his command post the notices around town. Then he met Edwin at the stables, and the pair spent the afternoon canvassing places of business they had not visited before.

When they were coming out of a furniture maker's shop on Nicholson Street, Kane spied a small young woman with dark auburn tresses going into a millinery shop across the street. His heart leapt into his throat. No! It couldn't be Glynna, he knew, yet he had to find out. The street seemed a mile wide as he strode across it. Edwin followed, somewhat puzzled by Kane's haste since he had not seen the woman. Before Edwin got to the door, however, Kane came out of it, a dark scowl on his face. "Don't ask," was the only explanation he offered.

By nightfall, the two had become convinced that Glynna was not, nor had she ever been, in Williamsburg. Their high hopes dashed, they sat gloomily over supper at Wetherburn's.

"The *Gazette* is our last hope," Kane said. "If you want, you may start home tomorrow."

Edwin's eyebrows rose. "And what will you do?"

"Stay here for a few more days. Wait for the newspaper to come out."

"And then?"

"Have Samarra print more advertisements. Take them to—God! I don't know these colonies! Where should I go?" As he dropped it, Kane's fork clattered on the stoneware plate. He shook his head in dejection. "I'm not giving up, Edwin. I will not give up. If I have to go to the ends of the earth, spend the remainder of my life searching, I will not give up!"

Edwin's tone was comforting. "We'll find her,

Kane. I'm not going home tomorrow. I'll go with you."

"What about the farm?"

"To hell with the farm! Father has plenty of help. Besides, when I marry Beth, I won't be around to work for him anyway." Edwin speared the last morsel of food on his plate, laid his own fork down, and, when he had finished chewing, gave Kane his full attention. "But I think we're wasting our time. She's not here. In fact, I don't think she ever left the frontier."

"All the more reason, then, for you to go home tomorrow. I'll use the public coach for transportation, move from town to town. Whoever took her could be in Philadelphia or New York or Boston by now."

"Or Norfolk or Annapolis or Newport . . . or on his way to Charleston or Savannah. By the time you reach those places, he could have sailed with her to London or the West Indies or New Orleans."

"But there must be a trail—somewhere! She's alive, Edwin. I know she is." Kane's chin was set determinedly, and his gray eyes were obsessively bright.

"Pardon me, Mr. Rafferty." The soft, breathless voice came from Kane's side. Samarra Seldon stood there, one hand flattened against her mobile chest, the other holding an envelope. She had obviously been running. "A mailbag came from London this afternoon, and this was in it. I thought it might be important."

Kane had stood up as soon as he saw Samarra, and now he took the envelope from her proffered hand, broke the wax seal, and unfolded the missive. By the light of the candle on the table, his eyes scanned the contents, his expression changing

241

from annoyance to concern. His jaw at first tightened as he clenched his teeth, causing his temples to pulsate, and then it slackened and his complexion paled. He refolded the letter and placed it in his waistcoat pocket, then bowed low.

"My undying gratitude goes to you, dear lady, for personally delivering this missive. Were it not for your concern, it would have gone on to Cavanaugh's, and I'm not certain when I shall return there myself. Won't you join us for dessert?"

"Thank you, but I must decline," she said, her breathing now even. "My own supper is done and awaiting my return. I hope"—she paused, wondering if she was being too bold and then plunging ahead anyway—"that your news is not too distressing."

"I'm afraid it is. I must leave the colonies for Ireland on the first ship going that way."

"But your search for Miss O'Rourke—"

"I will place in the capable hands of Mr. McLaird here and those of Lieutenant Reed at the governor's office. Thank you, Sam. Thanks for everything." On impulse, he hugged her briefly, momentarily forgetting the other occupants in the public room. Stunned by his action, Samarra Seldon slowly walked away.

When they had reseated themselves, Kane motioned to the waitress, ordered a carafe of sherry, then stared at Edwin as though he were looking right through him. Edwin sat quietly, patiently awaiting an explanation. The sherry arrived, Kane poured out two glasses, downed his, then poured himself another.

"That's no way to treat good sherry," Edwin could not help observing, picking up his own glass and taking a sip.

"You're right, of course. I should have ordered Irish whiskey." He took another long draught, his head averted, his eyes staring off into nothingness.

"Are you going to tell me what's in that letter, or are you going to leave me guessing all night?"

"My father is ill. Perhaps dying. I must go home."

At that moment Glynna, too, looked without seeing. She stared listlessly into the fire as she stirred the soup one last time before ladling some of it into a bowl. This she set before Mitchell, along with a small pan of spoonbread and a tall tankard of fresh milk. She had spent the morning at the creek, washing clothes again, and the afternoon pressing them. Her eyes drooped wearily and when she breathed deeply, a sharp pain caught her between the shoulder blades. Her stomach churned, and her chest felt as if someone had tied a knot in it.

Glynna suffered from a weariness of the mind as great as that of her body. A dull void occupied her cranium, and Mitchell had to speak to her thrice before she heard him.

"You ain't eating?"

She shook her head in negation, taking only a tin cup of milk to her corner.

A grimace distorted his florid features as he swallowed a large spoonful of soup. "Don't blame you, girlie! Whatever did you put in this soup to make it so bitter?" He drank deeply from the tankard, then crumbled a large piece of spoonbread into the broth and tasted the soup again, nodding as he swallowed this bite. "That's better. Think I can eat it now."

A niggling bit of conscience pierced Glynna's lassitude. Could she sit quietly by and allow him to eat her concoction? Her right hand moved of its own accord to her wounded cheek, the fingertips pressing softly against still tender skin. Much of the discoloration had faded, leaving a dark yellow patch dappled with purple markings where the bones of his hand had struck her. Her eye was almost clear now, but it continued to manufacture healing tears that Glynna had grown tired of wiping away. It itched, too, and her vision out of it had yet to clear.

These were scars that would heal with time. The injuries he had inflicted upon her soul would never heal.

Yes. She could let him eat her soup.

She prayed that she had prepared it properly, for if she had not and he guessed her intention, she might never live to make it again.

Chapter Sixteen

How long will it take? Glynna wondered.

Mitchell had eaten two large bowls of soup, and his only reaction thus far had been a rather loud belch. She watched him covertly as she cleaned the kitchen, her movements unhurried yet marked with a nervousness she fought to control. A tin plate slipped through her fingers as she removed it from the dishpan; it bounced on the edge of the dry sink and clattered to the floor.

Mitchell ridiculed her. "What's got into you, girlie? You're as nervous as a she-cat in heat."

Glynna ignored his jeers, picked up the plate, and returned it to the dishwater, then wiped up the soapy puddle from the bare wood floor. If he would just be sick! He didn't have to die. Glynna had no real desire to kill him.

She had utilized her time at the creek that day searching out poisonous plants. The bouquet idea had seemed adequate the previous week, when she'd thought she had ample time, but she no longer could afford to allow the flowers to wilt before using them, and she dared not risk having

245

Mitchell wonder where fresh flowers had gone. Besides, he might not allow her to gather them on the way back from the creek, and then she would have to wait another whole week before being given the opportunity to go outdoors again — except to the necessary, where she was always escorted by her captor.

No, she had to devise some other method. Along the banks of the creek, she had found Indian hemp growing, its clusters of greenish-white flowers clinging to the ends of thin branches. She recalled that Katie had once said this plant belonged to the same family as oleander. She knew oleander to be poisonous, so maybe Indian hemp was, too. And its leaves had the added advantage of resembling those of sweet bay. She had gathered a handful and tied them in a handkerchief, which she'd secreted inside the waistline of the salmon-colored gown. The linen towel she had knotted around her middle had held the bundle securely while the excess fabric of the bodice camouflaged its slight bulk.

Mitchell did not make a habit of checking food as it cooked, but that was another risk she dared not take. A distillation of leaves, roots, berries, or flowers would have served her purpose better, but that required time, equipment, and privacy. She had none of these. So she used the leaves of the Indian hemp, hoping, should he spy them, that Mitchell would think they were those of the sweet bay, which were often used for seasoning. Her caution had been unnecessary; even their bitterness he had dismissed as evidence of her deficient culinary talents.

Had simmering the leaves in the soup's broth provided adequate poison? she wondered anew, her thoughts racing ahead to the problem of dealing with Lucifer should the soup accomplish its intention.

Kane Rafferty lay awake in his room at Henry Wetherburn's Tavern, his open palms cradling his head, his eyes staring through the gloom to the shadowy ceiling overhead, his thoughts muddled. A myriad of questions pricked his consciousness, their niggling dagger points effectively eliminating relaxation. He coerced the fragmented questions into some semblance of order so he could manage them with sound logic and reasoning.

He chose first to deal with his most recent revelation—that of his father's alleged illness. Had his mother written the letter Samarra had delivered that evening, Kane would not have doubted its veracity. But Valerie had penned the missive, and Valerie he did not trust. In the privacy of his room, he had reread the letter several times, his agile mind scrutinizing its contents for proof of fabrication. She had used his mother's distraught state as justification for writing in Catherine's stead. Though his mother generally remained calm in the face of adversity, he could believe her composure had disintegrated—if what Valerie had written was true.

Kane did not want to think of his father as afflicted with apoplexy which caused the loss of a good portion of his mental faculties as well as physical control over the right side of his body. If such were the case, Catherine had ample reason to be distraught. According to Valerie, his mother would allow no one else to tend Thomas Rafferty, and Kane could not help being concerned for

247

Catherine's health as well as that of his father. He thought of Darcie Cavanaugh's constant care of her son, her refusal to leave Brian's side for more than a few minutes at a time, her wilted appearance and weary countenance.

Although he did not relish the possibility, Kane had to consider the fact that his father might not live long enough to see his eldest again. Valerie's letter had been brief, her message urgent. Catherine needed Kane by her side, regardless of the outcome. He could not ignore the situation, could not shirk his responsibility to his parents, to his heritage, no matter how much he wanted to remain in Virginia at present.

The tie of blood called him home, but the tether of love bade him stay. No matter what happened with his father, Kane silently vowed to return to Virginia—and to the unexpected jewel he had found nestled in the velvety clutches of the wilderness, a jewel of far greater value than the ones his mother had sent him to find.

That this priceless jewel might be lost to him forever, he refused to consider. She was alive—he knew it, deep down in his gut he knew it. And he was certain that someday they would be reunited.

With that gossamer thread of reassurance keeping him sane, Kane Rafferty finally succumbed to the rest his body and soul so desperately needed.

Glynna's hopes plummeted with every step she made up the stairs to Mitchell's bedchamber. Throughout the evening his health had remained hearty; if anything, it seemed to have improved. His color was high, his spirits higher, his grating laughter echoing through the house. Perhaps he mopped his sweaty brow a bit more often than usual; perhaps he guzzled more of his watered-down rum—"baptized brew," he called it. But the evening was quite warm and humid, and Glynna found herself sweatier and thirstier than was her wont.

By the time they reached the landing, however, Mitchell had begun to sway, the flame of the candle in his hand flickering precariously. "My God, it's hot!" he bellowed. "And I left my flask below. Go fetch it."

Glynna retrieved the candle from his bedside table, used the one he held to ignite it, and left him standing on the landing as she descended the staircase. Lucifer's snarl caused her to start when she entered the parlor, but the mongrel made no move to prohibit her from retrieving the flask. She longed to fetch herself another dipper of water from the kitchen, started toward that room, then abruptly halted as Lucifer sat up, his pointed ears pricked, his teeth bared. The snarl changed to a low growl, was suddenly joined by a piercing scream from upstairs, and Lucifer bolted from the room.

"You mustn't tell anyone about this," Galen demanded, his dark eyes narrowed in anger.

"No, Galen. Not this time." Darcie's voice was gentle and soft as always, but firm. "Our past is riddled with secrets, and we're neither running nor hiding from the truth, not ever again."

Glynna could not recall her aunt's ever contradicting Galen before, at least not since she had come to live with them. She sat up straighter in her chair, her gaze ricocheting between the pair with her in the dimly lit keeping hall. Her uncle's shoulders sagged, deep furrows etched his brow, and his mouth was tight and grim. In contrast, Darcie sat ramrod straight, her hands folded in her lap, her blue eyes soft with concern.

Although it was well past midnight, Darcie had made a fresh pot of tea, and the three found some small measure of comfort in the hot, sweet liquid. For want of nothing better to do, Glynna picked up the spoon and stirred her tea. She should have been tired, she knew, but though her spirit was weary, her brain refused to grant her surcease.

Without having been told, Glynna knew her uncle carried memories of some threat from a past he pretended was nonexistent. What crime had sent him halfway around the world, causing him to uproot his family and leave his ancestral home? Whatever it was, it had almost caught up with him in Williamsburg, but he had run again. Would they tell her now, or would they merely use the past as an example of what not to do in the future?

"Our daughter's reputation will be ruined," she heard him argue, her thoughts centering on his calling her daughter—the first time he had ever done so in her presence. "No one will believe she wasn't ravished."

"Kane Rafferty will believe it."

Glynna realized with a shock that it was she who had uttered these words. Encouraged by her own boldness, she continued, "And he's the only other person, besides you two, who matters." Oh, she realized, Katie counted, and so did Beth and Edwin, but they were her friends. They would believe her. They would support her. People like Mother McLaird were going to believe the worst anyway, and nothing she or Galen or Darcie could do or say would change their minds.

"What good will come of besmirching Samuel Mitchell's name?" Galen argued, but he could see from the set faces of the two women before him that his position was weakening.

"What story would you concoct, Galen, to replace the truth?" Darcie countered. "I see no way to be clear of this matter short of running away again. And why should we be forced to leave our home for the sake of a dead man's reputation?" She sighed wearily. "Glynna has journeyed to hell and back, Galen. God has seen fit to remove the devil's spawn from our midst. Let's leave it at that."

In the days that followed, Glynna began to realize how accurate Darcie's observation had been. If hell was anything like the ten days she had spent with Samuel Mitchell, she didn't ever want to go there permanently. The horror of that time shadowed her every move, and she could not seem to shake her skittishness. She had never been fond of dogs, but now she abhorred them. The only ones Galen owned were sheepdogs—calm, placid animals, she knew, yet she could not bring herself to go near them. One morning Darcie found Glynna in the root cellar, screaming at the top of her lungs. Later, she could not recall why she had gone there. She refused to ride Sheena and never wanted to be alone, even at night. An extra bed was moved into her room, and Rosie, one of Katie's daughters, slept there.

But the thing that bothered Glynna most was fire. Even the tiny flame of a candle made her shiver.

When Kane comes back, she told herself, every-

251

thing will be all right.

The days and nights blended into each other as she waited for him. She had begged Galen to travel to Williamsburg, but he had shrugged away her concern for her tutor. "You'll be here when he gets back," he had said. "He and Edwin are most likely on their way home now. They must have learned that you weren't taken to the coast, and I cannot believe they would dally. Your Mr. Rafferty seems to be a sensible man, and I know Edwin McLaird to be one."

She occupied herself with assisting Darcie in caring for Brian. The child had greeted her ecstatically. "Oh, Glynna," he had gushed, tears of joy welling in his blue eyes, "you're home!" Darcie insisted that he had begun to improve remarkably from the second he saw her. "We all worried about you, but no one suffered from your absence the way Brian did," she said.

He was, indeed, nearing full recovery. His back would remain forever scarred, but better his back than certain other portions of his anatomy, they all agreed.

Glynna could not help thinking how fire had shaped so much of her own life. Her parents had been killed in a blaze, and now another had proved the instrument of her salvation.

She never knew exactly how the fire had started at Mitchell's place. He must have fallen upon the bed with the lighted candle in his hand. He had been unsteady on his feet when she had left him. At times, Glynna castigated herself for not running upstairs to his aid. She had gone back to his room, but she had not hurried to get there, though the noxious odor of burning feathers and the roar of the flames consuming the bed had alerted her to the cause of Mitchell's screams. And he had screamed. Over and over, loudly and pitifully.

I murdered him, she thought, feeling completely liable for his death. The poisonous leaves of the Indian hemp had done their work, attacking his central nervous system, causing the hot flashes, extreme thirst, and partial delirium. She could not have explained this, but she knew the poison was responsible for the lack of self-control that was responsible for his dying in the fire. For days—and nights—one thought haunted her. *I murdered him.*

Katie found her huddled on one of the garden benches late one afternoon, sobbing so hard she had started to hiccough. The cook went down on her knees and pulled Glynna into her massive embrace, hugging her and crooning to her until the sobs subsided. "I knows 'xactly what you be needin'," Katie told her then, helping Glynna to her feet and guiding her into the kitchen where she made a pot of chamomile tea to soothe Glynna's distress.

Glynna had not told Darcie and Galen every gruesome detail of her captivity. Some parts she had omitted because she could not bring herself to talk about them, some cruelties she had blocked out of her memory; but the guilt she carried for Mitchell's death was her most guarded secret. Although she trusted her aunt and uncle, Glynna feared the consequences of discovery. Others had swung from the gallows pole for lesser offenses.

Katie's meaty hand covered Glynna's fine-boned one, her black thumb gently rubbing the knuckles along the back of it as she said, "Tell ole Katie 'bout it, chile. You needs to git it out."

"I can't, Katie." Glynna shook her head despairingly, a tear rolling out of her eye and trickling down her cheek. "It's too awful."

"It cain't be that bad, missy. You wouldn've kilt him delib'rately."

Glynna batted her damp eyelashes, her gaze scrutinizing the round, ebony face that mirrored her friend's knowledge. How . . . how did you know?" she gulped.

"I know you didn't set that fire, so why you so upset?"

"I . . . I didn't even try to save him."

"And die yo'self?" Katie laughed then, a warm, comfortable sound in the stillness of the kitchen. Glynna listened to it reverberate in the brick room, heard the bubbling in the pots hanging over the fire, heard the fire crackle and pop, heard a piece of wood fall into the ashes as it burned in two. And she was soothed by it all. A hint of a smile touched her lips for the first time since she had come home.

"What are you laughing about, Katie?"

"The thought of itty-bitty you tryin' to haul that horse of a man out of that room!"

Glynna's face clouded then. "Lucifer tried to do just that."

"And what did that mangy ole cur git for his efforts?"

"He died, too." Her voice was flat and dull.

Katie poured the herb tea and handed Glynna a cup. They sat quietly for a few minutes, sipping the tea, listening to the frogs croak and the crickets chirp, and watching the room grow dark as the sun went down behind the mountains.

Katie's mellow voice broke the silence. "Seems to me he did it to hisself. Leading a double life that way. God was bound to strike him down sooner or later. Lucky for you it came when it did. I jes' wish it had come sooner."

"God didn't poison him."

The words hung in the eerie stillness. Glynna wished she could have called them back. Now she was done for. As soon as she said them, she hung her head, fixing her gaze upon the gray stonewear mug and watching steam rise from her tea. If she had glanced up, she would have witnessed the barely suppressed merriment in Katie's black eyes and the twitching of her ample mouth.

"What'd you use for poison?"

Why not tell her? "Indian hemp leaves."

"How'd you git him to eat 'em?"

"Cooked some in the soup."

Katie coughed, and then began to hiccough herself as she choked on her laughter. "And you think that did it?"

Glynna looked up then, saw the twinkle in Katie's eyes. "No?"

"Not 'less you fed him a pan full of 'em, and they's so bitter you'd had to hog-tie him and force 'em down his throat."

"Then why?"

"Imbibin' the spirits, mos' likely."

They broke into gales of laughter, reaching for each other's hands and squeezing them tightly. All the tears in the world could not have cleansed Glynna's soul as that laughter did.

The grapevine of gossip is strong and far-reaching. Despite the distance between the farms surrounding Cavanaugh's Tavern, word got around. By the time Sunday arrived, virtually everyone knew about Reverend Mitchell's death and

Glynna's safe return home. Since the two had occurred at the same time, people drew their own conclusions. The permanent residents at Cavanaugh's knew about the grapevine. Glynna did not expect anyone to come to Sunday services until Mitchell had been replaced, but Darcie warned her they would come anyway—out of natural curiosity if nothing else. Galen had asked Deacon McLaird to prepare and conduct a memorial service for Samuel Mitchell, thus nurturing the grapevine and further encouraging the members of the community to come on Sunday.

And come they did.

Glynna wasn't sure who hugged the other tighter—she or Beth. They clung to each other all day, Beth protecting her best friend from cruel gossip as best she could. There was no protection from the accusing stares, the hushed whispers, but Glynna had anticipated worse.

The memorial service consumed the morning. After dinner, the men rode over to Mitchell's farm and began to clear away the debris, even though it was Sunday. These men had their own work to tend to during the week, and most of them had already spent a good deal of time away from their farms searching for Glynna. Earlier in the week, Galen had sent a few of his slaves to retrieve the cow, the draft horse, and the hogs and chickens. Glynna had ridden Gabriel home that fateful Monday night, so now all of Mitchell's farm animals were sheltered at the tavern.

The fire had been confined to the farmhouse, the outbuildings being too far away to suffer damage on that windless night. But no one knew of any kin Mitchell might have had, and any will he might have written had probably burned with the house. Prior to the memorial service, the men had met briefly in the gentlemen's parlor to discuss the disposition of Mitchell's remaining possessions. They decided that the fairest thing to do would be to hold an auction, then place the money in trust and later apply it to the building and maintenance of a meetinghouse at some future date. In the event someone came forth and claimed to be the minister's heir, that person would have to accept the money as his inheritance.

While the men were gone, Glynna and Beth escaped to Glynna's bedchamber. Sensing her friend's reluctance to discuss the details of the incarceration at Mitchell's hand, Beth filled the afternoon with bright chatter about nothing in particular. Glynna was certain the matrons were pumping Darcie for information, but she knew her aunt could be evasive if the situation called for it.

Glynna's main source of distress had nothing to do with the nosy matrons closeted in the ladies' parlor. She pined for Kane Rafferty—for his companionship, his tutoring, and yes, she admitted, his kisses. Beth, she discovered, harbored similar feelings brought on by Edwin's prolonged absence.

The two men should already have been back.

Though Glynna and Beth both knew this and could not set aside their concerns for the men's safety and well-being, this was another subject they purposely avoided.

It rained again Sunday night—a soft, gentle rain that nourished the fast-growing crops and purified the air, giving it a sweet scent. Monday morning, however, brought an unrelenting summer sun intent on absorbing the moisture left by the rain. A glittering haze pervaded the lower atmosphere, making both vision and breathing difficult.

Glynna was sitting with Brian when she heard the ruckus downstairs. "I'll be all right," he assured her. "I promise not to move. Go and see what's happening."

A large wagon laden with the goods Galen had ordered from Williamsburg had pulled up in front of the tavern. Glynna stood on the second-floor balcony and watched her uncle supervising the unloading. She had to squint to see through the brilliant haze, and she did not understand for a moment the significance of the wagon's arrival.

The realization of it came swiftly. *Williamsburg!* She could not descend the stairs quickly enough. If Kane was not with these men, then maybe he had sent word. She had to find out.

Her heart pounded in her chest, but she took no note of its hard palpitations as she rushed outside. She paused briefly on the porch, her sparkling green gaze quickly surveying the men busily unloading the wagon. One of them straightened, and her heart lurched. No one else was that tall.

"Edwin!" she called, her legs moving swiftly again as she ran toward him.

He almost dropped the wooden crate in his arms when he saw her. He did drop his gaze—all the way to the toes of his boots. "I . . . I was coming up to . . . to see you," he stammered nervously. "Right after I took this crate inside. I brought some things to Mother, and I didn't want them mixed up with your uncle's things." It was a lame excuse, he knew, for the crate he held was marked McLaird in bold black letters. He was attempting to purchase time, time to bolster his courage before he faced her.

He moved around Glynna, his long legs taking him toward the house. She looked around, saw neither Kane nor his horse, then turned and followed Edwin.

"Where is he?" she demanded.

"Where is who?"

"Edwin McLaird, you stop right there and answer me! You know *who!*"

He seemed to wilt before her eyes, his shoulders remaining slumped even after he set the crate upon the porch floor, his eyelids hooding his gaze. Let's go inside," he said, opening the door wide for her.

Something was wrong. A hard little knot pulled at her stomach, and her throat felt thick.

They sat at a table in the ordinary and Edwin stared at its polished surface. The little speech he had planned deserted him. Glynna forced the hated question from her throat. "Is he dead?"

Edwin took a deep breath and let it out slowly. "No," was all he managed.

Glynna was becoming exasperated. "Then where is he, Edwin?"

There was no brooking the command in her voice now, but still he avoided answering her directly. "He wrote you a letter." Edwin brought forth the epistle, which was folded with one of the advertisements, from inside his waistcoat. "This explains everything."

Chapter Seventeen

The lazy tide of long summer days dragged by, pulling Glynna with it toward a private isle of eternal refuge. She went willingly, inundating herself in the delusion of activity while subconsciously allowing the floodwaters of despair to drown her spirit, their whirlpool drawing her deeper and deeper into the vortex of her soul.

Once Brian was able to be up and about, Darcie went back to work at turning the former storage room into a general store. Glynna assisted her, utilizing her eye for line and color to create pleasing displays while Darcie set up account books and mulled over inventories. Brian's morning lessons were resumed, Galen's mill was completed, and the McGintys' relatives from the Shenandoah Valley finally came to collect them.

Darcie and Galen hosted a farewell party for the couple on a fine Saturday in early July. The McGintys had become fixtures at the tavern, and everyone in the community hated to see them leave. Huge barbecue pits had been dug between the kitchen and the slave quarters; spitted above these were a rack of venison, several legs of lamb, and a dozen chickens. The womenfolk brought fresh vegetables from their gardens, a variety of jarred sauces and relishes, and desserts of every description. Everyone brought a small and, in most cases, practical gift for the McGintys.

As was the custom, the men gathered around the pits, discussing politics and farming, while the women cared for the smaller children and prepared the tables the slaves had moved outdoors. The McGintys' relatives provided additional news of the trouble brewing beyond the mountains, and this served as the major topic of conversation among both groups. Since no word had as yet been received from Williamsburg concerning the governor's disposition on the matter, the men decided to send Dinwiddie another message.

The celebration ended with a dance, a high-stepping, foot-stomping affair to the accompaniment of violin and harpsichord, that was in no way reminiscent of the formal ball held a few months before.

Nevertheless, Glynna remembered the ball, and though Beth and Edwin begged her to join in the lively jigs and reels, she insisted on remaining seated at the sidelines.

It was in the midst of this joyous occasion that Edwin announced his betrothal to Beth. Their marriage vows would be solemnized in the ballroom in early August, and since Beth asked Glynna to be her maid of honor, the two began to spend more time together than they were routinely allowed, sewing their dresses, fashioning their headpieces, and planning the decorations and refreshments. Beth's activity was characterized by her usual zest, augmented by excitement over the upcoming event. In contrast, Glynna pasted a smile on her face and performed her tasks with false enthusiasm. Her absent-mindedness made her industrious facade transparent, but she staunchly refused to allow herself the pain of feeling.

Without a conscious attempt, the invisible wall of self-preservation had been rebuilt, and nothing short of Kane Rafferty's return would bring it down.

Katie's shrewd counsel had effectively dispelled the guilt Glynna had carried, and a large measure of her anxiety. She had begun to ride Sheena again, but did not ride far—and never without an escort. Josh, the lazy stableboy, accompanied her with uncharacteristic alacrity, for his mistress required nothing more of him than his presence. Her days she peopled with those she loved and trusted, shrinking from the very thought of being left alone with her swirling emotions, from the deep-seated fear of being, again, taken against her will.

In contrast, she embraced the hours of darkness as one would a long and trusted friend. This attitude was due, perhaps, to a combination of facts. She slept alone—Rosie snored, and the flighty girl would more than likely prove to be an ineffective bodyguard anyway. There was a lock on her door, in which she turned her key nightly. Brian and Darcie and Galen were near enough to hear her scream should she need them, and, finally, her mind and body required some measure of solitude and privacy. Regardless of the reason or the combination of reasons—none of which Glynna consciously acknowledged—Rosie's bed had been removed from Glynna's chamber. And she now slept peacefully for the most part, her deep, dreamless slumber induced by toddies Katie concocted of honey and rum.

The one fear Glynna could not seem to eradicate was that of dogs. Even the sight of playful puppies sent her into paroxysms of terror, for she saw them not as babies but as the adult animals they would become. In her mind, they all had long gray coats, yellow eyes, and sharp, pointed teeth. The rational part of her knew that Lucifer was dead, that he could never snarl at her or attack her again. But rationality did not control her emotions.

Dogs she could avoid. Beth's insistence that she attend their house-raising she could not.

Glynna had stayed home the day of the auction, and she had asked no questions concerning its outcome. If Galen had purchased anything of Mitchell's, she didn't want to know about it. When Beth told her that Edwin had bought Mitchell's farm, however, she experienced a feeling of dread that made her fear of dogs pale in comparison.

She had thought Edwin would build a house on a piece of McLaird property, which was close enough to the tavern for Glynna and Beth to enjoy weekday visits. They had talked about how wonderful this proximity would be for both of them. Although Beth had known about Edwin's purchase, she had not apprised Glynna of it until the plans for the house-raising were announced.

"How could you, Beth?" Glynna wailed.

Her friend looked at her askance. "How could I what?"

"How could you agree to live on that man's property, knowing what he was, what he did? How could Edwin buy it? I thought you and

Edwin were my friends. And why did you wait so long to tell me?"

Beth laid her sewing aside and reached for Glynna, hugging her close and waiting until the tremors had left her friend's small frame before answering. "We were trying to give you time to readjust, to overcome your nightmare. You may as well know Edwin and I both discussed this move at length. We considered your reaction, but we mutually agreed that it was what we wanted."

Glynna pulled away from Beth's arms as though she had been stung. "How could you?" she repeated, her voice revealing her feeling of betrayal, her green eyes awash with unshed tears, her jaw set mutinously.

Refusing to let go of Glynna completely, Beth let her hands trail the length of her friend's arms and then grasped Glynna's hands in her own. Her countenance as well as her voice pleaded for understanding. "We didn't intend to hurt you. But just think of what this purchase is saving us. The property has been cleared, the outbuildings are intact, the creek is nearby, and we'll be close to the tavern. But most of all, we won't be so close to Mother McLaird. We can't live our lives in her shadow, Glynna. This way, we'll have our own piece of land. *Ours,* Glynna! Our house will be different. And the place lacks a woman's touch. In a few years, when my flowers and shrubs have taken root, you won't even recognize it."

Beth had watched Glynna's reactions closely as she'd talked, and had noted a slight yielding to reason, a loosening of her set jaw, a softening in her green eyes. "Come to the house-raising," she implored. "I want you there . . . I *need* you there. Please say yes."

Glynna agreed only to think about it.

But she went. On the surface she insisted her action stemmed from her love and respect for both Beth and Edwin, but, deep down, she knew her attendance marked a milestone in her emotional recovery. If she could go back to that farm, there wasn't any other mental obstacle she couldn't surmount.

Except, perhaps, her grief over Kane's return to Ireland. In her mind, he had deserted her in her hour of greatest need, and Glynna did not honestly believe he would ever come back to Virginia.

Kane had booked passage on a merchantman bound for Dublin and Liverpool, the color of his coin buying him the most commodious passenger quarters available. Even then, his cabin was small, his bunk hard, the food barely making up in edibility what it lacked in plentitude. He spent much of his time on deck, drawing in great gulps of salty air and soaking up health-giving rays of sunlight. By the time he disembarked in Dublin, his complexion glowed with a deep bronze hue, the darkening of his skin seeming to lighten his gray eyes and make his teeth appear even whiter.

Despite his healthy glow, Kane felt anything but healthy. Never before had he experienced heartache, but he felt it now. Not knowing what had happened to Glynna, whether she had yet been found—whether she was even alive—tore at his insides. During the twenty-seven days he had spent aboard ship—and he had counted every one of them—his thoughts had vacillated between the love of his life and the condition in which he would find his father when he reached the estate.

He took the overland coach from Dublin to Galway, chafing at the slow pace of the draft horses, wishing he had been lucky enough to find a ship heading to Galway Bay in the first place. He left the coach at the village of Athenry, some fifteen miles east of the western coast, and hired a horse, which he rode to his father's estate ten miles north of the village.

For the past several days, rest had eluded him. The closer he came to his father, the more his thoughts centered on his parents—and his future. What if Thomas Rafferty were dead? Kane had to consider the possibility. Would his younger brother, Michael, accept the title of Baron of Ulrich and assume his father's place in Kane's stead? Had Michael any inclination toward supervising the estate or becoming a member of Parliament? Kane wished he had spent more time with his brother, that he knew him better. Ten years his junior, Michael had been but a lad when Kane had left Ireland for the university. By the time Kane had come home from his extended Grand Tour, Michael himself was away at school. As Kane jounced across hill and dale atop the rented horse, he realized with chagrin that he did not know his brother.

Or his sister either, for that matter.

Alaina he remembered as a bright, precocious child who seemed never to be still. She had had a mass of red-gold curls, and as she'd grown, they had lengthened into natural ringlets, their color, if possible, intensifying. She had also had a penchant for bobbing her head, making her ringlets bounce into disarray so that Catherine was hard put to keep them arranged neatly. When Kane had been home, she had pestered him with a myriad of questions, her curiosity insatiable.

And that was the sum total of what he knew of Alaina. He wasn't even sure how old she was now—only that she was younger than Michael.

A little better than halfway from Athenry to the baron's estate, Kane's horse threw a shoe. He slowed his pace in deference to the exposed hoof, cursing under his breath at the further delay. The hour had grown late, the sun now making its final descent into the oblivion of the horizon. He had been forced to wait almost a week in Williamsburg before the ship embarked, had spent a night in Dublin awaiting the departure of the coach and another on the road to Galway. Taking everything into consideration, he supposed he could not have made better connections, and yet an urgency to arrive at his home nagged at him, pushed him on, drove him.

Just after midday on July 16, 1753, the *Charming Bess* dropped anchor in the York River, having sailed to Virginia by way of Barbados. Using the quarterdeck as a rehearsal stage on calm days, the members of the Prescott theatrical troupe had practiced their roles—to the delight of the off-duty sailors. Now that they had finally arrived in the New World, they were forced to wait on board ship while their manager, William Prescott, went ashore to make arrangements for their transportation to Williamsburg.

On July 18, the *Virginia Gazette* carried an announcement that the Prescott Company had arrived in Williamsburg "with a select Company of Comedians. The Scenes, Cloaths and Decorations are all entirely new, extremely rich, and finished in the highest Taste. The Scenes having been painted by the best Hands in London are excell'd by none in Beauty and Elegance, so that the Ladies and Gentlemen may depend on being entertain'd in as polite a Manner as at the Theatres in London, the Company being perfected in all the best Plays, Operas, Farces, and pantomimes that have been exhibited in any of the Theatres for these ten years past."

Prescott had obtained Governor Dinwiddie's permission to perform before he had leased the forty-year-old playhouse on the Palace Green, which the actors set about remodeling. They planned to put on their opening performance— *The Merchant of Venice*—in early fall, just in time to take advantage of the crowds coming to town for the October Court.

The members of the troupe were amazed at Jarvis Whitfield's sudden propensity for laziness, at his slovenly workmanship when he did deign to appear at the playhouse. He had worked so hard, so diligently, in London, but now that they had reached their destination, he seemed to have lost interest. He had also grown short-tempered at rehearsals, showing little tolerance for those who failed to perform well or forgot their lines. The actors began to shun his company, which suited him fine. As soon as he learned the whereabouts of Galen Carmichael, he was leaving Williamsburg anyway. Prescott would just have to find someone else to play Shylock.

A thunderous booming stirred Catherine Rafferty from a deep sleep. She rolled over, burying her face in her pillow and pulling its softness over her ears in an attempt to shut out the incessant noise.

As abruptly as it had begun, the thunder ceased, and she relaxed once more, snuggling deeper into the feather mattress and taking deep, cleansing breaths that brought her near to total repose until once more she was disturbed by thunder. This time it was closer, its intensity and strength rattling the diamond-shaped panes concealed by heavy velvet draperies. Instinctively, she reached for Thomas, her hand grasping air before falling upon the empty muslin sheet.

The resounding roll seemed to be coming from the bowels of the house, so loudly did it bellow. Even the heavy oak portal that sealed her chamber clattered on its hinges, and a voice as deep as the thunder itself bade permission to enter.

Oh my God! What has happened? The thought flew across her brain, sweeping away the cobwebs as she threw back the lightweight cover and reached for candle and flintbox, her trembling hands making several attempts before succeeding in producing a light.

"Mother, please, open this door!" the masculine voice demanded, and she called out so Michael would know she was up.

Behind the heavy door, additional voices joined those of her son, giving further indication that something was amiss. Had lightning struck a tree? she wondered. Or perhaps the stables? The thunderous approach of the storm seemed to have subsided now. She fought the urge to pull back the heavy drapes and see for herself what was causing the furor, instead pulling on her dressing gown and hurrying across the room.

A small group huddled in the hallway just outside her chamber door. Michael stood with his back to her, his arms locked around a trembling Alaina, who was squalling loudly. Catherine raised her candle, its flame illuminating the faces of those behind her daughter: Hadley, the butler, in his nightcap and robe; Mrs. Beaumont, the housekeeper, her wire-rimmed glasses upon her nose; and Michael, coming toward her, his hands gently pushing the beloved servants aside.

Michael! If the man whose back was turned to her, the man clutching Alaina was not Michael, then who . . .

A small gasp erupted from her throat. *No! It can't be!*

But it was. He disengaged himself from Alaina's embrace and turned around, his countenance a study in contrasts: a mixture of delight and chagrin.

"Mother!" her eldest exclaimed, taking the candle from her and handing it to Alaina, then pulling Catherine into his now-empty arms and squeezing her tightly. She felt his heart pound against her own throbbing chest, felt the hot rush as tears escaped her eyes; and she melted against his tall leanness. He smelled of horseflesh and leather, and Catherine thought she had never smelled anything so delightful. Kane's hands slid from her back to her upper arms, grasping them and gently pushing her away. The embrace ended all too quickly for her, and she raised her tear-streaked face to his troubled visage, her own gaze searching his for an explanation for this sudden distance. What had happened to distress him so much? Why had he come home now?

His gray eyes stared past her, into her bedchamber, fixing upon the empty bed. She watched his jaw clench, saw the sheen of unshed tears moisten his eyes. "I'm too late," he whispered, his voice laden with a combination of sadness, pathos, and regret.

Catherine peered around him, saw on the faces in the hallway a lack of comprehension. "Too late for what, Kane?" she asked quietly.

"Father."

She waited, but her son offered no further comment. "What about your father, Kane?"

He swallowed hard, his Adam's apple working in his throat. "When . . . when did he go?"

Catherine frowned in puzzlement at his obvious discomfiture. "Four days ago."

His voice broke then, and he let go of her arms to place his head in his open palms. Deep sobs racked his tall frame while his mother stood helplessly in front of him, wishing she knew what demon caused his grief. "I came so close!" he railed, his splayed hands suddenly leaving his face and reaching ceilingward, his handsome features contorted in rage. "Damn! If I had just gotten here sooner!"

Catherine touched his cheek, her gentle fingers wiping away a tear. "You know your father's business takes him away from time to time, Kane. There's no cause for such anger," she offered soothingly, still confused by her son's attitude.

Kane acted as though he didn't hear her. "I should have been here, Mother. I should have been here for him. And for you—and for me. Don't you understand?"

"No, Kane, I don't. You're talking as though he were dead. He merely went to Dublin on some matter concerning the estate accounts. He should be home tomorrow, or the following day at the very latest."

Kane's arms slowly fell to his sides, and he shook his head sluggishly. "Don't trifle with my feelings, Mother. I can cope with the truth."

"I wouldn't lie to you, Kane."

He turned around then, searched the faces of those behind him and saw mirrored in them the truth his mother spoke. "Goddamn Valerie Sherman's hide to hell! That bitch lied to me!" He clenched his fists tightly at his sides, and his gray eyes turned to steel. "And she may not live long enough to regret it!"

"You owe my mother your undying gratitude for being alive," Kane told Valerie the next morning. "When I discovered your 'little white lie,' as you put it, I wanted to wring your neck. Do you have any inkling of what mental anguish you have put me through—over *nothing?*"

Valerie batted her long, honey-colored lashes at him and turned up the corners of her full, pink mouth into a smile intended to charm. "It was the only way I knew to get you home, where you belong, darling. You'll get over being angry with me in a few days and realize I did the right thing." Butter would not have melted in her mouth.

"Don't hold your breath, Miss Sherman!" Kane snapped, turning on his heel and stalking away from her.

"Kane!" she called, her voice suddenly panic-stricken. "Don't leave yet! Molly is bringing some refreshment, and I do so want to hear about your adventures in Virginia."

His right hand already on the doorknob, he

stopped and twisted his head around to bestow upon her a withering glare. "What you don't seem to understand, Valerie, is that I don't *ever* want to lay my eyes upon you again. I was telling the truth—*I* don't lie—when I said that my mother is responsible for your continued good health. She did talk me out of killing you. But that was only part of the truth. I lay awake most of the night, thinking about your little prevarication, about how much you want to become the next Baroness of Ulrich, and I realized that is all you want. Not me, just the title. I also realized that the best punishment I could inflict upon you would be to deny you that opportunity—now and forever. Good-bye, Valerie."

He left her then, her pink mouth agape, her eyes narrowed in anger. You'll be sorry for this, Kane Rafferty, she silently vowed. You'll be sorry. If it's the last thing I ever do, I'll make you pay for this.

Kane did regale his family with an edited account of his sojourn in the colony of Virginia. They laughed with him over Mrs. McGinty's chickens and over his mistaking Glynna for a serving girl, but they glowed with parental and sibling pride when he told them about fighting the fire at the McGinty's farm and then of saving Brian from being burned to death. Their hearts ached with his when they learned of Glynna's disappearance and of his attempts to find her. Although he avoided discussing his true feelings for Glynna, not knowing how well his family would accept his living permanently in Virginia, his love for her shone through his every word, his every

273

expression.

When he had been home a week, Kane and his father rode over to Galway to check on the availability of passage on a ship heading for the colonies. They found the *White Wave* in port and learned from her captain that she would set sail for Annapolis, Maryland, in another fortnight, or thereabouts. Once he reached the New World, Kane would have to secure his own transportation to the colony of Virginia, but the captain assured him this would not be a problem as a number of colonial boats worked the coastline, and Kane should be able to take one of these to Yorktown.

Having seen his family and assured himself they were all healthy and happy, Kane wanted desperately to return to the Virginia frontier, to see Glynna again if he could find her and to be assured of her health and well-being. His family appeared to understand this desperate need and did not scold him for leaving so soon.

Later that evening, Thomas Rafferty summoned his eldest to his study. When Kane was comfortably seated and Thomas had poured each of them a snifter of brandy, he got right to the point.

"I went to the post office while we were in Galway today, and this was there waiting for me." He had removed a letter from his desk drawer as he'd talked, and now he handed it to his son.

Kane's heart lurched when he recognized the handwriting. It was Glynna's. She must have been found while he was still in Williamsburg for a letter to have gotten to Ireland so quickly. He sat for a moment with his eyes closed, absorbing this thought, letting the waves of relief wash over him, through him, the hand with which he held the letter trembling with joy.

"I think you had better read it, son, before you go jumping to conclusions," Thomas quietly suggested.

A part of Kane heard the warning in his father's voice, yet he refused to acknowledge it. He swirled the amber liquid Thomas had provided, sipped it, and felt its pleasant warmth trickle down to his stomach before he opened the parchment. His eyes traveled first to the date, just a few days prior to Glynna's disappearance, and then to the salutation.

His spirits plummeted. He should have known better, he mentally fretted. But why had she written to the baron?

With questioning eyes he read through the letter, lifted his puzzled gaze to his father for a moment, then read it again, this time more slowly, allowing the meaning of Glynna's written words to penetrate.

"I . . . I don't understand," he choked out. "I thought she loved me, too."

The fourteenth Baron of Ulrich looked long and hard at the son he had thought for thirty-four years would be the fifteenth Rafferty to carry the title. "She does love you, Kane. Were that fact not obvious, I would not have shown you her letter."

"But she wants me replaced."

"No, Kane. Read the letter again. She wants you removed—or she thinks she does."

"But why?"

"Because she's afraid. Love is a very powerful emotion, and when one experiences it for the first time, it can be extremely frightening. Loving someone else wholly and completely requires sacrifice. Your Glynna may not be quite ready to relinquish her entire self and the remainder of her life to you, but she will in time. Trust me on this matter." Thomas paused, sipping his brandy as he watched doubt register on Kane's features. "You may not be ready yet, either. But there's another sacrifice we need to discuss right now. Mine."

Chapter Eighteen

"It was a beautiful wedding, wasn't it, Glynna?"

"I'm sorry. I wasn't paying attention. What did you say?"

Beth cast her pale blue eyes upon her dearest friend, regretfully acknowledging Glynna's wan features, the dullness of her green eyes, her extreme thinness. Everyone had thought she would bounce back, but Glynna had yet to exhibit any resiliency. Instead of lessening her distress, the passage of time seemed to worsen it. Glynna had pulled herself deeper into her shell, and those who loved her were becoming more than a little bit concerned about her mental stability. They had granted her enough time, enough space. The time for interference had come.

The long summer was drawing to a close, gradually giving way to shorter days and cooler nights as autumn approached. The sumac leaves had already turned a bright red, and the maples wouldn't be far behind.

Beth wanted to say, "He'll be back, Glynna. Have faith. Kane loves you." But it would just be a repetition of previous assurances—assurances which upset Glynna more than they comforted her. Instead, she said brightly, "Edwin and I are going to Williamsburg early next week. We want you to go with us."

Glynna shook her head in negation. "Thanks for asking me, though." Her voice sounded colorless, defeated.

"I'm not asking, Glynna. I'm telling you that you *are* going with us." The announcement produced a genuine reaction—the first she had provoked from her friend in weeks.

Glynna's eyebrows shot upward, and her jaw fell slack in shock. "Never in all our years of friendship have we made any demands on each other, Beth. There's no reason to start now." It was the longest speech Beth could remember hearing from Glynna in a while. And the most sensible.

"If there were no reason, I wouldn't be doing it. We aren't going to let you mope around here any longer. If you aren't going to do something about it, we are."

"Who're *we?*"

"Edwin and I, your aunt and uncle, Katie—all of us who love you. Even Brian agreed it would be good for you to get away for a spell."

"So you've all been talking about me behind my back! I should have known you would." She paused to consider this revelation, then continued, "But I don't suppose I've stopped to think about anyone other than Kane . . . or anything other than my own misery lately." Glynna's gaze dropped to her lap. Fingering the fabric of her skirt, she almost whispered, "I haven't been much fun to be around, have I? I don't know why you tolerate my ill moods."

Beth placed a hand on Glynna's forearm and squeezed it lightly. "Because I love you. And I'm not going to stop loving you just because you've become an old grouch."

Glynna smiled then, a half-smile that didn't reach her eyes, but a smile nonetheless. "I have been difficult."

"Difficult! That's not the half of it! You've been incorrigible! But all that's about to change. You pack your bags and be ready to leave at first light on Monday. And be sure you bring a variety of garments and accessories, including a ballgown."

"Why? What are we going to do in Williamsburg? And how long will we be gone?"

"Wonderful! You're going willingly!" Beth's eyes glowed with a combination of awe and gratitude as she hugged Glynna tightly. "You'll see when we get there."

Kane clutched the taffrail so hard his knuckles bulged white against his dark tan. He welcomed the cleansing salt spray spewing on his face, for he felt dirty—dirtier than he had ever felt in his life.

If he had known—had any inkling even that the *White Wave* was a slaver—he would never have stepped foot on board. There would have been another ship, eventually. He should have known better than to trust a Yankee! He should have gone on board when the ship was anchored in Galway Bay, talked to some of the sailors, instead of trusting that Yankee, Captain Jackson! He could still hear him promising, "Won't be but a few weeks, me lad, 'fore we drop anchor in Chesapeake Bay. God willing and the wind be right, we'll be there 'fore you know it."

But there was more to Kane's anger than the pretense that they would sail directly to Maryland, than the delay that resulted from their sailing to West Africa first. There were the slaves themselves, shackled in the hold like so many animals and treated not half as well. How could he not have known that the stench he smelled when he came aboard was not that of horseflesh but of human flesh? Kane blamed his dull wit on his eagerness to return to Virginia, but that thought offered little comfort now. Small wonder the mate had whispered "Danger of plague . . . Let's get them on deck while the weather holds . . . they keep better that way."

They keep better that way! The words echoed relentlessly in his ears. They keep better—as though they were oranges or mangoes that required fresh air to keep them from molding. Kane shivered in the cool night air, pulling the folds of his warm cloak around his torso in an effort to combat a chill that had no relation to the temperature.

He had had his suspicions when he realized they were sailing south instead of west, but Jackson, ever glib of tongue, had passed off the observation by insisting they were tacking. When this argument no longer possessed merit, he had finally admitted to Kane that the *White Wave* was a slaver.

"Then why did you take me as a passenger? And why in hell did you not tell me this in the beginning?" Kane had asked angrily as he and the skipper shared a private dinner one evening.

"I liked the color of your coin. Specie's hard to come by these days," Jackson had answered candidly. Kane wished the man had been so honest in Galway. "You don't understand colonial commerce," Jackson had continued. "Money's scarce in the colonies. Oh, there's a motley collection of Spanish and other European coins there, but little English currency."

Kane recalled how delighted the merchants in Williamsburg had been when he had opened his coin purse. Their reaction had meant nothing to him at the time, his concern for Glynna overshadowing analysis of such a minor matter. "So they operate with bills of exchange?"

"On what they export to England. But the king, you see, and the Lords in Parliament stay up nights devising ways to ruin the colonists financially. Take the tobacco planters, for instance. They've got this law working against them, see. It says they can export tobacco only to the British Isles. That means no matter how much tobacco they grow, they can't get the highest bid for it 'cause they ain't allowed to sell it to nobody else. England can't use all that tobacco, so it's reexported to other places, at a profit, while the hardworking planters get left out in the cold."

All the while he was explaining this, Jackson had been tamping tobacco into his pipe, and now he lit it, the smoke curling upward, its pungent fragrance filling the confines of the small dining saloon. Jackson lost some of his crudeness in speech when no sailors were around, and Kane could not say he found the man's company unpleasant. He wished he could say as much for the man's morals.

"The planter sells his annual crop to an English merchant, who credits him with its value—after deducting charges for shipping, insurance, and commissions. Then the planter buys slaves and manufactured goods through the merchant, who deducts their costs from the planter's credit on the books, so the planter doesn't ever have any money. Not really. Same thing's true for the colonial merchants and shipowners. If we abide by the law and pay all the duty England requires, we end up in the hole, so to speak."

Jackson held up one of his large, calloused hands, the fingers splayed. Gradually, he pulled his fingertips into his palm, saying, "The Crown keeps tightening its hold, squeezing the colonies harder and harder. One day they won't take it no more. Mark my words. One day the planters and merchants and shipowners are all gonna say they've had enough. I just hope I live long enough to see it happen."

Kane had heard about the Navigation and Molasses Acts, but he had never before considered their impact on the American colonies. If what Jackson said was true—and it certainly seemed to be—then the Crown and its colonies were hurtling toward an all-out war that Kane wasn't at all sure he wanted to live long enough to see.

But he did want to see Glynna. Nothing else mattered as much.

Glynna absently tucked a wayward wisp of auburn hair under her bonnet, then returned the hand that had committed the deed to the edge of the tailgate, clutching it tightly to keep from falling off.

"You know, Glynna, if you wouldn't sit with your back so ramrod straight," Beth observed, "you'd be a lot more comfortable."

Glynna stole a surreptitious glance at her friend, who reclined lazily against the muslin sacks of cured tobacco stacked in the back of the buckboard. Beth's feet were curled up beneath her skirts; her bonnet brim was pulled down over her eyes. Glynna had thought Beth was asleep and had been ignoring her.

"Are you going to fume all the way to Williamsburg, or are you going to tell me what's bothering you?"

From beneath the wide brim of her white bonnet, Beth watched Glynna's reaction to her question, and was duly rewarded with the sight of a jutting jaw and narrowed eyes. "If you don't tell me, I'm just going to pester you until I wear your resistance down, so you may as well get it over with."

I may have to talk, but I don't have to relax, Glynna thought rebelliously. Beth and Edwin seemed deliriously happy, and while Glynna did find it in her heart to be happy for them, she persisted in refusing to embrace such bliss herself. "Do you remember when Aunt Darcie decided to open her general store, and we—Brian, Kane, and I—helped her clean out the storeroom?"

"Yes."

"Aunt Darcie found a crate of things that had belonged to my parents. She sent it to my room, and in all the confusion after . . . well, you know . . . I forgot about it. Someone had shoved it under my bed, and last night when I was looking for a misplaced glove, I found the crate."

Beth waited patiently for Glynna to continue, then decided she required assistance. "And something in that crate has disturbed you?"

If Beth hadn't been watching Glynna's face, she would have missed the tiny movement of her head as she nodded in agreement. After several long minutes, during which time Beth silently willed her

283

friend to say something, Glynna declared, "My father kept a journal. I found it in the crate." She then took a deep breath to still her intense anger, but to no avail. She collapsed against one of the sacks and burst into tears.

"Do I need to stop the rig?" Edwin called from his seat at the front of the buckboard.

"No," Beth answered. "We're all right." She turned her attention to Glynna, trying to put comforting arms around her friend's quaking form, but Glynna pushed her away. "Sometimes a good cry cleanses the soul," Beth said gently, backing away and repositioning herself against the pungent tobacco. Although she ached for her friend, she silently acknowledged that this display of emotion—whatever its cause—was part of the healing process.

At long last, Glynna's deep sobs ebbed, and when she had loudly blown her nose into the handkerchief Beth provided, she wiped her eyes and apologized for her outburst. "I thought I had it all under control, but I don't. When I get really riled up, I cry. I wish I didn't."

"That's just part of being a woman, Glynna. Can you tell me now?"

Glynna blew her reddened nose again and nodded slowly. "I think so. Kane . . . Kane lied to me."

Beth's pale eyes registered surprise. "What about?"

"Who he was—*is*."

"Kane Rafferty's not his real name?"

Glynna shrugged melodramatically. "I suppose that is his name. But his father, Thomas Rafferty, was one of my father's best friends. He is a baron, Beth! A baron!"

"So?"

"And Kane is his eldest son."

"So one day you will be a baroness." Beth could not suppress the laughter bubbling in her throat. "It's what you've always dreamed of, Glynna. Why are you upset?"

"Because Kane didn't tell me. He led me to believe he was my tutor!"

"He *was* your tutor. And a very good one, I believe."

"But I don't want to leave Virginia! I don't want to leave you and Edwin and Aunt Darcie—and everyone else here."

"You could always come back and visit us," Beth suggested, wondering anew at the way minor incidents triggered Glynna's ire. That had always been her friend's worst flaw. "A short fuse," Mrs. Jenkins had called it.

"Don't you understand, Beth?" Glynna asked tearfully, her voice cracking again. Beth held her breath for a moment, waiting for the deluge, but Glynna took a deep gulp of air and plunged ahead. "There has to be a reason why Kane was sent here instead of a real tutor. If he truly loves me, he should have trusted me enough to tell me who he really is and why he came."

"Maybe he'll tell you when he returns."

"Oh, Beth," Glynna gushed, reaching out to hug her friend, "you're such an optimist! What would I do without you? Kane isn't coming back. Why would he?"

"What makes you think he accomplished his mission—assuming there really was one?"

Glynna pulled back, gazing with wonder at Beth's studiedly placid face. "And if he didn't . . ." Glynna's green eyes sparkled brightly, then narrowed again as a flurry of possibilities flitted across her brain. "But I can't just act as though I don't know about him now."

"Of course, you can. If Kane Rafferty is playing some kind of game—and I believe with all my heart that he is in love with you and that that is not part of his game—play along with him. At some point, you may be forced to ask him what he's doing and why, but first give him the opportunity to tell you. Whatever you do, don't confront him with it immediately."

Glynna digested this advice, relaxing for the first time since they had left the tavern hours before. By the time Edwin pulled the buckboard off the road and under the spreading arms of a mighty oak so that they might eat their lunch, her normal good humor had returned. She smiled inwardly when she saw the relief on her friends' faces. "I know what you two are thinking," she said, her smile evident in her voice even before it touched her lips, "and you're right. It's about time I put the past behind me and got on with my life. Now tell me, you closemouthed so-and-sos, what are we going to do in Williamsburg that requires fancy clothes?"

Beth and Edwin shared secretive smiles, then tactfully changed the subject.

Edwin had prepared for the trip well in advance. The Raleigh Tavern had two adjacent rooms prepared for them upon their arrival Thursday afternoon, and within the space of an hour Glynna found herself taking a luxurious soak in a large hipbath with Beth in attendance.

"Oooh," Glynna breathed. "This is heaven after

that long, grimy, bone-jarring trip."

Beth turned from the bed, where she was removing wads of tissue paper from the folds of Glynna's ballgown. "Sorry you came?"

"Not at all."

"Good! Now I don't have to feel guilty about insisting upon it."

"You wouldn't anyway," Glynna teased.

Smiling, Beth returned to her task, shaking out the pale green brocade gown and slipping a wooden hanger into its wide neckline. "Now hurry up and get out of that tub!" she implored. "I want to use it, too, and my dear, sweet Winnie will be knocking at your door soon enough."

"You'd best summon one of the maids, then." Glynna's laughter tinkled through the room as she stood and reached for a large linen towel. "This tub looks like it was filled with swamp water!"

The next few days were a whirlwind of activity, made more exciting if more cumbersome by the crowds that were steadily thronging into Williamsburg. Beth and Glynna spent those days combing the shops, ordering hats from the milliner, and purchasing yards of ribbon and lace from the dry goods. They delighted in the fine, crisp, linen writing paper, sharp new quills, scented sealing wax, and bottles of colored ink they bought from the stationer.

"Now we can sit at our desks, wearing our new frilly bonnets, and write beautiful letters to everyone we know," Beth said haughtily, her nose raised imperiously for effect.

"And what shall we do with our ribbons and laces meanwhile?" Glynna asked, attempting a serious mien, but smiling in spite of herself.

"Why, paste little strips of them on the stationery, of course." Like Glynna's, Beth's lips curved in amusement. "Or we could make our letters look like little kites with ribbon and lace tails."

Their spontaneous laughter drew the disapproving attention of a stiff-backed crone sitting at the table next to theirs at Christiana Campbell's Tavern, but Glynna and Beth paid her no mind.

"How do you like your rum-cream pie?" Beth asked when she had regained her composure.

"It's awfully rich! But divinely delicious."

Beth gloated in her success at bringing Glynna out of her depression.

Despite her friend's pleas, she and Edwin had refused to disclose the need for a ballgown until they were almost finished with the noontide meal on Monday, and only did it then because Glynna forced the issue.

"I want to go back to that silversmith's this afternoon, Beth—you remember, the one near the Palace Green. He has a lovely little salt cellar I've decided to buy for Aunt Darcie. Do you want to go with me?" Glynna asked.

"No . . . well, yes." Beth seemed uncertain. "I mean, I want to go with you, but not this afternoon."

Glynna lightly shrugged away her friend's lack of cooperation. "I will go by myself, then."

"No, you won't!" Beth insisted, her eyes flickering to Edwin, begging for his intervention.

"You're going to be otherwise occupied this afternoon—and evening, Glynna," he explained, knowing all the while further information would be demanded from him, thus spoiling the surprise he and Beth had so carefully planned. As he had suspected she would, Glynna badgered him until he gave in.

Thus, when she was supposed to be napping later, Glynna's heart fluttered with excitement and her eyes refused to remain closed for more than a few seconds at the time. *The theater!* Beth and Edwin were taking her to the theater! Never would she have guessed, despite the advertisements she had seen posted around town, that Edwin could have obtained tickets with such a huge crowd in town. She had worked herself into a frenzy of excitement by the time Beth knocked on her door in midafternoon. They took turns bathing and crimping each other's hair with the curling irons, then dressing their locks into cascades of smooth, sleek ringlets. They manicured their nails, powdered their bosoms, and dabbled hints of floral fragrance behind their ears. They laced stays, adjusted panniers, and smoothed the fabric of their skirts. At five o'clock, they left the Raleigh Tavern, entered a waiting carriage, and rode the few blocks up Duke of Gloucester Street to the Palace Green.

"Where's Edwin?" Glynna asked. "Isn't he coming?"

"He wouldn't miss it for the world," Beth replied. "In fact, he's been at the theater now for two hours or so."

A look of disappointment crossed Glynna's face. "Have we missed a performance? I do so want to see everything they have to offer there."

"No . . . no. Edwin's friend, who secured the tickets for us told him someone in the party must arrive well in advance to secure and hold choice box seats." A wistful smile touched Beth's lips. "Poor Winnie. He's been sitting there all alone, waiting for us all this time."

The young women had expected a sedate crowd,

the elite of Williamsburg and the surrounding countryside, to attend the theater. The noise that greeted them quickly dispelled that notion. The fashionable boxes, one of which Edwin had obtained, curved in a horseshoe around the lower floor, where those from the middle class sat closely on backless benches, chattering loudly as they attempted to avoid the wax dripping from the chandeliers overhead. The gallery above the boxes was crowded with servants and those of the lower classes. These last were calling to one another and were heckling the poor souls on the lower floor by throwing fruit pits at them, giving them something else to avoid besides the dripping wax.

Glynna and Beth had no difficulty spying Edwin, for he stood in their box, his head and shoulders towering above the crowd. Glynna was surprised, however, when she and his wife finally reached him, to see that he was not alone. With him were a young, petite woman, a red-coated soldier, and an older man whose white hair seemed oddly at variance with his smooth complexion. Glynna looked askance at Beth, but the secretive smile was back on her friend's face and Beth's sparkling eyes avoided Glynna's, raking instead the trio of strangers.

"May I present my wife, Hepzibeth, and our dear friend Miss Glynna O'Rourke?" Edwin graciously asked, extending a long arm toward the two.

Beth and Glynna curtsied, bowing their heads slightly in deference to their new acquaintances.

"And may I introduce to you sweet ladies another of your breed: Miss Samarra Seldon, female extraordinaire, master printer and engraver."

A secretive smile also touched Samarra's lips before she tucked her head and curtsied. Glynna had little time to ponder this, or Edwin's announcement of Miss Seldon's occupation, before he continued with the introductions. The older man was Samarra's father, Randolph Seldon. It was he who had secured the theater tickets. The soldier, a British army lieutenant assigned to the governor's office, was MacKenzie Reed.

"We feel that we know you already, Miss O'Rourke," Samarra said. "Mr. Rafferty sought our assistance in advertising your disappearance a few months ago. We were all immensely relieved when Mr. McLaird sent us word that you were safely at home and unharmed."

The swift dawning of who Miss Seldon was overshadowed the sharp pain the woman's words sent to Glynna's heart. "Then you . . . you're not the printer . . ."

Samarra nodded, her round face aglow with warranted pride in her workmanship. Glynna saw the poster in her mind's eye, again aware of its remarkable likeness to herself, and she now understood the secretive smiles. Suddenly, she realized she was gawking at Miss Seldon in utter amazement. Edwin had brought some of the advertisements home with him and had told her about his and Kane's efforts to locate her in Williamsburg, but he had not even mentioned Samarra.

They made a congenial group, however. For the space of half an hour, they shared small talk and tidbits of fruit and cakes purchased from the vendors outside the door. The men had congregated on one side of the box, leaving the other to the women, an arrangement which relieved Glynna of having to accept the company of either Randolph or MacKenzie for the evening. She enjoyed Samarra's easy chatter, and began to feel as though she had known this young woman for some time.

At precisely six o'clock, the stage manager blew his whistle and the entertainment began. The performance opened with the first act of Shakespeare's *The Merchant of Venice*. Although Glynna had read the work years before, this was the first time she had seen it, or any other play, performed on stage. From the first line, she found herself caught up in the drama, though without being consciously aware of it she linked the evil, wolflike Shylock with Samuel Mitchell. She had forgotten how intellectual yet decidedly feminine Portia was, and felt drawn to this heroine who was so much like herself.

Between acts, the theatergoers were entertained with singing and dancing, and following the final act of the featured play, the company performed a rollicking comic opera designed to send everyone home in a festive mood.

It was almost midnight when the final curtain fell, but Glynna didn't feel the least bit tired. It had been a most exhilarating evening.

She was hungry, however, having completely missed supper.

The six companions piled into Randolph Seldon's carriage—the one he had sent for Glynna and Beth earlier—and within a short time they were all enjoying a late supper at the Raleigh Tavern.

"Look," Samarra whispered to Glynna as their dishes were being cleared away. "Isn't that the actor who portrayed Shylock?"

The man stood directly in Glynna's line of vision, and even without his stage makeup and costume, he was quite recognizable as the lead player.

His gray eyes, so like Kane's now that he was close enough for Glynna to see them, bored into her.

She shivered, whether from his uncanny resemblance to Kane or from some indistinct memory of this man she didn't know.

"Have you made his acquaintance?" Samarra inquired.

"No!" The sharpness of her own response startled Glynna. She willed softness into her voice before she spoke again. "Why do you ask?"

"Because he seems to know you."

A pain caught in Glynna's throat and held it like a vise. She saw the actor walking toward her as though he were part of a dream—or a nightmare.

Chapter Nineteen

Jarvis Whitfield could not believe the vision had substance.

She sat there amid the others, smiling, talking, eating—performing human deeds, interacting with her companions. Could a ghost do that? he wondered briefly, then quickly put the notion aside, for he knew her to be real.

Glynna O'Rourke blinked several times in an effort to clear her vision, but the man continued to move toward her. She had not conjured him up. He was real.

As Jarvis came nearer, he noticed subtle differences in her face—the forehead was not quite so high, the chin was a bit more pointed, the mouth was slightly wider. But her coloring was exactly that of her mother, and the differences in features too minor to be of any importance. This young woman had to be the offspring of Glynndon and Brenna O'Rourke. A swift calculation confirmed his belief.

Never had Glynna seen Kane in a wig. His preference for his natural hair, minus even a hint of white powder, had pleased her. Yet this man wore a white peruke styled with full, smooth hair which rose high off his forehead, its only curls sitting on the upper half of his ears, its length caught at his nape with a black velvet ribbon. His height and build were remarkably similar to Kane's; yet this man's gait was not so confident, his movements were not so agile. But those eyes, so like Kane's, continued to hold hers as he took her hand, breaking his gaze only for a moment as he bowed low over it, his mouth not quite touching her fingers.

He is only an actor from the theater company, and I see Kane in him only because I want to.

She is the key to that one I seek. If she is in Virginia, then so must be her uncle Galen, Whitfield thought.

"Pardon my intrusion upon your company." The actor's rich, mellow voice gave his words a poetic cadence. "But I could not find within myself containment of the urge to meet such a lovely lady. I am Jarvis Whitfield, lately of London, more recently of Williamsburg, a mere actor, 'tis true, but an admirer of beauty in any form."

A gentleman would not have presented himself so boldly, would have sought a more indirect approach to gain an introduction to a young lady, but an actor could employ such a stratagem without fear of censure. Randolph Seldon introduced those around the table. Then a flurry of questions and comments were directed at Whitfield, and someone asked the actor to join them for dessert. All the while, Whitfield played out his part, not allowing even a flicker of the inner workings of his mind to show on his countenance.

By the time the party quitted the supper table,

Whitfield had acquired all the knowledge he needed to proceed.

Glynna wanted to believe that Kane was coming back. Enough time had passed for a letter to have arrived from him, a letter which would confirm or deny his intention to return, but, alas, none had appeared at the post office in Williamsburg before they had been forced to take their departure.

It had been easy enough to get caught up in the torrent of activity revolving around the fall Public Time, easy to put aside her fears and misgivings while she had been among so many people. But once Glynna started home with Beth and Edwin, the doubts returned to plague her.

They had been back scarcely a week when Wilson's coach pulled up before the tavern. Glynna's heart almost stopped, then recovered rapidly to thump with frenzied savagery as she stood on the porch with Darcie, awaiting the sight of Kane's tall lean form. Her mouth had gone dry and her throat felt parched, and when she could stand the suspense no longer, she quickly descended the steps and ran toward the coach.

Her heart lurched again when she saw him—he was not Kane—and her spirits fell in direct proportion to her immense frustration. Glynna masked her disappointment as best she could, pasting a bright if insincere smile upon her lips as she greeted Jarvis Whitfield.

Darcie, too, employed her usual hostess's charm, and with as much effort as her niece. Glynna had told her about meeting the actor in Williamsburg, and Darcie was puzzled by his sudden appearance on the edge of the wilderness. In addition, there was something about this man that bothered her, something almost evil. She shooed away the feeling, attributing it to her generalized distrust of the male species since Glynna's ordeal.

"But how will William Prescott's theatrical troupe manage without their Shylock?" Darcie heard Glynna ask of their new guest as they entered the tavern.

"We had only two more scheduled performances of *The Merchant of Venice* after the evening you attended, Miss O'Rourke, and I did not feel myself well suited to the new role they had assigned me. Besides, I came to Virginia with the intention of settling here if the country pleased me, as it certainly has. I was told there was land available for purchase here and across the mountains in the valley."

But his actions over the next few days convinced both Glynna and Darcie that he had not come in pursuit of land, rather in pursuit of Glynna. He sought her out, no matter where she fled, insisting that she ride with him over Galen's plantation or accompany him to a neighboring farm to introduce him to the "locals," as he called them. When they visited her friends, she would desert him as soon as was prudently allowed, leaving him to discuss land use and values with the men of the household while she talked to the women and girls. On more than one of these occasions, she returned to the parlor before Whitfield was expecting her and overheard him discussing her uncle's affairs.

Glynna puzzled over this and finally plucked up enough courage to ask Whitfield about it. His explanation was simple enough—and quite believable, for Galen had a reputation for being reticent.

"Your uncle is, by far, the most successful planter and businessman in this area, but he will share little of his expertise with me. It appears that no one else is the wiser, either, for I have been able to gain nothing from my inquiries. Perhaps if I stay long enough at the tavern, I will learn his methods from observation if not from conversation."

True to his word, Jarvis Whitfield seemed to be in no hurry to purchase his land and leave the hospitality of the tavern, but the more Glynna was in his company, the more she longed for Kane. October was drawing to a close, and though she had heretofore thrived on the cooling temperatures and nature's rampant use of color at this time of year, this autumn her discontent overpowered any outside forces from working their wiles upon her.

One crisp, bright morning near noontide, they returned to the tavern from a visit with the elder McLairds to find Wilson's coach parked in front of the stables. Without taking the time to explain, Glynna left Sheena in Josh's capable hands and raced uphill toward the house, leaving Whitfield still seated upon his gelding. In some vexation his gray gaze followed her progress.

No sooner had the front door banged shut behind her than Kane Rafferty appeared in the front hall, his steps as hurried as hers as he emerged from the gentlemen's parlor. Without conscious thought, Glynna flew into his open arms, her senses reeling with the nearness of this man she had thought never to see again. For a long moment they clung to each other, each savoring the warmth and physical closeness of the other, the commingling of their individual smells, the pounding of their heartbeats against the press of their joined breasts. Neither wanted to let go of the other, yet their eyes longed for the intoxicating embrace in which their arms indulged.

After a while, Glynna removed her cheek from the fabric of Kane's waistcoat and tilted her head back so that she might see his face. Her cheek tingled where it had so recently touched him, and she relished the sensation, wanting it to go on forever, knowing the only way to relieve the tingling was again to place her cheek upon his person. She thought she would drown in the desire-glazed depths of his gray eyes as her own jeweled orbs locked with his gaze. Her heart and lungs performed their involuntary chores, but Glynna felt as though she no longer lived within her own body, that it functioned only because Kane's presence had breathed life into her again. In the span of a few seconds, their spirits had melded and then soared, creating an aura that was almost tangible in its intensity.

How long they might have stood there in the hall, clinging to each other, they neither knew nor cared. But a guttural exclamation behind them broke both their interlocked bodies and eyes, and with reluctance they stood apart, turning to see that one who had dared intrude upon the sweetness of their reunion.

Jarvis Whitfield stood just inside the doorway, his eyes wary as he regarded Kane. "You didn't tell me you have an older brother, Glynna," he remarked smoothly.

Never before had Whitfield ignored etiquette and called her by her Christian name. She had found his demands on her time irritating enough, but for the man to act as though there were any intimacy between them eradicated any tolerance of him she'd had. Her green eyes flashed sparks, her shoulders squared themselves, and her words dripped icily from coldly set lips. "You may be a guest in this house, *sir*, but that does not give you the right to speak to me so familiarly!"

Behind her, Kane observed Whitfield closely and noted the slight narrowing of the other man's eyes and the tightening around his mouth before he regained control of his features.

Kane and Darcie had spent the hour during which he had awaited Glynna's return filling each other in on the events of the previous few months; Whitfield's presence at the inn, therefore, had not come as a surprise to him. He did wonder, though, in light of recent events, why both Darcie and Galen trusted this stranger enough to allow his solitary escort of Glynna—and why Glynna, too, trusted Whitfield. Perhaps they saw only the popinjay facade the man presented to the world, whereas Kane had the distinct impression that it was a false front hiding a cold, calculating heart.

Judging from Glynna's reaction, Kane did not believe Whitfield had truly angered her before this moment, and he silently applauded her outburst. Outwardly, he possessively placed his hands upon her shoulders, his stance defying opposition.

When Glynna did not introduce the two men, Kane added frostily, "Perhaps, sir, you may at some time have occasion to meet my sister, but Miss O'Rourke and I share no common blood. Now"—Kane gently turned Glynna toward the open parlor door—"if you will excuse us . . ."

Jarvis Whitfield's eyebrows shot upward and his mouth gaped open at the affront. Who was this man? And how dare he take Glynna away from him? Whitfield silently vowed retribution. He would have his pound of flesh.

Greatly amused by Whitfield's uncharacteristic discomfiture and overjoyed by Kane's sudden appearance, Glynna managed somehow to contain her bubbling laughter until Kane had used his heel to push the portal closed behind them, but even then she was not allowed its release. As she turned into Kane's arms, his mouth swiftly covered hers, his lips pressing firmly, possessively against her own, taking her breath away. She melted against him, slipping her arms around his neck and pulling his head down as she arched her back, allowing him better access to the honeyed sweetness of her mouth. Her heart kept singing, I never thought to experience your touch again, but you came back! You're here, holding me, kissing me! Kane Rafferty, I love you!

She gasped for air when, at long last, he released her mouth. His arms continued to hold her close, his right hand moving upward to press her head against his heaving chest.

"Darcie has packed us a picnic lunch," he whispered, "and I can see you're dressed for riding. Do you think you are ready to get back on Sheena?" Kane felt her head nod enthusiastically beneath his hand.

He held her elbow as they left the tavern and walked at a less than sedate pace downhill to the stables. Glynna had thought they would have to wait for Josh to resaddle Sheena and then saddle the large bay stallion Kane favored, but both horses were outfitted and awaiting their mounts. Josh handed up the basket of food to Kane, who heeled his horse into a gallop as he raced after Glynna.

She wore the bottle green velvet habit, her only

one now since Mitchell had destroyed the black bombazine. Kane remembered the soft green velvet from that first day they had gone riding and tumbled down the hill together. The lavender and cream plumes in her saucy little hat bounced and fluttered in the wind, and Kane's fingers itched when he thought of removing that hat along with the pins that held her hair. The picnic basket he held in front of him inhibited his ability to push the stallion to the limit of its strength, but Kane also held back purposely, enjoying the view of her straight back and curved hips as she rode before him.

When Glynna thought they had ridden far enough, she reined Sheena to a halt in a stand of oaks and maples, and awaited Kane's assistance in helping her dismount. The brief pressure of his hands on either side of her rib cage sent delightful little shivers through her, and she stood impatiently as he looped the reins of their horses over a low-hanging limb before removing a blanket from the basket and spreading it upon a carpet of fallen leaves and withering grasses.

Feeling as though she were moving through a dream, Glynna joined Kane on the blanket. She pulled the full skirts of her habit out of the way before she sat on her knees, her eyes never leaving his face. "I have so much to tell you," she said, not really wanting to break the warm, comfortable silence yet knowing they had many things to discuss.

"And I have much to tell you. Shall we throw a die to see who goes first?"

His suggestion brought a devilish grin to her lips, parting them to show small, perfect teeth and the tip of her pink tongue pressed against her upper lip. "Do you have one?"

His gaze, too, had not wavered from hers, but her words drew his eyes to the sight of her open mouth, which seemed to invite him to taste its sweetness again. He leaned toward her, drawn to her as a moth is drawn to a flickering flame. "Do I have what?" he whispered.

"A die."

"No."

A breeze sailed through the trees, divesting them of some of their colorful leaves, many of which were lifted and carried on the wind like little kites. The dry leaves still clinging tenaciously to the branches rattled for a moment, then were still. Pale gold shafts of sunlight sifted through the half-bare limbs over their heads to fall in dappled array onto the blanket and its occupants, who took no notice of nature's dazzling display.

Glynna shivered in anticipation when Kane's fingers reached upward to remove her hat, which he held upside down in one hand while the other slowly worked the hairpins loose until her dark, burnished locks fell capriciously upon her shoulders. The pins he placed in the crown of her hat before he laid it aside, just beyond the outer edge of the blanket, that act evoking sweet memories for both of them.

Then Kane lowered his head to hers, his lips brushing Glynna's with feathery softness before moving upward to briefly touch the tip of her nose. She felt his arm across her shoulders, felt the gentle pressure of his torso as he lowered her to the blanket. She rolled slightly to the side, pulling her folded lower legs from beneath her thighs and buttocks and straightening them, wanting to feel Kane's length pressed against hers. This time

303

she welcomed the feel of the quickly hardening bulge of his manhood as it moved against the softness of her thigh. Whatever misgivings she had harbored before had fled, a deep yearning born of her love for Kane having replaced them.

His lips continued their wayfaring journey across her face, nibbling at her cheekbones, her eyelids, the corners of her mouth. When she could no longer tolerate the sparks of the fire he had so gently ignited, Glynna reached upward to hold his freshly shaved cheeks and to maneuver his warm lips onto hers, seeking the heat of their blaze. At her insistence, his kiss became impassioned, his tongue raking her front teeth before plunging into the honeyed recesses of her mouth and exploring its depths. She responded with a fervency that matched Kane's, her tongue flickering out to tantalize him even as his tantalized her.

Nothing had ever felt so right to her before.

Fearing his withdrawal, Glynna gasped when he lifted his chest from hers, then sighed contentedly when his nimble fingers began loosening the silk frogs of her jacket. She relished the slight roughness of his palm as it grazed the sheer fabric of her blouse, his fingers performing the same chore upon its fastenings. When his hand slipped under the edge of her chemise and moved downward to cup her breast, his thumb rubbing its peak into hardness, she instinctively arched her back against his exploration.

Glynna had never thought of herself as wanton, but that was how she felt now. Months before, Kane's first kiss had awakened a passion in her she had not known existed, and the time they had been separated had served to fuel her physical desire for him. She had worried that Mitchell's mistreatment of her body would inhibit that desire, but it had burst forth the moment she had seen Kane, the memory of her ordeal remaining buried in the ashes of the past.

His hand moved again, this time to slide the narrow strap of her chemise down her shoulder and push its silky folds beneath the soft mound of her breast. His tongue withdrew from her mouth then, to trace a hot, wet trail across her cheek, down the length of her throat, and finally to seek an exposed, throbbing crest. A soft moan erupted from her throat when she felt the moist texture of his tongue flicker across the taut peak. His hand molded itself around the underside of her breast and gently pushed its quivering flesh into the fiery cavern of his mouth.

Glynna thought she would surely melt from the heat of the scorching flames which seemed bent on devouring her, yet she willingly embraced the conflagration. Of their own accord, her hands pressed against the back of Kane's head, holding it firmly in place as his mouth worked its wonder upon her breast. The now-familiar ache deep within her burned brightly; it was a thirst that demanded to be quenched.

When Kane raised his head from her breast, her trembling fingers moved to the front of his waistcoat and began to undo the brass buttons holding it closed. When the coat parted and Glynna ran her palms across the thin fabric of his shirt, Kane laid his cheek against the side of her neck. She could hear his ragged breathing close to her ear, and the short rushes of air from his mouth tickled the downy hair behind her earlobes. She sensed his reluctance to separate his body even a few inches from hers when he raised himself onto his elbows and whispered, "Glynna, look at me."

She raised the curtain of her eyelids and witnessed the sparkle of her own desire mirrored in Kane's darkened eyes. The raspiness of his voice further attested to his physical need of her. "Do you want to stop?" he asked.

It was a question she had not allowed herself to ask, but it was also one to which she needed to allot little thought. "No."

"I don't want to hurt you."

"You could never hurt me, Kane . . . not unless you leave me again."

"I won't, my dear, sweet Glynna. Not ever again. From this moment forward, wherever I go, whatever I do, I want you by my side."

Kane sat up on his haunches then, pulling Glynna up with him. With utmost tenderness, he slipped the soft velvet sleeves of her jacket down her arms and over her hands. It joined the hat beside the blanket. Her blouse and chemise followed it, and Kane paused then, his eyes soaking up the beauty of her small but supple breasts with their dark pink nipples pointing skyward. Glynna knew a moment of self-consciousness as, with reverence, Kane's eyes and hands caressed her, his palms barely grazing her quivering flesh as they moved over her bosom.

She had never seen him look so peaceful, so completely content. His jaw hung slack, leaving his mouth partially open, and she shivered as she watched the tip of his tongue travel lazily across his upper lip. His lids hooded his eyes, but when he lifted his gaze to hers, she saw that their irises had grown almost black with the escalation of his ardor.

His voice was a husky whisper when he spoke.

306

"I meant what I said, Glynna. If you'll have me, I want you for now . . . and for always."

She answered him with a kiss that left no doubt of her total and absolute commitment, a kiss that fanned the flames of their mutual desire into a conflagration of passion. Still, Kane maintained a lazy pace, insisting on slow, deliberate movements as he pulled Glynna to her feet.

"I've been wanting to do this since that day I followed you into your bedchamber," he told her softly as he unfastened the waistband of her skirt, his gaze following the garments' path to the blanket, where it puddled at her feet. The mass of her petticoats followed suit, and when Glynna had stepped out of them and Kane had whisked them away and tossed them upon the steadily growing pile of clothing, she stood before him in pantalettes, stockings, and riding boots.

Glynna gasped in awe when his shirt was discarded and, at long last, the brown expanse of his chest was exposed to her appreciative view. "Oh, Kane . . ." she whispered. "You are magnificent."

Kane's body did, indeed, prove more splendorous to Glynna's eyes than she had imagined it would be. Sifting rays of sunlight danced upon the rich, coppery tan he had acquired during his recent ocean voyages. His shoulders were broad and muscled, though not heavily so, and the curly black hair, which his opened shirt had revealed to her so many months before, continued across his chest, swirling around the dark brown hue of his nipples and tapering to a point below his navel.

He coaxed her to the blanket again and removed her boots. A chill sliced through her as his warm hands smoothed the silken stocking covering her calves and then returned to her feet to massage them lightly. Then he reached beneath her panta-lettes, grasped her garters, and slowly, inexorably slid both garters and stockings down the lengths of her legs. Glynna forgot how to breathe and thought she would surely die of suffocation before Kane brought this tender act of love to fruition. She closed her eyes against the exquisite pain, felt him stand up, heard the soft *swoosh* his trousers made as they traveled the length of his long legs, felt him sit upon his knees beside her. "Open your eyes, Glynna," he requested, "and look at me."

She began her slow perusal of him with his face, allowing her gaze to journey downward until it rested upon his thrusting virility. The blush of returning self-consciousness suffused her cheeks as she quickly lifted her eyes upward, fixing them on the slight depression just below his breastbone.

Having bathed and dressed Brian on a number of occasions, Glynna was not unaccustomed to male anatomy, but never in her wildest imagina-tions had she envisioned a man's desire to mani-fest itself so.

Mistaking her discomfiture for the repugnance he had expected, Kane leaned over, touched a fore-finger beneath her chin, and gently drew her head upward, forcing Glynna's eyes to look into his. The tiny frown lines on his brow disappeared when he witnessed her fascination. Encouraged, he took her right hand in his left and guided it to that part of him which her eyes had so recently ca-ressed. Her touch sent a welcomed jolt through the length of his body.

Although Kane refused to let the thought sur-face, a part of him could not help wondering what had happened to her while Mitchell had held her captive. Kane steeled himself for the moment she would link him with Mitchell in her mind and suddenly loathe him simply because he was a man.

His words followed his thoughts. "I am a man, my darling, nothing more, nothing less."

"No," she whispered, her hand gently squeezing his distended flesh, "you are *my* man, and I am your woman. You are my knight in shining armor. I am your damsel in distress." She moved her hands to his chest, with her fingers combed the springy hair there, feasting upon the shudder that ran through him and the growl that caught in his throat as her fingertips caressed his nipples, then dipped lower to circle his navel.

"And you are the sun and moon and earth to me, the air I breathe, the very sustenance of my being," he replied hoarsely, his mouth lowering ever closer to hers until their breaths mingled.

His kiss was tender, his hands gentle as they moved over her. He found the split in the front of her pantalettes, slid one hand into the parted fabric, and rubbed her tautening stomach before letting his hand glide downward, his fingers touching, caressing her most intimate flesh. Glynna's ache for him, which had been transferred to her loins, throbbed painfully, and she pulled Kane against her, her body begging for surcease.

"Not yet, my love," he murmured into the delicate shell of her ear, his own pain evident in the rasp of his voice. He untied the ribbons at the waist of the pantalettes, and she raised her buttocks as he shimmied the garment over her hips and down her legs. His hands moved upon her trembling flesh then, his mouth following the trail of his fingertips, caressing each of her breasts in turn before traveling hotly across her rib cage and back to her navel, then downward again over her stomach, stopping just short of the downy mound of her womanhood.

Glynna writhed beneath him, gasping in unfamiliar pleasure as she felt the sudden dampness seep between her thighs. He raised his body completely from hers, and a fresh breeze wafted across her aroused flesh. She gasped again when she felt his wet mouth upon the arch of her left foot, felt its moist path traverse her ankle and then her calf. She squeezed her eyes closed against the rippling sensation as his mouth reached her knee and finally the delicate skin of her inner thighs. He paused there, using his teeth to lightly bite the sensitive flesh and his tongue to trace semicircles upon it.

"Have mercy, Kane!" she cried. "Please!"

But he ignored her entreaty, gliding his tongue over the top of her thigh, across her hip, and upward to the taut crests of her breasts. His gentle suckling, releasing, suckling rhythm brought tears to her eyes, and she begged him again to end her pain.

With excruciating slowness, he parted her thighs, brought his knees up between them, and lowered himself over her. She felt the wet tip of his manhood touch her most private place, and wondered, for the first time since she had flown into his arms that morning, if this was what she really wanted.

But his softly spoken avowal erased her unease. "I love you, Glynna O'Rourke."

She writhed beneath him then, the sheath of her womanhood accepting his sword, her hips undulating to the rhythm his had created. She cried out when the sharp pain of his entry pierced her flesh, and Kane swiftly covered her mouth with his own.

The pain was mercifully short-lived, a pleasure more intense than any she had ever imagined quickly replacing it.

Together, they plunged into a dark, swirling abyss. Together, they discovered a multitude of ways to please each other. Together, they communicated their love with sighs and moans and rustling movements. Together, they learned that the intensity of that ultimate physical gratification resulting from their joining was possible only because of their mutual love. And, together, they lay in the aftermath of that manifestation, their tangled bodies wilted from their satisfaction, their heartbeats gradually slowing, their breathing returning to normal.

Chapter Twenty

The cool breeze that washed over their dampened skin refreshed them at first, but as the heat of their fervor waned, their chill increased. Kane groaned in frustration, stirred to pluck at the edge of the blanket and pull the cover over and around them; then he propped himself up on his lower arms. His length covered Glynna's, and he lovingly watched her peaceful repose for a moment.

The dark fringes of her lashes fluttered lightly against the paleness of her complexion, its creamy coloring also broken by the delicate violet hue of her eyelids and the pink bloom of her cheeks. Her nostrils flared slightly as she breathed in and out, and were it not for the occasional twitch at the corners of her love-swollen lips, Kane would have thought she was asleep. He reached out and plucked a blade of grass and, with gossamer strokes, pulled its end across her smooth forehead, down the bridge of her nose, and around her mouth.

Glynna wriggled beneath him, her lips spreading into a wide, contented smile even as her eyelids floated upward, stopping at midiris.

" 'Tis not the statue of a goddess, then, upon which I recline, but one fashioned of flesh and blood, sinew and bone," he teased.

She wriggled again, more forcefully this time, her eyes twinkling with merriment when she felt his response grow firmly against her thigh. "Wouldest thou have called me cold as marble, Sir Knight? Surely marble hath not the power to move"—she arched her back, her pointed breasts barely grazing the hair upon his chest—"or breathe." She pursed her lips and blew her sweet, warm breath into his face. "Or bite!" she said quickly, raising her head and pretending to sink her teeth into his neck, using them instead to nibble at it. Her tongue laved the spot, then her open lips clamped onto the beard-roughened skin, and she sucked it gently into her mouth.

His moan provided her answer, his physical response her surcease.

Later, when they had thoroughly satisfied their hunger for passion, Kane retrieved her pantalettes and chemise along with his breeches from the pile of garments, and, dressed, they satisfied their hunger for food.

Darcie had packed more than the two could possibly eat, along with a bottle of red wine. Glynna, already quite intoxicated from their love-play, sipped slowly from her glass, watching Kane partake heartily of both wine and food. "It will be time for tea soon," she said matter-of-factly, "and we have yet to engage in conversation."

"There is time. I told Darcie we would be away the entire afternoon."

Glynna's surprise registered on her face. "Aunt Darcie—" She stopped herself. Her aunt was no

313

fool; she had deliberately provided the time and opportunity for much more than a pleasant horseback ride and picnic.

Kane wiped his mouth on a linen napkin, then began to replace the leftover food in the picnic basket. "It's all right, Glynna. I had Wilson stop by the mill, and I talked to your uncle. He is quite willing for us to marry, as is your aunt."

"Marry?" she asked in some confusion. It was the natural thing for two people in love to do, and yet there were so many questions to which she needed answers.

"Of course! What did you think?"

"I . . . I don't know."

"I assumed . . . I didn't ask you, did I?"

She shook her head in negation, her hair flailing wildly about her shoulders as laughter bubbled in her throat. Kane scooped her up and sat her upon the top of the split-oak basket; then he knelt before her and took her hands in his. His gray eyes searched her emerald ones as he spoke.

"I, Thomas Kane Rafferty, love you with all my heart and want you to be my wife, Glynna O'Rourke. Will you marry me?"

His words filled her with warmth and wellbeing, yet she could not in good faith answer him positively. "Maybe," she breathed.

"Maybe?" he echoed, taken aback by her reply.

"Where will we live?"

"Where do you want to live?"

She answered hesitantly. "I'm not sure I want to leave Virginia."

"We don't have to."

But the question of where they would reside was only one of many Glynna wanted to ask. She wanted him to tell her about himself, who he really was, and she wanted him to tell her of his own accord. She carefully considered her next words. "I don't know much about you, Kane."

He shrugged his bare shoulders, and Glynna watched his muscles ripple, fascinated. "What do you want to know?"

"Everything—but first, may I come down off this basket? The slats are permanently denting my backside."

Kane grinned wickedly as he lifted her down. "Heaven forbid any damage be done to your lovely form."

When he had settled her comfortably upon the blanket, he poured out more wine for both of them and then began a recitation of the major events of his life. "I am the eldest of the three children born to Thomas and Catherine Rafferty of County Galway, Ireland." He told her about his early education at Eton, his years at Cambridge, his extended Grand Tour of the Continent. Later he had studied law, he said, and had spent several years working as a clerk for the House of Lords, "of which, you may as well know, my father, as Baron of Ulrich, is a member."

He watched her reaction to this information closely. Glynna carefully schooled her features to acknowledge surprise. "And you are his eldest son."

"But not his heir."

"I don't understand."

"You know that, when I left Williamsburg so hastily in June, I thought my father was dying. I had received a letter from a . . . close friend of my family." He groaned in frustration. "If I don't tell you everything, this won't make sense."

"If you don't tell me everything, I won't marry

315

you."

Although her words were marked with a teasing lilt, Kane knew she meant it. He took a deep breath and exhaled slowly. "The letter came from Valerie Sherman. I was supposed to marry her when I returned to Ireland with you next spring. Valerie never wanted me to come to Virginia. I know now that she is a vicious, self-serving witch. My father is in excellent health. Her letter was a lie, its intention to ensure my return to Ireland — and to her side."

Glynna could not prevent the stab of jealousy that pierced her heart any more than she could prevent the question forming on her lips. "Do you love her?"

Kane set their wine glasses upon the flat top of the basket, then took her hands in his once more and gently squeezed them between his larger palms. "I didn't know what love was before I met you, Glynna."

She would not allow the warmth suffusing through her to deter her from hearing what she had to know. "You haven't told me why you will not inherit your father's title."

"You must meet my father, Glynna. He is a most remarkable person. I only wish it hadn't taken me so many years to realize that fact. He knows about you, approves of my desire to marry you, and has offered — with my wholehearted permission — the title and lands to my younger brother, Michael."

Glynna did not know what she had expected to hear, but it was not this. "You are willing to give all that up . . . for me?" she asked in amazement.

"All that and more. Whatever you want of me, I am willing to give."

He had not mentioned Thomas Rafferty's friendship with Glynndon O'Rourke, had not told her why he had come to Virginia to tutor her instead of sending someone else. Her brow furrowed in consternation as she thought of these things, which were closely intertwined in her mind. She had avoided pointed questions, but now she realized that if she expected him to be perfectly candid with her, perhaps she had best be completely honest as well. Glynna searched his face, saw there the utter sincerity of his declaration; and she wanted desperately to believe he was not trying to hide anything.

"Do you remember when we were cleaning out the storeroom with Aunt Darcie and we found a crate that contained some of my parents' possessions?" she asked, her eyes never leaving his. Her brow furrowed slightly when she witnessed his wide smile. What had he expected her to discover among her parents' personal items?

"Yes."

"I didn't go through that crate until after you were gone." Glynna took a deep breath, then plunged ahead. "My father kept a journal. Aunt Darcie had told me before I ever met you that he and the baron were close friends; then I learned from his journal that you were the baron's son. Why didn't you tell me yourself before you left?"

"Would it have made a difference?"

"Possibly. I don't know. But you knew about their relationship, *you* knew all about me when you came here. You thought just then that I had found whatever it is you were sent here to find, didn't you? The tutoring was all a hoax, wasn't it? And you a wolf in sheep's clothing?" They were painful questions to ask, but she must have an-

317

swers to them.

Kane dropped his eyes and whispered, "Yes to the first two questions, no to the last. Never a wolf, Glynna." But he quickly recovered, lifting his gaze to hers again, and she saw a pain equal to hers in the sheen of his dove gray eyes. "I . . . I can't tell you about that yet."

"And I can't agree to marriage until you do." A solitary tear escaped from one of Glynna's eyes and rolled down her cheek.

Kane gathered her in his arms and rocked her gently, whispering into her fragrant hair. "Tonight, my love, we will discuss this matter with your aunt and uncle. My reason for coming here involves them as much as—perhaps more than—it does you." When she had calmed, he ventured quietly, "You said earlier that you had much to tell me. Do you feel like doing it now?" He felt her nod reluctantly against his bare chest, felt his desire stirring again, and tenderly put her from him.

Glynna plucked the soft wool of the blanket, her eyes downcast. "Before you left, I . . . I was angry with you. No, I think I was more confused about my feelings for you than anything else. And I was afraid of those feelings."

When she paused, he said, "Would it help if you knew that I was as confused, as afraid?"

Her eyes met his then; she saw the pureness of his love shining from their gray depths, giving her courage. "I wrote a letter to the baron, asking him to remove you as my tutor."

Kane wanted to say "I know," but he had to let her tell him about the letter in her own way.

"I sent the letter with Mr. Wilson. No sooner had he left than I regretted having written it. That's why I left so early that Saturday morning. I thought I could catch him and get the letter back."

"But Sheena threw you in that bog," he supplied, sensing her hesitancy, "and while you were walking home, Mitchell happened by and offered you a ride. I knew that bastard had you all along! But I couldn't find you at his place. Where did he keep you?"

Glynna shivered as memories rushed over her. Kane found her velvet jacket among the pile of garments and placed it around her shoulders. When she answered him, her voice sounded as though she were forcefully tearing the words from her throat. "Tied and gagged in the root cellar."

"Oh, my God!" He pulled her quivering form to his chest again and held her tightly. Darcie had not told him very much about Glynna's experiences before he had heard Glynna and Whitfield ride up. "Perhaps it is best," Darcie had suggested, "for Glynna to tell you herself."

With her cheek against his warm chest, her torso enfolded within his comforting arms, Glynna poured out her tale. "But I don't understand why he wanted to hurt me," she finished. "He was supposed to be righteous and upright."

"I do."

She raised her head then, confusion written across her brow and in the emerald gleam of her eyes.

"Edwin told me . . . a ghastly tale. Did you also wonder why the people around here didn't censure you afterward?"

Glynna nodded. "There were cold stares from some, but never a true cut from anyone."

"I thought someone would have told you. Perhaps Edwin thought your aunt and uncle had; perhaps they feel guilt, along with the rest of the community, for not believing the rumor when they first heard it and for allowing Mitchell to remain their minister."

"What rumor?"

"Apparently you are not the first young lady he abducted. According to local gossip, Mitchell was married years ago, but his wife left him for another man. He was living in Massachusetts then. That was when he became a man of the cloth, using religion as a cover for his carnal desires, I suppose. He must have had perverted attitudes toward women even then. A young woman disappeared, and the villagers searched for her as we searched for you, but they found her. They should have hanged him then and there, but they felt a more fitting punishment was required, so they castrated him and ran him out of town. Several years later, someone staying at your uncle's tavern recognized Mitchell and told the tale."

"And no one really believed it."

Kane shook his head. "By that time, Mitchell had established himself as a respected member of the community, and he had never given any indication that he could be capable of such vile behavior. The man who had recounted the story seemed, himself, a man of disrepute, so his story was discounted as one of spite. And no one thought any more about it — until I told Edwin I thought Mitchell had abducted you, and even then he didn't really believe it. When we could find nothing to prove you were, indeed, being held captive at Mitchell's farm, even I relinquished my theory." His words were tinged with regret, and his eyes begged forgiveness. "I'm so very sorry, Glynna."

" 'Tis not your fault I rode out after Wilson's

coach, or that I was foolish enough to take short-cuts. You did what you could, Kane, and more. Let's forget the whole sordid incident—if that is possible. We can't let our future be jeopardized by regrets."

Kane agreed without reservation, his mind and heart focusing on "our future." He sealed the bargain with a kiss, and as the sun dimmed, he proved to Glynna once more how very much he wanted her, needed her, loved her.

Nature orchestrated their loveplay, but they did not hear the warble of the songbirds or the harmony of the insects. They did not hear the soughing of the pines and the crackling of the hardwoods' dry leaves as an early evening breeze wafted through them. Their ears were receptive only to their own soft moans, their own rustling movements.

From a nearby hill, Jarvis Whitfield watched them in disgust, in the encroaching darkness, trees masking his form. Whitfield wanted Glynna for himself, and he would have her, too, he vowed. No one would tell him anything about this interloper, but he was a patient man. In time, he would know everything.

He had wanted to hear their conversation, but had feared discovery if he crept too close. He chafed at the delay in finding them and felt certain his hostess had contrived to keep him away from the couple. The noontide meal had been postponed, the flimsy excuse of burned bread having been given. Then, when he had requested the lazy stableboy to saddle a horse for him, the foolish youngster had spooked Whitfield's favorite mount and had spent some time catching the gelding.

Whitfield had watched Glynna and Kane ride northward, and had planned to use the elder McLaird's farm as his supposed destination, but Darcie Cavanaugh had thwarted him again when she had asked him to deliver a package to Beth and Edwin. The two had insisted he remain for tea; then his progress had been further delayed when he had skirted the Cavanaugh plantation to avoid having anyone see him. That there had been a conspiracy afloat he harbored little doubt.

Whitfield was angered, too, at his not having been able to catch Galen Cavanaugh alone. He was certain now that Cavanaugh was actually Carmichael. There were too many coincidences: the same initials, a wife named Darcie, the lack of explanation for Galen's wealth, and a niece named O'Rourke who strongly resembled one Brenna O'Rourke, now deceased. That particular death was the only he'd caused that he regretted. Brenna O'Rourke had been a beautiful woman.

Nonetheless, now the sweetness of anticipated revenge filled his being. For almost two decades he had eluded accusations. No one could have been more careful, more cautious than he. Not once had he left a witness to his crimes, and the authorities would never suspect his motivation.

He had begun to consider allowing Galen Cavanaugh to survive—for the time being. The more he toyed with the idea of marrying Glynna and settling down at the tavern, the more he liked it. Opportunities would present themselves for the systematic elimination of everyone Galen loved: Darcie, Brian, and even, perhaps, Glynna. Once they were all gone and Whitfield had fallen heir to Glynna's estate and had established himself as heir to Galen's, he would then take care of his most hated adversary. What an ultimate coup that would be, telling Galen Cavanaugh who he really was and admitting his responsibility for all those deaths . . . just before he plunged the knife into Galen's heart.

Jarvis Whitfield wrenched his eyes from the scene before him and, with a stealth he had mastered over the years, made his way down the south side of the hill to the tethered gelding at its base. He walked the horse for almost a quarter of a mile before he mounted and pushed the animal into a hard gallop toward the tavern. His first chore would be the permanent removal of Kane Rafferty, a task he relished as he contemplated how best to accomplish it.

Glynna and Kane sought to drag out the minutes left to them before darkness claimed the earth. Kane wet his handkerchief from the jug of water Darcie had packed, and the two lovingly took turns bathing the sheen of perspiration from each other's bodies. Their clothing they donned reluctantly, their now less than eager fingers lingering over fastenings, Glynna's pausing to caress the wide expanse of Kane's shoulders before his shirt covered them, his pushing the opening of her blouse aside so he might again cup her soft breasts. He could not seem to resist touching her lips with his from time to time, and when his mouth slanted over hers, deepening one of those kisses, he groaned in frustration.

"We cannot worry the Cavanaughs unnecessarily, but, God, I don't want to go back right now!"

"Nor do I," Glynna breathed against his lips, her own claiming his again for a moment, "but I suppose we must."

Not willing to part from her yet, Kane tied the oak basket to Sheena's saddle and the mare's reins to the stallion's saddlehorn. When he had mounted his horse, he pulled Glynna up in front of him and trusted the bay to find his own way back to the stable.

Glynna, surprised to find Katie awaiting her in her bedchamber, steeled herself for a tongue-lashing. Instead, a wide grin split Katie's ebony face as she turned from the large wooden tub in which she had been stirring fragrant bath salts into steaming water.

"Oh, how heavenly!" Glynna gushed. "Thank you, Katie."

"You mos' welcome, Miss Glynna. Let me help you with them clothes."

Glynna could not count the number of times Katie had seen her naked, yet she found herself suddenly embarrassed by the prospect of Katie's seeing her in the altogether. "Don't you have supper to finish? I'm starved!"

"My girls are watchin' it. It'll wait." Katie took Glynna's jacket and brushed a few blades of dried grass from its back before putting it away. "Did you and Massah Kane have a good ride?"

Unwilling to meet Katie's eyes, Glynna busied herself with sliding the green velvet skirt off her hips. "You know we did. Oh, Katie!" she cried, stepping out of the garment and throwing her arms around the beloved servant's wide girth. "I'm so glad he's back! And he wants me to be his wife!"

"Well, it's about time he asked you!" Katie

hugged her tightly for a moment. "If you doan git in that water, Miss Glynna, the heat gonna be done gone."

"I . . . I would like to be alone now, Katie, if you don't mind."

Katie squeezed Glynna again, then, without argument, left the room.

Relishing her memories of the afternoon and dreaming about being Kane Rafferty's wife, Glynna lingered in the tub longer than she had intended. Rosie's timid knock brought her out of her reverie, and she shivered as she stepped from water that had, indeed, grown cold. The girl assisted Glynna with her toilette, giggling when Glynna fussed over recalcitrant strands of damp auburn hair which seemed determined to defy all efforts at restraining them.

Glynna had chosen a fetching gown of royal blue velvet adorned with an overskirt of white satin; cascades of wide white lace paraded down a bodice insert and fell from the elbow-length sleeves. It was a more formal gown than those she usually wore for supper, but Glynna wanted to slay Kane with her appearance. When she walked sedately into the ordinary, head held proudly, she knew she had accomplished just that. His fixed gaze allayed her irritation over her coiffure and sent a delightful warmth coursing through her.

Kane led her to a private table in a darkened corner of the room, and they spent more time and energy feasting upon the sight of the other than consuming the delicious meal of roast mutton, cabbage, and potatoes that Katie had prepared. Later, when Brian had been dutifully tucked into bed, Glynna and Kane joined Darcie and Galen in the keeping hall.

Anticipating their need for private conversation, Darcie had had two wing-back chairs and a settee moved into this room. She and Galen settled themselves into the chairs, leaving the cushioned, high-backed settee for Glynna and Kane. The furniture had been placed in a semicircle in front of the fireplace, the soft amber light of the fire the only illumination in the room. A silver tray bearing a decanter of brandy and two crystal snifters sat upon a small, low table, along with Galen's pipe rack and a receptacle for ashes. The carefully created ambience failed to eliminate the tension in the room, however, and the four found themselves sitting stiffly as they chatted too brightly about matters of no real significance.

When Kane had poured his second glass of brandy, he reclined more comfortably against the back of the small sofa, then broached the subject of their marriage plans. "As you may have guessed by now," he began, "Glynna has agreed to my proposal—with some reservation, which I shall, I trust, resolve shortly. We want to stay here, in Virginia."

This declaration brought looks of surprise mixed with undisguised pleasure from the Cavanaughs. "But, how . . . ?" Galen asked, letting his voice trail off as he caught himself, wondering how much Kane had told Glynna about the Raffertys.

Kane laughed lightly. "My father has hoped for years that someday I would meet your niece and fall in love with her. Apparently, he and her father had discussed just such a liaison between their two families, but my father knew better than to push me into a relationship. It seems I have played the part of rebellious son over the years. As much as my father would like me to return to my inheritance in Ireland, he understands my rebelliousness, and he wants this union. I was taken unawares when he offered to allow my brother, Michael, to assume my role as Baron of Ulrich, and I surprised myself by accepting his proposal."

"And what do you plan to do here, in Virginia?" Galen asked.

"Much the same thing I would have done had I returned to Ireland, I suppose. Become a plantation owner, raise horses, busy myself with the delightful demands of being a husband—and hopefully—a father." Kane glanced at Glynna then and chuckled at the blush that suffused her cheeks.

In the interim, Galen and Darcie exchanged nods across the expanse separating their chairs.

"And what land had you planned to purchase?" Galen inquired.

A light shrug touched Kane's wide shoulders. "We hadn't given that any consideration as yet. There *is* land available?"

Glynna noted the twinkle in her aunt's blue eyes, the hint of a smile upon her uncle's lips. That they had hatched some scheme she was certain, but just what that scheme might be she had no earthly idea. Her mouth gaped open in absolute awe when her uncle spoke again.

"Most assuredly, but none so good as my own. Would you consider purchasing this tavern and the vast acres that go with it?"

Kane was rendered as speechless as Glynna.

"Darcie and I would retain a few acres, of course—not too close to the tavern, mind you. We've been thinking about building a house in the valley, close to the creek. About a mile or so from here."

"Why?" Glynna and Kane asked in unison.

"We have accomplished a great deal here, but we have also grown tired of the constant demands this business requires. We would never sell to strangers, and would stay on here until Brian becomes of age if necessary, but we want you two to have it."

Kane swished his brandy, watched the light bounce off the crystal bowl of the snifter and the amber liquid inside it. With a quick flick of his wrist, he then brought the glass upward, tilted it, and drank all of its contents. "I think," he said at last, "we had best discuss another matter first. When you hear the story I must tell you, you may not want to sell to me. And Glynna may change her mind, as well."

Chapter Twenty-one

With one eye pressed against the keyhole, Jarvis Whitfield crouched beside the door to the keeping hall. Silently he cursed the pain that had settled into his bent knees. The joints ached, and his neck was stiff from maintaining the position his acute attentiveness required. He knew if he did not change his position soon, he might not be able to move quickly should retreat become essential.

He grasped the doorjamb with both hands and pulled himself upward, then quietly took a nearby chair and set it close to the portal. Whitfield discovered that he could hear the conversation just as well, if not better, with an ear pressed against the wooden panel. He relaxed somewhat, smiling broadly at the words that came from Kane Rafferty.

". . . jeweled tiara that has been in the possession of the Raffertys for four centuries. When my mother was unable to locate it in Ireland following Glynndon O'Rourke's death, she was certain he had secreted it among his belongings, and that it had, thusly, traveled with his daughter to the colonies."

"But we have never seen this tiara," Darcie said. "Do you still think it is here, at the tavern?"

"The possibility certainly exists," Kane contended. "Glynndon could have hidden it inside something—maybe a trunk with a false bottom, or a pillow . . . perhaps even in a book with the pages cut to accommodate it."

"I don't understand why you did not tell us about the tiara when you first arrived," Glynna said, her voice raspy with pain at not having been trusted.

"Strictly out of loyalty to my mother, my dear. You see, the investigator she hired to find the tiara seventeen years ago uncovered a mystery surrounding your uncle. Perhaps he can explain better than I why my mother insisted on secrecy."

If it were possible, Whitfield listened even more intently now. For a long moment, nothing was said, and he wondered if he should move around to the back door of the keeping hall so that he would be closer to the furniture grouping. But the night had grown cold, and if anyone still worked in the kitchen, he might be discovered. No, he decided, he would remain in the shadowed darkness of the ordinary.

Had Whitfield been able to view the interior of the dimly lit keeping hall, he would have seen Galen rise from his chair and tend the fire. When another log had been added and the embers stoked, Galen turned his back to the fireplace and held his hands behind him. His gaze roved the three other occupants of the room during the pregnant pause, and he allowed it to rest on each one in turn.

"Aye, lad," he said at last. "I have left the past buried far too long. 'Tis time Glynna heard the tale, since it involves Glynndon and Brenna as well. No one else in the colonies knows the story I am about to tell you, and should the facts of this tale ever leave this room, my life could be in grave danger. I tell you this now, Glynna, because I think you are old enough—mature enough—to allow reason to dictate your response."

Glynna's skin suddenly felt cold and clammy. When Darcie's hand touched hers, she squeezed it gently, grateful for the warmth and reassurance the pressure sent coursing through her. A brief glance at her aunt's calm demeanor further alleviated her misgivings. She had always thought she wanted to know what had gone wrong for her uncle Galen, what he was running away from when he had left Williamsburg so suddenly. Now she wondered if she really wanted to be apprised of the details of his past. But Kane thought it necessary. And, apparently, so did Galen.

"Kane Rafferty, you obviously know a bit about my life already, though I venture 'tis not the entire story."

"Your assumption is correct," Kane agreed.

"My father was naught but a poor fisherman on the Isle of Man," Galen continued, "and I one of his eight children. As a lad, I dreamed of dieting on something besides fish, of living in a fine, warm house, and of being able to afford an education for my children. When I had attained my majority, I joined many another Manxman in a highly profitable trade—smuggling."

Glynna gasped involuntarily. Her uncle . . . a *smuggler?*

"Ah, I can see, lassie, that you do not approve, but hear me out. 'Twas with the aid of the Parliament who, in their typically supreme idiocy attempted to limit importation that we were able to

331

profit. The British do not control Man, so it was easy enough to secure the fine silks and champagnes the wealthy English and Scotch and Irish wanted, then to run them over when Manannan's Mantle cloaked the waters. I soon learned how much money a man could make if he owned his own boat, and I saved until I could afford one myself. Within a few years, I had attained more wealth than I knew how to spend, but I still felt empty and unfulfilled."

Galen retrieved his pipe and pouch from the table and spent a moment tamping tobacco into the bowl and lighting up. While he made several long pulls on the clay pipe, his eyes lovingly caressed Darcie.

"Every smuggler needs a contact for each shore. My Irish contact was your father, Glynna. One day he introduced me to your mother's sister, and I knew immediately what was missing from my life. Darcie was well aware of how I earned a living when she agreed to marry me and live on Man. We built that fine house and started the family I had always wanted. Although she never said so, I knew Darcie worried about my safety.

"Certainly there were risks involved. Occasionally, there was a skirmish with the British Royal Navy, but we exercised extreme caution. When the trouble came, it was not from the Navy."

Galen returned to his chair and poured out another draught of brandy. His brow beetled in remembered anger for a moment, and then he consciously cleared his face of all emotion and took a sip of the liquor before continuing his story.

"There were many other smugglers—and trade enough for the lot of us. But there was one renegade, an Englishman who called himself Sir Charles Robertson, who was a greedy bastard. He set out to eliminate as much of the competition as he could. One dark night, just as we were approaching the Irish shore, his sloop opened fire on us. We were caught between him and land, and the wind was against us, leaving us no alternative but to return fire. My boat was heavily armed, my crew excellent marksmen. With a few well-placed shots, we destroyed his sloop and came away with only minor injuries to both men and boat."

From his position in the ordinary, Jarvis Whitfield nodded slowly against the wood-paneled door. By his own admission, Galen Cavanaugh was the Manx smuggler who had been the object of his search, lo, these many years — the man who had killed his father. Whitfield considered leaving his post and retiring to his room to solidify his plans, but then he remembered the tiara. Greed got the best of him. He decided to listen for a while longer.

"I thought little of the incident until your parents died, Glynna. Although some twenty people lost their lives in that fire, which the authorities thought had been deliberately set, I knew in my heart the target had been Glynndon O'Rourke. The newspapers had carried reports of the disappearance of Sir Charles, and while I had thought him to be aboard his sloop that night and surely dead, I began to wonder if perhaps that were so. The man was without scruple, and would stop at nothing to achieve his goals. I had no wish to endanger my family, and had already begun to make plans to leave Man when word started trickling in of the vicious murders of various sailors, all of whom were or had been smugglers. Without further delay, I sold everything—my boat, the house, the land, all the furniture. I then changed my name from Carmichael to Cavanaugh, and we set sail for Virginia.

"Garth was barely two then, Glynna three. Darcie was carrying another child, a daughter born prematurely on that rough ocean voyage. She didn't live but a few hours, poor child. Darcie and I grieved over her loss, over having to bury her at sea." Galen's dark eyes shone with unshed tears for a moment, then he wiped the back of his hand across them and swallowed the remainder of his brandy.

It was the first time Glynna had heard anything about a daughter. Her heart wept for her aunt and uncle, who had witnessed the deaths of three of their four children. Whatever mischief Kane and his mother had concocted paled in comparison to that which had been perpetrated against Galen and Darcie. If they had not felt compelled to flee their homeland, those three children might still live. Whoever had been responsible deserved more than a swift kick in the breeches, and Glynna wanted to exact some payment from that person—and more. She was beginning to comprehend the evil that men do. The dragons from the fairy tales did have substance after all, but where there was a dragon, was there not also a dragon slayer?

"We had thought no further than seeking refuge when we arrived in Williamsburg, but we soon discovered how much money could be made—legally, this time—from the ownership of an inn. For ten years we ran such an enterprise in Williamsburg. We lived peacefully, had another son, and I was able to send my children to good schools, just as I had dreamed of doing. Then that dream was shattered again—when someone began asking questions about one Galen Carmichael."

"I'm sorry, Galen," Kane said softly, "that you did not know those inquiries came from the investigator my mother had hired to find Glynna."

"But it was not me she wanted to find." Glynna tore the words from her throat. "It was the tiara. She cared nothing about me."

Kane pulled her into his embrace then and explained gently, "She does not know you, Glynna, but she does know my father, and although we all love him, he can be a tyrant. She felt responsible for losing one of the family's most valued possessions, and she was afraid to tell my father what she had done. For years, she nurtured his desire to find you, hoping that, in doing so, the tiara might also be recovered. Please try to understand her motivation."

"And mine," Galen added. "We all do things we later regret. And we would all do things differently if we had our lives to live over, but who can say that another set of circumstances would not produce similar results? Each of us must follow our own dictates and learn from our own mistakes."

"I hope, Glynna," Kane said, sliding his palms down her arms and taking her hands in his, "that you can forgive my initial distrust and dishonesty."

"I already have, Kane," she whispered huskily, her eyes moist with tears. "I cannot imagine life without you."

"Does that mean you will marry me, in spite of the tiara?"

"Aye, me laddie," she teased, "in spite of the tiara."

"Have you ever seen the tiara, Kane?" Darcie asked. "Can you tell us what it looks like?"

"Traditionally the tiara has only been worn by Rafferty brides on their wedding day. My mother was the last to wear it, and it was locked away until she took it to Dublin and handed it over to Glynndon O'Rourke for safekeeping, so I have never actually seen it. But it has been painted a number of times. Our family gallery is filled with portraits of female ancestors who are wearing it. It is made of gold crafted in an openwork, filigree design. A large, pear-shaped emerald, which is surrounded by oval rubies, dominates the center point of the piece. The scrolls and swirls are encrusted with tiny sapphires, amethysts, and diamonds. It is truly a feminine piece, not overly large, but probably quite heavy."

Quietly, Jarvis Whitfield replaced the chair under the table and moved stealthily upstairs. He had heard enough to satisfy his curiosity, perhaps enough to satisfy his avarice as well. If the tiara were in Glynna's bedchamber, he should have time to find it before she retired. Having it might prove to be an even sweeter revenge than what he had planned. The tiara would certainly make him an extremely wealthy man far sooner than Glynna could, and it would enable him to return to his beloved London and to remain there, comfortably, for the rest of his life. The prospect of being forced to stay in this godforsaken land had not set well with him.

Darcie shook her head. "I don't recall ever having seen—"

"I have," Glynna interrupted, surprising everyone, including herself, with her admission. They all stared at her, waiting for more information while she appeared deep in thought for a moment. Finally, she shook her head in negation. "I know I have seen it . . . somewhere. But I can't quite remember where it was."

"Perhaps you saw it and didn't know you did," Kane suggested. "Or mayhap you read something about it. Did you read all of your father's journal?"

"Yes, but there was no mention of the tiara."

"Not overtly, perhaps, but there could be a clue. Would you mind if I read it?"

"Of course, you may read it. I'll get it for you."

Always the gentleman, Kane rose with her, but when she would have moved away, he pulled her against his length and lowered his head to brush his lips against hers. "I love you, Glynna O'Rourke, and I want you for my wife, whether or not we ever find the tiara."

"But I *want* to find it, Kane. I want to wear it on my wedding day. In fact," she teased, "I may not marry you until the tiara is found."

"What!"

"I will not have it said that *I* broke tradition."

He smiled broadly, his gray eyes twinkling as they gazed into her emerald ones. "Shall I go with you?" he offered.

"Thank you, but the stairs are well lighted, and I do not think it would be seemly for you to enter my bedchamber just yet."

"Will you look in on Brian for me?" Darcie requested.

"Certainly. I won't be long." Glynna smiled at the ease with which Kane resettled himself between her aunt and uncle.

"Tell me, Kane, what you heard in Williamsburg concerning our problem in the Ohio Valley. What is Governor Dinwiddie planning to do?" Glynna heard Galen ask as she closed the door and started upstairs.

Her kid slippers made soft swishing noises as she climbed the stairs and trod lightly across the bare ballroom floor; the stiff taffeta of her petticoats rustled in the stillness. Given different circumstances, Glynna might have noticed the thin thread of light emanating from beneath her door. But her heart sang joyfully and she thought only of her upcoming wedding and her life with Kane. She removed a candle from a wall sconce in the hallway and held it high in her left hand as she entered Brian's room.

The child lay on his stomach, his knees drawn up and his arms circling the pillow beneath his head. Glynna could hear his deep, even breathing in the quiet. Walking lightly to his side, she set the candle in a holder, and drew the bed coverings over his legs and feet. Suddenly, she became aware of a coldness she had not noticed before, and she rubbed the gooseflesh that had broken out on her lower arms before retrieving the candle and leaving Brian's room.

Jarvis Whitfield extinguished the candle and held her bedchamber door barely ajar as he watched her back out of Brian's room and softly close the door. At the same moment, he closed hers, then stepped behind it, his left arm clutching the bisque doll he had taken from her settee. Whitfield hoped this was just a precautionary measure, that Glynna had come upstairs for the sole purpose of looking in on Brian and would even now retrace her steps. He realized, too late, that in his frenzied greed he had now abolished all hopes of carrying his previous plan to fruition. At least he had found the tiara, and he felt certain its sale would bring enough to finance an easy life for many years to come.

With her right hand on the brass knob and her left holding her candle, Glynna hesitated before opening her door. An abrupt unease for which she could find no ready explanation had settled upon her in Brian's room, and she wanted nothing more now than to flee downstairs in all due haste. I'm just being silly, she assured herself. Uncle Galen says I should let reason dictate my responses, not emotion.

Perhaps the revelations she had heard that evening had robbed her of a feeling of security. So many lives altered or destroyed because of one man's petty revenge! Forcibly, she threw on a cloak of courage and pushed open her door.

The sight which greeted her obliterated that facade of boldness. Though she opened her mouth to scream, no sound issued forth. Nor would her feet move. She stood frozen, like a Biblical pillar of salt, the only movement that of her eyes ricocheting around her bedchamber.

The contents of her round wooden boxes had been dumped upon her bed, skeins of yarn, hanks of embroidery thread, packets of needles, wooden hoops, and partially worked tapestries mingling in tangled disarray upon the counterpane. The drawers of her chest gaped open; the stockings, undergarments, petticoats, and nightgowns which had so recently been folded neatly within them were strewn across the expanse of the rug. Tufts of soft white wool spilled from the long slits which had been cut in the crewelwork pillows she had so painstakingly created. Her tea table was littered with the dried flowers that had filled baskets, and the thatch-roofed dollhouse had been reduced to a pile of debris in a corner.

At once she was both angry and afraid. The anger fueled her limbs, and she whirled away from the unpleasant sight. But when she would have fled from it, a man's arms grabbed her from behind—the left circling her waist in a painful grip, the right holding the cold steel of a knife blade against her throat. Somehow she was not surprised at the identity of her attacker when she recognized the hoarse whisper of Jarvis Whitfield.

"If you so much as whimper, I will slit your pretty throat," he promised. And she believed him.

"I . . . I won't scream," she whispered back. "Just take whatever it is you want from my room and go. I'll give you time to get away before I go back downstairs."

He pulled her even more tightly against his chest. She stretched her neck upward in an attempt to loosen the pressure of the blade, but to no avail. He pressed it deeper, its sharp edge drawing a thin stream of blood as it pierced her tender skin. "I told you to be quiet," he hissed. "I'm going to take what I came in here for—and you, as well. I can think of no more appropriate revenge. Perhaps you will pleasure me as much as you did Kane Rafferty this afternoon."

"How dare you—" The increased pressure of the steel effectively terminated Glynna's angry words.

A weakness washed over her, and she realized, on some vague plane of consciousness, that she could not breathe. When Whitfield released his hold of her midriff, she instinctively sucked great gulps of air into her lungs. Her head had just begun to clear when he stuffed the middle of his silk cravat into her mouth, then took the candle from her left hand and blew it out. He laid it on the tea table with his knife. A thin sliver of light spilled in through the partially open door, casting an ominous pall over the disheveled room.

Glynna knew she would rather die than again be taken captive by a perverted man. She twisted and turned, struggling to get away from him as he grasped her wrists and pulled them behind her back and then upward until a sharp pain shot through her shoulders. For a moment she went limp, but she stiffened once more when he reached downward and picked up one of her silk stockings.

No-o-o-o! her mind screamed. She struggled again in earnest, tears streaming down her face when she felt the silk being wrapped around her wrists. With all her might, she worked her tongue and jaw in an attempt to dislodge the cravat from her mouth. Glynna knew a moment of triumph when the wet, cloying fabric touched her lips.

She did not have time to prepare herself for the blow which struck her lower jaw, clamping her mouth shut. Her tongue was caught between her teeth, and she thought at first that she had bitten its end off. The acrid taste of blood filled her mouth, but when she would have spit it out, Whitfield shoved the cravat back inside.

How long had she been gone? she wondered. It seemed like an eternity, but she acknowledged with chagrin that it had probably been only a matter of minutes. If something were to be done to stop Whitfield, she would have to do it, regardless of what it cost her.

Taking advantage of the fact that both of his hands were occupied with tying the ends of the cravat behind her head, Glynna kicked backwards with her right heel, hoping to place a stunning blow upon his shin. Her foot missed its mark and she lost her balance, but she had taken him by

341

surprise and he released his hold of the knotted silk. For a brief moment she felt airborne, her body hurtling through space before falling hard upon the littered tea table.

"Governor Dinwiddie is planning to send a message to the French commander in the Ohio River Valley," Kane told Galen. "A young army major named Washington has volunteered for the job."

"Not *George* Washington, surely?" Galen asked in disbelief.

"Yes, I do believe that is his name. Do you know him?"

"We met him . . . when was it Darcie? Three, four years ago?"

"It was in forty-nine, I believe."

"Lord Fairfax had hired him to survey a piece of land in the Shenandoah Valley and he stayed here on his way there. He must have been all of sixteen at the time, a most polite, intelligent young man mature beyond his years. He had wanted to join the British Royal Navy, but his mother, God bless her, refused to give her permission. He said if he couldn't be a sailor, then he wanted to see the frontier, so he dragged out his father's old surveying equipment and learned to use it. Damn good at it, too. He came back the next year to do more surveying as people were moving into the valley. We had hoped he and Glynna might fall for each other, but nothing more than friendship ever developed between them."

"Thank God for that!" Kane exclaimed.

"If I know George, he'll come through here on his way to the Ohio. He bought some land near here, and he does love my horses."

"And Katie's cooking," Darcie added. "Won't she be glad to see him?"

"Only because he flatters her and tells her she's the best cook this side of the Rappahannock," Galen said, and they all laughed at the expense of Katie's ego.

The resounding crash of splintering wood and shattering of china above them, abruptly ended their merriment.

"You bitch!" Whitfield ground out between clenched teeth. In his rage, he kicked out at her, the toe of his booted foot grazing her rib cage. He went down on his knees then, his hands groping among the debris for his dagger.

Glynna squeezed her eyes tightly shut against the anticipated pain, and tried to extricate herself from the rubble beneath her. But she had broken the porcelain tea service in her fall, and its menacing shards threatened to wreak havoc upon her tender skin. The final moments of her life slipped by as she waited for Jarvis Whitfield to end it, and she knew there was nothing she could do. Her blood was certain to be spilled, either from his dagger or the broken china. She found herself wishing she had known why. What had happened to this man with whom she had spent so many hours? He had seemed so . . . normal, even if he was a pest. Her only consolation lay in the running footfalls she heard from below, an obvious indication that her fall had raised a hue and cry. Would Kane reach her before Whitfield ended her life?

But Whitfield scrambled away from her, retrieved an object from behind the door, and fled down the hallway.

"Glynna!" Brian called out in terror from his bed.

She flinched, not wanting the child to get up and see her bound and gagged and bleeding, her face buried in the pile of rubbish that had moments before been a beautiful cherry table and a delicate porcelain tea service. She quivered in fear, not for herself anymore, but because Whitfield had found his knife and even now might be waiting in the darkness to strike out at Kane or Galen or Darcie when they rushed past him. Her eyes stung with tears of frustration at her total helplessness.

The sound of booted feet taking the stairs two at a time knifed through her consciousness. The floor vibrated beneath her as those same feet cleared the landing and bounded across the ballroom and down the hallway to her chamber. Her door was flung wide, and she thought she heard a harsh intake of breath before Darcie's screams pierced the air.

Chapter Twenty-two

Galen and Darcie did not possess Kane's agility. At the sound of the crash, he had rushed from the keeping hall without pausing to comment or question its source. By the time they reached the stairs, Kane was running down the second-story hallway. Although they had not taken the time to compare thoughts, all three had supposed that Glynna had fallen or tripped over something in the dark.

Whitfield, therefore, held the advantage of surprise when he leapt onto the landing from the shadows of the open doorway to the ladies' parlor and barreled into an astonished Galen Cavanaugh, throwing him upon the floor. The silvery blade of Whitfield's knife flashed in the dim candlelight as the younger man held it high, then thrust its point downward in a narrow arc.

Galen saw the knife, a long-bladed dagger, at the same time Darcie screamed. He rolled hard to the left, toward the ballroom, and felt a surge of cold air upon his cheek as the sharp point of the weapon whistled through emptiness and was buried in a wooden floor plank less than a hand's breadth from his head. With a quickness that belied his years, Galen jumped to his feet, but Whitfield acted with like swiftness, pulling the knife from the board and again raising it to attack position.

With both hands, Galen grasped the wrist that held the dagger, and he was amazed at the incredible strength in Whitfield's right arm as he struggled to wrest the blade from him. Whitfield used his left hand to push against Galen's right forearm. For a moment, time hung suspended as Galen summoned every ounce of his strength to hold the knife at bay.

Darcie stood rooted to the last stair, desperately wanting to aid her husband yet knowing any movement or further sound from her could break his concentration and mean his death. She clamped her teeth so firmly that the upper ones cut into the tender flesh behind her bottom lip, but she didn't feel any pain other than that which wrenched at her chest and throat.

"Why?" Galen gasped the single word. The muscles in his neck bulged above his collar band and the veins at his temples protruded in stark blue rivers as he pushed against Whitfield's wrist.

"You bastard . . . you killed . . . my . . . father!"

"I . . . never . . . killed . . . anyone."

"Liar!"

Years of toil had kept Galen's muscles in tone, but as the struggle continued it became more and more obvious that Whitfield far outdistanced him in stamina. The glittering point of the knife inched closer and closer to Galen's chest, which had begun to heave as his strength declined. Even if the act cost Darcie her life, she stood poised and ready to throw herself between them.

Then, out of the corner of her eye, she saw Kane step into the ballroom doorway and motion to her. With small, careful steps, she moved sideways to her left until she reached the wall. Pressing her spine and the palms of her hands against the wainscoting, she crept along its length until she stood next to Kane in the open doorway. Her eyes never strayed from the conflict on the landing.

"Glynna needs you," he murmured, his cheek twitching in barely suppressed anger.

In her concern for her husband, Darcie had momentarily forgotten her niece. Yet, she hesitated, not wanting to leave Galen.

"Go!" Kane hissed. "I won't let him hurt Galen."

She slipped behind Kane then and hurried to Glynna's bedchamber.

Kane had spent months training with fencing masters in France, had practiced swordsmanship for years, but he had little experience in brawling. What experience he did have had been long forgotten: an occasional rough-and-tumble play at Eton, a fist fight or two provoked by jealousy at Cambridge. He had been taught that there were better ways to best his fellow man than violent physical contact allowed. Wit was mightier than brawn, he had been told, but his rage toward Whitfield had eradicated his wit.

As soon as Darcie was safely out of the way, Kane moved quickly onto the landing, his right hand balled into a tight fist at his side. He moved with a natural, innate grace, already instinctively following a plan. With a mighty swing, he landed a swift punch into Whitfield's ribs and followed it with a left hook to the jaw. Whitfield released his hold of Galen's forearm and stumbled backward into a small table, sending a vase holding asters crashing down. But his right hand still held the knife.

"Let me have him!" Kane cried, and Galen, his pride unscathed, backed into the shadows of the ballroom. He had held Whitfield at bay longer than he had thought physically possible, and he knew that, without Kane's intervention, he would not have been able to do so much longer.

Kane lunged at Whitfield as the actor regained his stance, and the struggle for possession of the knife began anew.

Waiting and watching from the doorway, Galen winced when Whitfield, with his left hand, grasped the hair on the back of Kane's head and pulled hard. The tactic failed to achieve its aim, however, for Kane just pushed harder against the wrist holding the knife, ignoring the pain Whitfield's viselike grip caused. The dagger retreated a few inches, and then a few more.

For the first time in his life, Whitfield knew panic. His previous victims had all been weaker than he, either too old or too inebriated to put up much of a fight. He had connived to make each of them believe he was a friend and then had caught them unawares. Never before had he met an equal. But he knew he had now.

A vicious twist of Whitfield's wrist finally broke his hold on the blade, and it fell clattering to the floor. Kane instantly kicked it across the landing and down the stairs, and before Whitfield had time to recover from the loss of the weapon, he loosed a series of blows on Whitfield's torso and head, fighting like a madman, until Jarvis Whitfield crumpled to his knees and begged for mercy. "I ought to kill you for what you did to Glynna," Kane averred, barely winded himself.

Galen interrupted. "No, Kane. We're taking this scum of the earth to Williamsburg and turning him over to the governor. I think an investigation will prove he is guilty of far more than simple assault. I want to be there when they hang him for murder."

"Please, don't do this, Galen!" Darcie begged, hugging him tightly, her voice ragged with despair.

Although the hour was well past midnight, the two lay awake in their bed, sleep distant from both of them. Jarvis Whitfield had been securely shackled and then locked inside the smokehouse, two of Galen's largest and strongest slaves standing guard outside. Darcie had treated Glynna for shock and had tended the superficial cut on her neck. Kane and Galen planned to leave early on the morrow for Williamsburg, and Darcie was using every argument she could muster, every feminine wile at her disposal to talk Galen out of going.

"What else can I do?" His voice was weary. "Would you let him go free to murder again?"

"No, of course not, but—"

"*You* were the one who said we couldn't hide any longer."

"I don't want you to go to jail, Galen, and that is what will surely happen to you if you go to Williamsburg with Whitfield," she reasoned.

Galen sighed in resignation. "There is no other way, Darcie. The truth must be told now."

"Maybe he could just disappear. . . ."

"Darcie Cavanaugh! I am shocked!"

"He could, Galen, and no one would ever be the wiser. We could say we didn't know where he was going when he left here. If your theory is correct, Whitfield has no family. Who would care if he disappeared . . . forever?"

"You don't mean that, Darcie," he said soothingly. "You're distraught—and with good cause. I am not a vigilante. I will not carry the crime of murder on my conscience." His hands stroked her back and smoothed her hair. "Nor do I think you actually want me to. We've always known this time was coming. Since it had to happen, at least we're doing the world a favor now. My imprisonment will not go for naught."

Darcie was not the only distraught female in the Cavanaugh household that night. Glynna, as well, begged Kane to stay at the tavern.

"You promised, Kane! You promised never to leave me again," she cried softly.

"I'm not leaving you, sweetheart. I'm just going away for a few days," he whispered into her hair, his arms holding her trembling body close. "When I come back, we will be married. Have you thought who you would like to have perform the ceremony?"

The change of subject produced the desired effect. Glynna calmed immediately. She had not given this matter any consideration thus far, but she did now, voicing her thoughts as she did so. "After Mitchell died, Deacon McLaird contacted a circuit rider who works the settlements just to the east of here," she explained. "A Mr. Kinder, I believe his name was."

"And he presided over Edwin's and Beth's wedding? Did you like him?"

Glynna sighed softly, remembering the ineffectual little man with a voice and a demeanor as diminutive as his stature. "A preacher is a preacher, I suppose," she replied without enthusiasm.

"No, my dearest Glynna. This wedding must be special—as perfect as it possibly can be. Shall I bring a minister back with me?"

"Would you—could you, Kane?" she gushed.

"With a hefty enough purse, one can accomplish miracles," he assured her.

"But . . . what about the tiara?"

"If it is lost, then it is lost," he said philosophically, and she felt him shrug lightly as he lay against her. "We have to accept that fact, Glynna, and so must my mother. My father has mellowed over the years; perhaps he will bestow some measure of compassion upon her now. That he is capable of that emotion I am certain. The tiara could be anywhere, could have changed hands any number of times in the past two decades. We may never know what happened to it."

"I know I've seen it, Kane. Somewhere, sometime."

"Mayhap you saw it as a small child, after my mother entrusted it to your father and before he died," Kane suggested.

"No," she insisted. "Just recently I saw it. When you described it, I could see the tiara clearly in my mind. It was as though I had just today gazed upon its beauty."

They were quiet for a space, each savoring the nearness of the other, each dreading the short separation that was to follow, each contemplating the long days and longer nights they would spend together afterward.

"When I came here, Glynna, I harbored great hopes of finding the tiara and setting my mother's anxiety to rest. Little did I realize I would find a precious jewel, here on the frontier, that would prove itself of far greater value to me than a mere collection of cold gemstones set in colder precious metal. The most perfectly matched pair of emerald eyes set in a lustrous pearl complexion and crowned with ruby hair awaited me, and I shall forever bless the loss of a family heirloom whose very disappearance led me to you."

He kissed her then, a kiss which metamorphosed into one of depth and passion far beyond the tenderness that instigated it. Kane's mouth slanted over Glynna's, its tasting and nibbling becoming a plunging, probing force she welcomed with enthusiasm. At long last, he pulled his head away from hers, a feather's breadth, their hearts pounding in unison, their labored breathing mingling.

"Perhaps I should retire to the chair I promised Darcie and Galen I would spend the night in," he whispered hoarsely.

"Don't you dare move!" she threatened, her voice sweetly cajoling yet tinged with the promise of torment should he disobey her.

"But your injuries—"

"Are insignificant in comparison to the pain your withdrawal would cause."

"In that case, milady, I shall be thrilled beyond words to accommodate you," he murmured in her ear. And with no further speech between them, he did just that.

Later, they lay comfortably in each other's arms, relishing the aftermath almost as much as the actual act itself. Glynna had never felt so warm, so loved, so secure. Kane had never felt so completely sated, so cherished, so adored. And both felt at one with the world as they silently vowed to allow neither circumstance nor person ever to come between them again.

Shortly before the first weak rays of sunlight filtered through the drawn white curtains, Kane slipped from her side and began to dress himself for the trip to Williamsburg. He had pulled on his breeches and was fastening them when Glynna's anguished voice elicited his attention.

"Must you go now? Can this business not wait another day?"

"Were it left to me, I would not go at all," Kane assured her softly, moving back to her side and holding her small frame against his hard one. "But your uncle needs me, and he insists we begin our journey without delay." The pale light of early morning illuminated the disarray of her chamber, reminding Kane how close he had come to losing his beloved Glynna, his fiery Virginia jewel—and of the importance of bringing the felon Whitfield to justice. "Promise me you will not attempt to clean up this mess by yourself. Get one or both of Katie's girls to help you with it." When she did not respond, he added, "Promise?"

"Left to your own devices, you would spoil me," she answered.

"Humor me this one time."

"Done."

"What?" he attempted to simulate offense, but the teasing lilt in his voice belied that fact. "No argument? Where is your spirit, your defiance? I thought myself to be marrying a woman with a mind of her own."

"I would have sought assistance regardless of your plea," she teased, only a tiny quivering of her shoulders indicating her amusement. "I have no desire to tackle this chore alone. I had hoped you would help me with it.

"You're making this difficult . . . God!" He clutched her tightly. "I don't want this separation any more than you do."

A loud clattering on the front porch interrupted their embrace, and Kane quickly pulled on his shirt before running, barefoot, downstairs. Glynna heard another door close down the hallway and heavier footfalls join Kane's as she scrambled out of bed. Whatever could be causing such a ruckus? she wondered as she hastily fastened the bodice of a muslin daygown, praying that Whitfield had not escaped.

The sight which greeted her in the ordinary quickly allayed her fear. The common room was awash with redcoats, and she spied a familiar head among them as she sailed into the room. "George!" she called, a warm smile wreathing her face when a tall, lean soldier spun on a heel and opened his arms to her. He caught her against him in what appeared to Kane to be a less than brotherly manner and then spun her around, her feet leaving the floor as the major lifted her lithe form and laughed heartily.

"Glynna! Oh, my dear, sweet Glynna. I've missed you," he declared, planting a wet kiss upon her averted cheek before setting her upon her feet.

She backed away from him and let her eyes travel the length of his tall frame, from black kneeboots to crisp white breeches and sheathed longsword, from the double row of brass buttons on the breast of his red coat to the gold epaulets upon his broad shoulders and the gold-rimmed black tricorn upon his head. "What are you doing in uniform, George?" she asked in some awe.

The fringes of the epaulets were set atremble by a casual shrug of his shoulders. "A simple application to the governor and a commission this February past as a major. I was placed in charge of training militia in southern Virginia and volunteered to deliver a message from Robert Dinwiddie to the French commander in the Ohio Valley. So here I am!"

"But why so early in the morning? Did you ride all night?"

"Not all of it. Even a soldier needs his rest. But I smelled Katie's cooking yesterday," he teased, "and the hunger in my belly won the battle with my eyelids."

"We've heard nothing except 'Katie's cooking' since we left Williamsburg," one of the militiamen chimed in, a warm smile spreading his lips wide as the one of whom he spoke lumbered through the doorway, her meaty arms bearing a large platter of steaming scrambled eggs and fried smoked ham.

Glynna caught Kane's scowl from the corner of her eyes as George grasped her elbow and drew her toward a table. "There's someone here I want you to meet," she said, her free hand motioning to Kane in an invitation to join them. When he was by her side, she erased his frown by snaking an arm possessively around his waistline and bestowing a loving gaze upon his troubled visage. "This is my knight in shining armor, a man who has slain the dragon of resistance and won my undying avowal of love, a man who is sacrificing more than I can comprehend for my sake."

"A sacrifice perhaps from your point of view,

my dear, but not from mine. One cannot count as a sacrifice that which he willingly relinquishes in order to gain the prize," Kane gently corrected.

"And a prize she is," Washington agreed, his penetrating blue-gray scrutiny quietly assessing this man Glynna had chosen and wondering if he had been responsible for the darkening bruise on her lower jaw and the thin cut on her throat. Nothing was offered in explanation as the three chatted somewhat tensely over breakfast.

When Katie's daughters began clearing the tables, Galen asked George and Kane to join him in the gentleman's parlor. "We've had a spot of trouble here," he began when they were comfortably settled, then began the tale he had related to Kane and Glynna less than twelve hours before, ending with an account of Whitfield's attack upon Glynna and then Galen and Kane. He watched the major's jaw clench in anger as the latter was related.

"I've thought all these years that Sir Charles was behind the fire that killed Glynndon and Brenna and the murders of those sailors, but I am relatively certain now that he died that night aboard his sloop. This Jarvis Whitfield said I had killed his father. He had to be referring to Sir Charles. I tried to question him after we shackled him in the smokehouse, but he refused to tell me anything else. Kane and I had planned to take Whitfield to Williamsburg this morning, but we will wait now until you and your detachment leave."

Washington's lips had been set in a firm line as he listened to Galen's story. "Let me question this man," he said, offering no comment, either judgmental or sympathetic. Kane thought his attitude cold until the major met again with them a few hours later.

"I have dispatched two of my men to Williamsburg with this man Whitfield," he then told them. "They carry a signed confession from him along with a letter from me explaining what trouble he caused here. You may, perhaps, be summoned to the capital for questioning or testimony at some later time, but I think my insistence that Whitfield mistook you, Galen, for a former smuggler will quell any aspersions he may cast on your integrity. The man claims to be an illegitimate son of Sir Charles Robertson, and his many crimes were all committed, he says, on behalf of his father."

"George, I don't know how—"

"There's no need for gratitude, Galen. This is my job. Besides," he grinned, "we will have to wait here now for Thompson and O'Quinn to return. That means a whole week of Katie's cooking! I think I've died and gone to heaven!"

Chapter Twenty-three

Glynna and Kane spent the remainder of the day straightening and cleaning her bedchamber. Kane teased Glynna about her undergarments as they were refolded and returned to their appropriate drawers, and he comforted her over the loss of those items Whitfield had destroyed.

"I'm just a sentimental fool, I suppose," Glynna sniffed as she held a shard of the porcelain teapot, "but this service belonged to my mother."

"Why don't you keep one of those broken pieces?" Kane suggested. "It won't always remind you of last night."

Glynna nodded unenthusiastically, her gaze upon the pile of debris that had been her dollhouse. "Maybe I should keep a piece of that, too." Her voice caught in her throat. "My father gave that to me for my third birthday."

"I'm going to find a box for this, Glynna. I may be able to put it back together."

Glynna smiled indulgently at him as he rose from the floor and dusted off his breeches. "Don't you think I'm a little old for dollhouses?"

"*You*, definitely. But our daughter might like to have it. And that atrociously gaudy doll in the green dress, too."

His mention of the doll wiped the smile from Glynna's face, and a hand flew to her throat as she swallowed hard.

"What's wrong?"

"The doll." She dropped her hand, scurried to the settee, and began rummaging through the pile of pillow stuffing and ruined crewelwork. "It's not here!" Tears spilled from her eyes and her throat worked convulsively. Kane gently turned her around and hugged her.

"It's somewhere here, Glynna. We'll find it."

"But . . . you don't understand!" she wailed against his chest. "That doll is important."

"I know," he soothed. "Your father gave it to you—"

"When he gave me the dollhouse." She backed away from him a space, lifted the skirt of her apron, and used it to wipe her eyes. "I never could understand why he gave me the two together. A country cottage dollhouse and a bisque doll dressed like a doxie? The doll was an afterthought, Kane. I know it was. I told you I had seen the tiara recently. It's on that doll!"

"Are you sure?" His voice was crisp and fraught with his irritation. When she nodded her head in affirmation, he muttered, "Damn!"

"What's the matter?"

"Whitfield's on his way to Williamsburg, and we don't know what happened to the doll." Kane rushed to the door, rushed back and planted a brief kiss upon Glynna's open mouth, then rushed back to the door again. "Maybe I can catch up with them."

"Don't you dare try!" She found some humor in his agitation and smiled wanly. "I don't want to have to come and pull you out of a bog! Besides, I don't think he left here with it. He picked up something from behind the door last night just before he ran out of here. Where was he hiding when he jumped Uncle Galen?"

Her question gave him pause, then he grinned and returned to her side to grasp her elbow and gently pull her down the hallway. "Where are we going?" she asked, her heart beginning to beat erratically in her excitement.

"To find that doll."

Whitfield had dropped it on the floor in the ladies' parlor. For a moment, Kane and Glynna stood staring at it mutely, their eyes wide as they gazed down at its gaudily trimmed emerald satin dress. It was Glynna who finally bent down to retrieve the doll she had looked at every day for seventeen years. Her fingers caressed the faded folds of its gown, touched the rows of paste jewels and seed pearls that garnished the neckline, cascaded down the front of the skirt in an inverted V, then continued in a sprinkling around the hemline. Her eyes glazed with unshed tears as her fingers wandered to the doll's midriff and touched the adornment that encircled its waistline. The pointed center of the tiara pushed upward into the crevice between the doll's molded breasts, meeting the carefully patterned scattering of fake jewels spilling down from the neckline.

"Your parents could not have hidden the tiara in a better place," Kane said in some awe, his own fingers covering Glynna's trembling ones. "Who would ever have thought it was in plain sight all these years?"

"I can't believe I never noticed how luminous the real gems are. But I never paid any attention to their sheen, or to the fact that they are not stitched to the dress like the paste ones. Let's get it off and see what it looks like by itself."

They took the doll back to her room, and within minutes her nimble fingers had employed tiny embroidery scissors to cut the age-worn tacking threads and thereby had released the jeweled tiara. The doll's dress suffered no damage, but its lower bodice now showed darker green splotches where the gems and scrollwork of the tiara had covered it those many years. "Is it bad luck for the groom to see the bride in her headdress before the wedding?" Glynna asked, her emerald eyes sparkling with renewed merriment.

Kane shook his head. "We'll make our own luck, Glynna," he said quite soberly as he took the tiara and placed it upon her auburn locks. "Beautiful!" he whispered.

"Yes, it is," she agreed.

"I meant you." His mouth covered hers then in a kiss that promised her his love and devotion.

Near twilight on a cool, clear day in mid-November Kane and Glynna pledged their vows before the horde of guests who had gathered in the ballroom of Cavanaugh's Tavern.

Dressed in yards and yards of ivory satin and creamy bobbin lace crafted from fine linen thread, Glynna strolled proudly down the makeshift aisle at Galen's elbow. Her dress had been fashioned with a tightly fitted bodice and a deep, scooped neckline which exposed the upper curves of her breasts. The gown's long sleeves were gathered and poufed at the shoulders, tapering narrowly at her wrists and ending in points over the backs of her hands. The full, bell-shaped skirt had been adorned with inset rows of the bobbin lace, and a similarly adorned cathedral-length train trailed out behind her as she walked.

Her long strands of dark auburn hair had been twisted and coiled intricately, and were dressed high upon her head, lending her a regal appearance. The tiara surrounded this bonnet of curls, its freshly cleaned gems and polished gold scrolls twinkling as the final meager rays of that day's sun slanted through the long windows and caught their facets. Glynna's fine-boned hands, which trembled slightly, were folded around a simple nosegay of pale yellow and deep pink rosebuds. In memory of the one and in deference to the other, she wore her mother's pearls at her throat and carried one of Darcie's handkerchiefs with her bouquet.

More roses spilled from baskets strategically placed around the ballroom. Darcie had guarded the bushes, covering them at night and daring a frost to tarnish their blossoms before they were required. And massive arrangements of asters and chrysanthemums lent their vibrant shades of gold and purple to the corners of the room, with some white blooms of each variety mixed in. Multi-armed candelabra, their bases entwined with English ivy, had been placed on twin white pedestals at one end of the large room. The tall, cream-colored tapers they held burned brightly in the growing darkness, illuminating the faces of those awaiting the bride: the white-robed minister who had come from Williamsburg; Beth, dressed in her blue silk gown, clasping a nosegay similar to Glynna's; Edwin, dressed in his Sunday best; and Kane.

Glynna thought her heart would thump itself right out of her chest when she saw her husband-to-be. He stood straight and proud, his clear gray eyes glowing warmly in his tanned face, the dimple she loved embellishing his cheek as he smiled at her. The black velvet of his coat and trousers stood out in sharp contrast to his crisp white linen shirt, snowy cravat, and pristine white stockings. Unbidden tears welled in her eyes and her throat suddenly felt thick.

But as she gazed lovingly at him, Glynna could not help thinking of their initial meeting, of the streak of red clay which had clung to his shin that day. The memory banished tears, and a secretive smile lifted the corners of her mouth.

When Glynna came into his full view, the smile on Kane's face widened. His mind, too, conjured up an image of her as he had first seen her, down on her knees in the tomato patch, her face streaked with dark earth, the grimy kerchief hiding her glorious hair.

Her jeweled green orbs locked with his dove gray gaze as she took her place in front of Reverend Harper, and she saw in Kane's countenance the full portion of his love. The music which had accompanied her measured steps faded away, leaving in its wake the full realization of the significance of this ceremony. Glynna's scalp tingled beneath the tiara and a chill coursed down her spine. The minister's voice came as though from afar when he opened his prayer book and began to read. "Dearly beloved, we are gathered together . . ."

Glynna felt almost as if she were a witness rather than a participant. A part of her stood to the side, recording each word, each touch, each feeling for all time. She heard Galen reply "Her aunt and I" when the minister asked, "Who gives this woman to this man?" She felt him move away from her and knew he took his place beside that one with whom he had plighted his troth so many years before. She heard Kane's strong, mellow voice pledging to love, honor, and cherish her, heard herself respond in kind. And though her own voice came not so strongly as Kane's, she spoke with as much ardor and conviction as he.

When the time came for Kane to give her a ring, "as a token of his love and a semblance of eternity," Brian stepped forward bearing a small white pillow. Glynna gasped softly when she saw this token, for its narrow gold band bore the largest emerald she had ever seen. Her fingers trembled as she raised her left hand to receive the ring, but the trembling subsided when her palm touched the warmth of Kane's. He continued to hold her hand while the minister prayed for God's blessing upon their union, and his kiss when the prayer was finished carried the promise of passion in the hours and days and years to come.

Katie had prepared a banquet for the wedding guests, which was served in the brightly lit ordinary. The air bore the heady scents of flowers from Darcie's garden commingled with those of burning wax and Katie's delicacies. A myriad of toasts were offered, not the least of them from Kane, who teasingly wished they might have a dozen children with auburn hair and green eyes. By the time the towering white cake garnished with dark pink rosebuds was brought in, Glynna's head was reeling, whether from anticipation of the night to come or the quantity of sherry she had consumed she did not know.

She laughed when Kane clumsily fed her a piece of cake, shivered when his lips closed over her fingers as she poked cake into his mouth. It was the most furtive of caresses, and she felt a warm blush suffuse her cheeks as the tip of his tongue flickered over her fingertips. Whenever he leaned into her to impart some affectionate word or observational tidbit, their shoulders touched and her skin burned beneath the heavy satin until he moved away. By mutual agreement, they had remained celibate since the night Whitfield had attacked her, and Glynna found herself longing for the privacy of their bedchamber. The lack of intimate physical contact had served to heighten her sensuality, and she did not have to wonder if the same were true for Kane. His every look, his every gesture silently communicated his own impatience.

Without Glynna's knowledge, Darcie and Galen had incorporated a Manx wedding tradition into the evening's festivities: "tying up the bride." When the supper was over and Kane and Glynna moved ahead of the crowd to ascend the stairs first, Brian and the neighborhood children emerged from the landing to stretch a rope across their path. "Ransom, ransom," they cried, pulling the length of the rope around Glynna's waist and effectively halting her progress while Kane produced a small pouch from which he withdrew a handful of coins. These he threw to the "highwaymen," only partially appeasing them, for they raced ahead to repeat the "tying up" until Kane's purse had been emptied and they had gained the upper landing.

Glynna laughed heartily at their play, thinking this ransoming of the bride was certain to become a tradition in their community, her heart too full to allow the memory of a genuine abduction to cast a pall upon her good humor.

The guests formed a circle around the perimeter of the ballroom, much as they had at the ball in May when Kane and Glynna had demonstrated the minuet. As he had then, Kane took Glynna's small left hand in his larger right one and led her onto the open floor. They made a lovely couple, Kane's dark good looks and tall frame a perfect foil for Glynna's distinctive coloring and shorter stature. They dipped and swayed with the music, their every graceful movement fraught with the ever-pressing need for privacy, each seeing no other, their hearts melding.

When the first musical composition had ended and the quartet of players had started another, other couples moved into the open space. Kane danced with Darcie and Beth before several of the female guests vied for his attention. Likewise, Glynna danced with Galen and Edwin and what seemed to her a score of fervid males, most of them Galen's contemporaries. When Kane's strong arms claimed her lithe form again, she sighed contentedly and said softly, "I thought I had lost you."

"Never, my love. Might we slip away now?"

She nodded eagerly as he maneuvered her toward the landing door.

Ever-fading strands of three-quarter-time music accompanied them on their flight to the lower floor and out the heavy front portal to the porch, where Glynna begged softly for a short respite. "I'm exhausted, Kane. Let me catch my breath."

A full moon hung suspended in a clear sky, a myriad of tiny twinkling stars adding their luster to the velvety darkness. The pale light illuminated

Glynna's pearly complexion and sparkled in the jewels of her eyes. Kane's scrutiny absorbed her beauty, his gaze wandering downward to the quick rises and falls of her breasts. He groaned in frustration and scooped her into his arms. "Madam, I've waited quite long enough!" he ground out between clenched teeth.

Glynna looped her arms around his neck and giggled into his chest. "And what would you do if I told you I was sleepy?" she needled.

"I think I know a way to keep you awake."

His long legs strode the depth of the porch and down the brick steps to the walk, which he followed to the right until he reached a wing which had been added to the tavern when lack of sufficient space for guests had required it. The wing contained three rooms—one large bedchamber and two smaller ones. Darcie had worked vigorously preparing this area as an apartment for Kane and Glynna to use until the spring, when she and Galen would build their house near the creek. The old furnishings had been removed from both of the smaller rooms, one of which had been turned into a cozy sitting room. The other was now a dressing room complete with a large copper bathtub.

Kane pushed the outer door open with his hip; then, requiring a free hand but not wanting to set Glynna down just yet, he tossed her over one shoulder and held her securely with one arm across her upper thighs while he bolted the door. Glynna wriggled against him, her fists pummeling his lower back with soft punches and her feet kicking into thin air. "Put me down," she protested, the bubble of her laughter weakening her demand. "I'm not a sack of potatoes!"

A deep, guttural chuckle erupted from his throat in response. Down the hallway and into the dressing room he carried her, finally bending forward to set her firmly upon her satin-slippered feet. Much of Glynna's hair had come loose from its coils. She parted the wayward strands covering her face, tucked them behind her ears, and drew her brows together in a semblance of a frown. "I fear I have made a rather large mistake," she said, attempting but not quite achieving a serious mien.

One of Kane's brows rose almost to midforehead, and she saw that his gray eyes were growing increasingly darker as his ardor grew. "How so, milady?"

"If this little demonstration of your brawny strength is any indication of—"

His mouth swiftly descended upon hers, effectively cutting off her teasing protests. It was not a tender kiss, rather one calculated to prove both his superior strength and his supreme frustration at the continued delays. But when her lips softened and opened beneath his and the groan of her own frustration escaped her throat, his kiss gentled. Kane's lips plucked at hers; Glynna's responded in kind, and when his thrusting tongue invaded the sweet cavern of her mouth, her own welcomed its victorious triumph over her feeble defenses. She felt the evidence of his rising passion against her stomach and pressed her lithe frame more closely against his hard one, felt his hands glide down her satin-covered back to close over her buttocks and crush her to him.

At long last, and seemingly with some difficulty, his mouth released hers. Glynna leaned back in his embrace, her moist lips gleaming, her features relaxed, her dark lashes resting against her cheeks for a moment before fluttering open. The corners of her mouth lifted impishly as she regarded his own hooded eyes and fevered countenance. "Methinks thy conquering abuse, milord knight, has met with some success." Her voice was low, mellow, and provocative.

"I may have won the skirmish, milady, but never the war," he teased, lapsing into her rhetoric, his eyelids rising only the slightest bit as he gazed down at her. "The enemy's wiles far outnumber mine own, and her weapons prove more powerful than any at this poor knight's disposal."

As he spoke, Glynna's fingers worked loose the knot of his cravat, and when it was free, she clasped one end and tugged it slowly. The sheer fabric slipped around his neck, its soft gliding motion producing a shudder in his broad shoulders and drawing a low expletive from his mouth. "I was a fool," he breathed, "to ever think I held the upper hand with you, my little vixen. If it pleases you, I would stretch this night into eternity."

Glynna nodded her acquiescence, all the while moving her hands upon the strictures of his clothing, loosening the fastenings, first of his shirt and then his trousers. At the insistence of her fingers, he shrugged out of his jacket and then his shirt, letting them fall upon the small plush rug on which they stood. His own fingers removed the pins that held both the tiara and the remaining strands of hair atop her head. He groaned when burnished curls fell about her creamy shoulders, and setting the tiara aside, he turned those shoulders gently around to allow his fingers access to the fastenings of her gown.

Someone had laid a fire upon the hearth, its soft glow providing the only illumination in the room. The copper tub had been placed near the hearth, and two kettles of water hung over the flames. Using the poker's hook, Kane removed the kettles and poured their steaming contents into the fire-warmed tub. To this he added cooler water from a pair of oaken buckets which had been thoughtfully provided. "I've been wanting to do this," he said, his voice thick, "since that first afternoon of my arrival when I spied your urchin form in Katie's kitchen tub." His hands swished the water, mingling the hot with the cold. With deliberately slow movements, he dried his hands upon a linen towel hanging with others on a rack beside the tub before completing the task of removing Glynna's chemise, stockings, and petticoats. When he had shucked the remainder of his own garments, he extended a long arm toward the tub in an invitation to join him there.

Glynna hesitated long enough to twist the long skein of her hair upon her crown and tie it in a knot. Kane settled his larger bulk in the tub first; then she eased her form into the warm depths, her body facing his. Their legs moved around each others' hips to accommodate the slight crowding, and for a long moment they sat thusly, savoring their naked nearness and the sensuality of the warm water rippling over and around them.

Kane removed a handcloth from the rack and a bar of soap from a porcelain dish, and Glynna watched in fascination as his lean hands performed the simple task of applying soap to cloth until he had achieved a lather. She shivered when he reached forward and plied the cloth to her bare breasts, circling first one and then the other without touching their throbbing, distended crests. He moved the cloth downward to her stomach, then up again along her side, his thumb barely grazing the side of her breast as it journeyed past that tender spot to her shoulder and down her arm to her fingertips. She lowered her lashes against the onslaught of sensation his ministering hand aroused, and when she could stand it no further, she plucked the cloth from his hand and performed a similar chore upon his naked flesh.

The firelight danced upon the wet sheen of muscled arms and shoulders, droplets clinging to the swirling black hair upon his chest. Her gaze followed the movements of the cloth across his collarbone, down between the squarish mounds of his breasts, across his narrow waist, and down again, into the soap-clouded water.

"The knight's patience is sorely tested, milady," he groaned, lifting her now immobile hand from the water and removing the cloth from her trembling fingers. This he rinsed thoroughly before using it to splash the quickly cooling water over the soapy film on their bodies. Adversely, the coolness of the water heightened their mutual warmth, and it was with senses totally aroused that they stood in the tub and toweled away the clinging moisture.

They donned their dressing robes, which had hung ready on pegs, and moved as one to the larger chamber, where another fire burned brightly on the hearth and the bed coverings had been turned back enticingly. "Come," Kane invited as he turned toward the fire and sat cross-legged upon the hearthrug. From a small table which had been set nearby, he took a flagon and two small glasses. "Mead," he explained, pouring out the fermented drink and offering a glass to Glynna when she had settled herself opposite him on the rug. "I brought it back from Ireland — a month's supply to last through our honeymoon."

Glynna bestowed upon him a look of some confusion. " 'Tis a custom, milord, with which you needs must acquaint me, for, like the 'bride's ransoming,' 'tis one to which I have not before been exposed."

"I hold no regard with the cynical view many embrace for the meaning of the word 'honeymoon': that the sweetness of love, like the moon, is no sooner full than it begins to wane. I prefer legend's explanation for the coining of the word: that newly married couples once drank mead, which is made from honey, for one month, or moon, after the wedding, offering a toast each evening for happiness and long life."

Kane held his glass aloft and Glynna did likewise, touching her glass to his with a soft clink. "To my beloved husband," she offered. "May he live long and prosper." They each took a sip of the sweet liquor, then Kane spoke softly, "To my darling wife. May I always make her as happy as she has made me."

Momentarily their glasses were empty, and when Kane had replaced them on the table, he leaned into Glynna, his eyes raking the soft mounds of flesh exposed by the gap in her pink silk robe before moving upward to plumb the depths of her radiant orbs. His sweetened lips touched hers, softly at first, his tongue licking the remaining mead from her parted lips, then more firmly, his mouth slanting across hers, his tongue probing her teeth and gums.

Glynna felt his arm encircle her shoulders, felt the gentle press of his firm length as he lowered her spine to the rug. She offered the slim column of her neck to his roving mouth and arched her back when that selfsame mouth continued its downward journey into the valley between her breasts. His tongue played its melody upon the pliant mounds, his teeth biting the edges of her robe and moving them aside to allow him access to the fullness of her bosom. She moaned in ecstatic agony when the tip of his tongue flicked across first one hardened peak and then the other.

All the while, his large, strong hands moved upon her, taking their own slow, inexorable journey, touching her first through the fine silk robe and then slipping inside to caress her stomach, her hips, and, finally, the throbbing downy mound of her womanhood. His fingers barely grazed her love-moistened flesh before moving onward to work their wiles upon the silky inner flesh of her thighs. Glynna writhed beneath him when his lean fingers trailed upward again, finding their way home at last as one of them probed her womanly depths. Simultaneously, his mouth suckled a taunt crest and released it with the same rhythm his probing finger orchestrated.

"Kane!" she gasped. "Oh, Kane!"

The fire crackled and popped as a log burned through the middle and collapsed upon the embers, but the fire in Glynna's loins burned hotter than that upon the grate. Outside, the wind had begun to blow, and as it gained speed, it wailed around the corners and under the eaves of the wing, but its force was minuscule in comparison to the passionate throb of Glynna's pulse.

Kane's mouth released her breast and his tongue trailed hotly along her quivering flesh, moving ever downward until it encountered the obstruction of her loosely tied belt. His teeth worked their wonder upon the looped knot, the slight roughness of his chin pushing the slippery fabric across her stomach until it fell loosely at her sides. Her hands reached downward, her fingers finding his own belt and releasing its hold upon his velvet robe, and her open palms rubbed his chest. But when she would have reached farther, his body slipped downward again, his mouth bestowing nibbling kisses upon her navel and across her hipbone, pausing at the depression between it and her upper thigh before forging a wet path to the junction of her legs.

A myriad of sparks exploded behind her eyes as his mouth and hands worked their magic upon her quivering flesh. When she begged him for surcease, he flung the velvet robe from his body and moved over her, his knees gently parting her thighs, the heated staff of his manhood gliding into the moist cavern of her womanhood. When he had claimed her fully, he rolled to his side, pulling her with him, his back to the fire, his right arm beneath her, his left leg flung over her right knee.

The dim light of the fire cast a pearly luster upon her supple breasts, their aroused dusky pink buds thrusting upward to his touch as he rolled first one and then the other between thumb and forefinger. Her hands roamed his torso, seeking out his most sensuous spots and caressing them with her fingertips, then moving downward to grasp his firm buttocks and pull him deeper inside her. His hips gyrated in a primal rhythm practiced since the dawning of time, but never accomplished, Glynna thought, with so much loving tenderness. Her own rhythm matched his in a spiraling whirlwind of sensation until she gasped aloud, her mouth falling open and her green eyes widening at the wonder of it all. Kane's own racking shudders followed almost immediately, and when they had subsided, he pulled her close against his chest and whispered words of love in her ear.

The night stretched out into the eternity he had promised. Glynna made love to him much as he had to her, and when their bodies demanded rest, they napped in each other's arms. The wind continued to buffet the clapboard siding and ply its force upon the bare limbs of the trees, its wail a testament to the storm from within.

In the wee hours of morn, just before dawn's pale intrusion, Glynna lay upon the cool smoothness of the sheet, her yearning sated once more, Kane's fingers entwined in the mass of her hair, his leg flung across her stomach. "Will it always be like this?" she mused aloud, turning her face to gaze deeply into his dove gray eyes. "Or will you grow tired of me when my hair fades to gray and my skin wrinkles with age?"

"Never, my love, will the ravages of time alter my feelings for you. I love you, Glynna O'Rourke Rafferty, all of you—your wit, your compassion, your fiery spirit. The passage of time may work to more finely hone those qualities, but I cannot believe it would erode them." His fingers pressed more firmly against her scalp, easing her head ever closer to his. "And if I asked the same question of you?" he countered in a breathless whisper.

"Never, my love," Glynna promised as well and sealed her vow with a kiss which left no doubt in Kane's mind that she meant it.

Epilogue

The big black stallion's legs stretched out in lengthy strides as he raced after the spritely chestnut mare that seemed bent on eluding him. Months had passed since he had been allowed the chase, and both horse and rider reveled in the sport. The whistling air bore the merry tinkle of a woman's laughter, which was joined by a man's deeper chuckle as the horses mounted a steep hill and were reined to a halt.

The woman's dark auburn locks settled around her narrow shoulders as the mare side-stepped prissily, her snorts ruffling the full mane upon her arched neck. The stallion edged closer to the prize, his nose nuzzling the mare's heaving flanks in a wanton display of his ardor. "Sheena was in need of a good run," Glynna observed, her small, gloved hand reaching down to gently pat her mount's neck. "And for that matter, so was I."

"You and Sheena were not alone in your needs," Kane added, urging the stallion forward and then dismounting. He had purchased the black Thoroughbred several months before, the sire, he

376

hoped, of many fine colts and fillies to come. "Xerxes had need of the chase, and you, madam, have only recently begun to satisfy the needs of a starved husband." He looped the stallion's reins over a low-hanging branch and walked back to assist Glynna in dismounting.

His hands lingered at her sides as his clear gray gaze perused her slender waistline and full bosom. "No one would guess, my love, that you gave birth just two months ago," he whispered into her hair, his lips grazing her forehead before he released his hold of her and walked Sheena to the tree.

"He is rather a fine son." Glynna preened. "Mayhap milord would like a daughter next year."

Kane groaned loudly, his eyes rolling heavenward before settling on her smirking face. "Mayhap the year after. 'Tis true that I want children, several children, but I do not think I could tolerate having them all at once." His arm encircled her shoulders, his hand resting on the soft flesh of her upper arm and squeezing it gently through the velvet of her jacket. They stood upon the crest of the hill, their eyes surveying the rolling hills spreading out before them, the stark white rise of the tavern standing in miniature upon a distant summit.

Almost a year had passed since their wedding—a year filled with busy days and blissful nights.

In April, Glynna had celebrated her twenty-first birthday and had, thusly, come into her inheritance. She and Kane were amazed at the size of the legacy her father had left her.

Kane had insisted on using his own money to purchase the tavern from Galen and Darcie. That couple and their young son now resided in a lovely clapboard-sided, two-story house near the creek, where Galen spent his days puttering in a vegetable garden or, depending on the weather and the needs of his small family, fishing or hunting. Darcie had assumed the task of tutoring Brian, and, as always, ran her household with her unique combination of skill and finesse. They had taken some of the slaves with them to Manannan, the name Galen had given his new house, for there were still chickens to be fed and cows to be milked, horses to be groomed and food to be prepared.

But Katie had remained at the tavern. Her culinary talents had become widely known among the travelers to the frontier, and the decision to remain had been her own. The tavern had become her home.

Kane had never embraced the institution of slavery, and after his stint on the *White Wave*, he had become even more adamant in his thinking. Galen had warned him, however, of the dangers inherent in the immediate release of a people who had grown dependent in many ways upon their masters, so he devised a simple system of indenture, whereby the slaves were each assigned a pecuniary worth, which they might earn through their labors, thus "buying" their freedom.

Glynna shared her uncle's doubts that such a system would actually prove beneficial in the long run, but she put those doubts aside and gave Kane her full support. "Nothing attempted, nothing gained," he had reasoned, and she could find no fault with his logic. She had insisted, however, that the slaves be educated if they were some day to be free. In total agreement, Kane had established a grammar school for them, hiring a young man from Yorktown to teach the basics.

They had liked their apartment so well that they had decided to keep it when the Cavanaughs moved out. With the advent of their son's birth, and in anticipation of more children to come, Kane had supervised another addition to the main structure to accommodate a nursery and two more bedchambers. The original three rooms had been remodeled so that they now opened into each other, creating a master suite and affording privacy to the loving couple.

The mill and the general store were flourishing, and Kane had delivered his first tobacco crop to Williamsburg. He had returned from that city with less than pleasant news, however. Jarvis Whitfield had been taken to London to stand trial, and word had come to Lieutenant Reed that the man had jumped ship off the coast of Cornwall and no one had seen him since. Kane had also learned that George Washington had resigned his commission in the British army.

They had seen much of their friend this past year and had become more convinced with each visit that the man was a military genius. The previous December, Washington had arrived at Fort le Bœuf and had delivered Dinwiddie's message to the French commander, who had rejected the warning. Washington had then returned to Williamsburg in January with a letter from the French commander to Dinwiddie. At the major's urging, Dinwiddie had sent a force of frontiersmen to build a fort where the Ohio and Allegheny rivers join.

Washington, having been promoted to lieutenant colonel, had been assigned the task of holding the fort. He had encountered some difficulty in enlisting troops, finding Americans resentful because the British refused to pay them as much as regular British soldiers. Washington, himself, was not paid as much as a regular lieutenant colonel in the British Army. In April he had set out with one hundred sixty poorly trained troops. During the interim, the French had captured the British fort. Washington and his men had engaged the French in a skirmish, the French suffering heavy losses while only one of Washington's men was killed. Another British fort was built, and Washington was promoted to the rank of colonel.

In July the French had attacked this fort and American losses ran high. A third of Washington's men were sick at that time and the others were hungry. Washington had returned to Williamsburg a discouraged man. Despite the defeat at Fort Necessity, the colonists praised Washington and his men for their bravery. Washington had wanted a military career, but when Dinwiddie told him that all colonial officers' ranks were to be reduced, he had angrily resigned.

Kane and Glynna were, naturally, concerned over the continuing problem with the French and their Indian allies. In light of the year's developments, Kane had urged his parents to postpone their visit to Virginia, but they had ignored his plea and had sent word that they would arrive some time in September. As that month was drawing to a close, Wilson's coach, now bearing the elder Raffertys, had returned once more to the frontier tavern. Wilson had thrilled Kane and Glynna with his decision to open a regular coach route from Williamsburg to Cavanaugh's.

Glynna found Kane's parents delightful company. The four had spent many an hour cooing over the baby, who shared his father's and grandfather's name, and they had sat long over many a meal, reminiscing about Glynna's parents and Kane's youth. Valerie Sherman, they had reported with some humor, had bandied false tales about County Galway in an effort to ruin Kane socially, but had, in effect, seriously tarnished her own reputation. Kane's brother, Michael, had assumed responsibility for the Ulrich estate, and Thomas was greatly pleased with Michael's competence in that realm. Alaina was to be married next year to an English marquess—"Lord, grant him a willing ear and the patience of a saint!" Thomas had drolly declared.

The Raffertys had come prepared to stay through the long, cold winter months, and they had settled in well despite the less than urbane environment. While Kane and Glynna were glad to have them, the older couple's constant presence interfered with the spontaneity of their lovemaking and resulted in a loss of the privacy to which the younger pair had grown accustomed. Glynna's confinement during the latter stages of pregnancy and the weeks following the baby's delivery had, of necessity, temporarily inhibited physical intimacy. Therefore, Kane's suggestion that the two of them take their horses for a long ride into the hills had thrilled her.

Now, she leaned into her husband's embrace, lifting her face to gaze lovingly into his sparkling gray eyes. She had continued to marvel that he had accepted his new way of life with such equanimity—even, for the most part, with genuine enthusiasm.

"No regrets?" Glynna asked quietly.

"No regrets," Kane assured her, placing a finger under her chin and tilting it upward before planting a warm kiss upon her lips. Then he pulled back and hugged her to him, his gaze surveying the hills to the north. "I seem to remember spending a rather pleasant afternoon on a hill near here," he said thickly. "Do you think we can find it again?"

Author's Note

The inspiration for this book came from a visit several years ago to Historic Michie Tavern Museum, which stands, well preserved, on a mountain near Charlottesville, Virginia. This tavern is, perhaps, one of the oldest homesteads remaining in that state.